HEROES
OF THE
FIFTH SPIRE

Fallen Spires Book 1

TAVIAN ROYAL

To all my dear friends who supported me during the best of times and the worst of times

Contents

PART ONE

Chapter One

The Drift

In the realm of Tallendrall, there was a great desert known as the Drift. Many ancient ruins slept beneath its rolling sand dunes. Dreaming of times before the Age of Dragons, the ruins held only memories of sorrow and regret for an age that never came. With stories of curses and terrors inhabiting these bitter ruins, most people avoided them, especially those that valued their life. Breathing slowly, Faellan hoped those stories were not true as he stared into a dark descending stairwell of one of these ruins.

"I didn't sign up for this," Faellan said. Being slightly taller than the other mercenaries, he was a dark, imposing figure with broad shoulders and stout arms. He hardly ever backed down from a fight. Looking into the ruin's black abyss made him clench his fists nervously. Sweat dripped from his shaven head. A man with a thick mustache and eye brows approached him.

"When you signed your contract, you agreed to capture or kill Lady Enix's enemies and get paid very well for it." Captain Lurech's voice was stern but had a slight quiver to it. "Like I said, the plan is simple. You lure them out of the burial vault, and we will ambush the prisoners. But I warn you Faellan, Lady Enix will hold you personally responsible if you mess this up." Faellan knew he was afraid. They were all afraid of Lady Enix. When the prisoners escaped, she burned the incompetent guards alive in a fire that would not die nor would the guards. Their screams of agony could be heard throughout the spire. Gritting his teeth in anger and despair, Faellan turned towards the captain. For a moment, the only sound was their red uniforms flapping in the hot wind.

"When I agreed to to sign your contract, we only talked about raiding caravans and villages. No one mentioned lords, especially capturing or killing a totem champion or a wizard." Champions, a lord, were barbarian warriors with the head of an animal. This one had the head of a bull and wielded a giant two-bladed axe. "If the champion doesn't cut us into pieces, the wizard will burn us alive. We will never escape that vault."

"These crypts have winding passages. If you are fast enough, you can get out of the wizard's sight and escape the barbarian's axe."

"How do you know what a crypt even looks like?" Faellan had known the captain for only a few months. He was quick to blame others and hid from danger. Faellan was sure the man didn't have the guts to go into a crypt. The other mercenaries didn't like him either. His ability to pay them well was the only thing that kept their tongues and swords at bay. Seeing his face twist in frustration, Faellan figured most hired swords didn't stand up to him.

"I have used these ruins to raid caravans. Now, stop wasting time before we lose the element of surprise. Otherwise, I will let Lady Enix deal with you."

Faellan glanced eastward at the Fifth Spire. In the distant dark structure, he knew Lady Enix was watching them. He could feel her gaze like a thousand spiders crawling over his skin. The captain sensed something also as he shifted his stance nervously. Not having much of a choice, Faellan breathed deeply staring at the crypt.

"I am certain they already know we are here," Faellan said finally.

Signaling the two men next to him, Faellan lit a torch and led them down into the crypt. Each of their steps caused the edge of the stone stairs to crack and crumble. The falling debris echoed against the etched stone walls. Ancient markings were scattered along the wall. With his luck so far, Faellan suspected they were dire warnings against intruders. The stairs continued to descend deeper and deeper into the ruin.

With the dank, earthen air replacing the hot desert air, Faellan realized he was now inside the terrible, ancient crypt. To keep the terror from burrowing into his mind, he tried to think about his favorite inn in Bonewalk. It had the best roasted pork and Kinnish rolls in the Xandia province. He always tried to get down there at least once a year. Remembering the good company and drinks he had in that inn, Faellan smiled just for a moment. Then, he saw the twelve-foot door.

The stairs led into a large circular room with an enormous door positioned on the far wall. It was already partially opened. Faellan hoped the escaped prisoners had opened it and not something more terrible. Hearing the rest of the mercenaries making their way down into the crypt, Faellan and the two other mercenaries approached the massive door. Briefly, Faellan wondered what kind of horrors such a large door guarded against. They edged their way through the door and into the even darker burial vault.

Faellan found himself in a long hallway. The torchlight danced against the smooth, metal walls. The slow cadence of their footsteps echoed against the metal floor. Running his hand against the wall, he was astonished that the crypt wasn't built by ancient stone workers. Instead, the crypt appeared to be made of material similar to the Fifth Spire. Built thousands of years ago, the spires were known to have great power and dreadful secrets. He cautiously continued down the hallway fearing that this crypt may contain the same terrible mysteries as a spire.

Coming to another hallway on his left, Faellan thought he heard a voice drift out of it. It was faint and indiscernible. With a few quick hand gestures, he urged other two men to follow him. After several steps, they saw large indentions in the corridor's walls. Looking into one niche, Faellan discovered a perfectly preserved human skeleton. It had no gold or treasure. It simply slept unhindered. Grimacing, he quickly discovered that all the niches had human remains in them. The other two men hesitated when they saw the skeletons. Most likely, they believed the skeletons would come alive to tear their flesh off, if the stories about undead were to be believed. Faellan gave them a tense, angry stare and motioned them towards him. Without argument, they continued to follow. Several hallways broke from the one they were following, but Faellan was transfixed on a distant blue light. Getting closer, he realized the hall turned into another very large room.

Peering around the corner, Faellan saw two women standing in front of a bright blue whirlpool-like portal that stood at the center of the large circular room. Lines of white fire circled around the portal while spitting out arcs of blue lightning. In front of the crackling portal, one woman wore a white dress that clung to the her sinuous body. If she hadn't been an escaped prisoner, he would have mistaken her for an emperor's bride. Several guards mentioned her name was Estasia while obviously discussing her physical attributes. She was some kind of air wizard and noble woman. Feeling a tap on his shoulder, Faellan pulled his eyes off the beautiful woman and turned to the other mercenaries. With clinched jaws, they stared at him impatiently.

"What in the nine hells are you doing," one mercenary silently gestured.

"There are two women," Faellan gestured back. "I see no sign of the champion."

"Good, lets kill 'em quickly before the champion shows back up."

Frustrated, Faellan agreed but told them to wait a moment. He had to approach the two figures unnoticed. Searching the large room, there was no large objects that would hide him from their sight. The only other option was to charge them quickly. He had to reach the wizard before she could strike him down. Gathering his courage, he watched the beautiful woman for an opportunity to attack.

Despite her soft and inviting appearance, she seemed agitated with her long dark brunet hair waving in the air while speaking in a low inaudible tone. The other woman seemed just as agitated. Faellan noted that the other woman was dressed modestly in brown traveler's clothes and appeared unarmed. Goggles pushed her black hair off her forehead while it continued to flow down spilling over her shoulders and back. The modest woman was hunched over a console in front of the portal. The girl was named Calais, supposedly a powerful summoner. Fortunately, she seemed more occupied with the console than with the ranting beauty. Finding two of the three escaped prisoners, he scanned the room for the last one. The champion, known as Denarith, had to be close by. Behind him, Faellan heard something scrape against the metal floor.

Spinning around, Faellan found the other prisoner.

A tall, muscled man emerged from a dark crevice within the wall. He had a head of a bull covered in black fur that extended over the upper half of his body. His leather pants and boots covered the rest of his body. With a quick swipe, a huge two bladed axe cut one of the other hired mercenaries completely in half. Panicked, the other one tried to escape, but he was immediately smashed into a crimson mist. With the barbarian distracted, Faellan fled down the hall towards the stairwell.

Behind him, he heard the heavy footsteps of the champion pounding against the metal floor. Turning the corner back into the main corridor, Faellan ran faster, but the footsteps of the champion quickened. When the torchlight revealed the burial vault's exit, Faellan felt slightly relieved. Sliding past the huge door, he glanced back to the see the barbarian's shadowy form fast approaching.

Once outside the burial vault, Faellan found a group of mercenaries on each side of the door. They had their weapons drawn and waiting. Drawing his own weapon, he backed up to the stairs and watched the door. The light from the stairwell gave the room a dark blue hue. The torch created an orange aura around him. Then, the champion exploded from the door in a massive leap. Landing in the center of the room, he stared at Faellan for a brief moment. Looking into the champion's dark eyes, Faellan realized the champion knew what they were planning. Fear immobilized him while his gut twisted into knots.

"I am Lord Champion Denarith of the Tauru Totem, Hero of the Karjast Tribes, Slayer of the Gorlok army, Defiler of Myrlosh," the totem champion roared.

Both groups of mercenaries hesitated briefly, surprised by the ferocious barbarian. He swung his axe in one group's direction and released a massive wave of blue energy. His attack threw several mercenaries against the wall. Others were scattered on the floor. A second group attacked in unison. The only option they had was to overwhelm the large champion. Bringing his bull-head down, he charged the group. Astonished by his rapid speed, the mercenaries were thrown aside before they could hit him with their blades. Several men laid on the ground wounded from his horns. After his charge, the champion twisted around and killed three mercenaries in quick succession. Several other mercenaries tried to attack, but he deftly blocked each one and killed them quickly. Turning his attention to the first group who were preparing to attack, he pointed and yelled, "now Estasia!"

Faellan saw the beautiful woman standing in the door way. Her white dress swayed in the soft breeze. Lifting up her right hand, she released several lightning bolts. Faellan briefly turned away from the blinding light. Once his eyes readjusted, he saw several mercenaries reduced to charred remains. Confusion and fear swept over the remaining mercenaries. With additional lightning attacks, more mercenaries were killed while others were struck down by the barbarian. Not knowing what to do, Faellan raced back up the stairs.

Breathing heavily, he ran as fast as he could. He knew this was a bad idea. These were experienced warriors. They had only captured them by sheer luck or with Lady Enix's help. The champion was so drunk they carried him off. Estasia was captured while sleeping. The summoner surrendered once they cornered her, especially since she didn't have her summoner's book. Faellan never understood why the witch wanted these lords. All he knew is that she hated them for something they did to her ten years ago. Now, she wanted her revenge and planned to use them in some bizarre experiment involving a portal. He didn't care. He had to survive even if he didn't get paid.

Finally, he reached the top and stumbled onto the desert floor. The other mercenaries kept themselves and their horses at a distance. Faellan pushed himself back onto his feet while trying to catch his breath. In the corner of his eye, he could see Captain Lurech approaching him. Knowing that he had failed, he refused to look in the captain's direction and searched the ground for his next words.

"You failed us," the captain screamed. Faellan eyes scanned the nervous men around him. The captain leaned closer to Faellan's ear and whispered, "you failed us and now we are dead!" He could see the unmasked fear in the captain's face. Suddenly, the man's eyes widened and trembled.

"He has not failed you captain," a woman said. The captain slowly turned around to watch the mercenary group split to form a path. All the mercenaries bowed except the captain and Faellan. Faellan knew he should bow but terrifying thoughts overwhelmed him. Slowly, he raised his eyes to look upon the exotic woman that commanded them.

Lady Enix was very beautiful with a perfect figure. With long, firm legs and a tight body, she wore almost nothing except for a long blue tunic that barely hid her large bosom. Her hair was bright orange and blue while her skin was smooth and tanned. A feathered cloak hung around her. Most of the time, the cloak was red with some yellow and black. This time, her feathered cloak was black.

"Failure makes a man better," she continued. "It can strengthen him, quicker, faster and sometimes even smarter."

"Lady Enix," the captain said has he knelt down on one knee. "Please give us another chance. This time, we will all capture the prisoners."

"It is too late captain. They have used a portal and escaped this realm."

"Please, my lady, we will do better next time. Just give us another chance."

"Don't worry, my dear captain. I won't kill you. You and your mercenaries will live."

Faellan watched the other hired swords slightly relax. The captain breathed a sigh of relief. He even noticed some of the mercenaries smiling. The witch just smiled back at the captain.

"However, you will need to change. You will need to be stronger, faster and completely obedient."

Several mercenaries fell to the ground. Each one was grasping at his chest. Flames erupted from their skin. More and more of the men fell to the ground consumed by the red flames. Not even the horses were spared. Inside Faellan's chest, he felt a terrible burning. Dropping to his knees, he tore at his chest trying to dig it out. It was almost as if some fiery creature was eating his soul.

Chapter Two

Monty Awakens

She awoke in a strange, old house. Unlike an ordinary house, it had gray pipes and black wires streaming along the tall, angled ceiling. When they met the ceiling, they would jump in and out of the walls before completely disappearing into the floor. With lights flickering and whirring around her in this strange, metal jungle, she laid motionless on a silver bed. With a bit of effort, she sat up seeing herself for the first time in a small mirror hanging from pipes.

She wasn't like a normal girl. Instead, she had pure white skin hard as marble but as flexible as skin. Her eyes were white like her skin except for the pale blue irises and black pupils. In the mirror, she watched her silky white hair flow smoothly around her face and shoulders. Looking down, she touched the soft white dress that covered her slender, feminine body. Hearing footsteps, she turned to find an old man covered in a leather apron wearing thick leather gloves. He had a thin frame with wiry arms and legs. His bony, wrinkled face was accented by a long nose. He stared at her with glittering eyes and a wide, warm smile covered in a thick gray mustache. The man slowly approached her.

"Please do not be frightened," he said. "My name is Montague, and this is my house… and my workshop. You are safe here. Nothing will hurt you, or it really can't hurt you in any way. What I am trying to say is that I only want to help you. Tell me, how do you feel?"

"I feel warm," she said surprised. Somehow, she knew how to speak and move. She understood all the words Montague said. From the back of her mind, knowledge rushed through her mind like a river. Stunned for a moment, she recognized the different pipes and the wood used on the floor. Looking at Montague, she realized he was of a race called human. "How do I know what you are and what these pipes are? How is that I speak and understand you? Why am I here? Where am I?"

"Don't worry, I can answer most of your questions," Montague said calmly. "With the Divine's help, I created you."

"I don't understand," she said.

"I am an engineer, a crafter, you might say," Montague began. "I received a vision many years ago that showed me how to build you. Since then, I have tirelessly worked in this workshop to create you."

"I am still confused. Why did you create me?"

"I am not sure why the Divine chose me," Montague said reluctantly. "After a lifetime of making bad decisions, I was given the opportunity to finally do something right. You see, the vision told me that you would fix this realm and save it from darkness. That is why I had to make you."

"How do I stop this darkness from hurting the realm? Why doesn't the Divine just stop the darkness instead of making me?"

"The Divine works in mysterious ways I have been told," Montague said as he pulled tools from a nearby drawer. "That means you only know that answer when the Divine wants you too. For now, I will take care of you and help you the best I can to find your path. Now, let me to do some testing. I want to make sure everything is working perfectly."

The old man scanned her body with a glittering box covered in dials and gauges. Holding her left arm up, he moved it slowly from her hand to her shoulder. Then, he did the same procedure on her right arm and each of her legs. As he finished with her leg, she realized what the device was called.

"That is called an ethraedialscope," she said. "How do I know what it is, and that it measures energy?"

"I call it your deep memory," he said as he scanned her torso and abdomen. "Inside you, I put a soulforge. It is your heart and soul. After I constructed it, I performed a ritual I saw in a vision. Somehow, that ritual imbued it with mystical powers that also gave you all that knowledge. While I know many functions it can perform, it has many more powers that even I am not aware of. As you grow, you may even learn to harness more of those powers. Now, I will test your pain and reflexes. Does this hurt?" He put down the scanner and tapped a nail against her forearm.

"No," she said watching the nail. "I barely feel it." Then, he tried to jam the nail into her arm, but the hard skin prevented the nail from penetrating it. "It still does not hurt."

"Oh that's fantastic. You will be difficult to damage which mean you won't feel much pain. Now, catch!" He tossed a wrench up into the air and she quickly caught it with one hand. "Excellent! Now, stand up and go put it in the drawer over there."

The small statuette-like creature pulled herself off the table and onto the dusty floor. As her feet touched the floor, more knowledge flooded her brain that allowed her to quickly balance herself. Standing for the very first time, she was barely three feet tall and stared up at the kind, old man. Slowly, she took her first step, but found each step easier and easier. She glided across the floor like she had been walking for years. Remembering which drawer he had pulled the wrench from, she pulled open the same drawer and gently placed the wrench next to another group of wrenches.

"Very good, now, put up the rest of my tools for me." He threw each tool to the left or right side of her forcing her to jump and slide towards the flying tool. As she grabbed a tool from the air, she shoved it into the appropriate drawer while catching the next tool. Once all the tools were caught and put up, Montague was clapping excitedly. "You are amazing. You have the grace and speed of an elf along with the strength and endurance of an orc. You are a marvelous creation. You, you, you. Wait, I can't keep calling you, 'you'. Let me think, what should I call you? I have always been terrible at coming up with names."

While he pondered, she noticed a silver-framed picture sitting on his workbench. It was a picture of an older, elegant woman with a thin, narrow face. "That's a picture of my mother," Montague said. "Her name was Montrielle. Everyone called her Monty."

"She looks like a beautiful human. Where is she now?"

"She passed away many years ago. When she was alive, mother gave the best counsel when I needed it the most. I still miss her dearly." Putting down the picture, she noticed Montague regarding her with an endearing smile. "What if we named you Monty after her?"

"I would love that name," she said. It seemed short and quick like her. Noticing his sad face, she straightened up and curtsied. "I will honor her name to the best of my abilities."

"I don't have the faintest doubt in my mind you will bring great honor to her name. I just remembered that I have a better picture of her downstairs. Follow me and I will show it to you." He walked down a narrow set of stair positioned at the corner of the room. Monty followed and stopped at the edge of the stairs.

Looking down, she could see the stair case twisting downward with no visible end. Carefully, she tried to take her first step but found the steps were too high for her. Scanning the walls of the staircase, she saw no other help to walk down the stairs. Tentatively, she hopped down to the first step. Then, she hopped to the next. With each step, it became easier and faster to get to the next one. Like a rabbit, she continued to hop and skip down the stairs. Montague turned around surprised when she landed on the bottom floor.

"Remarkable," Montague exclaimed. "This is further proof you will accomplish a great many things. Now, let me see where I put that picture."

The bottom room was nothing like the upper room. With soft glowing lamps, she found it filled with wonders. With a gasp, she stared at pictures of beautiful animals and vistas along the walls. The floor was perfectly stained wood without a hint of dust Beautiful rugs covered most of the floor. Below the pictures, there were shelves decorated with strangle baubles. They spun and danced in midair without wires or glass. Two red couches were placed near the front of the room with Montague rummaging through a dark wooden desk positioned against one wall.

"What are all these amazing things," she asked as she poked a group of twisting rings.

"They are various instruments I created. When I was not working on you, I was designing and building machines to help people. Well, hopefully, help people. Most of the time, they want my gadgets to hurt people. Now, couches are for sitting and not standing."

"But they are so soft to stand on. Why would you want to sit on one when standing on one feels better on your feet?" She twirled around and jumped a few times. Then, one of her feet broke the cushion and disappeared into the white stuffing. "Oops, I didn't mean to hurt your couch."

"You see, those couches were made for sitting and not standing. Everything is made for a reason. Here it is." From out of the desk, he pulled a larger silver frame. Monty walked over and looked at the picture. It was much larger and more detailed. As Montague looked at the picture, Monty noticed several other pictures in the open desk drawer. Most of them were humans dressed in eloquent clothing. Then, she saw that there were other races as well. "Are these elves? Is this an orc?" The elves were like humans but they had long, pointed ears whereas the orc was green-skinned with a long nose and sharp teeth.

"The orc's name is Djinn," Montague said as he put down his mother's picture. "He is a dear friend of mine. Don't believe everything you hear. Not all orcs are bad."

"If I hear such things, I will not believe them."

"Yes, always remember people can be quite judgmental. So, you must hide your appearance until they get to know you. That is why I made you this cloak. It should cover you when you are traveling in the world." He pulled a small black cloak off of a nearby wall hook and handed it to her.

"Are we going somewhere," she said as she felt the soft black cloth.

"Not yet, but soon. We must do more testing which reminds me. But, first a fun test. Let us see if you can eat."

She followed him to a small breakfast nook adjacent to the main room. In the center of the nook, there was a small table with two metal chairs that was surrounded by large windows covered with thin, white drapes. On the table, several breads and puddings were prepared. She climbed into one chair and placed the cloth on her lap. The plates were glistening from the warm sunlight that spilled into the room.

"Normally, we eat this for breakfast," Montague said as he sat in the other chair. "Even though it is almost dark, we can break the rule this one time and have breakfast for dinner."

"This looks wonderful," Monty said as her eyes jumped from dish to dish. "What should I try first?"

"Take a bite of each one and tell me what you think."

"This bread is very sweet," she said while sampling a small slice of yellow bread. Then, she picked up a slice of pink bread. "This is salty and crunchy." She saw a utensil she recognized as a spoon and used it to take a bite of the pudding. "This is very tart and lemony."

"Try this bread, this is my favorite." Montague grabbed a piece of bread that had black filling.

Monty grabbed a piece as well and chewed it quickly. "That is wonderful. It is not too sweet and I think you call the filling blackberries which have a wonderful taste."

"That's right. I love blackberries. My mom used to grow bushes outside our house. I would always eat a few every day despite my mom's threats of punishments. She said they were for desserts and not for snacking."

"Why can't you eat desserts all the time?"

"For us humans, we need meat and vegetables to stay strong and healthy. Desserts are just a fancy that lets us enjoy life a little more."

Finishing the bread, Monty heard the clacking noise of a wagon outside the window. Turning around, she saw an ornate wagon being pulled by two brown horses. "What is this place?"

"That is the city of Smithhaven," Montague said sitting back as he studied another sweet bread. "It is in the Sinjara barony which is in the province of Adia. It is one of four provinces part of the empire. The empire rules this realm we call Tallendrall."

As he gave his brief lecture, Monty continued to watch the strange wagon make its way towards a large group of tall, distant buildings. Instead of slowing down, it forced groups of people in the streets to disburse. Some people jeered at it while others ignored it.

"What is in that wagon?" Monty said while leaning on the window sill. "People don't seem to like it."

"Of course not," Montague said. "That wagon carries a rich noble. They serve mostly themselves and sometimes the empire. Their hunger for power and schemes make them despicable people which makes everyone else even more miserable. It is best to avoid them."

As the sun set, she watched the wagon disappear into the growing darkness. Most people left the streets making their way into one building or another. With the world being overtaken by shadows, she saw a group of soldiers coming down the street. Then, Montague shut the window in front of her.

"Why did you shut the window," Monty said surprised.

"I am afraid our time has been cut short," Montague said as he shut the other windows in the breakfast nook. "I have to leave now."

"Why are you leaving? Who were those soldiers?"

Montague led her back to the main room with the couches and knelt down next to her. "Many years ago, I helped some friends stop a horrible evil. Now, that evil has returned and is seeking revenge. One of the reasons you were made was to stop this evil, but you are not ready. If they find you now, you will be destroyed. That is why you must hide. Whatever happens to me, you must stay hidden. Promise me you will not show yourself."

"I can help," Monty protested. "I don't want them to hurt you or take you away."

"It is okay," Montague said reassuringly. "You are my greatest achievement. I am so happy and proud that I have been given the chance to talk to you and play with you and eat with you. I love you so much and there is nothing more I need from this life." He hugged Monty tightly while tears ran from her eyes.

"I don't know what to do," Monty said as she cried into his shoulder.

"Don't worry, I have friends that will help you." He pulled her away so he could look straight into her eyes. "When the soldiers are gone, and it is safe to come out, you must find the Ninth Spire and it will take you to the wingless angel Enikus. He will show you your path."

"How do I find this Ninth Spire?"

"The medallion on this necklace will lead you to it. I don't have time to show you how it works, but you are very smart and you will figure it out. One more thing, you are a good person. Everyone will try to tell you that your evil, but you must not believe them. Trust you heart, and it will not lead you astray."

Monty reluctantly nodded and then he led her to a small cabinet. After he opened the doors, he eyed different areas inside the cabinet. Then, he pressed on a few jewels on the side of the cabinet. The air inside it became electrified. Monty stared at the sizzling air nervously, but his warm smile reassured her.

"Monty, go inside... into this cabinet. It will protect you. Trust me, I made it specifically to protect anything inside from any danger outside. Think of it as some kind of vault. Now, when you are inside, you must stay as quiet as possible, no matter what happens. When you are ready to leave, you just have to press this button and it will let you out."

"I'm scared." Looking into his eyes, he never cried, and he showed no anger or fear. He just beamed back at her with his warm smile and glittering eyes. He knelt down and embraced her with a hug again that filled her with a warmth that she would never forget. With no other words, Monty held her black cloak tightly in her arms while walking into the cabinet. Gently, Montague closed the doors.

*   *   *   *

From inside the dark cabinet, there was still a ray of light coming through a crack. By peering into it, she could see some of the room with Montague standing next to the couch. For several moments, everything was quiet. Then, she heard a gradual crescendo of footsteps nearby that suddenly stopped. Montague stood motionless as he waited. After distant yells, the door exploded as several men in black armor burst into the room. They ran upstairs and weaved in and out of different rooms. Regardless of the ensuing chaos, Montague just patiently watched an approaching man protected by a black and gold-encrusted armor. A flowing red cloak fell from his back.

"Hello Tomas," Montague said to the man. "I am disappointed. You should have known better."

"Ah, Montague," the man said. He was just a little taller than Montague but had short black hair with a long angular face. His devilish grin made Monty uneasy. "After ten years, you are still trying to lecture me. Well, you won't have to worry about me anymore, because your time is up. I am here for your soulstone so I can return it to Lady Enix."

"So, it is true. Lady Enix has returned. Unfortunately, there may be no stopping her now."

"Why would we want to stop her," Tomas said as he began circling Montague like a vulture. "I know the truth now. Lady Enix has shown me know how you lied to us. While the realm called us heroes of the Fifth Spire for stopping Lady Enix, you only delayed the realm's inevitable destruction. You and the other heroes wanted to overthrow the empire yourself. It was all because of stupid, useless politics."

"You're a fool, Tomas. It is true that I disagree with how harsh the empire has been treating its citizens, but I would risk hurting none of them. Do not let her words poison your mind. While we squabble among each other, she will unleash hell onto this realm. Everyone will be killed or enslaved by demonic hordes."

"No, the real enemy is this plague that is turning people into monstrous creatures known as the corrupted. To stop them, she needs the soulstones you and our friends took from her."

14

"Sir, I found something," a soldier said as he rushed downstairs carrying a large, jewel-lined box with a long, protruding barrel. From her deep memories, Monty knew it was similar to other cannons that had been used to fight dragons.

"So, this is what you have been up to," Tomas said as he examined the weapon. "You know it is treasonous act to make ethaerium weapons outside the Arcanium."

"I only built that weapon to destroy Lady Enix if she were to return."

"Lady Enix is an ally of the Emperor and any plot to kill an ally is yet another treasonous act. For that, we will have to confiscate everything in this house and arrest you. However, the empire needs your soulstone more. So, we will leave your house and all your stuff if you give up your soulstone."

"Never," Montague said strongly.

"Very well," Tomas said with a sigh. Then, he ordered his men to grab anything that looked like machines, tools or even plans. Monty could not see where the men went as they would disappear from view only to return with filled sacks. Montague just stood by as he watched them throw the sacks outside. While the soldiers collected various devices, Tomas ordered them to take everything off the shelves and walls. Then, he noticed the closed cabinet that Monty was hiding in. When he motioned towards it, Montague quickly intercepted the soldiers.

"That is enough," Montague said. "I cannot watch you decimate my work any longer. While these devices may not seemed like much to you, I have spent most of my life developing them. I would rather you take me prisoner, so some of my work can survive." Tomas waived the soldiers away and walked towards Montague.

"You know I was lying, and I was never going to arrest you," Tomas said drawing his sword. "There are only two ways to get a soulstone. One is by death and one is by a machine. After what you did to her ten years ago, Lady Enix prefers death."

"You don't have to do this, Tomas. You still have a choice. Don't be fooled by her lies."

"You're wrong," Tomas said. "I don't have a choice, because you took everything from me." Tomas screamed as he plunged his sword into Montague's heart. Monty covered her mouth and choked on her own scream while tears ran down her cheeks. She wanted to cry out, but she promised Montague that she would remain hidden. Shrinking backing into a corner, she helplessly watched the old man collapse onto the floor as Montague withdrew the sword.

Out of his pocket, a small sphere rolled onto the floor and flashed. Tomas' eyes grew large and ordered everyone to evacuate the house. It was too late. Monty watched the house explode. While Tomas and a few soldiers dived through windows, most of the other soldiers were caught in the blast. The magical cabinet protected Monty from the explosion and roaring flames that consumed the house's remains. Wrapping her arms around her, all she could do was cry.

Chapter Three

Caellan's Empty Glass

Caellan sat in a dim tavern staring at the empty bottom of his glass. With this being his fourth drink, he pondered his glass' emptiness. At the back of his mind, he could still hear the screams of the dead. Over the years, it became harder and harder to drown the voices out. To make things worse, he was still angry after fighting with his wife two days ago. He needed a few more drinks before he went home and faced her again. He motioned to a server to bring him another strong ale.

As a noble from the south, Caellan had lighter skin, broad shoulders with a muscular frame. His face was accented by a square jaw, strong nose, and shoulder-length, black hair. Unlike everyone else, he had deep eyes that were the color of gold.

"Hold that drink," a familiar voice called out.

"It is not wise to stand between a paladin and his ale," Caellan growled.

"Since when have I ever been wise," the dark-skinned man said as he sat across the table. The other man had a slimmer frame and a black-bearded face with a clean shaven head. His smile glistened with ivory-color teeth. "Besides, I am merely helping you stay within your paladin vows to not be drunk."

"For your information," Caellan paused as he shook his finger at the man. "I am not drunk." The other man just returned an unconvincing look. Not willing to push the matter further, Caellan slumped back in his chair. "Okay, Jarmel, what do you want?"

"I need nothing," Jarmel said innocently. "I am just wanting to see how my dear drunken friend is doing. I have not seen you much since the wedding. How is your lovely wife doing these days?"

"Jewel is constantly fighting with me," Caellan said frustrated. "I can never make her happy. She doesn't seem to like anything I do. I prefer fighting dragons than dealing with her."

"Ah women," Jarmal laughed. "Do not worry yourself. You face the plight of all husbands. When I first got married, it was like a battle. Then, we eventually conceded. She gets everything I owned, and I get a good night's rest. It also helps to serve in the militia and be away from home for several months. When I get back, she has forgotten everything and is happy to see me. When she is mad again, I just go on another tour."

Caellan had only heard half of what Jarmal said. It troubled him that his wife didn't appear happy. He had given her a title and a mansion, but she still was unhappy. He tried to be a good husband and take care of her, but it never seemed enough. Something deep inside him suggested that she would be better off without him.

"How is Jerick," Jarmal said after watching him for a few moments.

"I have not seen him since the wedding," Caellan said regretfully. Jerick was his best friend for years. Everything changed when they met Jewell. Jerick had no land or title and was not suitable to marry the niece of a baron. Since he was a son of a baron, Jewell married him. After the wedding, Jerick disappeared. Caellan regretted losing a friend over the marriage arrangement. Sometimes, he wondered if she regretted it for another reason.

"That is too bad," Jarmal said. "He was a good fighter and a good man. He could fight a hundred men and still win."

"If you are trying to cheer me up, you are failing spectacularly," Caellan said. While Caellan had been wearing a dark green long jacket over simple trousers and a white shirt, Jarmal wore battle armor and a heavy cloak. "Let me order another drink and you can tell me why you are really here."

"I need your help. We have received several reports that Kellenor is under attack by demon spawn and undead. Considering your past with demons and dragons, I thought you might help."

"The other militia men don't trust me," Caellan said bitterly. "Even after several years of helping this barony and hailed as one of the heroes of the Fifth Spire, they still whisper behind my back about my dragon curse. They think of me as some kind of freak who can't even summon his own armor."

For the last several hours, sweaty, grimy men had been filing into tavern. All of them avoided Caellan's gaze and whispered among each other. With no laughter, they groaned about the empire, supervisors and their pitiful wages. Humans had become disparate as they sat in the gloomy shadows, holding their breath every time the candles flickered. Even the nobility's laughter was a facade to hide their endless scheming. Despite his station as a nobleman and paladin, he didn't want to be involved in any of it.

"I am sorry my friend," Caellan said. "I cannot help you on your mission. May the Divine protect you in your journeys."

With a sigh, Jarmal rose to his feet and readjusted his cloak and tunic. "My men and I are leaving tonight," he said. "If you change your mind, you will know where to find us. I hope you find your armor again. Farewell, Lord Knight Caellan Pellandarr." After a slight bow, Jarmal left the tavern, and Caellan stared back at the bottom of his empty glass.

*   *   *   *

After a long ride back home, Caellan's horse carried him slowly pass the opened, iron gates. With only a few lanterns to light his way, Caellan directed his horse to the gloomy stables. A young stable hand stumbled out of the stable's shadows with a deep, arm-stretching, yawn. When the boy saw Caellan, he quickly recomposed himself and bowed. Shaking his head, Caellan dismounted his horse, and relinquished the animal to the boy. While Caellan was miserable, he did his best not to make his servants miserable. Turning to a stone path, he made his way to the manor.

The manor was an old military outpost converted to a summer home. Unfortunately, most of the amenities were applied to the interior while leaving the exterior to rot. Caellan and his wife stayed in it because it was a gift from the baron. Like a stone sentinel standing over the surrounding forest; it watched him approach. Pulling open the large wooden doors, Caellan entered the outpost's dark gaping maw.

Since the few manor's servants had already finished their nightly duties, there were only a few lit-lanterns holding the darkness at bay. His steps created a slow cadence that echoed across the manor. Once he arrived at his bedroom's door, he hesitated before opening it as he was uncertain of what to expect from his estranged wife. With a soft click of the door knob's mechanism, he slipped into the bedroom trying not to wake her. In a dark corner, he unbuttoned his jacket and shirt. From the red moonlight streaming through the window, he tried to find his wife among the blankets, but saw no one in the bed. Looking around the room, he saw no sign of her. He also noticed her large clothing chest was gone as well. Wondering where she might have gone, he stepped out of his bedroom and searched other rooms for a servant or butler.

"Can I help you sir," the butler said from behind him. He was an older, portly man with thinning hair and a buttoned nose.

"Gerren, do you know where my wife is," Caellan said turning around.

"She left this morning sir," the butler said impassively. "I am surprised she didn't tell you."

The butler knew exactly why she didn't tell him. Being a servant most of his life for his wife's family, he was always watching Caellan like a hawk. Gerren knew they spoke little and were usually fighting when they did.

19

While he said nothing, Caellan could always feel the man's disapproving stare burrowing into his soul.

"Where did she go now," Caellan sighed. Most of the so-called business arrangements benefited only the baron and his perpetual duplicity.

"The lady was meeting the baroness for some business arrangement in Kellenor."

When he heard the city's name, Caellan gasped. It was the same city that Jarmal had told him about earlier where all the trouble had been reported. Now, he wished he had asked Jarmal about the details. He hoped that she was not involved, or the reports were wrong. However, a cold chill running down his spine warned him, otherwise.

"I have to go find her," Caellan said rushing by the butler.

"Has something happened," the butler said as he followed Caellan back into the master bedroom.

"The city was attacked, and I must make sure she is okay," Caellan said as he redressed himself for travel. Watching Caellan adorn light armor and his heavy battle cloak, Gerren look changed from doubt to distress. "I won't be back for several days, and you will need to reschedule all my appointments." He hated the business of being a noble. It usually entailed boring accounting and long, tiresome meetings where everyone talked too much. At least now, he will have a reprieve for a couple of days.

"Of course," the butler said dryly. Caellan only told him out of proper decorum. Choosing not to waste anymore time, Caellan rode the horse from the manor and onto the dark path that would lead to Kellenor. Normally, the trip would take a full day, but Caellan could make the trip much faster. He hoped he wasn't too late.

CHAPTER FOUR

Escape from Smithhaven

Monty continued to watch out of the small hole in the dark cabinet where Montague had placed her. It had been several hours since the fire had ended. No smoke or fire ever entered the cabinet, so she just watched the flames dwindle to nothing that left only darkness. Eventually, a cool night breeze blew threw the cabinet. Then, the sun rose in the east. It created beautiful golden rays that caused the morning dew to glisten. Distant bird calls filled the air.

She hummed her song again. Monty had been singing intermittently all night, but she didn't know why. It created a warmth inside her that provided comfort and hope. As Montague's last words churned in her mind, she dreamed of spires and angels.

She knew there were twenty-four spires located in the middle of the Drift, a deep wasteland that was somewhere east of her. While walking was an option, Montague had insisted on using this medallion that hung around her neck. Examining the medallion, it was hollow while covered with gold and silver interlacing strands. There were no visible buttons to push or twist. Trying to pull or push on the medallion itself yielded no results. Then, she heard a noise outside.

Dropping the medallion, she frantically looked through the small hole for the source of the new sound. It was close. Earlier, Monty heard distance voices, horses, and wagons, but these sounds were in the house. Continuing to look through the small hole, she only saw charred wood and ash. It wasn't moving fast like rodents or bugs. This was much bigger. Suddenly, the cabinet door flew open.

Wearing a very large brimmed hat, the tall, gangly figure stood above her. He had a very thin frame that was wrapped in cloth bandage and a ragged robe. His skin was dark green and his eyes were a deep red. He pulled down a large red scarf to reveal a wide smile filled with sharp, jagged teeth.

"Ah," the figure exclaimed in a deep voice. "I finally found you. I knew he would put you somewhere safe."

Studying his face, Monty suddenly recognized the orc from the picture frame. "Your Montague's friend," Monty said cautiously.

"The great wizard, Djinn, is at your service," the orc said as he bowed to her. "What name did Montague give you?"

"I am Monty," Monty said returning the bow. "How did you find me?"

"Great question, but no time," he replied. "Now, quickly, come with me. It is very important that we hurry." He motioned to her to follow him as he stumbled his way back through the debris. Remembering what Montague said about not being seen when traveling, Monty put on her cloak and followed Djinn through the debris.

As they emerged outside, Monty found Montague's house was one of many houses. There were small and large houses spread out around different dirt streets. Looking to the west, she gazed at the very tall stone buildings decorated with lights and large pipes. Back to the east, she discovered a large forest pierced by city's main road. People with wagons or satchels bustled about the streets. As she continued to look around, a horse-drawn black carriage approached them.

"Quick, we must hide," the Djinn said pulling her across the street behind a smaller house. Then, she heard the carriage slow nearby. The orc was already peeking around the house corner although half of his hat was sticking out in the open. Monty knelt down so she could squeeze through his ragged robes and see the carriage for herself.

A large woman in a bright blue dress with white lace pulled herself from the carriage. From the other side of the carriage, a short bearded man with black and yellow robes walked to Montague's house. He had much nicer robes than the orc did. The large woman was fanning herself fervently as she walked over to the shorter man.

"Can we get on with this, Lord Master Illario," the large woman said. "It has already gotten hot this morning, and I hate the dirty outskirts of this city. My dress is already torn. It will take a week to get the seamstresses to fix this. Look at all these poor people out here. I never understood why they want to stay out here in the wilderness when they could come to the city where they would be taken care of."

"I disagree," the short man said. "I would rather keep these ruffians out of the city. They would just dirty it up or cause more problems."

"Well," the large woman continued. "You shouldn't have to worry much longer. Since the Governor has declared that only people in the sanctioned cities will be protected, I suspect we won't be coming out here much longer. They will probably just kill themselves or eat each other or something. Now, do you have the paperwork I need to sign?"

"Once I am finished," the man said. "You can sign the paper work as a witness. Don't worry, Lady Henthrow. I am an earth wizard, and this will only take a few minutes. I am only creating a simple two-story workshop."

The short man stretched out his hands and closed his eyes. Focusing on the house, his hands glowed and a massive whirlpool of sand, dirt, and water appeared underneath the rubble. Monty gasped as she watched the house of her creation slowly disappear into a black whirlpool.

Panicked at losing the only home she knew, Monty rushed out from behind the house. Surprised, Djinn gestured, and whispered fervently while she approached the two people from the carriage. When she made it across the street, the last remnants of Montague's house disappeared into a black pit. Then, large steel beams and stone columns grew upward from the whirlpool. As they twisted and danced around each other, they slowly connected into a steel lattice work. "Please stop this," Monty yelled. "That was my home. I was made here!"

The short man and large woman startled at the sight of her so much that the short man stopped his spell. The house slowly stopped building itself and left a half constructed house with beams and stones strangely angled. "What is that abomination," the large woman shrieked. Then, Monty realized that her hood had fallen down. "Is it some kind of corrupted being? Maybe it's a strange white nymph that will kill us where we stand. Lord Master Illario, you must do something!"

"Calm, yourself, Lady Henthrow," the short man said. "This is nothing more than one of Montague's gadget. He was known for being eccentric and always made the most odd devices."

"I am not a gadget," Monty said. "I am Monty. Montague was my friend, and this was his house."

"This is not his house anymore," Illario said. "This now belongs to the city because of city ordinance... wait, why am I talking to a gizmo. Let me destroy this thing so we can finish up quickly and get out of this dirty place."

"Wait," Djinn said. "You cannot destroy her. She is not a gizmo. She was inspired by the Divine himself."

"Orc," the large woman shrieked again. "Guards! Guards! Quick, we are under attack!"

"It is okay, madam," the orc said as he bowed. "I will not hurt you. I am Lord Master Djinn."

"You stupid orc," the short man said. "It is high treason to impersonate a member of the Lords' Council especially one of the heroes of the Fifth Spire. Now, we have two reasons to kill you."

"I absolutely agree with you that no one should impersonate a lord," Djinn confirmed. "As I said, I am Lord Master Djinn and... wait, two reasons. What's the other reason?"

"We will kill you because you're an orc," the large woman said.

"Funny, I thought this was an enlightened society that accepted all beings," Djinn said.

"That's right," Illario said. "Human beings become more enlightened as we kill more orcs."

"That doesn't seem very enlightening at all."

Monty noticed several guards in black uniforms approaching them. They carried spears, shields and swords. To Monty, they all looked similar to the men from last night. She became very nervous and backed away slowly.

"Why must you punish us," Monty said. "We did nothing wrong."

"You don't need your guards," Djinn said. "We will just go along our way. Come little one, let us move along."

"Guards, kill him and that thing," Lady Henthrow yelled.

"Run, little one, run," Djinn said motioning to the forest. He turned and waived his hands. "I shall stop them with a great fireball." Reluctantly, all the guards took a step back. Monty stared to run to the forest and then heard a loud boom. Turning around, she saw the guards, Lord Master Illario and Lady Henthrow covered in snow and ice. "Oh, look its snow. Well, close enough to a fireball." Holding himself and shivering, the short man pointed furiously at the orc.

"Ki-Ki-Ki-Killlll this charrrlaaatan," Illario said with a shivering lip. Stiffly, the guards moved to Djinn with their spears lowered. Djinn turned around and ran past Monty to the edge of the forest.

"Wait don't leave me," Monty said as she chased the orc. Looking behind her, she saw several other guards running past the chilled guards.

As Monty and Djinn neared the path leading into the forest, Djinn stopped. "Into the bushes, little one," Djinn said shoving her into the underbrush. "I will slow them down with a lightning spell." While trying to watch Djinn waive his hands around again, Monty slowly pushed her way through the underbrush. Fortunately, her hard skin made her impervious to scratches or injury from the plants, but her cloak seemed to catch on everything. Then, Djinn launched a loud, crackling blue spell at the pursuing guards. Instead of lightning, the spell released a black oil all over the ground that caused the running guards to slip and fall. "That wasn't supposed to happen."

"Do your spells ever work correctly," Monty said curiously from the bushes.

"Obviously, they work," Djinn said indignantly. "You see, I slowed them down." The guards were slipping and sliding in the oil as they tried to regain their footing.

"I see other guards," Monty said from deeper in the bushes. "Will you slow them down as well?" As Monty continued to navigate the thick underbrush, she looked back to see the orc squinting back towards the town at another group of approaching guards.

"Quickly, into the woods, little one," Djinn said as he came stomping through the bushes. Instead of pushing her own way through each bush, Monty found it easier to follow the orc's path of destruction as he tore through the forest. After a time, Monty could hear the guards crashing through the forest behind them.

"What are we doing," Monty said. "Is there a place we can hide?"

"Yes," Djinn said. "Follow me, I think we need to go to this way. Don't worry, I have a plan." Suddenly, something clicked and Djinn was yanked up into the air. Hanging upside down, he swinged back and forth as he his left leg was hung up in a rope. "You see, all part of the plan." Several guards emerged from the underbrush and approached. With their spears pointed at them, Monty backed up against Djinn while the guards chuckled. Nervously, Monty looked around for a way to free Djinn but couldn't see the source of the rope. Refusing to leave Montague's friend, she stood her ground between the spear and the orc. "Stand back, or I will cast another spell. It will be a spell of great power."

"What now, feathers," the guard laughed. "If you are a wizard, you have to be the worst wizard ever."

"Surrender now, or face her wrath," Djinn said as he pointed at a bush. For a moment, nothing happened, and the men chuckled to each other. Their eyes hungered for the orc's death. Then, a jaguar, black as night, silently emerged from the bush. The guards stopped their laughing and watched the large cat with wide fearful eyes.

"You heard Djinn," the cat said. "Go back to your farms or factories, militia men. You don't want to die here in these woods for a smelly orc."

"Marvelous, a talking cat," Monty exclaimed.

"It's a corrupted," a guard muttered.

"It's a wereling, a type of corrupted," an older guard said. "I heard they can turn into animal-human monsters. Grow claws longer than a man's arm. Their jaws could bite a man in half."

"You would only be so lucky," the cat said. "I am something far worse. I am a druid. A protector of all things natural; created by the Divine. You have no right to kill this orc. He did not break your laws, and last time I checked; humans need not eat orcs."

"Druid, wereling, whatever you are," the guard sneered. "We will kill all of you so I can sleep better knowing there are three fewer freaks in the world."

The cat did not move. Instead, the cat's eyes glowed with a fiery white light. Monty noticed several tree branches and vines moving around them as If the forest had come to life. Each guard was grabbed by a branch and yanked into the air only to be grabbed by another branch. The trees continued to toss and catch the guards until they were finally thrown out of the forest. In the distance, Monty could hear several guards screaming and running farther away.

"Thank you, kitty," Monty said as she walked up to it.

"You are welcome, child," the cat said. "My name is Nora and the orc hanging upside down is my traveling companion, Djinn."

"Oh yes, she already knows my name," Djinn said. "Her name is Monty. Nora, can you help me down? I'm getting a muscle cramp in my leg."

Nora looked at him thoughtfully as she sat down. "Why don't you use a spell of great power. I am sure it will help you."

"It was all part of the plan where I distracted them while you killed and ate them."

"Oh, was that the plan? I don't recall discussing it, or being asked."

"Next time, I will be happy to discuss anything you want. Now, can you be a good cat and get me down?"

"Oh fine," Nora winked at the tree and the vine dropped Djinn to the ground with a heavy grunt. Standing back up, he quickly brushed the grass of his ragged robe. "Did you find the old craftsman?"

"We were too late," Djinn said sadly. He sat down on a nearby log and pulled his hat off his head. Lowering his head, he covered his face with his hand and hat.

"Oh my dear orc," Nora said pulling herself off the ground. She padded over to the orc and placed a paw on his shoulder. "We did what we could. Do not grieve. Montague is in a better place now. Do you know what happened, child?"

"A human named Tomas killed him," Monty choked as the memories of Montague's death reignited tears in her eyes.

"Tomas is a coward," Nora growled. "I should have known he would turn on us."

"Why did he kill him? Why does he want a soulstone, and who is Lady Enix?"

"Please be calm, child. Ten years ago, Lady Enix almost destroyed this realm. She had become too powerful to stop, so we used the soulstones to banish her to another dimension. Recently, we received a message from

Montague warning us that Lady Enix had been freed. He said he had created you to stop her and that we must reunite with our companions again to destroy her. This time, it seems that some of our old companions have chosen her side."

"If Tomas is an ally, it means she has allied with the empire again," Djinn surmised.

"It makes our task that more dangerous," Nora said. "Child, did Montague share his plan with you on how to destroy her?"

"He said I must find the Ninth Spire. It is supposed to lead me to the wingless angel, Enikus."

"The Ninth Spire cannot be found," Nora said. "It finds you whether you want to be found or not."

"Montague said that this medallion will call the Ninth Spire," Monty said as she removed the necklace from around her neck. Nora walked over and inspected the medallion. "I have never seen such an artifact. If it can call the Ninth Spire, it must be powerful. Djinn, do you know what this is?"

"It is an old artifact from before the Age of Dragons," Djinn said as he lifted up his head. He stood up and put his huge hat back on his head. "I know of only one man we can trust to help us."

"Who is it," Monty said placing the necklace back around her neck.

"We call him the Sage," Djinn declared. "He lives in Parn."

Nora groaned.

"Is that far from here," Monty said. Her deep memories knew of the city, but they didn't tell her how far away it was from their current location.

"Not very far from here," Djinn said. "We should leave now."

"No," Nora said. "This is not our task to complete. This is Monty's task, and she must decide. You should know, Monty, that the sage is very strange and may not help us. He may not even want to help us. Also, Parn has a large militia with a strong imperial presence. It will be very dangerous."

"Is there another way," Monty said.

"I cannot think of one," Nora said regretfully.

"Then, I shall go to this sage."

"Excellent," Djinn said. "Let us begin our journey."

"No, Djinn," Nora said again. "You need to stop being so pushy. It is Monty's decision if she wants us to join." She turned to Monty. "We are friends of Montague, but we are not what you would consider good people. We will protect you, but you must know that we have done some horrible things in our past. It is up to you if you want us to join you."

Monty had never had a friend before. Looking into her deep memories, she knew friends were supposed to helped each other. So far, they had saved her from being captured or killed. If they spoke the truth, their experience would be invaluable on her journey. Otherwise, they may betray her, and she would fail Montague. She knew it was a gamble, but she had little choice. Monty did not understand where she was or how to find this sage. With a long slow exhale of breath, she made her choice. "You may come with me, but you must leave if I ask you too."

"It will be my honor to accompany you," Djinn said with a bow.

"You have my word we will protect you," Nora said.

"Thank you," Monty said. While Monty felt slightly relieved, her thoughts still dwelled on Tomas' betrayal. She could still see Montague's eyes as he fell to the ground. The empty, lifeless eyes were so different from when she first met him.

"Are you okay," Nora said. The cat studied her for a moment and even sniffed her.

"I just miss Montague."

"He was a good man, child, even though he was an engineer. I disagreed with him on the usefulness of human technology, but he made a few good devices that helped people. I will miss him too. Now, we must leave before other militia men come looking for us."

Monty just nodded and looked at the thick brush surrounding them. "How do we get to this sage?"

"We take a train," Djinn said.

"I hate trains," Nora groaned.

CHAPTER FIVE

Airwalkers

"Denarith," Calais yelled. "Do you see anything?"

"All clear," the bull-headed champion declared.

"Oh good, we've made it," Calais said with a deep sigh of relief. After running for days from that witch and her mercenaries, they finally escaped. Unfortunately, they had to travel to another realm through an old, forgotten portal. Thankfully, her calculations were correct. Not having the current planar measurements at hand, she could use only approximations. The planar movements were usually predictable except for the occasional ethereal storm. When that happened, portals could take a traveler to any random destination or just disintegrate them. Obviously, they were not disintegrated and weren't being immediately attacked. So, the trip was a success.

Like a large swirling blue and white vortex, the portal's crashing waves of light and sound finally dissipated and left them in a completely dark room. However, it wasn't dark for long as a small orb of light appeared behind her. The orb's light showed a thousand shadows dancing around the ruined remains of tables and weapon racks surrounded by cracked cave walls. On the other side of the room, Calais noticed a passageway leading further into an endless darkness.

"What dirty tomb did you take me to now, Calais," the woman in the white dress said.

"It's not a tomb, Estasia," the champion said. "It's an old combat preparation area."

"Not much better from what I can tell," Estasia said as she delicately stepped around the rubble on the floor. Estasia's orb of light passed in front of Calais as it tried to illuminate her path. "We are lucky that this place hadn't collapsed on us."

"We can always go back to the Lady Enix's prison instead," Calais offered. As she tried to follow Estasia's light, she kept stumbling on large rocks as her eyes couldn't adjust between the bright orb light and dark floor. Frustrated, she gave up on the floor and made her way to the top of the dusty stone tables. After making sure they could hold her weight, Calais stood on the table top and looked around the room. She recognized some of the old runes and carvings that were still present even after a millennium. Besides being further proof that Calais got them to their intended destination, she marveled at the history of this room.

"Incredible," the champion said. "I haven't ever wielded weapons like these. I have only heard great stories about how they were used to destroy dragons." He picked up a long ornate spear that stood over twelve feet long.

"Denarith, you found a dragon spear," Calais said as she leaned forward to get a better look at it. "Do you see how it's perfectly balanced? It was magically enchanted so that it could be thrown up to a thousand yards. If you hit a dragon, it would cause the creature a great amount of agony, but they never destroyed a dragon. If the dragon were caused enough pain, it would dissipate only to appear later, and it usually wasn't very happy when it did."

"Great," Estasia said. "I have another stain on my dress. You know, magic keeps this dress only so clean. It would have been pleasant if we could have gone somewhere where there was a warm bed, a hot bath, and had clean clothes." She paused as she tried to brush off the stain. With little success, she sighed and turned back to Calais. "I am sorry my dear. I appreciate your getting us out of that prison and away from Lady Enix. I am just tired. I didn't want to spend my last few months before my wedding always running from a demon. So, where did you take us and how soon can we get back home?"

"This should be the realm of Eirondrall," Calais said. "Historically, this cave was used as a staging area to help people escape the dragons' furies and to stage hit-and-run attacks. To the end of the Age of Dragons, they could infiltrate these outer planes and wipe out most of the resistance. As for home, I plan on finding another portal that will take us close to your father's barony and then we should be safe."

"Good," Estasia said. "Now, lets get on our way before we run into anything else. Eirondrall's savanna's and mountains are known to be full of large, hungry monsters."

"This will be just like one of my tribe's great hunts. We will slay these monsters and have a great feast."

"Technically, Denarith, they are not monsters. So far, there have been five groups of animals cataloged on this plane. The first group is known for…"

"Come along," Estasia said as she walked out of the chamber and into a dark cave. Her glowing orb floated above her head as it tried to light her path.

Calais shrugged and turned back to Denarith. While still holding the dragon spear, he touched two jewels halfway down the shaft. The entire spear shuttered and collapsed into a foot long handle that didn't include the large two-foot long serrated spear tip. Calais thought it almost looked like an exotic sword. He wrapped it up in some cloth he pulled from his satchel. Then, he put the wrapped spear into his satchel and threw the satchel over this shoulder.

"Another souvenir," Calais asked.

"You never know when you might have to fight a dragon."

"Ow," Estasia yelled from further down the cave. "Stupid rock!"

"Shall we rescue the lady," Calais said.

"Why else am I here?"

*   *   *   *

Traveling for several hours through a dark cave, Estasia led the way with Calais and Denarith following. While Estasia lighted the way ahead of them with her blue light orb, there was barely enough light for Calais to maneuver through the rocky path. When Calais mentioned something about the light, Estasia claimed she didn't want anyone else to see them. Calais knew better.

Estasia was not a very strong wizard. Both belonging to noble families, Calais and Estasia had been friends since childhood. While Calais loved her studies of summoning, Estasia preferred to socialize and disappoint suitors. She never really wanted to be a wizard, but it was extremely rare for a noble woman to have a talent for wizardry. With pressure from the empire and the Lord's council, Estasia was pushed into being a wizard by her parents. While her parents saw it as a badge of honor among the noble families, Estasia was derided by her social peers. Despite Calais' friendship, she avoided her studies to maintain her social standings. In the end, Estasia barely passed her wizard test and was never offered a position at the Arcanium or helping the Lord's Council. While it would have been disappointing to others, Estasia was relieved and focused on her social standing. While it was great for her to be married to an important baron, it left Calais and Denarith with a weak, ill-prepared wizard when they really needed something more. Finally seeing a light at the end of the cave, Denarith placed his hand on Calais' shoulder as a signal to stop. Without taking another step, Calais slowly turned around to look at him.

31

"There is someone else here," he whispered while pointing to his black nostrils. "I can smell them." Denarith moved in front of her as he slowly readied his axe. Despite his large, bulky size, Calais always found it interesting that he could move with soft steps. She assumed it was that stealth was a required skill in animal hunting. The barbarian clans relied almost solely on their hunters for most of their food supply. Since the empire forced the barbarians into areas with less fertile soil, they didn't engage in very much farming. Lost in thought, Calais didn't notice the figures appear behind her until she felt the sharp point pushed into her back. It was just enough pressure for her to notice but not to wound or kill her. Calais stood motionless as her eyes glanced side to the side as she tried to identify her attackers. Denarith somehow noticed the figures behind her and quickly spun around.

"Elves," Denarith growled as he raised his axe.

"Not another step barbarian," an elf said above them in a small niche. The elf had pulled back his bow and aimed his arrow at the champion's chest. "We will gladly kill you and your companions."

"Wait," Calais said but stiffened as the blade dug deeper into her back. "Um, we are friends. You don't need to kill us."

"You are no friend of mine," the elf said.

"And you're pissing me off," Denarith countered. "I think it's time to crack open some elven heads."

"Wait Denarith," Calais said. "Airwalkers, with respect, we are here to speak with Revannick, son of Regilus. May we speak with him?"

"Fortunately human," the elf said. "You don't have to go far."

"Calais," a voice said further down the cave. "Hold your weapons. I know her." Still not wanting to move with the blade in her back, she could see only a shadowy figure pushing its way through some other elves. "Don't worry, my big friend, I won't hurt you." As he patted the Tauren champion's shoulder, Denarith reluctantly moved to the side. With Estasia and her floating light following the figure, Calais immediately recognized Rev and his roguish smile. She sighed in relief as the figure behind her moved the blade away from her back. They laughed as the two old friends hugged each other. Calais was always attracted to him, but never knew what to say to the free-spirited elf.

"Why didn't you say you were here to see me in the first place," Rev asked.

"Well," Calais began. "You know I was never that good with words, unlike my father. As a baron, he could sway the entire empire. Undoubtedly, you knew that when you visited me during the summer."

"Oh Calais," Rev said. "I have missed you and your wonderful creatures. Did you bring any new ones?"

"No. I was captured by Lady Enix and had to hide my summoner's book. So, I don't have it or any scrolls."

"Lady Enix? Why has that wicked creature come back?"

"Someone released her from her inter-dimensional prison. That's the only way she could have gotten out. Now, she wants her soul stones back, but she has to kill us or capture us for some gruesome ritual."

"Do not worry. You and your friends are welcome in my home."

"Oh great," Denarith grumbled.

"Don't worry cow man," Rev said. "It's only a bad place if you are afraid of heights."

"His name is Denarith," Calais said. "Behind you is my friend, Lady Estasia, daughter of Baron Eston Verrandrin."

"My lady," Rev said as he kissed her hand.

"Sir elf," Estasia said. "I am honored to be your guest."

"We prefer the term airwalkers. We feel the word, elf, is derogatory."

"My apologies, airwalker."

Calais noticed that Estasia gave Rev one of her flirtatious looks. She felt a burning anger in her chest as she watched them. Calais wasn't about to let Estasia crawl into his heart. Normally, she didn't care whom Estasia chose, but Estasia could not have Rev. "Ok, we should really get moving. Lady Enix may send her mercenaries after us."

"Don't worry. No human mercenary shall find their way to our city. Ever since the Age of Dragons, we have learned to hide ourselves quite well."

By touching something on the wall, the part of the cave wall silently gave way to a passageway of stairs. Even with Estasia's light spell, Calais could barely see the stairs leading upward into more darkness. Rev motioned to follow him up the stairs.

The stairs were narrow and went up forever. As her leg muscles began to ache, Calais started to notice how tired she was becoming. After all, she had been on the run for two days from the Fifth Spire. Lady Enix had commandeered the magnificent structure for her own evil uses. Thankfully, Estasia knew a few spells to get them across the Drift quickly. Looking back, Estasia was slowly falling behind the group as she looked more and more weary. With a loud crack of thunder, Calais looked back at the stairs to see flashes of light in the distance. Finally, they were about to get to the top. Denarith head and horns formed a silhouette against the scattered lightning. He was ahead of the line almost racing the elves to the top.

Once Calais emerged from the stairway, she found her self on top of a mountain range. The mountain tops were smoothed down and flattened by howling, eroding winds. While a gray sky was above her, black clouds roiled below the mountain peaks to cover the distant land beneath them. As lightning struck out of the tumultuous clouds, the group fell into a long vertical column as they started to make their way across the long, narrow peaks. Calais fell in line near Rev and her companions as they began to make their way along the edge of a mountain.

"How much farther is your city," Estasia said.

"Do not worry, my beautiful lady," Rev said. "We do not have much farther to walk. You know, Calais, my father still talks about you. He really missed you and wished you had retained your noble status. He claims we would have been a perfect match."

"Ha," Calais said. "You would get too bored married. You couldn't sit still for more than a few hours let alone a few decades."

"Who would give up on this incredible life of fame, fortune, and adventure? You never know what's around the next corner. It could be pirates, demon spawns, and even cow men."

"I am a Tauru champion of the Karjast tribes," Denarith growled.

"Of course, my friend. Do not worry. My intention is not to offend you but to have fun. Life is too short to be angry. Relax great warrior. For tonight, we shall have a great celebration."

"Celebration," Denarith asked. "Finally, we get something to eat. There will be meat right?"

"Of course, there will be food. There will be mountains of food. You happen to come when we are celebrating the Festival of Alignments."

"As long as there is food, I am happy," Denarith said.

"Ah yes," Calais said. "The realms align around this time that will cause various energies and forces to increase in their strength and focus. With the right methods, the power of a spell could be increased by tenfold."

"Planar mechanics was never very interesting, but enough of that. We have made it!"

Calais looked around as they stopped at the side of a mountain cliff. More black clouds spit out lightning below them and large grey clouds floated in front of them. Her companions looked around confused as they saw no sign of any structures or cities. Calais quietly smiled to herself and waited for the entrance to appear.

"So where are we at," Estasia said.

"This is my home," Rev said as he pointed out into the distance.

"Is this some kind of joke?"

In front of them, Calais watched a bridge of light and clouds connect their cliff to golden city gates within the dark cloud. The elf party eagerly strode into the city as Calais' companions looked warily at the translucent bridge.

"Welcome to Eirodias," Rev declared, "the city of the clouds."

"This is impossible," Estasia said. "No magic spell is this powerful."

"And that is the reason for our festival. Now, come on. Let's have some fun."

"Using the aligned planes, they are able to re-enchant their city every 300 hundred years," Calais informed her companions. "It is constantly moving and hidden from all outsiders."

"So, that's how they avoided the dragons and their armies," Denarith said.

"Enough history," Estasia said. "Do you smell that?"

"Cooking meat and freshly baked bread," Denarith said licking his lips. "It's time to eat!"

CHAPTER SIX

The Designs of Lady Enix

In the Drift, a tower of gray stone and black obsidian stood tall against a storm of purple and blue clouds. From a massive whole in the ground, a symphony of clouds and lightning rose high into the sky. Undaunted, the tower remained unmoved with only its face reflecting the chaos of the maelstrom behind it.

Within this tower, an imperial commander, an elite member of the imperial guard, stood alone in the dimly lit hallway. Trying to hide his deep uncertainty, he fiddled with his gold-engraved breastplate. As he heard the entrance gate's gears start churning, he tried to straighten out his black and silver-lined tunic and pants. With a metal cadence, he watched the gate slowly climb upward releasing an explosion of light into the large hallway. Wincing from the painful light, the man turned his head until his sight readjusted. As the gate continued its march upward, a black cloaked figure waited patiently from the outside. After another several moments, he heard the gate stopped with a deafening silence. The figure proceeded into the long dark hallway.

"Caezik, my old friend," the commander said as he fell in step next to the hooded, cloaked figure. "Welcome to the Fifth Spire. It has been too long since we last saw each other. How are your brothers and sister?"

"I am only here because I was summoned by Lady Enix," Caezik said without breaking his stride. "Where is she?"

"She is in the audience chamber. I believe you remember where that is." After a long pause, Tomas felt the uneasy silence close around them. Caezik was always cold and reserved. As a member of the Black Hand that was one of the many orders in the Lord's Council, Caezik acted as executioner for the empire. Tomas figured that anyone who had to kill heinous criminals would become very jaded. From what he knew of Lady Enix's plans, he didn't understand how an executioner would fit in. He was already doing most of her dirty work. "I must admit that I am surprised to see you. Lady Enix didn't inform me that you were coming."

"Why are you helping her," Caezik said as he stopped mid-stride turning to Tomas. Removing his hood to reveal a rugged, bearded face, he stared at Tomas with deep-set, gold-colored eyes. He was shorter than Tomas with a thinner build. Unlike Tomas' heavier plate armor, Caezik wore lighter, black leather armor over tightly wrapped, black clothing. His heavy hood and cloak hid most of his dark, short hair. No weapons were visible, but that was normal for a Black Hand. They wanted to surprise their targets to make it easier to kill them, but Tomas knew that Caezik carried his signature bow that never missed its target. "What treachery is the empire planning this time?"

"It's okay, my friend. You can trust me."

"Trust? A lot can change in ten years, especially a man's soul. Are you still a member of that blood-thirsty group of knaves?"

"It's called the Viper squadron and no, I am not a member of it anymore," Tomas began in a softer, pleading tone. "I am here because I have to be. Lady Enix and I have an agreement that she is bound too. There is no empire, and there are no orders. I am doing this because I need her."

"You still haven't answered my question."

Tomas paused for several moments searching the ground for answers. His friends would never understand his arrangement with Lady Enix. If they did find out, they would reject him and he would be alone. Even among the ranks of the Imperial Guard, he had very few friends. However, he had to tell Caezik something or he would keep pressing for answers.

"It's my wife. She is very sick, and only Lady Enix can help her."

"Making deals with that witch is risky business. I hope you got a plan." With that, Caezik continued down the hallway as Tomas followed. As they got closer to the tower's control room, Tomas could see Caezik loosening up as if he were about to enter battle. While Tomas tried to make small talk, Caezik wouldn't answer or gave very short grunts. While his friends harbored bad memories of this tower from their experience ten years ago, Tomas had grown accustomed to the strange tower and the fickle witch.

The control room was a very large round room with a vaulted ceiling above it. Above the ground floor, Tomas could see large multilevel balconies encircled the room Each one was supported by large pillars. At the center of the room, a large diadem formed a raised platform surrounded by several large stone columns jutting above it. A set of stairways extended from the edge of the platform to a large stone ornate chair that was suspended in midair. When they had entered the chamber, Lady Enix was walking down the white stone stairway to them. Unlike the desert, she wore her blue, orange and red feathered cloak along with a blue open robe that barely covered her tanned, curving body. Tomas always felt uneasy around her. Sometimes, it was her sensual appearance, and other times he felt like prey standing in a room with a hungry predator. Regardless, he always tried to keep his uneasiness and doubts hidden from her. He had to stick to the plan if he were going to save his wife.

"Lord Commander Tomas," Lady Enix said in warm tone. "I see you have brought back our old friend, Lord Black Caezik. How long has it been since we last saw each other Cae?"

"Not long enough Enix," Caezik said coldly. "I see you are still playing with portals. I thought you would have learned your lesson the last time when we trapped you in that prison."

"Cae," she said as she stepped off the raised platform and slowly approached Tomas and Caezik. "I do not harbor any bad feelings to you and your friends. You did what you had too."

"Why did you summon me?"

"Always straight to the point," Lady Enix said affectionately. "I need your services. Over there on the table, there are three black letters that require your attention."

Raising an eyebrow suspiciously, Caezik walked to the nearby small stone table while watching her closely. He picked up the letters that were made of a thick, black parchment that was folded up into thirds. Each one was sealed with the gold imperial seal in which only a judge could reproduce. Reluctantly, he touched a seal causing it to reshape itself so that he could open the letter. The imperial seal was an old, magic that was developed during the Age of Dragons to prevent secret messages from being discovered. Now, only the empire's judges and members of the Black Hands used them for sentencing criminals to death. If any other person besides a judge or a member tried to open the letter, it would kill them. Those that survived such an attempt were maimed for life. Meticulously, Caezik reviewed each letter.

"Dragoncraft," Caezik said. While Caezik did not show any emotion, Tomas was astonished. Working with dragons and their magic was forbidden throughout the empire. Although it had been over three hundred years since the dragons were exiled, all people in the realm still had a deep distrust for the creatures.

"We worked so well before and, oh yes, your father has experience with dragoncraft." While Caezik scowled, Lady Enix returned only a playful smile. In Tomas' experience, it was a treacherous smile. However, Caezik remained unfazed. Tomas watched him close each letter and place them in a black bag that he wore at his belt.

"I am not interested in you or your games. How did you get these scrolls?"

"I am still sanctioned by the empire. I have all the same authorities I once had. If you would like, I can show you my imperial letter."

"So, the empire is still interested in demons and portals."

"Not officially," Tomas interjected. "While she is not under any direct orders from the emperor, she still has his blessing for now. I can vouch for her and I promise you that she has not done anything to jeopardize the empire or our companions."

"Tomas," Caezik said pointedly. "You can take your politics and shove it. As for you, witch, I will complete these tasks when I see fit." With that, Caezik turned around and left. After a few moments, Tomas could hear the outer gates open and close.

"Please my lady," Tomas said. "That was unnecessary. Caezik has been a good friend. I value his opinion and skills."

"Oh, do not worry, Tomas. I have not sent him on a dangerous mission. In fact, he is very important to our mission."

"You mean the mission to save my wife, right?"

"Of course, my dear. Once I have obtained enough soulstones, I will be able to reopen the portal and save your wife. The plan has not changed."

"So how many more soulstones do you need? You promised that you would not harm my friends unless they stood against us. You know that my friends are very important to me."

"So why do you lie to them," Lady Enix said nonchalantly.

"It is necessary," Tomas said dourly. Not wanting to discuss it any further, he decided to leave the room. As he left, he could feel Lady Enix silently laughing at him. Needing to clear his head, he went to a place in the tower that was as far from her as possible.

*   *   *   *

The defense station was a large balcony with several control stations. Each station controlled magical cannons mounted at various points around the tower. The cannons were an old technology was more powerful than any weapon created since the Age of Dragons. No one knew what they were meant for, but Tomas shuddered at the thought of facing such foes.

He carefully fingered the controls so he wouldn't activate them. To control a group of cannons, a person just had to hold the controls and their mind would be merged with the cannons. By just looking toward a target, the person could will the cannons to fire. They had perfect aim.

Tomas had only seen one test to another spire where the defenders flawlessly destroyed all the attacking ships. With three of the four stations each controlling a different group of cannons, they filled the sky with red bolts. While it took only two bolts to destroy an airship, the cannons fired their energy ammunition rapidly and endlessly. The test didn't last long. The fourth station was a defensive station that could create small energy shields that would block each attack. While the airships could only fire a few shots at the tower, each cannon volley was easily thwarted since they just had to see the attack to block it. Despite the Lord's Council's long history with the spires, no one could discern the tower's inner workings or weapons. Tomas was grateful since the empire's ambitions have grown darker over the years. Before he could contemplate the terrible atrocities, the empire would perform with such power any further, he was interrupted by one of Lady Enix's mercenaries.

"The lady wants you, lord commander," the mercenary spat. Tomas didn't know the man's name. While he considered a mercenary to be below his station, he took notice of their faces for security reasons. He recognized the man by his leathery face and flat nose. Besides a wide grin, he wore the standard mercenary armor that comprised a loose red shirt and pants accented by black leather armor. While each one was armed with different weapons, this one had a long sword and several daggers strapped to his belt. "Well, are you coming or not?"

"Take me to her," Tomas said. Earlier, he had scolded the mercenaries for their indignant tone, but he had grown sympathetic to them and their plight. Despite their best efforts, Lady Enix was never satisfied and converted many of them into fiery creatures called fire knights. Other mercenaries were tortured for days in endless fire. Now, there were only a few mercenaries left in the tower. They were as much of a prisoner as he was.

Tomas followed the mercenary to a section of the spire that was considered an archive or library. From his understanding, the spires had no such documentation or books. Making his way around the different bookshelves, Tomas found Lady Enix standing over a large circular table. With her finger, she traced the lines of several schematics that lay bare on the table. When they got closer to her, Lady Enix turned and dismissed the mercenary. Without a word or a nod, the man rushed out of the room probably grateful he wasn't killed.

"I am here, my lady," Tomas said with gritted teeth. "I presume you wish to mock me again."

"Do not fret, lord commander," Lady Enix said. "I will always mock you. There is nothing you can do about it. You think I am your puppet, but our agreement makes you my lovely puppet as well. What is even more interesting is that I am not the only one pulling on your strings? For instance, this letter we received from General Amirez. He reports that Castle Dragonlock's calibration is almost complete and will be ready for the ceremony. Plus, he reports his cannons will be in position as well." She handed him the letter with a devious smile. "I hope there isn't anything you aren't telling me."

"I have no secrets from you," Tomas said annoyed while grabbing the letter from her hand. He examined the broken seal and the parchment. Then, he opened the letter to confirm. "Besides, I would have reported this to you, anyway. There is no reason to distrust me. The plan is proceeding accordingly. I would think you would be overjoyed." Instead of giving it back to her, he put the letter in a small satchel hanging from his belt.

"I know your imperial bureaucrats are foolishly planning something, but it won't work. I know you humans all too well, and I already have measures in place to counter your treachery."

"You can read minds, and you would know if I lied."

"Please do not let that stop you," Lady Enix said while gently placing her hand on his cheek. "I truly love it when a man lies." She stroked his metal breastplate with a single finger. "It's as if I can feel their souls explode with their deepest desires."

"We have an agreement," Tomas said. He pulled her hand from his armor. "You do your part, and I will help you with your plans. We have no time for pleasure."

"How boring, lord commander," Lady Enix said mockingly. Turning her back to him, she sashayed back to the table with the drawings. "Trust me, this all pleasure for me."

"Is there anything else," Tomas said annoyed. He found it hard to resist her and did everything he could to avoid her seductions. He had already made one mistake with his wife, and he would not dishonor her any further.

"Of course, I need you for something else." Lady Enix walked to the opposite side of the table and leaned over to study the drawing. "Did you see any white statues moving or standing still when you were ransacking Montague's house?"

Tomas was taken aback. Everything had gone wrong that night. The old man was supposed to have cooperated and gone with him. Instead, Tomas learned that Lady Enix was right. The old man was conspiring against the empire and had been manipulating everyone from the beginning. Despite his treachery, Tomas regretted killing his old friend. Montague had always been pleasant and encouraging especially when Tomas worked with him ten years ago. Clouded by his anger and remorse, Tomas remembered little from that night.

"We saw nothing like that," he said. "Besides the cannon, he had tools, trinkets, and drawings."

"Fortunately for us, this drawing is the key to our success. Do you see what it is?"

Tomas approached the table slowly, but maintained his distance from her. "I do not recognize it," he said after reviewing the drawing. In truth, he had little interest in schematics or engineering. None of it ever made sense. To him, it appeared like a drawing of a strange heart that appeared crystalline in nature. Around the main drawing, Tomas observed several other smaller drawings of gears and waves.

"This is a soulforge. It is an artificial soul that is infused with energy from the Divine. By connecting the spire to it, we can use the full power of the Dragonshield to finally close the maelstrom."

"So, we don't need the soulstones anymore?"

"Not all of them. We will still need some of the soulstones for the calibration process."

"How many more," Thomas said anxiously.

"We only need seven more before the planar alignment."

"With your allies giving you their soulstones, we would only have to kill two more."

"No, we have to kill seven more of our enemies. The soulstones give you certain powers and immunities. Is it not better to have fewer enemies with powerful allies?"

"I suppose," Tomas said regretfully. While he didn't want to see his friends die, he had no choice if he wanted to save his wife. "How do I find this soulforge?"

"The old fool stored it inside a construct made of marble and stone."

"He made a maru!" They were creatures of legends that brought terrible destruction with them. Many believed that they were more terrible than the corrupted themselves. Some of them were destroyed while others disappeared. "How do we stop, let alone capture, a maru?"

"Calm down, my silly man," Lady Enix said soothingly. "I know how to deal with a maru. Right now, it is nothing but a child, stupid and powerless. It will be easy to capture."

"So, how do we find it?"

"I made these devices to locate the maru," Lady Enix said walking over to a nearby shelf. She picked up two devices that were the same. Each one was a metal box with several meters and knobs." It shouldn't be too far from the old man's house. Take these devices to Captain Rains and Baron Verrandrin since they know the area and should be able to locate it quickly. Once they do, it must be captured using any means necessary and then delivered here."

"You can't trust them. They will find a way to betray you for their own ends."

"Let them try," she said with a wicked smile. "As you well know, they will ultimately fail and will be rewarded with pain and suffering. Remind them of that when you see them." She handed them gently to Tomas. He turned around and started for the door. "Another thing, lord commander. When you have delivered those, please return. We have to plan your next visit with the wizard, Adrienne."

Tomas shuddered at the thought of another friend he would have to kill.

CHAPTER SEVEN

The Festival

Without a second thought, Denarith and Estasia almost ran across the bridge to get into the city. Calais followed as she gazed at the marvelous city. Out of all the cities in the realms she had visited, this was the most beautiful. She loved visiting the green gardens with their pink and yellow flowers that wrapped around the various white structures. Approaching the entrance, she heard the sound of music and dancing with laughter and cheering. She was amazed by airwalkers' jubilance despite all the evils that humans and dragons committed against them over the centuries.

Once Calais passed through the gold-ladened iron gate, she immediately saw a group of dancers spinning and flipping through the air. Instead of dancing on solid ground, the air dancers floated through air performing their various dance moves. The rest of the crowd was covered in bright clothing as they danced with the music. The spectacular sea of colors mesmerized Calais especially after hiking through gray fog on gray rock surrounded by black clouds.

When someone grabbed her arm, she jerked away uncontrollably. Once she saw that it was Rev, she calmed down and knew she had to relax. After the last couple of weeks of being imprisoned and then escaping, she was so tense and nervous that it almost hurt to loosen up. Of course, his dashing smile always helped her mood no matter what the circumstances were. He quickly handed her a glass, and then she noticed her companions also had cups of refreshments. However, they were examining the cups suspiciously instead of drinking.

"Its okay, my friends," Rev said. "You are our guest and we want you to enjoy yourselves. Relax, you are safe. Drink. I promise you they won't hurt you or kill you. See, I am drinking one as well." He quickly drank his mug and then exhaled loudly. "It is better than anything on your dull realm.." Calais drank the liquid. It was delicious with a sweet tangy flavor.

"Can I have another," Calais said.

"Of course, I will be right back."

Since Calais didn't collapse or die, Denarith finally relented and drank his glass as Estasia did the same. They both seemed surprised that they would like the drink. Then, they both yelled for Rev to get them more.

"This is an amazing place," Estasia said. "I don't know how this is possible."

"It is the spell they cast during the festival," Calais said. "As the realms align, they can harness the planar energies and cast this enchantment on their city every couple of hundred years. It was the only way they could avoid the dragons and their minions."

"So dragons and demons can't find us here," Denarith said. "Good! It's time to find some of that food. I will meet you both in the morning." Without waiting for an acknowledgement, he walked into the crowd to one of the inns.

"Oh food, wait up Denarith," Estasia called out as she tried to catch up to him.

Calais watched both of her companions disappear into the dancing crowd. Wondering what to do next, she looked at the surrounding streets. Having traveled so much, she didn't eat very much so she wasn't hungry yet. Still not seeing Rev, she could never find them in this festival. As usual, the surrounding dancers had another idea. Grabbing her hand, she was pulled into their twirling dances and quickly disappeared into a forest of red and pink dresses.

The dancing became so enjoyable that Calais had lost track of time and not noticed that the small sun had fallen below the horizon. Occasionally, she would look for Rev or her companions but never found them. Feeling the rhythmic beats, she danced to the intoxicating music. She didn't want the music to end until she realized she was dancing in the air.

Panicked, she flapped her arms and legs trying to swim but she kept floating higher and higher. The other dancers didn't notice and even joined in. Grabbing her arms, they spun and flipped her through the air. Calais' cries for help were met with cheering and laughter from the dancers. Almost totally disoriented, she could barely keep track of which way was up or down. After spinning around again, Calais saw a ledge close by. She quickly grabbed it and felt her body and legs swing upwards. Still clinging to the ledge, she could feel her body become almost completely weightless. She called for help several times until finally someone answered.

"There you are," Rev said while standing on the same ledge she was holding. "I got more gavo juice. It's freshly made. Where do you want me to put it?"

"Help me! I will float away and die in the cold air.

"Oh no," Rev said reassuringly. "The spell would end long before you get that high and you would fall to the ground instead."

"And Die!"

"Don't be so dramatic. We are airwalkers. We can fly and float wherever we want."

"I am a human, and I can't fly! Why am I flying?"

"It's probably the juice. It has magical properties but airwalkers are immune from it since we are part magic, anyway. Do you still want some more?"

"Help me!"

"Very well," Rev said dryly. He took a jewel from his gray jacket and pressed it against her arm. With a bright flash, she noticed the weightlessness was fell back to the ground. Barely grabbing the ledge in time, Calais found herself hanging from the ledge in the opposite direction.

"Help me!"

"I did. Ready for more juice?"

"No! I don't want the stupid drink. Help me up."

"Take my hand, my lady."

With a strong grip, he pulled her back onto the ledge. Breathing heavily, she thanked him and he kissed her hand in return. He led her off the ledge without using spells or flight. The ledge had led into a building where they traveled down a series of narrow stairs. When he needed to, he could walk on the air as he helped her get a cross some of the crumbling steps. Being air walkers, they didn't need to use stairs very much so stair maintenance was very low priority in the city. Once she was on the ground, Calais relaxed. Then, she suddenly remembered Estasia and Denarith. They had also drunk the juice.

"Rev, we need to find my friends. They both drank the juice. They could be floating away as we speak."

"Sure, let's go find them. A floating cow is something you don't see every day."

"He's not a cow."

"Cow. Bull. Barbarian. What's the difference?"

"Rev!"

"Follow me, my lady. I shall lead you to them."

As they moved through the crowds, Rev was singing, dancing, and drinking his way through. However, Calais was looking up as much as she could. As she pushed her way through crowd, she knew her companions would be floating up there somewhere. After not finding them in the sky, she wondered if they had travelled too far up to be seen anymore. Estasia's magic was not powerful enough to override the drink's enchantment, and barbarians couldn't fly unless they were one of those bird champions.

'There's Estasia," Rev finally said.

"May the divine help her," Calais said as she looked around the sky. "Where is she? I can't see her."

"She's over there," Rev said as he pointed straight ahead of them. Seeing Estasia's flapping white dress in her vigorous dance, Calais was greatly relieved and then she got closer. As they approached Estasia, Calais put her hand over her mouth and nose as she stared at the sight before her.

"Calais," Estasia said. "You decided to come out and have some fun. I met these three most wonderful guys. You must come with me to meet them. They are so cute." Seeing Calais' expression, Estasia stopped dancing and walked over to her friend. "Is everything ok?"

Speechless, Calais stared back and could only shake her head. She couldn't believe this could happen to Estasia and how could she not know or at least not notice her skin. Calais wanted to tell her friend, but she knew Estasia would be so angry that someone might get hit with a lightning bolt or fire a missile.

"Dance," Estasia urged. "Enjoy yourself. Just look at how much fun I am having." She danced again with her arms in the air.

"Like you, she is green with envy," Rev said.

"Rev," Calais exclaimed. "I can't believe you said that."

"Why? What's going on?"

"Ummm, you should take a look in the mirror… you might need to fix your makeup."

"Purple lipstick should go great with that green," Rev said.

"Oh no," Estasia said. "There's something green on me?"

Calais nodded silently as she was still stunned by the sight of Estasia. As Estasia noticed Calais' unblinking stare had not changed, Estasia rushed over to a nearby window to look at her reflection.

"In the name of the divine," Estasia said slowly. "Who did this to me? Who turned me into an orc!" Then, she let out an awful scream. While some applauded and cheered, most of the other elven patrons kept dancing and singing. "Rev! It was you!"

"Oh no, my lady. I did not give you this enchanted beauty."

"Change me back."

"I cannot, my lady. Where we are masters of the air, we are not masters of life. I could only turn off Calais' flight. Don't worry, it will wear off soon."

Estasia was almost in tears as she looked at her plump arms, very large bosom, flabby stomach, and large hips. Her white dress barely held it all in. Helplessly, she just stared at her reflection. Calais put her arms around her trying to comfort her sad friend. Estasia just stood there with a sad expression, barely acknowledging Calais' efforts. Rev returned to dancing with a nearby patron as they swung each other around.

"Who's the orc," Denarith said. Calais had not seen him approach because she was too focused on Estasia's plight. Then, she saw the champion's plight. Her mouth dropped when she saw what had happened to him. He was not floating. He had not been turned into an orc. Instead, all his fur and skin had turned bright blue. Between her sniffles, Estasia slowly turned to look at Denarith and just stared wide-eyed.

"That's Estasia," Rev said still spinning around. "Doesn't she look beautiful?"

"Really? I hear orcs have great stamina." Denarith nonchalantly bit into an apple as Estasia turned around and slowly walked off muttering something about a heavy drink. Calais stayed behind and just stared at her companions.

"What's wrong now," Denarith asked as he took a big drink from a very large mug.

"Take a look at your reflection." She watched him walk forward a few steps to the window. He gazed at his reflection for several moments. Then, he studied the liquid in his mug.   After glancing at Rev, he looked back at his reflection. Calais just knew Denarith would kill Rev. At any moment, he could pull out his axe and try to cut Rev in half. One thing she knew is that you never messed with a totem champion. They were proud warriors who took their honor and image very seriously.

Suddenly, Denarith dumped his entire mug of gavo juice over Rev's head. Immediately, Rev stopped dancing and shivered a moment from the cold drink. With his clothes still dripping, Calais watched Rev's skin and hair turn bright red. After a moment of studying his reflection, Rev turned his attention back to the champion.

They just started laughing.

CHAPTER EIGHT

The Druid and the Chaos Wizard

"Do all animals talk," Monty said as they walked down a narrow path in the forest. They had been walking for most of the day through a sea of endless trees. Being the first time in a forest, Monty loved listening to the birds and animals and the rustling trees. She felt the crunch of leaves and sticks beneath her feet, but she never heard the jaguar next to her make a sound as she moved.

"Of course animals can talk," Nora said. "They don't talk like we are talking but each animal has its own way. They can growl or hiss or purr or whistle or even laugh. If a druid has to talk to a human, elf or orc, then a druid can communicate in whatever animal form they have chosen."

"You mean you can be other animals besides a kitty. Soaring through the sky or swimming in rivers without boats or airships sounds fantastic."

"We must protect the animals and plants from evil," Nora said. "To do that, we can understand all creatures and plants. We become a part of nature and can take any form to help it. The Divine created nature and in that way, we serve the Divine."

"Can I become a druid," Monty said as she flapped down the path like a bird.

"No," Nora said flatly. "You have a different path. You were created for something else. I don't know what it will be, but, trust me, like Djinn, you are just as gifted as me. Speaking of which, I can hear him coming back to us now."

Djinn had disappeared hours ago. The strange orc hadn't been very conversational and ran off muttering something about mushrooms. It didn't seem to bother Nora so Monty said nothing. He didn't seem harmful and still could not figure out why the other men wanted to kill him. She tried to ask Nora, but she said it was just strange human behavior and then wouldn't talk about it further.

"I found onions and parsley," Djinn said as he burst from the bushes. "Dinner will be fantastic tonight. If only I could find some mushrooms and basil, then it would be even more terrific. If we only had a baking oven, I could make a cake. You would love my cakes, little one."

"A cake sounds wonderful," Monty said. "I have never tasted a cake. Do you think we can get some when we get to the city?"

"Of course," Djinn said. "I am sure there are some excellent bakeries."

"We are not going into the city," Nora said. "You saw what just happened in the last city. Humans just keep getting worse. I will ride with you on that dreadful train, but after that, we will stay on the edge of they city until your sage can meet with us there."

"But then, how will we get our cake," Djinn said dourly. "Speaking of food, I think it might be time for us to find a place to camp." Monty noticed that the sun was getting low on the horizon and that it would be night soon.

"Yes," Nora resigned. "We can make camp, but we must do it off the path in case a patrol or wagon come through here. More and more weapons and supplies are moving between the cities. Their blasted wagon contraptions destroy everything in their path."

It didn't take long to find a small area nearby to make camp. Nora paced around the perimeter with her eyes glowing again. Several bushes and vines formed a thick fence around most of the camp site. Then, she positioned her self at the entrance to the camp and took a nap. Djinn pulled out several pouches from under his robe and placed them on the ground.

"I need a fire," Djinn said.

"What," Nora said as she jumped up from her napping position.

"Don't worry," Djinn said. "I will keep it small so it won't attract any attention. It will just take me a moment to start one with magic."

"Quickly Monty," Nora said. "Follow me. We must take cover." She led Monty to take cover behind a large tree. Suddenly, the camp area exploded with flames flying past them. Then, Nora led her back to the camp where there was a small camp fire burning. Djinn's robes and hat were singed, but he didn't even seem to notice. "Oh good, you're still alive. Let me know if you plan to cast any more spells." She dropped down in the grass and went back to sleep.

"Is magic always this dangerous," Monty said.

"Dangerous," Djinn exclaimed. "There is nothing dangerous about my magic. It's just a little unpredictable at times."

"He is a chaos wizard," Nora said sleepily. "Their magic is always unpredictable since they channel their energies from the chaos plane. They need it to control ethaerium."

"What is ethaerium," Monty said.

"It's a magical energy, little one," Djinn said as he continued to work on his stew. "You know the purple stuff that zips and zaps. You see it exists between the planes. It was actually discovered during the Age of Dragons." He raised his hands for dramatic effect and waited. Monty continued to watch him, hungrily waiting for more. Nora continued to sleep. When nothing else happened, he scowled and went back to cutting onions. "It was harnessed to stop the dragons and seal them away forever. Lucky for us, we learned to use it and rebuild this great and ignoble civilization."

"So, what does a chaos wizard do," Monty said.

"Well, that's the trick, little one. Unlike other wizards, we combine normal magic with energies from the Plane of Chaos. We tame it and then make is usable for everyone else.

"It's the chaotic energies, child," Nora said with her eyes still closed. "While it gives them more power, it also alters their mind overtime."

"It's a win-win situation, little one. I go crazy while everyone else gets to live comfortably."

"That doesn't seem fair," Monty said sadly.

"Ha, it's done," Djinn said. Monty didn't even notice the soup he was making.   He had been cooking various ingredients in a metal soup pot that had been magically hovering over the fire. It was already bubbling with a spicy scent. Then, he pulled out three bowls from under his robe. He dipped one in and laid it next to Nora. Then, he dipped another bowl in the soup and handed it to her.

"Can you actually eat, child," Nora said as she sniffed the bowl.

"Yes, I can," Monty said. "Montague gave me some wonderful breads and sweets. Oh, this soup smells delicious." She carefully drank the hot concoction. The flavors burst into her mouth as the hot soup filled her with warmth. "And it tastes delicious."

"This is awful," Nora said.

"I take her side," Djinn said. "It's a wonderful soup."

"Uh huh," Nora said. "I am still waiting to see if she will leak."

"No, no," Djinn said. "She doesn't leak, but it would be funny if she did." He laughed to himself as he stared at the ground. "Actually, I believe her internal energy source can convert anything into energy. She could probably eat rocks and still get energy from them."

"Montague called it a soulforge," Monty said. "However, I don't know what it does."

Nora's eyes snapped wide open. "Djinn, is she talking about a soulforge, a legendary item that powered the maru of the past?"

"A maru," Djinn questioned with a forced grin. "I have no idea what you are talking about."

"What is a maru," Monty asked concerned.

"If you are a maru, then you are even more special than Djinn or I," Nora said finally. "One day we will tell you what it means, but for now, please do not ask about it again. And, please, do not mention it to anyone else. No one must know what you are. Montague was right to hide you and not tell anyone. His enemies would try to capture you and use you for evil. We must be cautious. Now, get some sleep. Tomorrow will be a long day. I know a shortcut that will get us to the train faster."

Using one of Djinn's blankets as a pillow, Monty laid down while looking at the stars Among the stars, there were four moons of varying sizes and color. From her deep memory, knowledge of the moons flooded her mind. The smallest moon was blood red with white splotches which was known as Fyyrondrall. Two smaller moons were positioned near the horizon. Ishkondrall was bright blue and with small bands of white. Elwyndrall was emerald green with black smudges. Eirondrall was the largest moon and also the most boring. It was mostly grey with black shadows. From the deep memory, she knew each moon was actually a realm that orbited the sun like her realm, Tallendrall. However, it seemed unusual to see four of them at once. Normally, only one or two would appear in the sky.

"Why are there four moons," Monty said as she turned toward the napping jaguar.

"It is because we are close to the planar alignment," Nora said with one eye opened. "Every two hundred years or so, all the realms in this plane will line up in a perfect straight line. Some people take it as a bad omen." Nora let out a huge yawn and closed both eyes. "Trust me, I saw it two hundred years ago and nothing bad happened."

"How old are you," Monty said surprised. Searching her deep memories, Monty found that humans and orcs generally lived less than a hundred years. Some elves had lived for almost two hundred years. "Are you an elf?"

"No," Nora said agitated. "I was born a human. As druids become part of nature, we are blessed with eternal life. I have seen many things and learned many things such as sleep is good for me. Now, go to sleep, child."

Monty laid back down and listened to the noise of the forest and Djinn's soft snoring. She had survived her second day since being awaken. After almost being killed by the men in black armor and escaping the town's guards, it would be a day she would not soon forget. While many terrible things happened, it was also the day she met her new friends. As she fell asleep, Monty hoped for more good things in the coming days.

*   *   *   *

Monty woke up the next morning to a bright sun in the eastern sky and a cool breeze blowing through the forest. She felt a burst of energy as the thought of a new day surged through her. After joyfully jumping onto her feet, she found herself alone in the small clearing.

"Hey, kitty, where are you," Monty said as she looked around. "It's such a beautiful morning."

"A morning person," Nora groaned from a tree branch above Monty. "I hate morning people. You and Djinn need to go back to sleep. The sage isn't going anywhere." Nora yawned and then went back to sleep.

"Oh really, where is Djinn? I don't see him. Hmmm, I wonder if he is over here." Putting on her cloak, Monty wondered out of the clearing looking around for any sign of the wizard. She continued to walk through more of the forest until she saw something on the ground. As she looked closer, she found a slaughtered deer laying near the path. It was completely bitten in half with most of its body parts missing. Stepping around the bloody area, she saw a trail of dead animals continuing along the path.

She slowly followed the bloody path and carefully avoided the carcasses. She looked up and down the path to find the cause of the destruction. Even some large trees were torn down. With swarms of bugs getting thicker and thicker, Monty made her way into a clearing where she found a small village.

At the center of the village, she gazed upon a large metal tower stretching into the sky with glowing antennas that adorned the tower's crown. Around it, there were several wooden buildings that were houses or stores. The narrow forest path transformed into a larger stone road that continued northward through the center of town. Looking for any signs of life, Monty was only met with the sight of dead bodies scattered among the buildings.   Some of them looked human, but most of the bodies were mutilated like the animal carcasses before. The thought of finding these horrible creatures made her shudder. As she turned around, she heard noise near the large metal building. Quietly, she made her way to the sound.

A young man was leaning against the metal tower near one of its closed doors. Carefully approaching him, Monty noticed he had a hollow look while just staring at a smashed house across the street. "What is your name," Monty said. He ignored her and just stared at the house. "It's okay. I am here to help you." Still, he did not respond. Monty lightly put her small hand on his shoulder, and his head snapped to her with wide eyes.

"The voices were right," he sneered. Then, the boy jumped to his feet while thrusting his finger at the house. "They got what they deserve. They never loved me. Never!"

"Stop," Monty said trying to be reassuring. "Let me help you. I know some people who might be able to help."

"I need no one else," the boy said as he glared at her. "I have a new family. I don't need anyone's help anymore. I truly found people who love me now and accept me for whom I am."

"Back away from him, child," Nora said behind her. "There is nothing you can do for him now. He is too far gone."

"What's wrong with him," she said while slowly backing away. He just stared at her.

"Don't be afraid," he said finally. "I told my sister not to be afraid. I am stronger now. I am more powerful than any lord." His voice crescendoed to a scream, and Monty just watched him helplessly. With a sudden burst of energy, the boy jumped around and wailed at the sky. Then, Monty saw what had happened to him.

His skin bulged violently with blood, muscles and bones. Then, his bones crackled and snapped as they quickly reshaped themselves. The boy's mouth reformed into a large snout. His skin erupted with long hair, and he grew taller and taller. Once his transformation completed, he was a large wolf-like monstrosity that stood even taller than Djinn. He had claws that were long and black. His teeth were yellow and bloody. The rest of his body dripped with blood from the change. Despite his large frame, Monty watched the monster lithely approach her.

"We are more powerful than the emperor himself," he said in guttural voice. Then, several other creatures appeared behind him. They had similar forms and looked just as angry. Nora and Monty continued to back away. He snarled and prepared for an attack. Suddenly, Monty was blinded by dust as something crashed in front of her. Once the dust cleared, she found a house had been dropped on the creature.

"I found it," Djinn yelled as he burst from a general store. "They had coriander. It will make my next meal even better than ever." He excitedly rushed up to Nora and Monty as he tried to show them the small seeds in his pouch. Then, he saw the fallen house next to them. "What an excellent idea! Why pack up your house and move when you could just move the whole house and then, you wouldn't have to worry about unpacking."

The monster burst out of the house's wall as the rest of the house finally collapsed behind him. The same creatures behind the house jumped onto the house rubble and snarled. "I can smell your fear. Don't worry, you won't suffer for long."

"Werelings," Djinn said. "I know just what to do."

"No Djinn," Nora commanded. "Take Monty into the tower. A storm is coming, and it will destroy these abominations."

"Very well," Djinn said while grabbing Monty's arm. "You be careful, my druid friend." Though Monty protested, he threw the door open and dragged her through it. Monty wanted to help, but she couldn't escape Djinn's grasp.

"Why did you do that," Monty yelled. "We have to help her. Let me go!"

"As you wish," Djinn said calmly while closing the door. As Monty jerked away from him, he released her, and she fell onto the floor. "You must trust me. We are only trying to protect you, little one. She is in no real danger. I can prove it. You can watch some of it through the door." Carefully, Djinn cracked the door open as he checked for any threats. "Come watch a powerful druid at work." Watching Djinn suspiciously, Monty made her way to the door and peeked through the cracked door.

As the creatures gnashed their teeth and growled at her, Nora crouched close to the ground preparing to pounce. Instead of attacking one of them, the cat's eyes began to glow like two suns. The creatures paused and watched the cat release a heavy deep roar into the sky. The deep, powerful roar was more like a lion than a jaguar. The skies turned black and circled her. The monstrosities became angrier and leaped at the cat, but it was too late. A cyclone erupted from the skies and fell onto the monsters. Monty could hear the wind and debris beat the tower's walls. Struggling to keep the door partially closed, Djinn finally shut it and locked it. Breathing deeply after holding the door, he leaned against the wall while trying to catch his breath.

"You see, little one," Djinn said between breaths. "The druid can take care of herself."

"What about the tornado," Monty said looking up at the orc. "Will it not kill her?"

"Of course not, little one. Tornadoes are a part of nature, and they know how to protect themselves from nature. She will be fine. Now, where are we?"

Monty found herself in a circular room lined with tall desks. Each desk had screens, buttons, and dials. She didn't know the devices' purposes and considered it. A bad idea to test the devices' functions. In the center of the room, Monty's eyes followed a large blue metal cylinder stretching from the floor to the top of the tower. The cylinder and the walls were smooth, bluish metal. On one side of the circular room, she found a stairway that went to a lower level. Djinn moved around the room studying the devices and the large cylinder.

"This is an ethaerium tower," Djinn said finally. "It generates power and sends it to the nearby cities. Underneath us, there is a chaos nexus where a motor pulls energy from it and sends it to the antenna above us. Fortunately, nothing appears to be damaged." Then, they heard a voice below them. Before Monty could ask, Djinn gestured for her silence. He carefully walked down the stairway. Monty followed him closely.

The stairway only went down to a small platform connected to the large cylinder while the rest of the room dropped to a bright glowing sphere. It was so bright; Monty had to cover her eyes. She barely could see needles that were stabbing the sphere at different intervals. Each time, it released a blue wave of energy that would move up the room before dissipating. Then, a deep cacophony of noise emanated from the sphere that caused part of the room to shake. As the sound subsided, she heard a voice from the platform below. A man was talking to another device that was set in the cylinder. He was younger human with a very thin frame. He wore black goggles over his eyes along with a scruffy beard around his bony cheeks and pointy chin. His brown hair was long and tangled. He was dressed in leather overalls and a black-smudged, white shirt. The man was stroking the device as if he were trying to soothe it.

"Don't worry," the man said. "I am trying to free you. I know you are in so much pain. It won't be long."

"What are you trying to free," Djinn said perplexed.

"You cannot be here," the man said frustrated. He screamed and tore his body off to reveal another wolf-man monstrosity. The change was much quicker and more violent than before. It was so quick that Monty was unprepared for his leaping attack. Monty fell back against the stairs while Djinn somersaulted to the platform. The creature crashed against the wall but clung to it with his large claws. The stairway below him partially crumbled away which kept Djinn from coming to Monty's aid. The creature turned and stared at her with glowing red eyes.

"The voices say I must destroy you," the creature growled. "You must die so it can be free."

"Stop this, young man," Djinn commanded. "I am a wizard, and I will destroy you if you come any closer to her."

"I can withstand a wizard's attack," the creature said. "Your lighting and fireballs will only burn me, but it won't stop me from killing her."

"I am not just any wizard. I am a chaos wizard."

"You are lying. Now, she must die."

The creature moved to the Monty. She tried to get up the stairs, but her black cloak was caught on the broken stairs. Looking at Djinn for help, she saw him raise his glowing hands. It almost seemed as if they were drawing their energy from the sphere below. With the creature getting closer, Djinn made his hands glow as bright as the sphere below. The creature stopped and turned to the wizard.

"He controls the voices' power," the creature said in awe. "You must free the voices."

Without answering, the wizard let loose a blast of energy that engulfed the monster. Monty covered her mouth in disgust while watching the creature slowly melted away. First, his skin disintegrated and then his muscles. Finally, the burning skeleton dissolved into nothing. The only sign of the creature was a large black hole in the wall where it had clung too. Hopping over the missing stairs, Djinn made his way back up to Monty. Helping to free her cloak, they made their way back up to the main room and closed the door.

"What are those things," Monty said. "They are called werelings. They are a type of corrupted. While each type of corrupted has their own talents, these creatures are powerful fighting machines that are almost impossible to kill."

"Do you hear that," Monty interrupted. There was only silence beyond the tower with no sign of the storm. Cautiously, Monty opened the door to sunshine. There were no clouds left in the sky, but there was no town either. Opening the door even further, Monty discovered the buildings around the town had been replaced with nothing but scorch marks. Even the bodies were missing. "What happened?"

"I destroyed the corrupted and cleansed this area," Nora said. She was sitting near the door while licking one of her paws.

Monty walked around blackened stone foundations where houses use to exist. She noticed a small silver bracelet on the ground. Picking it up, she studied it sadly. "Why did they kill all these people?"

"We don't know," Nora said. "The corrupted were once people until they became infected. Once infected, they become hateful and want to hurt everyone they can. As you saw, they also gain powerful abilities that make them extremely dangerous."

"If we knew how they were infected, we could stop them once and for all," Djinn surmised.

"The boy and the man in the tower said something about hearing voices?"

"What man in the tower," Nora said with a concerned tone.

"It was nothing," Djinn said shrugging his shoulders. "They say they hear these voices, but they can't tell you anything about them. Some people think it is just a symptom of their deranged mind. As a fellow crazy person, I am not so sure."

"If the voices are real, then maybe they can help us," Monty said.

"The voices could very well be the problem," Nora said. "Ten years ago, we worked with Lady Enix to cure the corrupted. When we tried to capture them for study, they often escaped as if someone or something were helping them. We never found the cause or these voices before Lady Enix betrayed us."

"You worked with Lady Enix?"

"We all did including Montague," Nora said. "That is how we met. The goal was to stop the corrupted, but Lady Enix wanted to use our research to open a portal to one of the planes of hell. People called us heroes of the Fifth Spire for stopping the portal, but they don't know the truth. While we stopped the portal, many, many innocent people died in the process and the empire didn't care."

Chapter Nine

The Search for Jewell

Caellan rode most of the night before he arrived at Kellenor. With one full moon and two half-moons, he could see the road without using lanterns. Even if it were darker, he always had keener senses then most people that included eyes that could see better in the dark. This allowed him to make the trip in the same time as he would have during the day. As he approached the city, he saw no lights among the tall dark structures and heard no sound. He hoped the city was just asleep, but his sense of smell told himotherwise.

With a faint smell of decay in the air, Caellan slowed down his weary horse as they entered the city. Clomping against the cobblestone street, the horse's hooves echoed throughout the dark, ominous buildings and ruins. Sages claimed it was one of the oldest cities in the realm. For whatever reason, it was destroyed and rebuilt in each new age. In this age, the city was a maze of crumbling stone walls and pristine buildings that shimmered with ethaerium power. Tonight, the new buildings were just as dark and silent as their ruined counterparts. After some time meandering through the dark streets, Caellan finally heard distant voices.

In the town's center, several men with horse-drawn wagons were moving up and down the connecting streets. As he peered into one of the passing wagons, he saw a heap of tangled, dead bodies with their lifeless eyes staring back at him. Aghast, Caellan rode to a militia command tent that had been erected near a large waterless fountain. Jumping off his horse, he handed the reins to a nearby confused militia man and hurried into the tent.

Inside, several men were pouring over a map of the city set up on a table in the center of the large tent. Other men were sorting through documents and placing them in different piles. His friend, Jarmal, was at the other end of the table looking at the map with a grim expression.

"What happened here," Caellan demanded.

"We were too late," Jarmal said. "By the time, we got here most of the people were dead."

"What killed them," Caellan said. "Is my wife among the dead?"

"We don't know," Jarmal said. "The few that survived speak of screaming shadows and fiery knights. Many were burnt alive while other fell over dead. We have not found Jewell's body, but we are still searching."

"I have heard of these shadows that you speak of," Caellan said trying to remember history lessons from his paladin training. "They are called wraiths. It is a type of undead."

"We hope you are wrong," Jarmal said grimly. "The shadows and knights speak of demons, and we have no way of fighting demons. The empire is sending dragon cannons and other weaponry, but it will take days for them to arrive, if they even work. All we can do is hope that these creatures have moved on and given the dead their proper burial. If not, we will join them soon."

"Where did these demons come from," Caellan said. "Surely, someone saw who might have been working with these creatures." Wraiths were controlled by a creature called a Wraethunu. He looked like a man or woman, but his soul had been possessed by a demon.

"I know what caused this," a voice said. Caellan turned around to see his old friend, Jerick, stepping into the tent. He had grown a dark beard around his thin, tan face. His body was covered by light armor and a red cloak indicative of a mercenary. His long black hair and deep brown eyes only added to his even darker expression.

"Jerick, I am so glad to see you," Caellan said smiling, but Jerick just stared back at him. Caellan could see the pain in his eyes. He loved Jewell just as much as Caellan did. Part of him hoped that Jerick and he could be friends again. Unfortunately, Jerick's hard expression reminded Caellan that things would never be the same between them. "Where have you been all this time?"

"I have been protecting caravans," Jerick said. "I am trying to make money so I could provide for my future wife. I was in town yesterday after finishing a job, and, despite my best efforts, I couldn't save Jewell."

"What do you mean," Caellan said shocked. "Is she alive? Where is she?"

"I think she is still alive," Jerick said. "Yesterday, I saw Jewell, and we talked for a while. After that, she brought me to the mayor's house where her aunt was negotiating taxation rates with the mayor and the city council. The mayor refused Baroness Krakenjall's demands. So, the baroness punished the mayor and this city. I know you will find this hard to believe, but she summoned these fiery creatures that destroyed everything. I tried to save Jewell, but one of the fiery creatures kidnapped her and threw her into the baroness' carriage. The baroness left with Jewell. I heard her screaming for help, but I was too weak and couldn't stop the creatures. I would be dead, but these shadows rose from the ground and destroyed the fiery creatures."

"You're right, I don't believe it," a militia man said at the table. "Why would the baroness kidnap her own niece? How is she cavorting with demons? The priests would have discovered it. Finally, why would the shadows be killing other demonic creatures?"

"I believe him," Caellan said hoping to gain his friend's trust again. "I have known him for many years, and he is an honorable man." Most of the other men in the tent just glared indignantly at Caellan.

"He speaks the truth," Jarmal interjected. "The baroness was in the city, and she was meeting with the mayor. We cannot vouch for what she said as everyone in that room was killed except for Jerick. All we know is that the baroness has returned safely to her castle. Their confirmation did not mention anything about Jewell."

"Since I am not needed here," Caellan said. "Jerick and I will question the baroness. If they are innocent, I will let you know. Meanwhile, if you see anything like shadows or fiery guards, I suggest you run."

"I am coming as well," Jarmal said as he followed them out of the tent.

"Wouldn't it be better for you to stay here," Caellan said.

"No," Jarmal said flatly. "If the baron has committed a crime, it would be better if an imperial officer were there to witness it. You don't have the best reputation in the empire and prosecuting a baron is most difficult."

"It's not as hard as you think," Caellan said under his breath. His father's failed trial was a terrible experience that still haunted him. Before thinking anymore of it, he refocused his mind on Jewell and their task of finding her. "We will need horses. Mine is too tired from the night's ride."

Jarmal gave orders to nearby militia men. They reacted sluggishly as they made their way to a makeshift stable. Instead of housing a garrison of troops in every city, the empire found it cheaper to commission a few officers to lead and train a barony's militia. Because the militia was made up of out-of-work volunteers and criminals, they were never as quick or effective as trained soldiers. Fortunately, the empire didn't have very many internal enemies to fight, so they didn't have to be effective. Most of the time, they were used to guard gates or patrol roads. That may all change with roving corrupted and the increasing attacks of undead. The whispers at parties said the empire was growing its army to maintain order instead of the militia. Caellan wondered if more soldiers were a good thing. Then, a militia man broke his train of thought when the man stumbled into him while bringing Caellan a horse. With a sigh, Caellan helped the man up and checked the horse. With no injuries to the animal, he pulled himself onto the horse. Caellan, Jarmal, Jerick, and two other officer's road out of town and to the baron's castle.

"Slow down, Jerick," Caellan yelled over the roar of hooves.

"We have to get to Jewell," Jerick yelled back.

"I said slow down," Caellan said as he grabbed Jerick's reins.

"What are you doing," Jerick said. "There is no time. Those black-hearted nobles could kill her at anytime. Or do worse."

"Stop and look," Caellan said pointing to sky. Several black shadows flew against the early morning sky to the distant castle. "We have to use caution and not attract any undue attention."

"It's not them we have to fear," Jerick said pointedly.

"What aren't you telling me," Caellan said suspiciously.

Without responding, Jerick forced his horseback into a slower gallop. Caellan and Jarmal followed, but the two officers just stared at the flying horror before falling in line behind them. Caellan wasn't sure if the officers followed them out of duty or fear of being alone. Either way, demons were present, and that bode ill for everyone.

*   *   *   *

The wraiths never changed their direction or notice the following horses. Over time, the men watched more and more shadows appeared in the sky above them. After several hours of riding, they finally reached the castle encircled by wraiths.

"We must get inside before they block our way," Caellan said. "Let none of them touch you."

Caellan forced his horse to charge through the gate and across the bridge into the main courtyard. The others followed before the orbiting wraiths blocked the entrance. Jerick jumped off his horse and forced his way through the main door. Shaking his head at his impetuous friend, Caellan followed with his drawn sword. Jarmal and the officers followed closely while watching the cloud of shadows above them.

"What are those things," one of the imperial officers said as he slammed the door shut.

"They are the fragments of a human soul," Caellan said. "Every time a wraith touches someone, a piece of their soul is ripped from their body and turned into another wraith. I would say most of the town is out there."

"Forget the wraiths," Jerick said. "We must find Jewell."

"We go to the baron first," Caellan demanded. "They have to answer for the town's destruction."

"Fine, you go to the baron," Jerick said. "I will find Jewel." Caellan simply nodded while trying to ignore Jarmal's disapproving glare. Without another word from his old friend, Jerick just walked away in silence.

"You should go with him," Jarmal said as they watched Jerick disappear into a descending stairwell. "A man's first duty is to his family and then to the empire."

"You don't know nobles as I know them," Caellan snapped. The thought of all those innocent people turned into monsters enraged him. "Those wraiths are only the first step. There will be more deaths and demonic creatures. In the end, this is just another twisted, depraved scheme for more power and more control. I have seen it first hand and trust me; their depravity knows no limits. They would turn servants into monsters to slaughter entire villages just to get back at another baron for some minor slight. They would carve and mutilate prisoners to present as art at some social function. Trust me, I know how these vile creatures work and I will not allow them to continue to treat people like some pawn on a game board. I will make them pay for all the people they have hurt."

"My friend, you must not cloud the present with the past. We will bring justice to those responsible for Kallenor's destruction. You need to focus on helping your wife and we will take care of the baron."

"Did you see those creatures flying around the castle? It is only a matter of time before they attack. If we don't stop the wraethenu first, it will not matter if I find my wife or not, because we will be all dead. No, the baron is mine."

Before Jarmal could reply, Caellan strode away into the castle depths. Shaking his head, Jarmal followed him while the two jittery militia men stayed with Jarmal. Moving slower than Caellan, the three militia men constantly scanned the dark castle interior for possible ambushes.

Caellan kept a steady and deliberate stride as he was not concerned about the wraiths. If they were meant to destroy Caellan, the wraiths would have already launched their assault. Instead, they just circled the castle as if they were waiting for something. Whatever it was, Caellan knew it was all part of some dark plan. He hoped he would find the baron before it was too late.

If the baron were involved with demons, he would mostly likely have learned this knowledge from ancient tomes hidden in his library. Most castles were built during the Age of Dragons. The castle stone and other materials were bi-products from the construction of the dragon's massive lair. The dragons needed only the castles as a place for their slaves to live and serve the dragons' tirelessly. For everyone else, they recognized the castles as symbols of the dragon's relentless tyranny. After the dragons left, the barons rebuilt only parts of the castle. To this day, many castles still held many secrets from that terrible time. Often, this included the libraries.

The dragons and their slaves created many tomes of knowledge about the planes and their realms. Many of these books proved to be unpractical for the needs of the peoples. However, some sages claim there were dark secrets hidden away in the writings. During balls and dinners, stories would be told of how a baron would use this forbidden knowledge to amass more power and destroy their rivals. Most people said the rumors weren't true, but there have been more than one barony destroyed mysteriously over the years only to be merged by a greedy competitor. Caellan was certain that the wraiths were a secret weapon that would destroy other baron just so he could take more land, wealth and power. When Caellan saw light shining through the library's entrance, he knew he could stop this baron before anyone else would be hurt.

"Come in, Caellan," the voice said from inside the library. "We have much to discuss."

*　*　*　*

The library was forty feet tall with a vaulted ceiling. Ladders of various lengths leaned against the book-lined walls. Near a large burning fireplace, Caellan noticed several cushioned chairs and small tables encircled the center of the room that had ornate rugs covering most of the stone floor. Sitting in one of the chairs near the fireplace, the baron was an old, withered man who stared at his new visitors with glittering, hungry blue eyes. Standing next to him, the baroness was a tall, slender, aged woman wearing a long, grey, dress. Her silver hair was tied up in a neat bun

Caellan, and the militiamen stood inside the doorway. While Jarmal and his officers nervously scanned the room for traps or ambushes, Caellan just glared at the baron for a few moments. Then, he unsheathed his two-handed sword walking to the baron.

"I shall have your head for all the people you killed today," Caellan growled.

"Stop, Caellan," Jarmal said as he rushed to Caellan's side. "This is not the way of justice. We will put him on trial where he will answer for his crimes."

"I have committed no crime," the baron said.

"Those impudent peasants refused to do the work that was required of them," the baroness said indignantly. "We were only asking them to do two additional shifts. A week and they thought they deserved something for their efforts. We showed all that they should be grateful to the empire for just letting them live."

"Instead of negotiating, you just killed them," Caellan said angrily.

"Of course," the baroness said. "They were willing to sacrifice the barony's well-being. I wouldn't live like a peasant just because they didn't want to work a little more." Each barony provided a small amount of manufactured resources of the empire to build armor, weapons, roads, and new technologies. In return, each barony was provided a certain amount of wealth and rare resources. The rest of the resources were traded among merchants as they traveled to different cities. Over the last decade, the empire's quotas grew each year and cities began failing to meet them. With the empire consolidating its power into fewer baronies and cities, many people were afraid to lose the empire's protection and practically worked themselves to death. The few that refused were eventually abandoned. A few barons created their own small empires while others were killed by the people when they learned the truth about their treacherous leaders. The baron was not loved and would surely be killed or forced to flee if the empire abandoned this barony.

"Our plan would have worked if those shadow creatures hadn't interrupted us," the baron said.

"What do you mean," Caellan said.

"We were going to fix their souls by turning them into obedient creatures," the baron said frustrated. "Instead, those shadows killed our fire soldiers and most of the people."

"If you are not responsible for the shadows, then who is," Caellan said worried. Caellan thought the creatures were controlled by the baron and were waiting for a signal. He thought killing them would end the plot, but now he didn't know who was responsible.

"Caellan," Jerick called from the library entrance. "I found her. Look, she is okay."

Caellan turned around surprised. Looking at Jewell, he felt a heavyweight lifted from his heart. Smiling, he quickly ran to her and embraced her. Her long black hair was partially wet and matted as it flowed over her stained red dress. "Oh, Jewell, I have missed you," Caellan breathed. Looking down at her, she was too weak to look back at him. "What have you done to her!" He returned Jewell to Jerick who comforted her while Caellan gazed angrily back at the baron.

"We needed part of the magic that was imbued in her," the baron said.

"What magic," Caellan said. She never told him about any of this.

"Do you think you were the only child experimented on by their parents," the baron said. "My brother had read the books about dragon magic that could enhance their children at birth. Just like you, he imbued her with ancient dragon blood, but she never showed any of the gifts like you. So, he was planning on killing her and taking her essence. Instead, his untimely death delayed the process, and we were forced to marry her off. We were hoping that your dragon essence would combine with her and create a powerful baby with even more power. Then, we would just kill them both off and gain more power."

"You were going to kill my wife and my child," Caellan said as he strode to the baron aiming the tip of his sword at the baron's chest.

"As a noble, you should know that you can have more kids and other wives," the baron said confused.

"Forget justice," Jarmal quipped. "Just kill him."

"We don't have time for this," Jerick said. "We have to get Jewell away from here before this magic kills her." Caellan was ready to kill him, but something inside him stopped Caellan's sword. Despite his rage and anger, Caellan stepped away from the baron and moved to Jewell. Then, the baroness burst into laughter.

"I can't believe you don't know," the baroness cackled. "You really don't know why she came here in the first place."

"Spit it out," Caellan said with a sigh.

"You're wonderful wife, whom you are so willing to die for, came here to annul your marriage," the baroness said still trying to smother her laughter. "She needed our permission with a writ of annulment. She hated you so much that she was even willing to give up her wealth and status."

"Is this true," Caellan said as his stomach began to churn. Something deep inside him told him that it must be true. It would explain why Jerick was in town then.

"Yes," Jewell said weakly.

The militia men were wide-eyed at the revelation. Jerick returned Caellan a sad look as he held up Jewell. Caellan stepped back almost dropping his sword. He felt like a twisting dagger had been jammed into his gut. Everything inside Caellan began to crumble as rage turned into despair, anguish, and bitterness.

"It is settled," the baron said as he stood up. "We keep the wench and you can keep your land and title while you find another wife."

"I think I will just kill you instead," Caellan said with a hollow tone. There was nothing but emptiness inside him as he prepared to strike down the baron.

"We can discuss this later," Jerick shouted. "We must protect Jewell." Caellan ignored his old friend and remained focused on his impending attack. He had no one to protect. He had only to kill.

Fiery energy exploded from the baron and threw Caellan across the room. With more blasts, Caellan steadied himself as the chairs and furniture burned away. From the corner of his eye, he noticed the militia men had been thrown against the wall or out of the room entirely. In front of him, the baron and baroness were engulfed in flames as they laughed.

"Don't you see," the baron said. "Our magic is more powerful than any lord, priest, or the Divine himself. This is true power." With that, they fired another flaming blast that knocked Caellan on the ground despite his attempt to block it.

"No," Jerick screamed. Looking back at the doorway, Caellan was horrified to see Jewell impaled by a piece of iron shrapnel. She lay on the ground with Jerick next to her as he tried to comfort her. "You were supposed to protect her, Caellan. You were supposed to protect all of us. You are weak, but I have the strength to protect her now. " He stood up as darkness enveloped his body. "I will save her and protect everyone."

"So you are the cause of the shadows," the baroness said above the roaring flames. "I should thank you for killing all those people."

"I released them from your tyranny," Jerick said darkly. "Now, I will finally destroy you so I can protect this barony."

With that, Caellan saw explosions and blasts of darkness and fire as Jerick fought the baron and his wife. Despite the storm of emotions inside him, Caellan made his way out of the room as his survival instincts took over. Several wraiths flew through the walls as they struck at the baron. Near the library entrance, Caellan found Jarmal still alive.

"You must get to the imperial army and warn them," Caellan said. "They must know what is going on here."

"Come with me," Jarmal said. "There is nothing else you can do here."

"I can't. I must help Jewell."

"Be strong my friend."

Then, Jarmal pulled himself up and made his way out of the castle. None of the wraiths noticed him as they were focused on battle inside the library. Crawling on the ground, Caellan made his way to Jewell.

Her life had almost slipped away. "I am sorry for causing you such pain," Jewell said with her final breaths. Caellan laid his hands on her hoping to heal her with the Divine's blessing but he was so empty inside that he couldn't do it. He just stared at her helplessly as the baron and his wife screamed in agony before exploding into nothing.

"I will save her," Jerick said. Before Caellan could stop him, Jerick released large amounts of dark energy into Jewell's body. Caellan quickly stood up and backed away from the dark ritual.

"Stop Jerick," Caellan said quietly. "You just going to infect her soul with a demon that will eventually take her over. She will not be the Jewell that you love anymore."

"You are so wrong," Jerick said. "I am giving her a gift. She will do so much now, and she will live with me forever."

"Why did you do this, Jerick? How did you become a wraethenu?"

"In my travels after the wedding, I discovered these dark secrets that gave me so much power than you or any lord. With this power, I could finally offer Jewell a real life so I came back to her. I thought the baron would agree, but I didn't realize how evil he was."

Jewell stood up once the ritual was done. The piece of shrapnel fell out of her chest as dark ribbons of energy healed her wounds. Much stronger now, she grasped Jerick's hand and gazed upon Caellan. For a moment, Caellan felt as though he was in a dream, but then he was knocked onto the ground by a nearby wraith.

"Interesting," Jerick said. "Why can't I turn you into a wraith? It's not your paladin abilities or your dragon essence. What is that inside you? I see it now. You have a soulstone. You spoke of your days with Lady Enix. So that was your reward."

"You mean a curse," Caellan said.

"No matter," Jerick said. "You will provide an even greater gift for our wedding."

"With me as the sole surviving heir, Jerick will be the new baron," Jewell said. "The land will finally know peace. Now, go to sleep, Caellan."

With a waive of her hand, everything went dark.

Chapter Ten

The Train Station

It had been over a day since the wereling attack. Fortunately, the rest of the journey to the train station was uneventful. Djinn continued to experiment with his cooking while Nora napped every chance she could. Along the way, Nora also told Monty about the trees and how they grew and eventually died. Then, she explained the different kind of animals and how everything lived in a balance. As they got within sight of the station, the group got very quiet.

The station was composed of a long white wooden building alongside a raised wooden platform. Train tracks ran along the raised platform and continued north and south into the horizon. Several smaller wooden buildings surrounded the train station with intersecting roads laid out between them. Near the raised platform, a beautiful white marble statue formed the center of the small outpost. "Don't worry, I will get us tickets for the train," Djinn said as he wondered for a building near the train tracks.

Nora just shook her head and looked at Monty. "Open your arms child," Nora said. Monty opened her arms, and the jaguar leaped to her. In a split second, the jaguar changed into a small black cat that landed gently into Monty's arms.

"That is marvelous," Monty exclaimed. "You are a little kitty now." She hugged the cat while stroking the cat's soft fur.

"Don't get used to it," Nora said. "I am only this animal since it will not alarm most of these humans." Monty noticed that these humans were dressed nicer than what she saw in Montague's town. They reminded her of the two pompous humans who almost got her and Djinn killed. They wore bright colored dresses that were lined with white lace. The men wore clean blue or red jackets with darker trousers. While waiting for the trains, they were milling about the platform next to the train tracks. Some talked while other read books. Noticing the nearby statue, Monty pulled her hood firmly over her head and ventured to the statue.

"What are you doing," Nora said alarmed.

"I want to see this," Monty said mesmerized by the sculpture.

She walked up to the statue of a woman in a flowing gown with long hair. The statue had a sad face that looked westward. Once Monty made sure nobody was looking; she carefully moved her hand along the bottom of the carved dress to a small foot sticking out at the bottom. Her white stone-like skin was exactly the same color as the statue.

"It's a statue of Queen Ann," an older man said. Monty didn't notice him come up next to her. She quickly pulled her hand back beneath her cloak. She watched him to see if he would say anything else. Instead, he just looked at the statue. He had a white speckled beard hiding an aged face with a large nose.

"She's beautiful," Monty said. For a moment, Monty wondered if she were as beautiful as the statue. "Who was she?"

"At the end of the Age of Peace," the older man said in a baritone voice. "Demons had broken the seals, and their armies were marching onto this world. The king and queen did everything they could to destroy the demons. In a daring quest, the king tried to rebuild the seals, but he failed and became lost on his quest. In a moment of desperation, the queen listened to the advice of an evil druid. She cast a massive spell powered by the Plane of Chaos, and it worked. It resealed the portals and stopped the demons. However, it destroyed part of her kingdom and opened up a massive portal to the dragons. Thus, the Age of Dragons began."

"Why did you make a statue of her, if she let in all the dragons?"

"Well, she is a very controversial figure in history. Some people look at her as a villain while others see her differently. Here, the artist is facing her westward because that is the way the king went. You see, the queen was looking for him. If she had waited for him, then she would not have made her mistake."

"So you are saying that a person should never give up and to keep fighting," Monty said.

"That's one way," he said. "But, you have to ask yourself, did she really have a choice at all?" He smiled at her and walked back over to sit on a bench in the shade. Monty found his last words perplexing. She thought everyone had a choice. How did Queen Ann not have a choice? As she continued to ponder the conversation, she saw the crowd suddenly part to allow the robed orc with the big brimmed hat to pass through. Several women whispered to each other while glaring at the orc.

"I got the tickets to Parn," Djinn declared.

"They sold an orc a ticket," Nora said skeptically.

"Absolutely" Djinn said. "It's true that the humans do have an enlightened, intelligent, and understanding society. That's why they put everyone else in the back of the train. Our line is over here." As Djinn continued to one end of the platform, Monty followed while trying not to trip on her cloak. Luckily, no one noticed that she wasn't human. She glanced back at the statue of Queen Ann as she pondered the old man's story.

"You know it was the king's fault, right," Nora said. "He shouldn't have left her in the first place, and then it wouldn't have happened at all."

"If he was lost, shouldn't she have looked for the king and tried to help him get back," Monty said.

"No," Nora said. "It's much easier to blame the man, because it's usually his fault, anyway."

Before Monty could think further about Nora's comments, the train approached. It was composed of long silvery cylindrical tubes that glided along the tracks. Some of the cylinders had large windows while others had protruding pipes and metal plates. As it approached, the train slowed to a complete stop and floated gently downward to become level with the platform. With a loud whirring sound, doors to several cylinders pulled open. Without hesitation, people lined up and worked their way onto the train.

Djinn led Monty to one of the last cylinders where several strange people were climbing into windowless cylinders. She gazed at the ragged people. Some of them were strangely colored humans with pointy ears while others were larger humans with thick beards and long hair. Despite their differences from the humans, they all shunned Djinn who didn't seem to notice. Most of them didn't notice Monty because she was so short. It allowed her to quickly get on the train and find a place to sit near the front of the cylinder.

"What is that smell," she gasped.

"Do you notice any bathrooms," Nora said. "Humans don't think that non-humans need all the same amenities."

"Why do they hate them so much," Monty said.

"Because we are different and better than them," a large man across from her said. Like some of the others, he had long black hair with an even longer black beard that covered his darker, sun-baked skin. "Do not be afraid. We are honored by your presence, mistress druid." He bowed slightly to them. Nora crawled out of Monty's arms and reverted to a jaguar. Surprisingly, no one seemed to notice and several others around them nodded or bowed to her.

"Thank you, blacksmith," Nora said. "Tell me, what news have you heard?"

"Please call me Hagash," the large man said smiling. Everyone was gently pulled backward as the train started moving. At first, Monty could feel the train picking up speed but then she was no longer pulled back. Strangely, it felt as if the train were standing still. She watched the light spilling through the top slits of the train car flicker faster and faster as the train picked up speed. "Darkness is spreading across the land, mistress. The orcs and barbarians have broken into war again as they fight for what land that is not filled with the corrupted or death. There are even stories of demons and their darkling armies building kingdoms while enslaving the few who still live."

"They are not stories," a dark slender man with pointed ears said. "A demon has taken over a large piece of land near the maelstrom. It had been the elves home since the Age of Dragons, but this demon and her fiery creatures killed my tribe. We fought back, but it had taken up refuge in one of the spires. Now, she controls the desert around the maelstrom."

"Impossible sand elf," a slender-faced, light-colored woman said who also had long pointy ears. "The empire would never let a demon get so close to Dragonlock. It is too critical to let a demon interfere with the airship and caravan traffic. Their mighty weapons would have banished the demon before it could do any damage."

"Unless the empire is working with the demon," someone else in the train car muttered.

"The emperor is not stupid enough to align with a demon," the woman replied.

"The emperor is a child," Hagash said. "He has no scars and has never waged war. He knows nothing of the evil that slithers through darkness. Instead, him and his kind cower behind their walls. Like all cowards, they will die behind their walls. I even hear that the corrupted are multiplying inside their grand cities."

"And they blame us elves for that," another woman with pointy ears said. "We once were accepted by most humans. Many of our families did quite well as traders between the humans and others. Now, they blame everyone else for the corruption and Imperial inquisitors patrol the cities destroying anything they think could be a corrupted. At least the Imperial guard has honor, the inquisitors are nothing but thugs. They kill or torture any nonhuman they come across. For all I care, the humans can wrought away in their glass and metal cities." The woman looked pained by some unspoken memory.

"The real question is can we survive," another male elf said. "There are bandit lords building their own kingdoms far away from the cities. Without imperial protection or supplies, we are all dead anyway. Either you will get killed by someone with a big magical weapon or will get eaten by some blasted corrupted. It's funny. No matter what the empire's propaganda says, many people joined the corrupted, because at least then, they have a fighting chance."

"Do not worry about the barbarian tribes," Hagash said. "While we may bicker and argue, we know how to survive and fight. We did it in the Age of Dragons, and we did it in the Age of Magic. This Age of Corruption will be no different. As for you elves, you must pick a side. And the orcs, will cower and eventually be slaughtered like the humans." Hagash glared at Djinn as he spoke. Monty noticed that everyone else actively avoided eye contact with Djinn except for Hagash.

"Don't worry," Djinn said. "Orcs will always fight on and on and on. They are great at that. Besides, we don't want the barbarians to get bored."

"What about the Lord's Council, Lord Warden," someone said from the back of the train.

"Do not place your hope in them," Nora said. "They do not take sides and have been trying to find a permanent solution to the corrupted for decades. They still don't even know what causes a person to become corrupted. Now, they just argue in meetings while the rest of us do what we can."

"Like I said, darkness is covering these lands," Hagash said. "Things are getting even worse than you know, mistress druid. The dead are rising and walking these lands. There are things like ghosts, walking corpses, and even a wraethenu was reported in castle Krakenjall."

"I tell you, the dragons are trying to come back," an elf in ragged clothing said as he waived his dirty hand. "They have found some way to break through the maelstrom and are coming back into this world. Before we know it, we will be all slaves again. Don't tell me the rest of you don't feel it. I can feel it in my bones. Their anger is surging, and the dragons will come back."

"We have always been plagued by the undead," Nora reminded them. "However... something is causing even more of them to stir and walk the land again. It could be the demons or something deeper, but I can assure you that it's not dragons. From what I have heard from summoners, they have moved on to other planes. They have no interest in coming back."

"How are you so sure," another passenger said.

"I helped the council explore a theory that the dragons could be behind the corrupted," Nora said. "Fortunately, it proved false, and we continued to look for a cure."

"Wait," someone said. "You're going to try to cure those monsters. They must all be destroyed. None of them should live. I have seen so much death by the corrupted. None of them deserve to live."

"Hey," another person said. "One of those corrupted was my brother. I would do anything to get him back. It's not his fault he is a corrupted."

"Your brother is a murder and deserves to be punished as a murderer," someone else yelled and jumped up onto his feet. Then, several other people jumped up and began yelling and shouting. Monty couldn't understand what anyone was saying as their voices merged into a deafening cacophony. Some even shoved each other around.

"Enough," Nora roared which caused everyone to stop yelling and stare at her. "Yet, we can only help release them from their curse. If it is possible to cure them, then we will determine their punishment later. Especially, since we still do not understand the corrupted. It might be, or it might not be their fault."

"Whatever you want, druid," an angry elf said as he sat down. "It's not as if you are helping, anyway."

"She killed a bunch of werelings and saved me," Monty said in an angry high-pitched voice. "She is trying, and she will help save us." The rest of the passengers seemed to notice her for the first time. As they stared at her strange face and eyes, Nora whispered to Monty to sit down. She slowly sat down trying to be unnoticeable again but couldn't shake the weight of their stunned eyes.

"My people have always trusted the druids, and we will continue to do so," Hagash said as he turned his gaze away from Monty and back to Nora. "They are brave and powerful warriors. I know they will fight with the barbarians until the last warrior has fallen."

"I hope it doesn't come to that," Nora said. "These are dark times. The only way any of us will survive is to help one another." There were only a few nods and agreements. The rest just solemnly stared at the floor. Monty could see fear and uncertainty in their eyes despite the reassurance of a powerful druid. Instead of pushing the matter further, Nora sat down into her usual cat nap position, but she remained awake with a troubled expression.

For a while, Monty continued to hide under her cloak trying to hide from the occasional glance. Neither Nora nor Djinn spoke with her or anyone else. Most of the passengers remained quiet with the occasional low spoken conversation. The train moved in and out of the tunnels with darkness consuming them momentarily and then releasing them. Each time no one stirred as light blasted into their train car.

Monty wondered if this is how most the world felt. Was it mired in so much anguish and fear that most people no longer had the will to fight the true evils that oppressed them? If only a few would stand against these evils, what chance do they have against such overwhelming odds? Monty found these questions disturbing and wondered if this is what Montague meant when he said she would save this realm. Before she could save anyone, she had to find the Ninth Spire. Looking down at the medallion and its intricate pattern, she knew she had to get this device working first. With a deep sleep overcoming her, Monty quietly hoped that they would reach the sage before any other terrible events happened, Unfortunately, it didn't work out that way.

Without warning, the train exploded.

PART TWO

Chapter Eleven

Shadows of the Lords' Council

Deep in the wilds of the Antellia Province, the Lord's Council was a large stone complex composed of multiple towers that varied in height. Tall, imposing, walls with various embattlements surrounded most of the towers from outside observers. When the few visible towers' windows were unlit at night, the black stone walls and towers appeared like a giant head of a terrible, horned beast. Unfortunately, a single window was lit this night in one of the tallest towers.

A priest slowly climbed the stairs to the lit room. Like many priests, he was thin and old. A thick white beard flowed down from his bald head and covered his bony cheeks and pointed chin. Under bushy, white eyebrows, he scowled at the partially open door. With his brown robe shuffling across the floor, he quickly made his way to the door and struggled to push it open. It was a large, dark wooden door common in most of the complex. After pushing it open into the small library, he was met with the sight of an old woman in gray robes impaled against the stone wall by a sword.

"Priest Ramier," Tomas said as he pulled his sword out of the dead woman's body. The body crumbled to the ground with a heavy thud. Aghast, the priest slammed the doors behind him.

"What have you done," the priest rasped. Stepping over the body, Tomas approached the priest while still holding the bloody sword. Nervously, Ramier stumbled backwards against the closed door as he searched for another escape.

"It is okay, my friend. I am not here to hurt you."

"She was my friend. She was helping you and Lady Enix. We both were. Why did you kill her?"

"Unfortunately, Adrienne had a change of heart," Tomas said shaking his head. "Like most wizards, she believed she knew best and would give our plans to the council."

"That can't be true," the priest said. "I have known her for over thirty years. She would never betray the empire. She believed in it more than she did the Lord's Council."

"If she loved the empire so much, why was she going to interfere with its planning?" Tomas studied his blade for a moment. Looking back to the priest, he determined that it wouldn't take much to kill this man. However, he didn't know whether he was immune to the priest's magic as he was immune to wizard's magic. When he noticed Ramier nervously glance at his blade, Tomas determined the priest's magic posed no threat. Tomas advanced toward the priest, but the priest tripped on his robes and fell backwards.

"When you killed Montague, the council began asking questions," Ramier said hurriedly. "We tried to delay or divert their attention, but the head of the council wouldn't let it go. He is infuriated that Montague was killed for treason. They are calling for a full investigation. What am I supposed to do?"

"Well, we can't have more lords crawling around the spires. That is why I brought you a distraction."

"What distraction?"

"Just listen," Tomas said. Ramier stood back up looking around the room. It was just a small room lined with books. It had one vertical window on the wall opposite the door. There were two tables and four chairs, but nothing else was moving or making noise. After a few minutes, Tomas could hear faint screams at the ground level of the complex. Ramier's wrinkled face tightened into an expression of horror.

"What have you done! There are innocent people down there. We had some of the best performers and artists in the entire empire. Their talents and experience will be lost forever."

"What you didn't know is that some of your so called 'artists' are actually corrupted. What will people say when they learn that the mighty Lords' Council can't even protect itself from the threat of the corrupted? They will have no one to turn to, but our benevolent empire. That is to say if the Lord's Council doesn't find a solution themselves."

"So that's your game," Ramier said with a thoughtful expression. "We've investigated this problem several times before. With this direct attack, the council will have to form a committee to investigate it again. They will ignore other problems like your Lady Enix until this is resolved."

The Lord's Council was a unique body in the empire. All its members commanded much power and believed that they were all entitled in the say of the council's governance. While each order had a representative on the council, it took a long time for each order to come to a consensus for action. Fortunately, the Imperial Guards were the only order that answered to the emperor who made them partially immune from the overly complicated machinations of the council.

"I have evidence of their movements and hideouts over there on the table." Tomas pointed to folder sitting on one of the small tables. The folder bulged with a large stack of paper held together only by string.

"Excellent," Ramier said. "With this evidence already in hand, we can start the process immediately. Trust me, it will take them months to agree on the stipulations."

"How long will it take them to kill the corrupted," Tomas said as he listened to further screams and explosions.

"Too long," the priest said. "I fear many lives will be lost tonight as most representatives are not the more powerful members of their orders."

Without warning, the doors flew open and a man wearing a thick, dark green cloak burst into the room. He had a strong, rugged face surrounded by a long dark beard and hair. Under his cloak, he wore a black leather jacket, black trousers and dark brown boots. In his thick, flexing hand, he held a large bow. After seeing the dead body, he turned his steely gaze to Tomas and Ramier.

"What did you do to her," the man raged. "Why is she dead!"

"She was a traitor to the empire," Tomas shrugged.

"Gullec," the priest said trying to soothe the man's anger. "We didn't want to kill her, but we had no choice. She had turned against us. She is the reason the corrupted got in here. She had to be stopped."

Tomas quietly smiled to himself while listening to Ramier's lies. For a priest that was supposed to uphold truth, the man was a terrific liar. He could persuade a village to hang a paladin if he wanted too. Ramier's lack of virtues was the main reason Lady Enix chose him ten years ago to help her.

While he went along with their revolt to imprison Lady Enix, Ramier cared only about riches and advancement and saw a fortuitous opportunity. He was the reason they were called heroes of the Fifth Spire, and he has used it to consolidate power over the years. As long as Lady Enix could line his pockets, Ramier was an invaluable ally.

"Just like Montague was a traitor," Gullec said. "I know you murdered him Tomas, and that you murdered Adrienne. Before I kill you, tell me why you did it."

"No," Tomas said. Gullec was part of the Order of Rangers. While they could take down any man or beast with one shot, Gullec was a drunken fool. Even now, he reeked of alcohol. With quick reflexes, Tomas could evade the drunk ranger's arrow and then kill the ranger with one strike. He had to act fast while his guard was down. "You are a fool that is why Lady Enix doesn't need your services."

"I thought Lady Enix was imprisoned," he said confused. Gullec also served Lady Enix ten years ago, but he hated her for always manipulating him. Fortunately, it wasn't a hard task. Grasping the hilt of his sword, Tomas motionlessly prepared his attack.

"She has returned, and she needs your soulstone," Tomas said. Drawing his sword, Tomas charged the ranger. Despite his drunken state, Gullec quickly raised his bow and fired an arrow made of blue light. It struck Tomas in the side and knocked him to the ground. Still alive, Tomas leapt back to his feet. Instead of attacking Tomas further, Gullec turned to the open doors as a group of corrupted werelings charged them from the hallway.

Each wereling looked like a man-beast hybrid. Two of them had the snout of a wolf and covered in thick, grey, bloody fur. Another corrupted had the head of a lizard with his body covered in thick scales and spines. The fourth one had a head of a lion with short, orange-yellow hair covering the creature's muscular body. Each of their hands had long black claws that dripped with blood. Despite the searing pain in his side, Tomas attacked the closest corrupted.

Like a whirlwind of blades, he spun and struck the lizard-man beast. The creature cried out in pain as the blade tore through its skin. Enraged, the beast struck back, but Tomas' sword severed the creatures hand from its arm. Cradling the bloody stump, the beast stared at the glowing blade.

Where paladin's had their magical armor, the imperial guard had magical blades that could cut through most materials. It made them deadly foes since their blades could slice through most weapons and armors. When fighting the corrupted or any beast, the sword would cut through their bones like warm butter. The trick was to kill the corrupted as fast as possible since he couldn't survive many direct strikes from the corrupted and their powerful claws and bites. Advancing onto the creatures to strike a final blow, Tomas realized the creature had another attack.

Opening its mouth, the corrupted spewed a jet of flame at Tomas. Rolling out of the flame's path, he charged the beast while it tried to redirect its attack. Tomas decapitated the beast, and a fountain of flame ignited from its neck. As the flame died down, the creature's body fell to the floor. Having killed his opponent, Tomas found himself surrounded by fire.

The creature's fire attack had covered the bookshelves and rugs in flames. The flames quickly spread along the walls as it consumed the old, dry books. Avoiding the flames, the priest fled the burning room while evading the other corrupted.

The other three creatures had attacked Gullec first. Noticing the fallen lion-man abomination at the doorway, Gullec must have posed a much greater threat since he took one down with a single shot. Now, he was dodging their constant swipes while firing blue energy arrows from his bow. As each bolt pierced the creature's hide, they would cry out in pain and slow down momentarily allowing the other creature to advance. While never liking the drunkard, Tomas hated the corrupted even more. Tomas approached the corrupted as he waited for it to turn and attack him.

Finally, one wolf-man creature noticed him and stopped attacking Gullec. Since the creature was distracted, Gullec fired a more powerful energy arrow at its back. Luckily, the shot was perfect, and the creature fell over dead with a gaping black hole in its back. Angry, the other creature charged Gullec despite being hit rapidly by Gullec's energy arrows. Focused on trying to kill the rampaging monster, Gullec couldn't dodge the attack and was impaled by the abomination's long claws. Still in an enraged charge, the creature pushed both of them through the window, and they plummeted to distant ground. Tomas ran over to the window see whether either one of them survived. Instead, he only saw two dark, motionless forms on the ground. With the room on fire and needing to verify that Gullec was truly dead, Tomas made his way out of the room and started his way down the tower's stairs where he met Ramier.

"It is wonderful to see you lived, my friend," the priest said. "Where is Gullec?"

"One of those things pushed him through the window," Tomas said as he stopped on a lower step. "I have to make sure that he is dead, so he tells no one our secret." He also needed to make sure that the man's soulstone was released with his death. With another soulstone, Tomas didn't need to kill the priest for his soulstone. While Tomas wasn't planning on telling Ramier, something in Ramier's expression told Tomas that he already knew.

"That is good," Ramier said. "Then, I will show this to the council." He held up the papers that had the reports of the corrupted movements. "With this information and so many deaths today, they will have no choice but to investigate these marauding corrupted so they will no longer bother you or the illustrious Lady Enix."

CHAPTER TWELVE

The Baron

After the train exploded, the events were a blur. Monty's train car had been tossed off the tracks as it threw her and the other passengers against the inner wall. With a sudden jolt, Monty gripped the side of the train car watching the walls being torn asunder by large rocks followed by rushing water. It didn't take long for the train car to dissolve around her as the river ripped her away from the passengers who were screaming and drowning in the white foamy waters. Not knowing how to swim, Monty fought the river with her arms flailing, but she could not stay above the water. While she didn't need to breathe in water, she quickly lost sight of her companions.

Finally, Monty grabbed onto a rock near the shore and held on. After pulling herself above the water, Monty frantically looked around. Only limp, bloated bodies of some of the passengers floated by. As she tried to ignore the gruesome sight, she still couldn't find her friends floating in the water. On the twilight horizon, she could barely see the train's remains. Then, Monty noticed some people standing on the river banks. She began to wonder if Djinn and Nora had already escaped the river and were looking for her along the shore. Finding them was much better than sitting in a cold, fast moving river. Grabbing some nearby tree roots, she pulled herself ashore.

Her wet cloak hung heavily on her shoulders while her sopping dress clung to her skin. Still dripping, Monty made her way up the river bank to the group she saw earlier. Getting closer, she heard their distant, inaudible voices. They lighted several lanterns while looking around the water. Then, she saw the uniforms. They were the same uniforms as the men who killed Montague. Quickly looking around, she rushed into some nearby trees and hid.

Still, unable to hear what they were saying, Monty decided it was better to get away from the area than be captured. Trying to sneak away, she found her heavy wet cloak even more cumbersome. Using her small arms, she grabbed the bottom of the cloak and pulled it up to her waist. Looking like a small gray mushroom, she ran and hopped her way through the small forest. She wanted to stay near the river so she made sure that sounds of the rapids were always to her left. By nightfall, she finally exited the forest. With the clouds covering the moons, she searched the clearing before finding a path that happened to follow the river.

With still no sign of Nora or Djinn, she continued to walk along the path alone. Thinking it couldn't get much worse, thunder and lightning erupted from the sky heralding a heavy down pour of rain. While being wet and cold didn't bother her, the muddy path made it much more difficult to traverse. The wind blew and tossed around the nearby vegetation. Unfortunately, the storm was so loud that she never heard the carriage come up behind her.

Monty jumped back when she noticed the two large carriage horses. Two guards wearing black and red cloaks jumped off the back and advanced slowly. While Monty tried to identify their uniforms in the gloomy rain, the men noticed her face and drew their weapons. Backing up, they looked at each other nervously. Monty just watched them as she huddled in her water-drenched cloak.

"What is it," a voice called out from the carriage. The guards looked at each other again and then glanced to the carriage.

"It's some kind of corrupted sir," one guard said. "At least, I think it is."

"Wait, wait," the voice said frantically. The door to the carriage swung open, and an older man jumped out. Quickly wrapping himself up in a cloak, he rushed over to Monty. She didn't move because she wasn't certain what to do. So far, no one was had attacked her, so she waited to see what they would do next. The two guards seemed afraid of her as they used their swords to protect them. The older man simply came up to her and pointed a strange bronzed colored box at her. Not feeling anything from the box, she watched him move the device up and down slowly.

"Why are you pointing that device at me," Monty said. "I do not recognize it. "Ignoring her question, the old man remained focus on the device. It glowed and sparkled at times and then all the lights disappeared. After that, he put it back underneath his cloak.

"It's all right," he called to the guards. "She isn't a corrupted."

"What is she," a guard asked.

"Not sure," the older man said. "First, we need to get out of this dreadful weather. Come with me and I will protect you." He held out his hand in a friendly gesture.

"How do I know I can trust you," she said. The rain continued to pour down around her.

"I am Baron Eston Verrandrin," he said. "I am the lord of these lands and the city of Parn. I give you my word I will protect all those on my land who is not a criminal or corrupted. Besides, anywhere is better than out here." When he said Parn, a spark of hope ignited inside her. She was close to finding the sage. Would he help her? Reluctantly, she gave him her hand, and he led her back to the carriage. The guards sheathed their swords and jumped back onto the back of the carriage. Followed by the baron, she climbed into the red velvet lined carriage. The seats were included heavy red cushions. As she and her clothes slopped down onto one of the cushions, the baron carefully sat down across from her. The carriage had glass windows that kept out the howling wind and rain. It was still dark, so she could barely see any of his features as he looked at her. "Now, that we are out of the rain, what is your name?"

"I am Monty," she said. She started to say something else, but stopped. She didn't know him and wondered if he would be a friend like Djinn and Nora. Could he be more like the two pompous humans who took away Montague's house? So, she waited to see what he would do next.

"You have nothing to worry about," he said. "I am the owner of these woods, and we will be back home soon. You can barely see them in the dark, but we are passing by the white fingers. At least, that's what we call them, because they are a grove of white trees that grew on the edge of the forest like crooked fingers. It is a strange sight, but I love looking at them in the spring when they are covered with pink and yellow flowers. I have seen nothing like them anywhere else. I know, because I have traveled throughout the realm."

Despite his casual and warm tone, Monty remained guarded.

"If you don't mind my asking, were you on the train that crashed nearby? If not, did you see what happened?"

"No." She lied. It felt horrible, but she didn't know what else to do. He might be with those guards at the river bank. With that thought, she felt a sickening feeling In the pit of her stomach.

"That's disappointing," he said. She wondered if he noticed her lie because his expression never changed. "I hoped that you could shed some light on what happened. Those blasted imperial guards would not tell us anything and wouldn't let us organize a search party. It is so frustrating." Still refusing to trust him, she remained silent. "Ah, theirs the gate. We are finally home." Through the dim rain, Monty watched two tall towers pass by the carriage. They were only lit by a few lanterns causing the light to wrap around their uneven stones like long bony fingers. As the carriage pulled up to the front of the very large house, the carriage interior became fully illuminated from several lantern posts around the house's entrance.

The man wore a dark red jacket with a black undershirt and pants. His clothes were accented with white lace ruffles and silver buttons. Despite her strange appearance, his gray bearded face just smiled at her. Like Djinn, he had little hair left on his head. The door opened, and he pulled himself out of the carriage. Then, he helped her out.

Monty found herself near two large doors of an enormous house. It was built of gray stone that reached high into the sky and spread outward to her left and right. Lighted windows were spread out evenly along the walls. To protect them from the rain, the baron directed Monty to stand underneath awning. The courtyard had a giant circular drive covered in cobble stones. From the main gate; two roads intersected the drive. Then, the large doors opened, and the baron led her into the house.

*   *   *   *

The inside of the house was covered in marble floors, reddish wood walls, and an impossibly high ceiling. Looking into the various adjoining rooms, she saw furniture lining the walls whereas couches and chair were positioned in the center of each room. Several people poured into the entryway to help the baron with his clothes, but they all gasped when they saw her. Monty just smiled back while she dripped on the floor.

"Do you know how late it is Eston," an older woman's voice said as she came around the corner. She had a long slender face with a tiny nose. Her grey hair was tied up in a large bun, and she wore a long, maroon dress. Then, she saw what the rest of the servants were staring at. "By the Divine! What is it? Is this another one of your projects, Eston?"

"Relax my dear," the baron said. "She is completely safe. I found her in the woods, and I couldn't let her stay in the rain. Also, I tested her, and she is not a corrupted." As he said this, he pointed to the same bronze box from earlier.

"Fine," she said angrily. "First, we must get her out of those wet clothes. She is ruining the floor. Miranda, take her to the guest room and get her cleaned up for supper. My husband is lucky we are still having supper as late as it is." Miranda was a servant girl who had black hair with a short plump body and a round smiling face. She wore a dark blue uniform like the other servants. The uniforms were very plain except for bright yellow seams that ran along the shoulder and arms. The men wore pants whereas the women wore long skirts. Finally, the servants adjusted to Monty's appearance and several of them began assisting the baron with this jacket while another one mopped up the wet floor. Despite all the commotion, the baron remained focused on his wife and never looked at any of them.

"Oh come now, my dear," he said. "I was just surveying the train wreck. The imperial guard makes everything ten times more difficult."

"Oh please," she said. "It was just another corrupted attack. It was hardly worth your time. You need to be preparing Parn instead. Hopefully, we won't need those trains much longer." She stopped and noticed Monty again. "Why are you still standing there? Off with you at once." As she shooed Monty away, Miranda led her upstairs into a room after walking through several corridors. It was decorated with an armoire, a dressing area, a wash Basin, and a small bed. Miranda carefully removed the cloak from Monty and hung it on a hook near the dressing area.

"Wow, you look amazing," Miranda said astonished. She gently lifted up her arm and looked down at her sides and back. Monty felt strange as she was examined. "Your skin feels like the statue in the hallway, but you move like a dancer. And your hair is so soft. If you were human, the boys would be falling all over themselves trying to get your attention. You are just so pretty."

"Thank you," she said meekly.

"Its okay, the servant said. "Just let little sweet Miranda take care of you and you will be as bright as new. Now, let's see what we got in here." She began to rummage through an armoire while muttering to herself. She tossed several dresses onto the bed that looked way too big for Monty. "So what color do you like? We have a red dress here. We also got this yellow dress, but I think it's a little too light for your complexion. What about this blue one? It matches your eyes." Monty looked at the blue dress. It was a satin blue dress with white lace along the front and bottom.

"I like blue," Monty said. She was surprised that she just said that. She hadn't really thought about colors, but the blue dress looked the best out of all the dresses.

"Go try it on," Miranda said as she pointed to a changing area that was protected by a screen. After a few minutes of fighting with the dress, Monty finally got it on and walked to a body mirror. As Monty looked in the mirror, she found the dress way too big. It hung low around her shoulders and was bunched up on the ground.

"Hmm, that's the shortest dress we got. Let me see what I else I can find." Miranda walked out of the room. Monty just stared at herself in the mirror. She still had smudges on her skin from all. The traveling and her hair was much dirtier than it was at Montague's house. She knew she would have been much dirtier if it hadn't been for the river and the rain storm. Then, Miranda came rushing back into the room. I just found you another dress. It will fit much better this time. First, we got to give you a bath. Come with me." Miranda grabbed her hand and took Monty into another room with a large tub that was filled with suds and water. " Take that off and wash up here. Just yell for me when you're done." With that, the woman left the room and closed the door.

Monty removed her clothes and stepped gently in a bronze-colored bathtub. Being only three feet tall, the soapy, warm water easily came up to her chest while still standing up. Surrounded by mountains of soap bubbles, she became fascinated by the bubbles and how they easily floated through the air. After several minutes of tossing and catching the bubbles, she remembered that she had to get clean. Finding soap, a cloth, and a soft brush nearby, she scrubbed the patches of dirt off her. Fortunately, the dirt came off her stone-like skin easily. Once she finished cleaning her body and hair, she climbed out of the bath tub.

As she sought out her towel, she found her reflection in a full size mirror. She looked up and down her slick, shiny body. While she was sculpted with a slender, female body, she found it extremely unsettling how much she looked like some of the marbles statues she had seen earlier. Not wanting to be still and lifeless like them, she dried off her body with the nearby towel and looked for her clothing. Unlike the statues, she could hide her appearance with clothing.

Near the door, Monty saw a beautiful blue dress with white satin ribbons. As she picked it up, her hand ran down the soft cloth. After marveling at it for a few moments, she started to unbutton it so she could put it on. Once she got it on, she loved how soft and plush it felt against her skin. It was so much better than her other dress. Finding the full sized mirror again, she twirled around in it watching the dress fly around with her. It made her feel so much alive than she was without it. She looked nothing like those statues now and almost looked human. Smiling, she left the mirror and opened the door to leave the bathing room. Before she could step out, Miranda was already standing in the doorway.

"You look so good," Miranda squealed. "You are just so cute. I cannot tell you how cute you look. Now, lets see what we can do about your face."

"What's wrong with my face," she said.

"Well, it's a little pale", Miranda said. "But, we can fix that. Trust me, I know exactly what to do. Follow me." Following Miranda down the hallway, Monty entered another smaller room filled with more furniture. Miranda took her to a table and chair against the wall. The table was filled with vials and brushes with a giant mirror overlooking it. As Miranda lighted several large lanterns, Monty pulled herself up into a chair next to the table. "We are going to the make you just beautiful. Now, hold still."

Using brushes and pads, Miranda quickly applied different colors to her cheeks, eyelids, and lips. As Miranda's arm moved back and forth, Monty tried to get a glimpse of the progress, but the woman was too quick. Eventually, Monty gave up and just stared at the different colors on the table. She found all the different shades of blues, pinks and purples fascinating. Occasionally, she would reach over and pick up a vial of makeup just to watch the liquid roll around in it. After a time, Miranda declared that she was done.

Looking into the mirror, Monty smiled deeply at her newly painted face. Her lips had become bright red while her cheeks were accented with a soft pink blush. The black eye liner surrounded her blue eyes with deep purple eyelids. It almost made her look just like everyone else and not like a statue. "I love it," she said mesmerized.

"I am so happy to hear that," Miranda said. "You now look as if you are ready for a royal ball. You would just knock those suitors right out of their boots when they saw how pretty you were. Now, we are running a bit behind so I need to get you down to dinner. The baron had the cooks make a special meal just for you. You will love it. Follow me." Helping her down, Miranda followed her out of the room and back down the gray marble stairs covered in a dark red carpet.

Monty was led to dining room with a very long dining table made of a dark-stained wood. Miranda pulled out a large wooden chair near the head of the table so that Monty could sit down. Once she was comfortable in the chair, Miranda said goodbye with a smile and a wink. At the head of the table, the baron sat in a gold-laden wooden chair as he swirled around his drink in a gold goblet.

"I hope you found your accommodations to your liking," the baron said once the Miranda and the other servants left.

"I love the new dress and makeup," she said excitedly. Hearing her eager voice echo through the silent chamber, she felt embarrassed and adopted a meeker tone. "Thank you, good sir, for your help, and kindness. I was lost, and I couldn't find my way to Parn. Do you know how to get there?"

"Of course," he said. "I will be glad to help you on your way to Parn. It's only a day's ride from my house to the city. As the ruler of these lands and the great city of Parn, I spend much time there. It is a smaller city, but clean and beautiful. A tribute to the hero it was named after. Have heard of the great hero, Parn?" Two servants entered the room each caring a small bowl and placed them in front of the baron and Monty. She grabbed the spoon next to the bowl and began eating the white soup. It was very different from Djinn's soup, but it still tasted just as good. As she quickly ate part of the soup, she realized that she had almost forgotten the barons question.

"No," she said between bites. "No one has told me about this hero. What was he like?" A thought flashed in her mind that this hero might be just like her. Could she be a hero too?

"Parn was one of the greatest heroes during the Age of Heroes," he said as he placed the goblet back down. From her deep memories, she knew that the Age of Heroes occurred before the Age of Peace. "While there are no exact dates that scholars can identify, the age was approximately a thousand years ago. He was not some nobleman but actually a human peasant. He traveled to different villages and protected them from various monsters. It was said that he was a grandmaster of all sorts of weapons, but he wore only peasant garb. He never wore armor. He wanted to show the people that he was just like them. He did this for years until he eventually died in a great battle.

"In this battle, the greatest heroes of that age joined together to defeat armies of demons. It was said that they fought for weeks nonstop, without food and some say even with no water. That's just silly since all humans need water. They eventually, defeated the armies, but he actually died after the battle.

"You remember the mysterious portals that were opened? They were actually opened by a maru. When the heroes found this evil creature, they fought him for a day, but only Parn knew how to defeat it. While the creature seemed completely armored and impervious to weapons, Parn found a weak spot between its armor, but he knew it would cost him his life. With a simple dagger and a brave heart, he killed the creature with one blow. However, before Parn could escape the death throes of the dying creature, it took its powerful fist and smashed the hero. As the maru died, the portals closed, and the demons were pulled from this realm. Because of the unholy magic of a maru, the heroes could not save their friend and buried him in an unmarked grave. He was the only one to die out of the seven heroes who fought in that battle."

Monty was stunned. Parn was nothing like her. She wasn't a human and didn't know how to use any weapons. Worse, it was her kind that actually killed him. Her kind was actually the villain in the story. Part of her wondered if there were other maru in history that were actually heroes. As she pondered this idea, several servants reentered the room and replaced her soup with a dinner plate. This time, it was some kind of fish lightly covered in a white sauce. Unlike the soup, this dish had a sour, acidic taste.

"Tell me more about the maru," she said hesitantly. Did he know that she was a maru?

"The maru is very rare. It generally only shows up once or twice an age. Usually, minions working for demons or dragons build them for their unholy missions."

"What kind of missions?" A part of her didn't want to know, but she had to find out more about her kind.

"Well, there is the story about a maru during the Age of Dragons. You see, humans attempted many failed rebellions. There was a city, oddly enough, named Haven. It was the headquarters for a rebellion and might have actually succeeded. However, the dragons sent a maru that was over 40 feet tall and destroyed the entire city. When traders traveled to the city, the buildings and walls had been completely disintegrated. The only thing left were hundreds of skeletons partially buried in dust and dirt. Fortunately, no one ever saw the maru again.

"The other story I seem to recall was about a maru slaughtering students at the academy of magic known as the Arcanium. During the Age of Magic, the technology was advancing quickly, and we were constantly learning new methods of magic to improve our lives. One of the most powerful magic schools was developing a technology that would have created a Utopia for all humans. Unfortunately, a maru destroyed the school and everyone in it. Hundreds of children were killed in the attack. After that, the maru was hunted down and destroyed by the empire."

Maru killing entire cities and children disgusted Monty. She didn't want to hurt anyone, but all these other maru killed so many people. The thought of a similar destiny for her appalled her. She no longer wanted to eat, and she didn't want to be at the table. She found herself looking around for a place to go hide and be alone.

"Did you want dessert," he said after take a sip from his goblet. His fish was still uneaten.

"No," she said quickly. "I am ready to go to my bed."

"Of course," he said empathetically. He called for Miranda, and she quickly entered the room. "Miranda will take you to your bed. I will see you in the morning. My cook makes the best breakfast." Without hesitation, Monty hopped out of her chair and followed Miranda back upstairs. After walking down a hallway, Miranda led her into a small bedroom with giant canopy bed taking up most of the room.

This is one of the better beds in this place, Miranda said. Then, she paused for a moment as Monty stared distantly at a wall. "What's the matter? Are you all right? The baron didn't say anything did he?"

"How do you know whether you are evil or not," Monty said sadly.

"Honey, don't worry about such things. Just because they may say that one human is evil doesn't make all humans evil. Now, you listen to Miranda, sweet girls like you are not evil and don't let anyone tell you differently. Now, try to get some sleep, because things are always better in the morning. You'll see." Miranda bent down and hugged Monty. In a way, it made her feel better, but she still had some doubts. Then, Miranda wished her a good night and closed the door. Monty climbed into the bed and sank deep into the mattress and blankets.

As she fell asleep, she made a promise to herself that she would never hurt anyone.

Chapter Thirteen

The Fire Knights

Calais stood in the Eirodias' library. Wrapping herself in the dark, silent solitude, she managed to finally escape the loud revelry that pervaded the city. With the festival going on for days, the elves refused to sleep and continued their celebration unabated. After spending several exhausting hours of listening to Estasia whine about her fat, green body, the enchantment ended and gave Estasia back her beautiful body. She was so excited that she immediately rejoined the dancers and drinkers. Although Calais didn't think they would have noticed her appearance since most of the city was completely drunk. Exhausted, Calais had tried to find a quiet place to rest but that was near impossible. No matter where she went, she was bombarded with music and dancing lights. After some searching, she found the library.

With most of the city's sounds muffled, she walked quietly through the rows of tall shelves. Since the airwalkers could hover for a short time, they built their bookshelves very high, but also very thick, and wider than human-equivalent. Surrounded by thousands of volumes of histories and fables, she felt a small since of excitement. She had only been in this building once before and only for a short time.

Rev had spent much of his childhood in this place that didn't include very many fond memories. Princes were required to be familiar with the history of their people so they didn't make the same mistakes. Rev found books boring and would rather run through the countryside on some adventure. During her visit, Rev showed her a few books then wanted to show her other sights in the city. Not wanting to disappoint him, she followed reluctantly. Now, she had time to look at whatever she wanted.

The airwalkers were officially classified by scholars as air elves. While there were elves before the dragons, their race was changed dramatically. The dragons had killed or mutated most of the elves until finally there were five distinct groups with each one representing a different element. Originally, they were used as soldiers and spies for the dragons to enforce their will on other races. This created a great distrust of elves who endured even today. However, most of the groups finally escaped their dragon rulers and fled to the planes beyond. Some helped the resistance while others disappeared. The airwalkers had written extensively about the time of the dragons so that the generations would never forget their hardships. After the dragons were sealed away, the other races did not welcome them back, and the airwalkers remained on this plane. Insulated from the rise of great technologies and wars, they had a much simpler life and kept more objective records. Although, the few books she found that were written about the other races were often skewed or misunderstood. They were content to sit on the periphery and watch the tumult on Tallendrall.

Calais scanned the books wondering what she should read. If she had enough time, she would read all the books but that was unlikely. She wondered if she should read a great fable, a history of the dragon's experiments or the stories of the brave resistance fighters. Unfortunately, she knew she had to read about something much darker.

She needed to look for something about portals and prisons. She had her doubts on whether she would discover any clue on how to kill Lady Enix, but she wondered how the witch even escaped her dimensional prison. With her reduced energy, she should not have been able to break it. More than likely, someone or something helped her escape. The more important question is how to put her back in the prison without a way for her to escape. After some time of climbing shelves and browsing various volumes, she found several that might help her. Dropping the dusty volumes on a nearby table, Calais pulled up a chair and read about portal's harmonic energies and vibrations. After several hours, her eyelids became heavy while fighting through another few lines of text. Finally, sleep over took her.

Shaking her awake, Calais felt a strong hand grasping her shoulder. After a moment of her eyes refocusing, she recognized Denarith standing over her. Calais wondered how long she had been asleep. Before she could speak, Calais was overcome by big yawn. She must have been more tired than she thought.

"Do you know how long I have been looking for you," Denarith said. Calais couldn't tell whether he was annoyed or teasing her. "This is a big city. This is what happens when you give a bunch of elves a couple of stones and a cloud. They just keep building and don't stop. Then, I have to go looking for a summoner who has hidden herself away in a library, the last place I would have looked."

"I would have thought it would have been the first place to look for me."

"Hey, I haven't been in a library in over ten years. I forgot they even existed. Besides, you should have been enjoying yourself and not reading old books."

"But Denarith," Calais began. "I have found some very interesting ideas. When we first used the portal to trap Lady Enix, Montague setup a pulse repeater which realigned the portal. While it created a sufficient inter-dimensional plane to trap her, we actually needed something more complex. It had to be an emitter that could fluctuate the portal's energy patterns in variable intervals and increase and decrease the portal's energy frequencies at different levels. This kind of technology doesn't exist, but if it did, we could actually trap her permanently."

"Ok, stop right there," Denarith said. "Do you see me? A man with a bull-head, body covered in rippling muscles and gifts that make women think I am a god. What part of that makes you think I understand anything you just said. I need not look at books, and I really don't care unless frequency is something I can smash and maybe eat."

"Actually…"

"Okay, no more. My brain is already starting to hurt. Now come on. Rev says the king wants to see us."

"Why?"

"I don't know, and I don't care about what royal elves want. But I must say, these elves really know how to have fun."

"Do you have any idea what you have done," the king yelled as Estasia, Denarith and Calais entered his throne room. It was a large cavernous room with a vaulted ceiling. High above them, the king was perched on his throne, positioned on a large ornate column near the back wall. A crowd of ornately dressed spectators had assembled in the room. Wearing outfits of various colors, Calais couldn't identify their stations or importance. Carefully making her way through the crowd, Calais found Rev at the front with an annoyed look on his face. He acknowledged her only with a glance.

"It was my understanding that the members of the Lord's Council were protectors and enforcers of imperial law. Instead, you bring death and destruction to my city."

"King Regilus," Calais said cautiously as a dreadful thought came to her mind. "What's happened?"

"Ha," King Regilus exclaimed and then continued in a much lower tone. "A group of fire knights, sent from Lady Enix herself, will crash through my city walls presumably looking for you. However, in their search, they will kill thousands of people and destroy half the city. How do you answer to these crimes?"

"Father," Rev said. "They didn't know fire knights were coming, and they didn't lead them here. We checked the portal, and nothing was coming through."

"You are fool, my son. Your friend, Calais, is a powerful summoner that can create an entire army of creatures. Denarith is a totem warrior and Lady Estasia is a wizard. Their powers are like beacons on this desolate plane that led these demon spawns straight here."

"How were they able to find us," Estasia said. "The city's magic should have cloaked our presence?"

"So my son didn't tell you. During the ritual, he should have told you that our city defenses are down. The ritual takes so much power that the city's defensive and offensive capabilities are nonfunctional. To prevent attacks, we posted patrols at all the portals to keep them blocked. Somehow, they got through the portal and now they will butcher my people. All because you don't want to accept the consequences of your actions."

"So this is pretty easy," Denarith said. "We will just kill the fire knights and everyone can go back to partying and completing rituals."

"Denarith," Calais said. "We can't fight them here. Too many people will die. But, we can lead them away from here and take the fight elsewhere."

"We will not help you with this fight," the king growled. "Once you leave, you may never return."

"If you won't let us fight the demon spawns then let me help them in other ways," Rev offered.

"Revannick," the king said. "Do what you can stop this, but you will still have to answer for this when the ritual is complete." For a moment, Calais saw despair and sadness in Rev's eyes. Then, he turned to her with his old, familiar smile and glistening eyes.

"Let me show you your escape plan," Rev said.

* * * *

From the one of the city's outer tower, four metal flyers burst into the orange sky. Known as spiderlights, the flyer had a thin streamlined front with a bulbous back that contained the engine and protected the rider's legs. Because of the lightning coils in the engine, harmless purple lightning bolts would occasionally strike out to nearby objects giving the flyer the appearance of having giant spider legs. At first, Calais had a hard time holding on, but she quickly figured out the controls on the handlebars at the front and the pedals at her feet. While the airwalkers could float in midair and even fly slowly, she knew they used these vehicles for reconnaissance, fast attacks, and racing. Calais and her companions each piloted a spiderlight and followed Rev that was piloting his own spiderlight. As they flew over the beautiful white city, they saw the monstrous creatures known as fire knights approaching the city's gates.

The fire knights wore full plate armor that glowed red-hot like embers in a fire pit. Their heads were covered by cylindrical helmets with thin eye slits that contained two smoldering eyes. Instead of chainmail underneath the plated armor, there was only raging fire. Though they stood almost seven feet tall and wore awkward-looking armor, they moved quickly. In their hands, some held large swords, and axes while others carried flame-covered spears. With these weapons, Calais could see that their attacks on the walls had been devastating.

They were tearing their way through the city's wall as they somehow stood on the city's cloud foundation. Unable to withstand the heat and the creatures' might, the wall was melting away like butter. From what Calais could see, the wall was on the verge of being breached and the elves were about to be slaughtered.

In a dizzying move, Rev spun around and dove into the group of fire knights nearest the wall. Using the blades on the spiderlight, he sliced through several monsters that sent them crashing to the ground. Denarith tried to follow suit, but he was still struggling with the flyer's controls. While Denarith cursed the spiderlight, Rev was already back in the sky preparing for another attack run. This time, Rev used the spiderlight's bolt thrower that shot a bright red lightning bolt that burned its way across the ground. Many fire knights were stunned by the electricity while two were disintegrated. Calais could only imagine the horrible destruction these vehicles could bring against a normal army. She turned back to Denarith who was still fighting with the spiderlight's controls. Then, Rev gave the signal to follow as the fire knights turned their full attention on the flyers.

The fire knights rode a large horse-like creature covered in bone, flesh, and fire. Unlike normal horses, these creatures could gallop into the sky leaving a trail of fire. Calais could count at least a dozen of these creatures while she tried to follow Rev. Fortunately, for the city, the plan was working. All the fire knights had abandoned their attack on the city and were now following them.

The next part of the plan was a little trickier. All they had to do was move faster than the fire knights and reach a series of caves that contained an old portal leading back to Tallendrall. Using the vehicle's lightning attacks they could jumpstart the portal to open a gateway and then have only a few seconds to fly through. It was an old tactic that was used in previous wars but a dangerous maneuver, nonetheless. Calais knew that the portal could explode if too much energy were applied or it would close before they could fly through. Therefore, she knew it would take a couple of hours to recalibrate the portal and start it up again. She didn't think the demons would wait for that. The worst case scenario is that the portal could be calibrated for a different location than the airwalkers claimed. Then, they could end up on any other realm and most realms were not very hospitable. After a brief shudder, she forced herself to focus on the mission as she flew faster and faster trying to keep up with Rev.

They raced along the clouds to their destination, but Calais could see the fiery riders were gaining despite their spiderlight's insane speed. As the fire knights slowly got closer, they unleashed balls of fire that screamed past the flyers. Rev deftly moved around the fireballs with smooth maneuvers while Denarith jerked and wobbled out of the fireballs path. While Calais smiled at Denarith antics, she was not piloting much better as she moved left and right trying to evade the fireballs. She noticed that Estasia was having a much easier time then Denarith or her. She could almost keep up with Rev with her new light-brown traveler robes were flapping in the wind. Suddenly, Calais' flyer was struck releasing a fiery explosion around her.

Other than her hair and clothes slightly singed, she was physically fine but still a little shaken. Unfortunately, her spiderlight was not doing as well. The engine sputtered and coughed, and she lost speed. Calais' mind raced through ideas. Having no weapons to fight back, her options were limited. From the corner of her eye, she watched them draw very large swords made of fire and steel. With screeching wails, she knew they were closing in for the kill.

Chapter Fourteen

Crashing Portals

"Jump," Rev yelled.

Instinctively, Calais looked at the distant rocky ground below her. Stunned by the fear of falling to her death, she gripped the handlebars tightly and tried not to panic. Then, another fireball struck her spiderlight. As the searing heat and flames surrounded her, Calais leaped off her vehicle.

The cold wind swept past her face, but she could still feel the intense heat around her. Panicked, she realized her clothes were still on fire. Rolling around in the air, she began slapping the various flames into warm smoke. Remembering the ground that was rushing towards her, she screamed while watching her friends and the flaming riders become distant specks. From the corner of her eye, she barely saw the other spiderlight.

With no effort, Rev grabbed her arm as they raced to the ground. Calais was grabbing onto anything she could while Rev pulled her behind him. She instantly wrapped her arms around his abdomen and held on with all his strength. Clinching her teeth, she saw that they were still flying downward instead of pulling back up. Grunting with pain from Calais' grip, Rev steered the vehicle down the slope of a large mountain. Besides boulders, Rev deftly navigated around the rocky terrain. With purple lightning arcing from the vehicle to the ground, Rev slowly pulled the vehicle up. Unable to pull out of their descent, he was forced to fly into a large canyon. He waved one of his hands and caused a large gust of wind to blow them upward.

Leveling back out, Rev forced the spiderlight to race along the canyon's floor while whipping it back and forth to avoid the rocks jutting out of the canyon's walls. The spiderlight's lighting lit the canyon up with deep purple flashes while it walked along the floor and walls. Unfortunately, they were not alone as the canyon walls exploded behind them.

Above the canyon, two fire knights continued to pursue them. The vehicle lurched upward causing Calais' stomach to twist and turn. He guided the vehicle to the knights and did the same maneuver as before. Several long blades popped out of the sides. Before getting much closer, Rev fired a bolt of lightning from the nose of the vehicle. It successfully struck the fire knights with an explosion of purple energy. Stunned from the attack, they were too slow to dodge the charging vehicle. It sliced the two knights into pieces. Everything became dark again as they climbed back into the dark sky.

"You can let go now," Rev grunted. Realizing that she had been holding him tight, she slowly loosened her grip.

"How much further," Calais shouted against the wind. Slightly flinching away from her, he pointed to a dark mountain that was growing bigger.

Near the base of the mountain, there was a cave that led to a portal which would be very similar to the one they arrived in. When a portal was discovered, people tried to make them easier to access and defend against. The tunnel would be winding and treacherous as defenders needed to halt an attacking force's advance. In the end, they only had to worry about such tactics if the force could survive the traps and weapons.

From what Rev had said during their planning, the portal they arrived in was only recently discovered by the airwalkers. They hadn't set up their usual turrets and traps, but they had sensors put in place to notify them of the portal's activation. That is how Rev found Calais and her companions so quickly. Fortunately, the airwalkers created a system to disable the defenses if they ever had to use the portals. The only problem was that this new portal's equipment hadn't been checked in over twenty years. They may not be able to switch off the defenses.

Looking for her friends, she saw the other two spiderlights approaching them from above. Unfortunately, a trail of fiery riders still pursued them. Getting closer, Calais waved to her companions. Estasia waved back eagerly while Denarith still fought with the vehicle's controls. With the mountain filling the sky, more fireballs began to fly past them.

Instead of fighting back, Rev increased his speed and dove to the ground. Calais was thankful for the different tactic since it was much easier on her stomach. Denarith and Estasia did their best to follow but didn't go as low as Rev. All three of them continued to dodge the fireball attacks. The fireball exploded against the ground as it rushed below them in a dim blur. There was only darkness in front of her and behind her as no moons lit the landscape like her home, Tallendrall.

While she couldn't see the approaching cave entrance, Calais knew that Rev could see well in the dark as if it were daylight. It was a gift from the dragons. Like the dragons, they need their elite soldier to operate in the darkness effectively. The elves found it extremely advantageous while humans found it disturbing or unmerited. It was one of the many reasons that humans were so prejudiced against the elves that the humans caused many needless deaths and conflicts since the Age of Dragons.

Her train of thought was broken when Rev fired a bolt of lighting from his vehicle to strike the entrance of the tunnel. Seeing a rock glowing eerily above the cave, Calais realized that Rev had to mark their destination for Denarith and Estasia who were trying to catch up. She also knew that it was marking the way for the relentless fire knights. Hopefully, some of the defenses still worked and would destroy the fire knights.

The spiderlights' engines roared as they entered the large cave. Behind them, Calais flinched at the fire knights' shriek echoing against the cave's walls. As the cave turned to the left and right, Rev piloted the craft deftly while Denarith and Estasia had a much harder time. Denarith even struck the wall a few times with his spiderlight screaming in protest. The fireballs would strike the cave walls as they made each turn. Entering a carved hallway that ran straight, the fire knights fired several fireballs at once.

Reaching around Rev, she began pressing several buttons to activate the portal. While her elven was rusty, the glyphs showed her that the portal was activating, but it wasn't going quick. Looking back at the blinding orbs, Calais knew they were still too far away from the portal and there was no where to go to escape the attack.

Then, Calais saw Denarith's silhouette against the incoming attack. Letting go of one of the handles, champion swung his axe repeatedly and released waves of blue energy at the incoming fireballs. The fireballs detonated in a massive explosion that caused the surrounding area to shake. While most of the fireballs were destroyed, a few flew past them and struck the distant portal room. Looking over Rev's shoulder, Calais saw that the portal's readings began to fluctuate.

"Just fly through as fast as you can," Calais yelled over the explosions and engine noise. Denarith would have heard her because he had excellent hearing. However, Estasia might not have heard her. Hopefully, she would have stuck to the plan. Calais just hoped they had enough time. If they didn't get through fast enough, the portal would explode and kill them all.

Seeing the glowing portal ahead of them, Calais activated the defenses to attack the fire knights. Unfortunately, the defenses were not responding. Most likely, they were malfunctioning from lack of maintenance or damage from the fireballs. With no defenses, it looked like the fire knights were coming with them. Focused on piloting through the small bright hole, fireballs exploded around the portal. Undaunted, Rev sped up and Calais clenched her teeth as they flew into the light.

*   *   *   *

A tall stone statue stood on large mound surrounded by a yellow plain of tall grass. The statue was a warrior who stood in a wide stance on top of a circular stone base. It looked over a cliff where the grassy plains ended, and the drift started. As if he were challenging the Drift, the weathered soldier wore light armor while holding two large swords in each hand high above his head. A small white light shone through the grass blades at the base of the mound. It slowly grew larger and larger, until finally, the side of the mound exploded.

The three spiderlights soared into the air before an explosion of flame and dirt encompassed them. Heavily damaged, the smoking spiderlights could not sustain their altitude and fell back to the ground. Fortunately, the vehicles had an emergency system that slowed their descent before sliding along the ground. Ejected by the force of the crash, the four passengers lay in the tall grass near their perspective vehicles.

Calais sat up and surveyed the damage. The portal was nothing but a large, smoking hole that burrowed deep into the side of the mound. While the base of the statue remained intact, the rest of the statue was destroyed except for the two legs that remained connected to the base. Noticing the cliff as it overlooked the Drift, she realized that the statue was known as the Statue of Brandolier.

Not much was known about the hero. He lived during the Age of Heroes and was a companion of the great Parn. It was said that he was one of the heroes that ushered in the Age of Peace and helped build Castle Dragonlock. Some say he was an ancestor of the emperor's family, but no record exists for such claims. Generally, he was a ranger and an explorer. Many sailors and travelers considered him good luck, so they built the statue on the edge of the Drift.

Calais knew the Drift was not always sand and silt. Looking over the distant dunes, she always wondered what it must have looked like before the Age of Dragons. It was written that it was a large sea that connected the four main continents. Large sailing ships would travel back and forth while braving the dangerous creatures that swam underneath the cool waters. Dragonlock was an island in the middle of the sea where the King and Queen would rule over all the lands. Unlike the dirty, rough oceans that surrounded the continents, the old records said the sea was a bright blue with white, small waves. The beaches would have been golden yellow with squawking seagulls fishing near the shore. With the thought of the beautiful smell of sea air, Calais wrapped herself up with the dream of paradise while forgetting about the crash. Then, she heard Rev calling out her name.

"I am all right," she replied quietly as the image of the blue sea was replaced by the brown desert.

"Are you hurt," Rev said stumbling to her. She nodded and stood up to assess the situation. Rev's spiderlight was still in good condition, but the other spiderlights was twisted up from their poor landing. Estasia sat up and was brushing the dirt off her clothing before being thrown back to the ground with a yelp.

"You're welcome for the soft landing," Denarith grumbled while standing up.

"I was getting up," Estasia said as she rolled over to her side. Still hidden by the thick grass, Calais could only imagine Estasia's smug look. "A lady has to make herself presentable."

"A lady," Denarith laughed heartily. "You forget, I've seen you at the parties."

"Well, nothing wrong with having a little fun," Estasia said, "especially when you will be married."

"The poor man," Denarith said. "He has no idea what he is in for."

"He definitely has no idea what he is in for," Estasia laughed. After a few moments, she stopped laughing and looked around. "Where are we now? Where are those fire creatures?"

"Don't worry about the fire creatures," Calais said walking over to the crater below the statue. "The portal is destroyed, and they won't be coming through here. If they are still around, it will take them days to find another portal."

"So what is that supposed to be," Estasia said pointing to the ruined statue.

"It is the Statue of Brandolier," Calais said.

"Isn't that supposed to be a good luck charm," Rev said.

"Not anymore," Denarith said. "Now, it's just two stone legs standing up in the middle of the plains.

"Don't you know it's bad luck to destroy a good luck charm," Estasia said.

Instead of immediately replying, one of Denarith's ears twitched. He looked up and smelled the air and walked slowly away from the statue.

"What is it," Calais said following him.

"Imperial horseman are coming," Denarith said.

Calais panicked and ran back to Rev. "You have to get out of here. They will take you hostage."

"Don't worry," Rev said. "I've dealt with imperials before. They are a little uptight, but I know how to smooth talk my way around them."

"No, you can't," Calais said. "For the last several years, they have been arresting or killing elves that are not citizens or officers of the empire. They blame the elves and the orcs for causing the corrupted."

"If we were only so lucky," Rev said. "To have such an army would make you invincible."

"Shut up and get on your spiderlight," Calais shouted. The thought of him being captured scared Calais. An elven prince would make the perfect scape goat for the empire's campaign of fear. She hated what they were doing, but she no longer had any influence in the government.

"All right," he said raising up his hands. She followed him to his vehicle.

"You can find a portal near the city of Ennoch to the northeast," Calais said while he started the spiderlight's engine. "There is an ancient temple where you will find a portal in the crypt below it. The combination to direct the portal to Eirondrall is…"

"I know the combinations," Rev barked. "It's not my first time to use the portals to get home." He paused for a moment as he dialed a few controls on his console. He must have seen her worried face and spoken softer. "Where will you be going?"

"I have to get my summoner books," Calais said. "They are in my brother's tower. He is the only one I can trust these days."

"You be careful," Rev said. "I have never liked Arturo. He always had a funny smell."

"Oh he is harmless," Calais said. "He would never hurt me." She put her hand on his shoulder. "You need to be careful, and I will find you when this is all over."

"Trust me, Calais, nothing will happen to me. I am just too good to be caught or killed." With a devilish smile, he activated the spiderlight and flew to the north. After watching him for a few moments, she ran back to Denarith.

"How far away are they," Calais said.

"Not far," Denarith said looking at his axe. "Should we kill them?"

"Their is no need to kill them," Estasia said. "I know how to deal with hot men in armor."

Scanning the horizon, Calais couldn't see Rev anymore. Breathing a sigh of relief, she looked over the hill and watched the small group of soldiers ride to them. Standing in the tall grass, they just waited.

The soldiers wore black imperial armor with metal helmets. They rode large chestnut horses. Since the horses were wearing light metal barding for faster movement, Calais surmised that they were a scouting party. Most likely, a much larger group of soldiers were nearby. As they got closer, the riders slowed their horses but didn't draw their weapons.

"Identify yourself," the lead soldier called out. On the side of his armor, Calais saw the solider's rank of lieutenant.

"I am Lord Master Estasia Verrandrin of the wind guard," Estasia said with bravado. "These are my traveling companions. This is Lord Champion Denarith." He nodded to the soldier while keeping his axe at his side. "And this is…"

"I am Calais, just a portal mechanic," Calais interrupted. It was a good idea to keep her identity secret to prevent further complications.

"I am Lieutenant Roan," the soldier said. "We noticed an explosion in the area. Are you okay, Lord Master Estasia? Your portal mechanic appears slightly frayed." Calais looked at her clothing and noticed that it was burnt and tattered from the earlier fireball. Embarrassed, she smiled while trying to smooth out her clothing.

"An experiment gone awry, I am afraid," Estasia said. "We were testing a newly discovered portal, and it unfortunately blew up. We were in the process of collecting further data from the failed portal. After that, we would request transport back to the Lords' Council which will take some time."

"You are in luck," Roan said. "We can take you back to our main camp. General Amirez would wish to speak with you." The mention of a general caught Calais off-guard. Generals led only large armies, and it was unusual that there was an army so close to the Drift. "I am sure the general could arrange much faster transportation."

"I would love to meet with your general," Estasia said. Calais was impressed that her friend maintained her composure despite what the soldier said.

"It will be our pleasure to take you to him," Roan said with a large smile. "You can ride with me, but I am afraid we do not have a horse big enough for your champion."

"I can keep up," Denarith said flatly.

"Mechanic," Estasia said waving her hand at Calais. "Go fetch the rest of our equipment so we may finally leave this dreadful place."

Annoyed, Calais walked back to the crashed spiderlights and looked for any salvageable equipment. Fortunately, the main weapon rod was still intact. Since they were powered by an internal gem of ethaerium, it could prove useful as a weapon. Next, she found part of the scanner still intact which may help them detect nearby people and energy sources. They were bulky, but she grabbed a few more components to hide the rod and scanner. Making her way back, Estasia was already mounted behind Roan and Denarith looked at her impatiently.

"Get her a satchel please," Estasia ordered. A soldier rode over to her and dropped a brown leather satchel in front of her. She always hated people who treated low society like dirt. Dropping the components into the bag, she cinched up the buckles to keep the contents hidden. After handing the satchel to Denarith, another soldier helped her up onto his horse. Riding behind him, she held onto his torso as they were ordered to move out.

Thinking about Rev, she looked back to the north. She hoped to see him again, but she knew it was unlikely with a Lady Enix and her fire knights still hunting them. It was only a matter of time before they succeeded in killing her unless she could get her books back.

CHAPTER FIFTEEN

Under the Mansion

Monty woke up the next morning but in a very different place. Instead of the soft bed, she lay on a stone floor. Actually, she was surrounded by stone covered walls except for one. It had vertical and horizontal iron bars that were closely knitted together. Through the bars, she could see that her small room was part of several other barred rooms that all connected to a much larger room. With a horrifying thought, she realized that this wasn't a room, but an actual jail cell where they kept bad people. Scanning the much larger room for any kind of help, she found that it had only a long set of stairs leading upward. The room was lit by several torches that covered the room in eerie shadows.

"Hello," she called out when she saw no one. This had to be a mistake. Why would anyone imprison her? "Is anybody there? Please help me!" No one came. She called out several more times, but still no one came. As she watched the shadows dance to music of the torches' burning flames, she slumped down against the wall. She was trapped and alone.

After what seemed like an eternity, Monty heard a noise coming down the stairs. After a few moments, a boy stepped out of the dark shadows of the stair well. He was young and only wore ragged brown clothes. While carrying a bucket in one hand, he hastily walked past Monty's cell and placed the bucket near another cell adjacent to her. "Help me," she pleaded. Instead, the boy kept his gaze to the ground and ran back upstairs. Then, she heard a large splash of water and then a scratching noise.

Since the bars were made to hold much larger people, Monty managed to push her head between the bars to see what was happening. While she couldn't see all of her neighbor's cell, most of the cell was a giant pool filled with dark water. Next to the bucket, a blue arm with a human like hand continuously reached out for it, but it only scratched the ground with long needle-like claws. As she watched the arm, Monty noticed that the bucket was filled with dead fish. Realizing the creature was hungry, Monty decided that the right thing to do was to help it.

Pulling herself out of the bars, she made her way down to the end of the cell and reached out to the bucket. Fortunately, the bucket was closer to her cell than her neighbors. Monty gently pushed the bucket to the blue arm. As she moved it closer, the blue arm withdrew. Once Monty pushed the bucket out of reach, she withdrew her arm, and waited. Without warning, the blue arm shot out and yanked the bucket back into the pool. After a few splashes, there was only silence. Monty watched the other cell to see if she could see her neighbor, but they never showed themselves. Eventually, Monty returned to the back wall of her cell and sat back down.

After a time, she hummed. It was that same song she had sung before. Soothing her soul, it brought her a bit of hope. The tone moved up and down in varying degrees. It always repeated similar patterns which she assumed was the melody. Even the flames eventually fell into step with its long and slow cadence. When she stopped humming her song, a new song arose from her neighbor's cell.

The new song was loud and pervasive. It filled the room with a deep, minor tone. Unlike Monty's song, this seemed to be a sad song. It was a song of longing and loneliness. Even the lyrics were sung in a strange alien tongue that weighed heavily on Monty's soul. It continued for a long time until Monty heard footsteps coming down the stairs.

A boy entered the room. He was different from the other boy. This one was well dressed with a clean haircut. He was moving slowly to Monty's neighbor. Before Monty said anything, she saw a strange, haunted look in the boy's eyes. Helpless, she watched the boy slowly walk to the cell with the water.

A beautiful woman rose out of the dark water with a light blue skin and a dark blue dress. She was tall and voluptuous. Her dark hair flowed down around her neck and shoulders. Still singing her strange song, Monty noticed that her purple lips were hiding sharp long teeth. Watching the entranced boy, she realized what would happen. The creature would kill him.

"Stop," Monty pleaded. "Please don't hurt him. You don't have to kill him." The creature stopped singing and just stared at the boy who was near the bars.

"I am yours, my love," the boy said with a soft tone. "Your song completes me. I now know you are the missing piece in my life. Come to me, and I will always be yours. Oh, how I will always love you!" Now, he was gripping the bars staring intently at the creature.

Monty rolled her eyes at the boy's comments. "You don't have to kill this idiot," she said. "At least send him away so I don't have to listen to his dribble."

"It is such nonsense, isn't it," the creature laughed in a soft voice. "I usually consume them quickly so I don't have to listen to their empty promises."

"I am serious," the boy cried. "I am yours forever! I need no one else. I will love you, and only you." Monty couldn't believe the boy had actual tears running down his cheeks. He was reaching through the bars trying to touch her. Then, the creature sighed.

"I release you," she whispered as she blew a kiss to him. The boy stopped crying and was bewildered. Confused, he said nothing and wondered back upstairs as if he were in a dream.

"You know he will probably die if his spirit is not strong enough," the creature said as she watched the boy disappear into the shadows of the stairwell. "Once they hear the song, they will never forget it, and it will either kill them or drive them mad."

"So why didn't you kill him," Monty said.

"To give him a chance to live, no matter how small the chance. Besides, I did it as a favor to you."

"You do not owe me a favor," Monty said.

"You helped me get my food bucket. I usually have to call one of these poor souls down here to push it to me, and then I would consume their soul."

"Why do you kill them? What did they do to you?"

"Nothing," the creature said sadly. "Before I got my gifts, I was ugly and they all ignored me. No one was kind to me. Then, the voices spoke to me and granted me new powers. With these powers, I can make them all love me and want me. I could fulfill their deepest desire, and when I am done with them, I take my revenge and consume their soul. As they are dying, I use to enjoy watching the terror in their eyes when they realized it was too late. I used to find satisfaction in my revenge on all those who ignored me. Now, I feel nothing."

"Why don't you find a new purpose? You don't have to kill people."

"I cannot change," she exclaimed. She sat down in the water as she shook her head in anguish. "I cannot change who I am. I am a corrupted, a nymph. I made my choice, and now I have all the power I want. No man can resist me. Almost nothing can hurt me. I will live forever as one of the most beautiful women in the world. Why would I want to give all that up to be normal and ugly?"

"It is wrong to kill people."

"Maybe I should. Maybe I am doing the world a favor. Those who come to me will probably cheat on their wives and girlfriends, anyway. I am just getting rid of all those nasty men so the women in the world will only have the good men to choose from."

"I don't understand. Was there no one able to help you? Surely, there was someone in your life that loved you. Montague told me to trust in the Divine."

"The Divine! I spit on him. He left me alone and hungry. It is his fault I am like this. If he had just made me pretty, everything would have been okay. My father wouldn't have sent me off to the factory because he couldn't marry his ugly troll for a daughter to a nice merchant who would treat her like an empress. Instead, I was beaten because I was too ugly and fat. I am through with that miserable life, and I am through with you." Then, the creature jumped into the water and disappeared.

Monty sat back against the wall. The angry woman reminded her of the angry boy in the village. She wondered if all the corrupted were just angry people who couldn't find peace. Monty couldn't help the boy in the village, and she didn't think she could help her neighbor. As the water in her cell placated itself, the room became silent again. Monty sat back down and began humming again.

After a while, Monty heard footsteps coming down the stairs to reveal the baron. This time, the baron was dressed in light-colored trousers and jacket. Monty felt relieved when she saw him and ran to the bars.

"Oh good, you are here," Monty said. "Please help me. Someone put me in this cell, and I can't get out."

He simply smiled at Monty while walking to an empty cell across from her. He opened the door and then touched random stones on the cell's wall. The wall popped and stone ground together as it slid to the side revealing a small alcove.

It had two tables along with a bookshelf. Several instruments and vials stood on each table. Various liquids filled the vials, and lights colored the various instruments. Walking to the bookshelf, he pulled out a large book. Turning around, he opened the book and put it on one of the tables.

"Tell me maru," the baron said impassively. "Do you feel pain?"

"I don't know what I am," she said confused. "I am not evil like them. Please help me get out of this cell. I must get to Parn."

"You are, in fact, a maru," the baron said. "I put you in there so you couldn't get away. I need you for my research."

"Why should I help you?"

"Frankly, you don't have a choice. I simply was curious if it will hurt when I rip the soulforge from your chest."

"Wait, how do you know I have a soulforge?"

"I detected it when I scanned you last night. Montague always talked about the theories behind the construction of the maru. Recently, he told me that he was close to discovering the soulforge. When Lady Enix sent me this device, I recognized it as one of Montague's inventions that detected the corrupted. Imagine my surprise when she told me it could detect a soulforge."

"You are working with Lady Enix," Monty said backing away from the bars.

"Trust me, it is only business," he chuckled.

"Why does Lady Enix want my soulforge?" A part of Monty didn't want to know the answer.

"I don't know, and I really don't care. She had her chance ten years ago. Now, it is my turn. I'll spare you all the gory details. Just know I plan to use it to unlock the secrets of the corrupted. Originally, I was trying to help Montague and the others to stop the corrupted. Then, I saw how powerful they were. One corrupted could destroy an entire town. They could be the ultimate weapons. However, we never figured out the secret behind the corrupted. With a soulforge we can now solve the great mystery of the corrupted. We could actually control the beasts and even make them even more powerful. It's even possible we could cure the corrupted if we wanted too."

"I see you are another friend of Montague who has betrayed him. He didn't want to hurt anybody."

"He was not as pleasant as you think. Like the rest of us, he was trying to save the world and stop the corrupted. But, you have to ask yourself, how good could he have been if he were an ally of that evil woman, Lady Enix? Please don't misunderstand me. I harbor no will to the great inventor. His mind and inventions were invaluable. He and that detestable wizard, Djinn, actually temporarily imprisoned Lady Enix and freed us of her wrath, at least for a time. Then, he made a maru so we could change the world."

"I will kill no one, and I will not help you. As I said, I am not evil like those other maru's."

"So you actually believe peasant nonsense I told you earlier. They tell those stories to scare young children. They are actually directly connected to the Divine since it takes the power of the Divine to create a soulforge. That's what make them so powerful, and that's why we need to pull it out of your chest before you figure out how to use it. Time is of the essence."

"No, please don't do this." She didn't know what else to say. This madman would take away her soulforge, and she would have failed Montague. Disheartened, she sank down with her back against the wall.

Noticing her despair, he closed the book and walked closer to her cell. "Part of me wish I didn't have to destroy you. You are truly a masterpiece. If the other engineer's saw you, you would be the talk of the empire. Everyone would know Montague's name and know he was the greatest engineer who ever lived. Alas, I like power far too much, and I must hurry before Lady Enix finds you." Stepping back, he pressed a few stones on the side of the wall, and the alcove closed back up into an empty cell. Taking the book with him, the baron proceeded up the stairs and disappeared back into the shadows.

"Can you really cure the corrupted," Monty's blue-skinned neighbor whispered.

"I don't know how. If I could, I would save you. I would save you all. I wished I knew how." She sobbed in the darkness.

CHAPTER SIXTEEN

The General

"We need a plan," Denarith said.

"We are just waiting for dinner," Calais said. "What could possibly go wrong?"

Roan had brought them to the regiment's camp. It was much larger than what Calais had expected. There were large tents distributed among the camp while smaller tents were clustered together. Hundreds of soldiers moved about the tents performing various tasks. Other soldiers milled about the area or surrounded small campfires while they laughed and talked. Around the camp, some soldiers patrolled the area while covered in battle armor.

Behind the camp, Calais saw large and small ethaerium cannons. The larger ones were almost sixty feet tall. The black and bronzed cannons were first invented during the Age of Dragons to defeat the dragons themselves. During the Age of Magic, they bombed rebelling cities and powerful monsters. They symbolized the empire's power and caused many enemies to retreat and surrender. Walking to a large tent, Calais remembered looking at the towering weapons and wondering what they would be used against.

When they had entered the enclosed tent, they found a large table set with plates, utensils, and cups. Then, Roan informed them that the general had asked them to join him for dinner and that they should wait here. Deciding to sit down, they had been waiting at the table for almost an hour before the general arrived.

"Oh, I know we will be fine while we eat," Denarith said. "It is when we leave this tent that our enemies might try to ambush us. The witch has spies everywhere."

"Hopefully, our enemies will wait for us to take a bath and get cleaned up," Estasia said.

Then, the tent flaps were pushed open as a large man entered. He wore a black silk uniform embroidered with a gold border. With a high white collar, white stripes extended along his shoulder and down his arm. Along the shoulder stripes, Calais noticed that they were decorated with the rank insignia of general. His face was weathered and rugged while surrounded by a short white beard touching his comb-backed white hair. He was only armed by a decorative sword that hung at his belt. He stood there for a moment while the three of them stood up per the rules of proper etiquette.

"It is an honor to finally meet the heroes of the Fifth Spire," the general said bowing before them. "I am General Ameriz, commander of the Adian army. I welcome you to my camp and offer you our services."

"Thank you, general," Estasia said with a curtsey. "I am Lord Master Estasia Verrandrin of the wind guard."

"I am Lord Champion Denarith of the Tauru Totem, Hero of the Karjast Tribes, Slayer of the Gorlok army, Defiler of Myrlosh," the totem champion proclaimed with his axe raised high.

The general looked at Calais, waiting. "I am just Calais, a portal technician," she said after a few moments.

"Don't be so modest, Lady Pellendarr," Ameriz said kindly. He approached her with his hands behind his back. "You are Lord Conjurer Calais Pellandarr, one of the greatest summoners to live. You have nothing to fear."

"Thank you, general," Calais said. "I am afraid that we have many enemies, and I am never sure who to trust." Calais hid her identity because her acts before the imprisoning Lady Enix still haunted her. After ten years, the guilt still stung. Since then, she had never felt worthy of being called a summoner. Being a portal technician was just a job to keep her busy while she worked through the endless guilt.

"You have my word that I will protect you," Ameriz said. "Please be seated. I had the cooks prepare a grand meal."

He sat at the head of the table while Denarith and Estasia sat on one side and Calais sat alone on the other side. Once they were settled, the cooks brought in the first course that was a light, herbal soup. Picking up the spoon, Calais took a few sips of the soup. It filled her body with warmth and was the first real human food she had in months. Overcome by hunger, she wanted to inhale the soup. Instead, she maintained her composure and ate it slowly. Denarith picked up the bowl and poured it down his mouth with some of it dribbling down his fur. Estasia giggled softly while trying not to look at the champion. The general appeared amused but said nothing.

"So tell me, Lord Calais, how is your family doing these days," Ameriz said. "I met your brother, Caellan, several years ago during one of my campaigns. At the time, he was engaged to a lady from the Krakenjall family. Did he finally get married?"

"Yes, he did, general," Calais said trying to stay calm. Her family was the one thing that caused her much anxiety. While she and her other brothers left the nobility entirely, Caellan tried to be a lord and a baron simultaneously. Caellan failed miserably despite her0 efforts to convince him he should abandon his noble heritage. Now, he sits with her in some dark castle, miserable. A fate she did not want to share. "Currently, he lives near Castle Krakenjall with his wife. I haven't spoken with him very much since the wedding."

"Is he still a paladin," the general said.

"Yes, he still serves the order and the Lord's Council," Calais said between bites. "Although, he enjoys his spirits more." A part of Calais felt bad for saying that out loud, but he never forgave himself for their father's death.

"That is disappointing," Ameriz said. "Your father was a good man despite the charges brought against him. I knew him well, and I tell you he would have been proud of you and your brothers." Calais stayed silent. She never knew whether he was a good man, but she knew the charges against him were real. She had seen his terrible dragon magic.

"Thank you," she said politely. "I will tell Caellan and Caezik when I see them next." She hadn't seen them in years and probably won't see them for several more years. Despite her mixed feelings toward them, she quietly hoped that Lady Enix hadn't killed them.

"How did you know Baron Pellandarr," Estasia inquired. "It seems unusual that a soldier from the Adia Province would know a baron from the southern part of the Antellia Province."

"Not unusual at all," Ameriz said. "He had a deep understanding of dragons, and he worked with me to crush the Elisian Dragon Cult. Without him, the cult might have summoned their dragon."

Calais shuddered at the stories of the cult. It was a fringe religion that believed dragons could be summoned back to this world and grant its followers with powers greater than any lord. For it to succeed, they believed that many people had to be sacrificed to their dragon crystals. Supposedly, these devices were powered by blood. With each sacrifice, the crystal gained only a small amount of power. They attacked several cities and killed the city's entire population. When the news of the massacres spreading, the empire pulled all their resources and swiftly destroyed the cult, but the death toll was enormous.

"Between the cults and the corrupted, those were very dark times," Estasia said. "Many people still speak of your great victory. Because of you, it allowed the empire time to implement the Great City Migration Plan."

"I have heard that your father had successfully petitioned the empire to include Parn as one of its protective cities," Ameriz said.

"Yes, general," Estasia said. "It was a great honor that the empire had bestowed on our humble barony. My father has already built the walls and defenses. The city will be well-defended, and the people will be protected."

"I also heard reports that your father is under investigation for dragoncraft," Ameriz said curiously after taking his final bite of soup.

"Oh general, my father is a little eccentric, but he is surely not dabbling in the evil arts of dragoncraft. He thinks only about the welfare of his people."

Denarith burst into laughter while Estasia glared at him. "Your father's a weasel," Denarith said. "He only cares about his bizarre experiments. Remember when he tried to experiment on me. It didn't go so well for him or his lab."

"Like I said before; he was just trying to learn more about totem champions."

"He is a crazy dirtbag," Denarith said shaking his head.

Calais knew very little about Estasia's father, and, sadly, Estasia knew little about her father either. He always sent Estasia away with servants and plenty of money. Calais knew Estasia well enough to know when the woman lied. Despite Calais' misgivings about her father, Estasia really believed her father was a good man. Unlike Caellan, Calais hoped that Estasia would never know the truth about her father, good or bad. Thankfully, the servants showed back up with more food to distract Denarith and Estasia.

The second course included a small piece of meat on a white porcelain dish. Denarith stared at the small amount of food in disbelief. Estasia proceeded to cut her meat into small pieces with the general doing the same. Calais thanked the servant when he put the plate in front of her and took away the empty soup bowl. She stared at her plate for several moments as she remembered a question that had been nagging her since they arrived. She had to tread carefully.

"Is there something wrong with your food, Lord Conjurer Calais," Ameriz said after a chewing a bite of food.

"Tell me general, why are you so close to the drift," Calais said hesitantly. Formerly, armies stayed away from the Drift unless they were planning a major offensive. With Lady Enix at the Fifth Spire and probably working with the empire, she worried that the general may work with the terrible witch.

"How much do you know about the Fifth Spire," the general said. Denarith stuffed the entire piece of meat in his mouth with his eyes darting around the room.

"I only know about what I learned ten years ago," she said coyly. Her stomach churned.

"Well, there is a plan to reopen the portal," Ameriz said calmly. "If the experiment fails, I will use the ethaerium cannons to destroy the Fifth Spire." Calais was not very good at political intrigue and didn't know how to take the general's forwardness. "Although, I suspect you know about the plan already."

Estasia stopped eating, and Calais looked around the empty tent nervously. "So, you are working for Lady Enix," Calais said. Denarith finished chewing his meat and stared at the general.

The general continued to eat unfazed. "I would hardly call that witch a lady. There is nothing noble about that creature. When you arrived, the imperial guard stationed with my army informed me of your supposed crimes. I explained to him it was my duty to treat you with the respect you deserved. He agreed to arrest you afterwards."

"Your plan was to lure us here and capture us," Estasia said angrily. "I thought you said that would protect us."

"And so I shall protect you," Ameriz said. "In a few moments, the imperial guard will come in here with soldiers to lead you to our stockade. You will go with him quietly. Later, someone will lead you out of my camp and you will be free to go on your way. Let me be clear, none of my men need to die. This is blasted politics, and no soldier needs to die over political maneuvering." Denarith nodded in agreement. "You must hurry and eat to keep up your strength. It's a pity. The chef makes a wonderful cabbage; onions and beets dish you will miss."

Calais forced down each bite as best she could. Her uncertainty continued to twist her stomach into knots, but they hadn't had a decent meal all day. Estasia finished her meal still eyeing the general carefully. Denarith just sat patiently. From what little Calais knew of Totem Champions, they would often enter a quiet meditative state before battle. It help honed their senses and mind so they could be even more effective killing machines. Calais finished her meal and waited.

The tent flaps flew open, and an imperial guard stormed into the tent followed by several soldiers. He wore the standard black and gold armor with his sword hanging off his belt. His face had a hawkish nose with long brown sideburns. He stared at them intently with steely eyes.

"I am Lord Commander Thorwyn," he said in a commanding voice. "You three are under arrest. Come with me peacefully or be prepared to die."

"What are the charges, Lord Commander," Estasia said politely.

"You will be arrested for the crimes of conspiracy and treason against the empire," Thorwyn said.

"Very well, we will come with you quietly," Estasia said standing up. "As a Lord of the Lord's Council and a lady-in-waiting, I assume that you have the Proclamation of the Issued Warrant for me to acknowledge." The imperial guards just stood there grinding his jaw. "If not, you must create a proclamation to notify my parents, my representatives in the government, the head of my order, and anyone who have a treatise with my family. I believe you will have to create eleven proclamations that must be sent out first light to notify all before my trial. Otherwise, you will have breached imperial law, and my parents will convince the emperor to demote you so low you will dig latrines." In the corner of her eye, Calais saw the general smile.

"Trust me, I will have all those copies ready for you to sign," Thorwyn said irritated. He grabbed Estasia's wrists and slapped metal cuffs on them. Then, he placed a gem in a slot that cause Estasia to wince in pain. The ethaerium gem continually drained the magic from a wizard. It was extremely painful and could drive wizards mad if they kept the cuffs on too long. Denarith handed over the axe to a nearby soldier while glaring at him. The soldier backed away from the angry barbarian. "Where is your book?" Thorwyn had walked over to her with his hand out.

"I do not have my book," Calais said.

"All summoners carry their books with them," Thorwyn said. "That is where all their power is."

"I am sorry, but I do not have my books," Calais said. "If I did, I would summon an army of creatures that would crush you."

"Fine," Thorwyn said. "We will just take you outside and strip you of your clothes to make sure you're not hiding anything."

"That is enough," General Ameriz said jumping to his feet. Denarith was about to go through the table, but Estasia put a hand on his shoulder. "This is my camp, and these are my soldiers. You will follow the proper protocols and treat her with respect. She has not yet been found guilty."

"When it comes to treason against the emperor, I am the ultimate authority in this camp. She either turns over her books or submits to being searched."

"Very well, she can be searched, but I will be the one to search her. She is still a guest in my camp."

"Fine, but I will choose what she wears after you are finished."

"I will agree to that. Now all of you get out. I will let you know when I am done."

Thorwyn grinned widely as he left the tent. The soldiers led Estasia and Denarith out to the stockade. When they were alone, Calais looked at the general nervously.

"Do not worry, Calais. I will be gentle."

*   *   *   *

Calais was chained to a wall inside a large steel wagon. After being stripped of all her clothing, she was given only a red top and a red breechcloth. She still felt flustered and humiliated after being marched through the camp as the soldiers mocked her. When she was brought into the wagon, Denarith said nothing disparaging and only asked about her well-being. She answered only with a nod while black iron shackles were placed around her ankle. Shivering from the cold steel floor and the iron manacle, she wrapped her arms around herself while keeping her top from sliding off her chest.

In the corner of the wagon, Estasia laid in a ball whimpering in pain. Denarith or Calais couldn't reach their friend. When they tried to talk to her, she only cried out in pain. Helpless, they sat and watched her. Calais hoped that morning would come soon and they would take the gem off the cuffs. Most casters are too drained from the pain to cast any spell for days if they keep their sanity through the night. Calais knew the Estasia was a strong-spirited woman. She would survive, but her revenge will be swift and terrible. It was always a bad idea to get on Estasia's bad side. Then, Denarith sang one of his tribal dirges.

Calais recognized the tribal song. She had only heard it a few times in her travels. It had a dark melodious tone. It spoke of dark times, defiant victories, and death. It would have been a beautiful song to listen too if it weren't being sung by a tone-deaf barbarian. His pitches where too high if he even hit the right notes at all. Some of the words didn't even make sense. While Calais could stomach the discordant requiem, but Estasia wailed back in pain. After yelling at him several times to stop and save her ears, Denarith finally relented and Estasia went back to whimpering. The silence was somehow soothing despite Calais shivering.

Then, the door lock mechanism turned. When the door opened, Roan, the scout lieutenant from earlier in the day, sneaked into the wagon. He wore a large heavy black cloak and appeared to be unarmed. Pulling a key out, he unlocked the manacles around Denarith and began working on freeing Calais.

"General Ameriz sends his regards," Roan whispered. "You must stay quiet and follow me."

Calais peered out the door while he freed Estasia. The wagon was part of a larger group of wagons encircling a burning campfire. There were guards spread throughout the area, but no one was paying attention to their wagon. Looking back, Denarith was carrying Estasia in his arms. Calais surmised that Estasia would remain very weak for quite some time. With a few quick glances, Roan led the three of them to a nearby tent where he ushered them inside.

"Take this cloak Lord Conjurer, it will keep you warm," Roan said while handing her a heavy black cloak. "We have to wait here for a little while until the patrols have moved to another area. She needs to drink some of this." He handed Denarith a bottle to give to Estasia. "It will give her some of her energy back. I must make sure everything is prepared. Also, this is a gift from the general." He handed Calais several pieces of parchment and a piece of charcoal for drawing. Calais looked at them hesitantly while the lieutenant made his way out of the tent.

"What about my weapon," Denarith whispered.

"I will get it to you soon," Roan said reassuringly.

"I need it now," Denarith said as he started to get up and follow the scout.

"I can barely carry the bloody thing. I had to put it on the horse which is where I am taking you. Now, stay here, and be quiet." Disgruntled, Denarith sat back down in the tent while Calais looked at the pieces of parchments and charcoal.

The secret of summoners is that they didn't need charcoal. They needed only a blank piece of paper or other smooth surface. She hated all the pain, and death her powers had caused so many years ago helping Lady Enix, but she knew what she had to do. Her friends needed her especially with Estasia injured and helpless. Denarith watched Estasia while monitoring the patrols outside. Calais had little time and not much parchment.

Looking out of the tent's opening, she focused on a set of small ethaerium cannons. Holding her finger on the parchment, she moved it in a circular pattern while staring at the cannons. Feeling energy pulsating through her body, black ink appeared on the page. Her finger slowly spiraled outward in small motions while the black spot grew on the page. It formed a silhouette of two cannons. Then, the image slowly lightened and darkened in different areas and gained the same hues of the cannons. With a final burst of energy, she closed her eyes as the two cannons finished forming on the page with photographic perfection. Breathing softly, she could feel the image's imbued power as if it were trying to jump off the page. Moving it to the back of her pile, she looked through the tent opening for other possibilities.

There was a group of armored soldiers practicing maneuvers near a group of torches. Focusing on them, Calais began the process again. From the corner of her eye, she could see Denarith watching her create a picture of five armored soldiers. When she finished, she found herself out of breath. The energies it took to create a drawing were extremely taxing. When the drawings were more realistic and detailed, it meant the summoned creature would be even more powerful than their models. The ability to create such detailed drawing took skill, talent, and power. Calais excelled at these traits. Not wanting to exhaust herself further, she laid down, and rested. Denarith remained unusually quiet.

Their culture revered summoners as the first ones came from the barbarian tribes. Instead of paper, they would put their images on small smooth stones and pieces of smoothed wood. Once the drawings were created, they would hang these objects around their body for accessibility. The stones, wood and even bone pieces became similar to jewelry and showcased their power. Some even learned to draw their images on their own skin. The tribes revered these individuals and made them figureheads in their tribe. Some say the totem champions were created by summoners although no one could prove that absolutely. Denarith always had a usually deep reverence for summoners, but he would never tell Calais why.

"It is time," Roan said putting his head in the tent. Calais jumped up startled. "Put your cloaks on and lets move."

Calais secured the parchment where it was still accessible. Denarith picked up Estasia while securing the cloak around her. Then, Calais and the others followed Roan out of the tent and to a group of trees. Denarith was too big for the cloak, so he slung it around his shoulders. There were no patrols or soldiers in sight. Quietly, the arrived at the trees and Roan continued to lead them along the tree line. After following it around, the came to another clearing with another group of tents. Silently, Roan told them to cross the clearing. Wrapped in their heavy cloaks, Roan and Calais made their way across to another group of tree. Then, they saw a patrol approach.

The patrol had three guards armed with spears. Calais' heart started beating quicker while watching the guards. Seeing Roan lower his head like a priest and still moving along the path, Calais followed suit. The guards didn't seem to take heed of the cloaked figures. Getting close to the other group of trees, Calais turned to look for Denarith. He was hiding in the trees as the guards passed. When the guards got out of sight, Denarith made his way across. Then, Calais heard another group of soldiers walking along the tree line. Denarith was still in the open. He made his way behind a tent. With the tent too small, he looked around and placed Estasia on the ground behind another nearby tent, Crouching down, he made only part of his back and head visible from behind a tent. The guards stopped and looked at him.

"Who's there," the guard said approaching Denarith.

"Moooooo," Denarith said in a flat tone.

"Oh, it's just another cow," the guard said irritated. "Those things get into everything."

"Should we shoo it away," the other guard said.

"I don't care," the first guard said irritated. "I chased five of them off last night. Let another patrol chase him off." He shook his head, and the patrol left the area.

Denarith picked Estasia back up and carried her over to Calais and Roan. "They called me a cow," Denarith said annoyed. "Do they not know what the difference between a cow and an awesome bull is."

"Don't make me shoo you away," Roan said in a loud whisper. "Be quiet and follow me."

"When I get my axe, I will show you what it looks like when someone tries to shoo me away," Denarith grumbled.

They continued to follow Roan through the trees until they reached the edge of a camp. Roan pointed to several horses tied to a makeshift hitching post. Dashing to the horses, Denarith looked for his axe among the various steeds. Finally, he found it and quickly examined it. Roan and Calais joined him and prepared the horses.

"These are branded horses," Roan said. "You must not take them near a city or a patrol. It is illegal for a non-imperial personnel to possess such an animal. When you ride, you can head north to Yellow City. Most of the army has already arrived so you shouldn't encounter any more soldiers." Calais thanked him and pulled herself up on one horse. Denarith handed her the reins of another horse while he continued to carry Estasia. Roan pulled off one of the nearby lanterns and handed it to Calais. Holding the lantern up, she rode off into the night with Denarith running behind her. Not hearing any other voices from the camp behind them, Calais slowed the horse down into a lope as they made their way through the dark plains.

Chapter Seventeen

Caellan and Jewell

Caellan woke up in a dark cell. With moonlight spilling into the cell from a small window, he quietly laid on the floor listening and watching. Besides the distant crackle of a torch, he heard nothing else nearby. Nothing moved. Even the shadows appeared to be painted onto his cell wall. Quietly, he sat up, and waited.

Seeing or hearing no other threats, he stood up in small cell and assessed the room. A wall of iron bars had only a door which led into the hallway. Scanning the rest of the hallway, he noticed that several empty cells lined its walls. At the end of the hallway, he saw a stairwell leading upward. Examining the stonework of the hallway, he found no distinguishing features that would identify his location. He knew he was in a castle but didn't know which one. Moving to the other side of the cell, he stood on his toes and peered out the small window.

Past the bars, he saw a long row of trees standing guard at the lake shore. Small waves playfully splashed the eroded shore and roots of the trees. Undaunted, the trees stood still in the night as dark shadows flew past their crowns. Watching the shadows fly around, Caellan watched there forms molt into skeletal shapes before reforming into more familiar human shapes. With the presence of the wraiths, he knew the was in the dungeon of Castle Krakenjall.

He slumped back down in his cell. He hoped that the truth about Jewell and Jerick was just a dream. With that idea shattered, he looked at the indomitable bars wondering if he should try to escape. He wondered if he deserved to escape. He had made so many mistakes that he wondered if he should die instead. Silently, he hoped his death would come quickly. With the slow footsteps approaching the cell, he knew death would not come and only suffering remained.

Jewell stopped in front of this cell. She was wearing a long flowing black gown that sparkled in the moonlight. Her hair was braided with entwining gold threads. Around her neck, she wore a gold necklace with is fingers extending out into a small web. Her wrists were guarded by gold, thin bracelets. With darks and red lips, she looked at him with pity.

"You look just as lost as the day I met you," she said. She grasped the bars and leaned to the cell. "I still think about the day we first met. Do you remember that?"

"How could I forget it," Caellan said. "It was a day we were almost killed by a crazy machine at the Celebration of the Excelatory."

"You couldn't even operate an ethaerium control unit let alone manage a walking mechanized construct." She let out a soft giggle. Despite everything that was happening, he smiled. She was right. He did not understand how to work any of the bizarre contraptions of the wizards. Looking at Jewell, she was just as beautiful now as she was back then. When he saw her for the first time five years ago, she was wearing a similar black dress.

*   *   *   *

Jewell stood in the marble hall with many other royalty. The men were wearing black jackets and trousers while the woman wore long gowns colored in various pastels. Instead of a pink or yellow ostentatious dress, Jewell wore an eloquent long black dress. With her alabaster skin, Caellan thought she was like a clear, fresh winter's day. Ignoring the nobles' disdainful looks for her different appearance, she walked among them as if she were an empress herself. Staring at the bewitching site, Caellan was finally shaken loose by a hand on his shoulder.

"What are you doing," Jerick said. He wore a black imperial officer uniform composed of a short jacket and pants. His uniform was decorated with silver, and gold highlights that showed his rank of captain. It was unusual for someone so young to make such a high rank, but he was an excellent swordsman and soldier that had proved himself in multiple battles. He was actually better with a sword than Caellan, but Caellan would not tell his friend that.

"I just saw the most beautiful creature," Caellan said. Like all paladins, he wore a simple white uniform that had a long coat and pants. They wore no cloak, and some even wore head wraps to hide their identity. Unlike the imperial officers, paladins always carried their weapons on their belts or back.

"The woman in black," Jerick said. Caellan just nodded. "That is Lady Jewell Krakenjall. A fine creature, indeed. When you become the emperor, she might notice you. I think Lady Arista Terrongrell over there is still available."

123

"Lady Arista is very gracious, but she doesn't meet the needs of my estate," Caellan said politely. "Lady Jewell is much better suited. I will have to find a way get her attention."

"So in paladin-speak, she is as ugly as a hog with warts."

"I would never think of a lady like that," Caellan said with a sly smile.

"How do you plan to get past her devious uncle, Baron Krakenjall?"

"That black heart," Caellan said surprised. "How did someone so perfect come from that twisted family line?"

"Maybe, they used demon magic. It doesn't matter to me. The world needs more beautiful women." Then, the bells rang and the doors to the presentation hall opened up. The crowd of nobility ambled through the doors. Caellan watched her to see where she would sit in the hall.

"She is sitting with Lord Engineer Rosaro in the Emperor's box," Caellan said after watching her walk with an elderly gentleman to a group of locked doors. He slowly unlocked them while he laughed with the small entourage that had gathered around him and Lady Jewell.

"Wait, THE Lord Engineer Rosaro who is the head of the Order of Engineering? You definitely don't have a chance with her."

"We should go to the second-level balcony," Caellan said ignoring his friend. "We should be closer to her there."

"What about our duty to protect and patrol the areas?"

"You are correct, my friend. I think we should patrol the second-level balcony."

Rolling his eyes, Jerick followed Caellan through the thick crowd. Every year, the crowds seemed to get worse. Many years ago, Caellan recalled that few nobles attended the exhibitions until the presenters started to show their inventions with bright lights and explosions. Now, the Celebration of the Excelatory was one of the biggest social events of the year. While insisting the inventions was only for the greater good, many inventors also became extremely rich when they were sponsored by a rich noble who would mass produce their inventions and sell them to the merchants. This year was especially bad with all the gossip about realm-changing inventions. They moved with the crowd to an open set of doors leading to an ascending stairway.

There were several floors of balconies on each side of the presentation hall. Over a hundred people spilled over the waist-height railings of each balcony as they struggle to see the stage. Below the balconies, Caellan scanned the nobles and their entourages as they sat in plush seats near the stage. The Emperor's Box was positioned on the wall opposite from the stage and at the same level of the second floor balcony.

The box was arrow-shaped with several tall seats within it. A solid wooden railing encircled the platform to prevent an attendee from falling out. Finally getting through the crowd to the edge of the balcony, Caellan could see Lord Engineer Rosaro, Lady Jewell, and several other chosen nobility making their way onto the platform from two tall half-doors. Usually, this area was reserved for the emperor and the heads of the orders that attended. Since the emperor was still very young, the steward rarely bothered with celebration. Instead, he just had a private showing of the best inventions at Castle Dragonlock. For the past few years, Rosaro used the event to lavish his attentions on certain nobles he felt would serve his best interests.

Rosaro sat down in the front row with another overly-dressed baron. Caellan knew most of the barons and their families but only by reputation. Since his paladin duties prevented him from attending many social events, he knew only of them though reports, gossip and stories. They would kill each other without a second thought if it meant more power or coin. It is one of the many reasons that Caellan liked being a paladin. Despite his rank as a baron since his father's death, his duties often called him into the field and allowed him to appoint a steward to manage his barony. With this being one of the few events that he could mingle with the other barons, he learned what he could and watched all of them very warily.

Studying Jewell carefully, Caellan wanted to know whether she was shallow and duplicitous like most nobles. She sat in the second row and conversed casually with the few people around them. One of the pompous nobles put his hand on her leg. In turn, she lifted his hand off her leg and squeezed it tightly. While she whispered in his ear, Caellan could see that the noble was in much pain despite his best efforts to hide it. Caellan was impressed by her moxie since it was unusual for a lady to be so direct. From that moment on, the noble just made simple pleasantries, but he actively avoided her. Obviously, his ego had been wounded, and someone usually paid for such a slight. However, Caellan didn't think this woman had anything to worry about. A deep, crashing thunder from the stage drew everyone out of their conversations as they directed their full attention to the announcer on the stage.

"Barons and Baronesses, beautiful ladies of the realm, mighty lords, and all the rest of the fine people of this realm," the announcer said in a deep voice. He wore a bright maroon and white jacket and black pants. Most of the orders of the Lords' Council tended to choose distinctive colors to represent them. Paladins wore white while the engineers wore maroon and white. Most lords didn't care about the colors and only wore them on special occasions. "We are pleased to continue our exhibitions today where we will amaze and astonish you with our grand innovations. I am pleased to present Lord Engineer Masery."

The spotlight dimmed, and the announcer faded away. Then, the edge of the stage exploded with several plumes of purple lights and smoke. The crowd screamed and cheered at the light show. From out of the fading smoke, several people appeared on stage. A man wearing a bright, satin maroon jacket stood at the center with several imperial soldiers standing at attention behind him. Each soldier had an ethaerium rifle in his hands.

"I am Lord Engineer Masery," the man in the center said in a high pitch voice. "I am here to inform you that you are now much safer in this realm. My improvements have made these rifles into powerful killing machines. They are no longer blundering tools that most heroes ignore. With my master genius, I have now made them as deadly as the swords at your belt." Caellan didn't know much about rifles. They had poor accuracy and varying power. Sometimes, a rifle could destroy the side of the building or it would just tickle their foes. Many soldiers nicknamed them blunderblasts. "By harnessing the power of ethaerium in new and different ways, we have increased the deadly power of each shot and given the weapon a range over a thousand yards." Some people gasped while Caellan watched skeptically. Looking over at Jewell, she studied the show intently but seemed unimpressed. "Let me show you our military's new weapons."

They brought two corrupted beings that were still in their wolf-hybrid forms. The crowds booed and jeered at the corrupted. They both had metal collars around their neck while their hands and feet were chained with thick black manacles. They growled but did not fight back. To Caellan, they almost seemed as if they had lost their will to fight. Since the corrupted were so powerful, it seemed odd that they would surrender. As the two soldiers kneeled down and pointed the rifles at the creatures, they just groaned with sad eyes. Caellan refused to feel sorry for such murderous beasts.

The soldiers fired the rifles. Purplish energy bolts flews out of the rifle barrels and to the corrupted. In an instant, he watched the exploding energy tear apart the corrupted's torso. Their blood painted the curtain behind them. The corrupted fell over dead with large gaping holes in their torsos. The crowds screamed and cheered. Then, the engineer issued another command and the two soldiers fired again at the corpses. The crowds were jumping and cheering while the rifles pulverized the bodies. Many were laughing as the gore was splattered across the stage. Some were looking away in disgust. Jewell watched the spectacle with a deeply, disturbed look. The surrounding people were standing up and applauding.

"As you can see," the engineer said. The applause and cheering slowly dimmed. "As you can see, these rifles are more powerful, consistent, and have longer range. In the next decade, I can see every imperial soldier being armed with this weapon and no danger from outside or inside this realm will ever pose a threat to us again. Long live the empire!" With that said, another group of explosions occurred around the edge of the stage. When the smoke cleared, the engineer, and the soldiers were gone. The auditorium was filled with a massive applause and cheering.

Caellan was always disgusted by how much the nobles loved the lights, explosions, and gore. Jewell just applauded lightly but didn't appear to be pleased by the presentation. This gave Caellan a spark of hope about the woman.

The lights faded again as the announcer reappeared in a bright spotlight at the center of the stage. He waited patiently for the applause to fade away. Several figures could be seen in the dark background trying to clean up the remnants of the mangled corpses.

"Please welcome our next presenter, Lord Engineer Zilvary," the announcer said. The spotlight faded away, and the presenter disappeared again. It was too dark to tell whether the cleanup crew had finished the grizzly task. The beaming spotlight reappeared, and this time a small man with a long maroon jacket was at the center of the stage. He had no hair and was extremely thin. His older appearance gave him a confident stare.

"My name is Lord Engineer Zilvary," the frail man said in a deep voice. "We have spent hundred of years improving our weapons and armor. We continue to train our soldiers and militia men to defeat our enemies and come home safely to their families. Every time a soldier dies, the empire loses another loyal and highly valued citizen of the empire." Caellan was impressed, but several people around him looked bored. They wanted explosions and not one of the dark truths about warfare. "The cost is too great. I propose that we no longer improve the soldiers, but make the soldiers. I present you our new guardian."

The curtains slowly opened up behind him with the lights undimming around the stage. With pounding steps, a large humanoid machine came up behind the small man. It looked like a giant human skeleton standing almost eight feet tall. Instead of bones, the creature was covered in metal rods, hoses, and twirling gears. Turrets were mounted on his arms and shoulders. The metal skeletal head had glowing purple eye sockets. Small rectangular wings were mounted on its back, and it carried two large swords on its belt. The crowd gasped and cheered when they saw the mechanical man.

"After extensively studying the human body and its soul, we used a process with ethaerium to duplicate the body and recreate it as a living metal body. Similar to the legendary maru, this mechanical guardian can endure significant damage while causing as much damage as a company of soldiers. Unable to be scared, angered or bribed, these guardians are the perfect protectors for our society. With no soldiers and militia men, more men can work in factories or in the fields which will make the empire even more productive and successful. To present his power, I have placed a target at the back of the stage. He will attack this armored dummy with his full force. Guardian, I command you to attack target one." The engineer pointed to the dummy in the back.

Turning around, the guardian fired several energy shots from a turret on its forearm at the practice dummy. The dummy exploded. The crowd cheered at the impressive fire power.

"Guardian, I command that you attack target number two," the engineer said as he pointed to another dummy at the back of the stage.

The mechanical creature paused. The engineer gave it another order, but the creature ignored it. It just stood there motionless like some kind of bizarre sculpture. The murmur of voices grew until the hall was filled with loud conversations. Finally, the guardian roared and stumbled like a deranged beast. It tried to smash the engineer, but he dodged the massive fist and dove off the stage. People began to scream and panic as the monster began wrecking the stage.

Everyone on the balcony with Caellan began rushing for the door. He shoved them out of the way as he tried to stay near the Emperor's Box since they were in trouble. Several people in the box were pounding on the closed half-doors while others were watching the rampaging mechanical beast. Caellan didn't know why doors weren't opening. Usually, standard procedure was to open the doors immediately unless there was a threat outside the hall. As a backup measure, the platform was protected by a force field, but it was rarely tested. Fortunately, it still worked.

The creature started blasting everything with its shoulder turrets and arm cannons. Caellan dove for the floor as several energy bolts flew above his head. Looking back over the railing, he saw that the auditorium was mostly empty while parts of the walls and chairs exploded. The platform was protected from the attacks, but the field looked strained as it glowed brightly. Caellan knew it was only a matter of time before the shield failed or the platform collapsed. The people in the box were pounding on the door or ducking below the railing. Jewell stood in the middle of the platform, studying the situation. Then, the balconies on the other side of the room collapsed into a heap of dust and splintered wood. Caellan knew he had little time before his balcony was demolished. Looking around the area, he didn't see an easy way to get to the creature. Several small fires around the auditorium had created a thick haze. With a high pitch crackling sound, he saw the force field around the platform collapse.

"What are you doing," Jerick said running up next to him.

"I have to get to the box and save those people," Caellan said looking at a nearby rope against the wall. The auditorium walls were encased in curtains to produce different effects. To move these large curtains, several ropes were positioned around the room. He grabbed the large hemp rope near the corner of the balcony and the wall.

"Are you crazy," Jerick yelled. "You will never make it."

"I have to try," Caellan said as he leaped onto the railing. "Use the curtain to get off this balcony. We need to figure out how to stop this thing."

Several soldiers had already attacked the creature with spears and swords. Unfortunately, their weapons did little damage. The beast turned his attention to them and drew his large swords. The soldiers leaped out of the paths of the heavy blades. With it distracted, Caellan put his plan into motion and swung over to the box, except his rope was too short. When he saw that he wouldn't make the platform, he hurdled himself off the rope and onto the edge of the platform. Several more blasts struck the walls around the platform while Caellan pulled himself into the box.

The blasts had caused one of the doors to collapse, and several people were climbing through a small hole to get out of the room. Then, another blasts caused the exit to collapse. Caellan didn't know whether any of the escapees had survived. Ducking below the railing to avoid further bolts of energy, Caellan saw Jewell make her way to him.

"Don't worry, I am here to save you," he said as explosions covered them with dust and splinters.

"You don't have any idea what you are doing," she said.

"Not in the least," he admitted. Then, he saw the curtains against the wall. Around the platform, several other people were huddled below the railing. Several bodies laid among the broken chairs. "Listen to me!" Several people lifted their heads and acknowledged him with their frightened stares. "We will use the curtains to get off this platform. We must hurry before the platform collapses."

"That monster will kill us," one survivor screamed.

"Oh shut up, Erik," Jewell yelled. "If you want to live, follow the paladin. Otherwise, stay here and die." It was a little more blunt than what Caellan was used too, but it worked.

He jumped on the curtain and did his best to slide down it. It was harder than he thought as the curtain burned his fingers. Unable to slow down, he fell the last few feet off the curtain and quickly rolled behind some nearby debris. Jewell and others followed him. Not as many as he hoped, but he knew that it was their choice in the end.

"Go through those doors," Caellan said pointing to the bottom floor exits. Several of those that followed him rushed through what was left of the doors. Despite his urging, Jewell remained at his side. "You must save yourself."

"No, I will stay and help you kill this monster," Jewell said.

"Very well, but stay close," Caellan said as they quickly made their way to the stage. He found Jerick positioned behind a large pile of debris that had fallen from the ceiling. When Jerick saw Jewell behind Caellan, his eyes grew large.

"You're supposed to take the damsel in distress away from danger," Jerick said.

"From what I can tell, you two are the only damsels in distress," Jewell said flatly.

"We've got the weapons," Jerick said. "You can't fight it."

"I know how to destroy it, captain," Jewell countered. "Without me, you will be smashed like the other soldiers."

"I like her," Jerick said smiling. "She has spunk."

"She is very brave, but she will die with the rest of us if we don't move quickly. My lady, how do we kill it?"

"Inside it's ribcage, you can see a bright light. That is the ethaerium generator. All we have to do is destroy the generator, and it will shut down."

"Seems simple enough," Jerick said. "Exactly, how do we get behind it's ribcage?"

"Do you see its legs," Jewell said. "They are too short, or they are not operating correctly. He should move with the same grace as a human. Instead, he is stumbling around like a sick animal. We can trip him and then access the core much easier." They both returned a questioning look as they waited for Jewell to explain further. "You both are almost as dense as some of those halfwit nobles. Over there in the corner of the stage, there are several of those ethaerium rifles from the last demonstration. One of you will distract him while the other will come with me to retrieve those rifles. All we have to do is shoot the floor where it steps and then shoot it again to knock it over. Once it is down, we can use the rifle to destroy the machine's core."

"I will distract the beast," Caellan said without a second thought. "Both of you should make a run for the rifle."

"Good luck," Jewell said as she kissed him on his cheek. For a moment, Caellan felt as though he could take on a demon army. His strength and resolve were refreshed, and he smiled back at the lady.

"Enough of that you too," Jerick said. "There will be time for the honeymoon later."

"Now's our chance," Jewell said ignoring Jerick as she looked over the debris.

Jewell and Jerick ran around the debris pile while leaving Caellan alone. After a few short breaths, he rose up and walked to the top of the debris pile that was shielding him. The mechanical beast was firing blasts of energy everywhere while roaring with the explosions. It wasn't focused on any person and was just stomping around the stage. Jumping off the debris, Caellan ran to the mechanical menace.

"Over here," Caellan hollered at the beast while drawing his two-handed sword from his back. With the beast still ignoring him, he ran to it and sliced through several hoses around the creature's kneecap. With another swing, he chipped the beasts knee joint. Oddly, it screamed in pain and swung an arm at Caellan. He easily stepped out of the way and continued to strike different metal components. After the beast missed him several times, Caellan saw its forearm cannons power up as it aimed them at Caellan's head. Disengaging from the beast, Caellan leaped away from several blasts as the stage exploded behind him. Then, he jumped back up to see direction of the next volley. Instead, ethaerium bolts from Jerick and Jewell struck the beast several times. Other bolts flew around the beast and Caellan. One even charred his ear as it flew past his head.

"You are supposed to be shooting it and the floor," Caellan yelled at the Jewell.

"This is a lot harder than it looks," Jewell yelled back.

He ducked instinctively as more energy bolts flew around him. The beast turned and fired a large volley of energy bolts at Jewell and Jerick. They both jumped out of the way and sought to cover. Noticing that the stage already had several holes in it, Caellan figured that the monster could make its own hole in the stage to fall through. He just hoped Jewell and Jerick were ready.

He ran to the beast and struck several gears that were its joints. It wailed again despite the lack of apparent damage. Swinging its arms around recklessly, Caellan continued to dodge the clumsy attacks while still striking the different leg parts. Finally, one gear broke off and the creature stumbled. As before, the beast used its forearm cannon to fire several volleys around its feet. Caellan leaped away avoiding the attack.

When the Caellan tried to stand up, his leg fell through part of the stage and he found himself trapped. The beast drew a large sword from its belt and stumbled forward. Preparing to swing the sword at the trapped paladin, Caellan held up his own sword to futilely defend himself. The damaged stage creaked and cracked under the strain of the heavy mechanical creature. It broke, and the creature fell forward to Caellan.

Unable to move, Caellan just held the sword up although he knew the beast would crush him. As the stage shattered around them, he felt a warm energy surround his body. While it happened only a few times before in his life, he knew it was his paladin armor. It surrounded only him long enough to protect him from the crushing weight while his sword and armor pierced its ribcage. As the sword smashed into the core, it exploded around him with a deafening roar. Then, everything was silent.

Finding himself standing on a stone floor, he looked at the broken stage above him. The mechanical creature's remains were scattered around him. Jewell and Jerick stood on the stage looking down at the paladin. Jerick was laughing and clapping at his friend. Jewell only returned a deep affectionate grin that he would never forget.

*   *   *   *

Caellan stood in the cell looking back at Jewell. That was only their first adventure before having many more. Eventually, she abandoned her interest in engineering and became a baroness with Caellan. It was not an ideal choice, but they both believed it was their duty. In retrospect, Caellan wondered if it were the right choice.

"Was I cruel or mean to you," Caellan said.

"You were distant," Jewell replied. "You have always had a hole in your heart, and I thought I could fill that hole. When we were first married, you seemed truly happy. As time went on, I slowly realized that no one could repair your heart. Caellan, you are a broken man who can't let go of the past. I thought I could be happy with just our titles and refinements. Instead, I was becoming hollow like the things around us and I hated myself for that. Several months ago, I sent letters to Jerick. After a time, I realized that he offered me happiness without the riches. After everything I had given up, I realized that I had made a mistake. I wanted to return to my studies and disappear from the nobility. With Jerick's help, I knew I could do that."

"Why didn't you leave," Caellan said slumping back down against the cell's back wall.

"When I saw the hatred and pain that my uncle and aunt were causing the people, I knew I had to stop them. These people work so very hard. They deserve to have a fair and just ruler. With Jerick's new power, I knew we could do that and stop all the injustices that the empire inflicts on its subjects. We could bring these people peace and prosperity. I know you only see his power's darkness, but we can use if for good."

"You only think you will do well. In the end, you will become just as evil as the rest of your family. Maybe that is what you wanted all along."

"Don't you dare compare me to those monsters," she shrieked with her eyes turning black and her skin glowing white. "I will bring justice to this world with you being the first one I shall put on trial. We will show the world your evils and how you are nothing like a paladin. When you are found guilty, I will cut off your head and then I will say 'I do' to my new loving husband as we stand in your blood."

With that, she flew up the hallway and out of view. Caellan did not see where she went, and he didn't care. He wished she would have told him the truth many months ago, but he wondered if he could've handled the truth. Maybe, he would've turned into the monster instead of them and spared their souls. If he had to do it again, he would have gladly died instead of seeing his true love get turned into an abomination.

CHAPTER EIGHTEEN

Monty's Escape

Monty sat in her torchlit cell as she waited for the inevitable return of the Baron. Her neighbor no longer said anything and only the crackling torch kept her company. Earlier, she had tried to find a way out but was unsuccessful. The iron bars were immoveable. She was too big to squeeze through them, and all the stone walls were impregnable. Eventually, she sat back down and began to hum her strange tune. After a time, she heard more footsteps. Monty's breath quickened as she waited in dreadful anticipation.

Instead of the Baron, the sweet maid, Miranda, jotted down the stairs. She quickly smiled at Monty and then looked around the dungeon. When she saw no one else, she tiptoed over to Monty's cell. "Are you okay," she said. "When I heard the Baron had taken you down here, I knew it was a mistake. You are surely no corrupted."

"Please help me," Monty pleaded. "The baron wants to take me apart and use me to make more monsters."

"Well, I knew the Baron was into some strange stuff. This time, he had gone too far. You are just too sweet to be an evil creature of doom. Now, where did he put that key?" She fumbled around part of the stone wall until she pressed some stone bricks as the Baron had done earlier. A compartment slid open to reveal a group of keys and large lever. She grabbed the keys and proceeded to unlock Monty's cell door. With a loud wail from the hinges, Monty pushed open the cell door and quickly made her way to the stairs. Miranda followed her and peered up into the dark stairwell.

"Please don't leave me," the blue creature in the watery cell said. "I was wrong. It was no one else's fault but my own. I should have been stronger and not let people make me believe I was something else."

"What changed your mind," Monty said. "You were very angry before."

"I was," the creature said. "Then, I found out that there may be a way to escape this curse. You might be able to give me a second chance. I would give up everything so that I didn't have to be this monster. I could be a normal person again, even if it is being an ugly fat girl."

"I told you," Monty said sadly. "I can't help you. I don't know how. I am not strong enough."

"But you will be stronger," the creature said emphatically. "It takes time to learn and grow, even for a corrupted. The longer I live, the more powers I gain. You are not a corrupted, but you will get stronger and I am sure you gain new powers. All I ask is that you continue to try to help people."

"Don't trust that thing," Miranda said. "They are nothing but lies and deceit. That thing just wants to hurt more people."

"My name is Nadalia," the creature said. "I promise you maru that I will not hurt anyone else even if you can't heal me. Maybe the Divine has a small place in his heart to offer me sanctuary."

"My name is Monty," the little maru said as she pulled the keys from Miranda's hand.

"Don't do this," Miranda said. "I don't trust that creature. This is not going to end well."

"I offer you a middle ground maid," Nadalia said. "Pull that lever instead. It will open the gate that keeps me from swimming out into the river. I escape, and you don't have to take me with you."

Monty looked back at Miranda that gave her a weary look. Then, Monty returned her gaze to the beautiful, sad blue face. Monty promised that she would help out anyone she could. She didn't know whether this nymph would kill again, but she wouldn't let the mad baron hurt her. Monty pulled the lever that announced a deep grating noise. Nadalia sank below the dark water with the first smile that Monty had ever seen on her face.

"Okay," Miranda said impatiently. "Are there any other monsters you want to release before we go?"

"No, we were the only ones."

"Good," Miranda said sourly. "Let us get out of here before anyone else shows up."

They walked up the stairs, and Monty was surprised to learn that the entrance to the stair well was a secret passage. After they entered a brightly lit hallway, Miranda pressed a switch on the wall and a panel closed behind them to conceal the dungeon's entrance. Monty followed Miranda down a group of hallways. There were doors that were opened to closets, storage rooms, and even a grand ballroom. Monty was completely lost as she had not seen this part of the mansion. From the few windows that they passed, she knew she was on the first floor and it was almost nighttime. Before

Monty could ask how long she had been trapped in the dungeon, Miranda stopped abruptly and waved her to back up.

They both peered around the corner to another hall, and Monty saw a group of sailors in baggy, ragged clothing turned away from them. "What's wrong," Monty whispered.

"Those aren't normal sailors," Miranda whispered back. "Those are vampires. And don't ask, I know a vampire when I see one." Then, another group of voices were growing more loudly behind them. Monty froze as she panicked. Grabbing Monty's arm, Miranda pulled her across the hall and into a nearby room. It was a very large study with a desk at one end of the room facing inward. Several bookcases lined the walls separated by various large pictures of people and landscapes. Throughout the room, there were several red cushioned chairs along with a couch and an end table. Fortunately, there were enough hiding places that Miranda and Monty found a place to hide unseen in the corner. Unfortunately, this was the same room that the voices came into.

The baron and his wife led some more sailors into the large study. These sailers were much better dressed, and Monty surmised that these were the officers and more than likely vampires. The baron seated himself behind a desk with his back against a dark window. The room was lit by six lights mounted on the walls.

"Have a seat," the baron said as he gestured to some chairs behind them. "Your men look weary, Captain Rains."

"We will stand," the vampire said in a surprisingly deep voice. He was wearing a heavy dark blue cloak, and black brimmed hat accented by a white feather. He had a pale, gaunt face and a slim figure. "Let us discuss business. We still have not received payment for attacking that train. It took quite a bit of ordinance that I will need to restock. Lady Enix made it clear that you would pay us for any expenses incurred in this venture. I don't care if she reimburses you or not. I just want out."

"My dear captain," the baron said. "You have not lived up to your side of the bargain. The agreement was that you find the wizard, the druid, and the maru. You still have not found any of them nor have you provided any proof of their death."

"You know what we are," Captain Rains snarled. "We searched for them throughout the country side. We can smell a person's blood miles away. If we didn't find them, then they were incinerated in the explosion. It's a little hard to prove that a pile of ash is someone's corpse. Besides, you're supposed to be friends with them. Wouldn't they come to you looking for help if they were stranded? So, if you haven't seen them, and I haven't found them, then they must be dead. Since they are dead, my crew and I get the money. Otherwise, you may not like us if we have to renegotiate." One vampire walked over to the baroness and pulled her closer to the others. The baroness' malicious gaze was like a dagger that could cut someone's heart.

"I do not care for your idle threats," the baron said nonchalantly. "You know whom we work for, and she would not be very forgiving if you tried to renegotiate. Besides, she would pay you a fortune for this simple task. You should have at least found the orc. How many orcs could there be in these woods?"

"Funny you should mention that," the vampire said with a slight laugh. "We found the orc, but we wanted to see whether you would renegotiate or not. Since you're not, we could just let him go and remind him where you live. Surely, you could handle an angry wizard."

"Fine, I will pay you a sixth of what we agreed now. Kill him and bring me his skull. Then, you will get another sixth. A sixth should keep you and your men happy for a little while." The baron took out a bag of money and weighed it on a set of scales located on his desk. Once the scale showed the weight of the bag, he handed it to the vampire. "It's a little more than a sixth, so consider it a bonus."

"Fine, we will kill the orc. I am looking forward to draining him."

"No," Monty muttered and then accidentally bumped into a piece of furniture. The whole room turned around and saw Miranda and Monty hiding in the corner.

"I see I wasn't the only one holding back," the vampire said. "I am impressed, Baron Verrandrin. However, how much will you pay me to keep me from killing her? She was part of the deal."

"Go ahead and kill her," the baron said casually. "I am not renegotiating the deal."

Another vampire approached Monty licking his lips. Monty frantically looked for a way to escape as she backed up against the wall. Refusing to see her fate, Miranda was paralyzed with her eyes shut tightly. Then, a black arrow pierced the vampire's back and tore through his chest.

The corrupted convulsed violently as he spit up large amounts of blood. His body became engulfed in black flames leaving only a charred skeleton that collapsed onto the ground in a pile of bones. The other vampires stared at the black arrow that lay on top of the remains.

"A black arrow," Captain Rains screamed. "It's a blasted trap! You brought us here to kill us. I knew better than to do business with Lady Enix. Quickly, kill them all, and get that assassin." The vampire sailor holding the baroness suddenly turned into a whirling tornado and consumed the screaming woman. While the cyclone became blood red, it ripped itself away from the skin-covered boney, dried corpse of Baroness Asianna Verrandrin and flew to Monty. When it got close to Monty, a black arrow pierced the tornado that caused it to burst into a black, fiery corpse. She briefly glimpsed a black-cloaked figure holding a black, glistening bow disappear into a group of shadows against the wall.

Several vampire sailers burst into the room and transformed into clouds of white fog with skeletal faces. Moving in large, fast arcs, the misty creatures flew at Monty and Miranda. Suddenly, a hand reached out of a nearby shadow and pulled them into it. After a moment of darkness, Monty found herself on the other side of the room near the baron, the cloaked figure, and a gasping, frightened Miranda.

With a quick, succession of arrows, several foggy creatures were quickly dispatched. The vampire leader leaped through the desk in a ghostly form and tried to grab the assassin. Flying into the wall instead, the assassin dodged into another shadow and appeared on the other side of the desk near a group of bookshelves. The vampire raced back to the archer at an incredible speed. Undaunted, the archer unleashed two arrows into the vampire that screamed as he died in a black fire.

"Caezik," the baron said joyously to the cloaked figure. "I am so happy you are here. The vampires were trying to blackmail me and forced me to say those things you heard before. I wasn't working for Lady Enix."

"I don't care about your lies," Caezik said gruffly. "However, you should care about this." He unfurled a parchment with a strange black seal. "It looks as if you picked the wrong side."

"That's not possible," the baron wailed. "It has to be a forgery. Lady Enix needs me. I am too important to her operation."

"I saw her operations," Caezik said. "She doesn't need us especially since we already got her soulstones."

"That's why you can't kill me. If you do, my soulstone's power will just return to her. You're too smart for that, my old friend."

"Well, I was never the smart one, and I would be happy to kill you. However, I can't kill you. My sister is friends with your daughter, Estasia. She would hate me if I killed you. Instead, I will let them kill you." Caezik glanced to the door to the study as two more vampires rushed to them as foggy tornados. Caezik threw the screaming baron into the whirling vampires and then fired two arrows. While the vampires consumed the old Baron Eston Verrandrin, they all exploded into a black cloud of ashes, blood and bones. Caezik turned back to Monty.

"Thank you for helping us," Monty said as she stared at the piles of bones and ashes throughout the room. "My name is Monty." She studied Caezik's hardened face.

"So you're the reason Djinn came down here," Caezik said after a long pause. "I guess that means he found Montague."

"No, he didn't," Monty said sadly. "He was already dead."

"Dead?"

"He was killed by a man named Tomas."

"That lying snake," Caezik said angrily. "I knew he was up to something."

"Do you work for Lady Enix too?"

"No."

"Then, I need your help to get to Parn?"

"I could, but this place is still swarming with vampires. We got to get you out of this mansion first."

"Don't worry about that," Miranda said stepping up besides Monty. "I've got a plan for that. We simply get you to a boat at the river dock. With the cover of darkness, you should be able to float along the river and straight to the city. "

"The plan could work," Caezik said. "I will provide the distraction while you make your way to the dock."

"Thank you," Miranda said. She pulled out a small white flower from her pockets and handed it to Caezik. "May my death be painless and swift, black hand."

"May you walk with the Divine in peace," Caezik said with a nod. Then, he walked to the door and scanned the hallway.

"What was that," Monty said quietly.

"He's a black hand," Miranda whispered. "His order is a part of the Lord's Council. They execute people who have been convicted of heinous and terrible crimes. It's an old tradition where people give them flowers as a thank you and a wish that they will be merciful. I am not sure how much it really matters, but I think it's better to be nice to assassins."

"It's all clear," Caezik said as he motioned for them to come to him. They followed him out into the bright hallway. With Miranda's frantically pointing the way, they made their way to a larger room that lead out to a boardwalk overlooking the river. It had several small boats hanging from the ceiling along with piles of woods and nets. Unluckily, the room had three vampires conversing with each other. They all ducked behind one boat as they tried to not be noticed.

"I see a boat over there," Miranda said quietly while pointing to a window. Through the window, Calais could see a small row boat, bouncing in the river's current and tied to the dock. "Now, you have to go without me. I need to stay here and help the black hand."

"Wait, Miranda," Monty whispered. "I don't want to be alone anymore. I keep losing my friends."

"Oh you sweet thing," Miranda said hugging her. "You will find lots of friends, and when you finish your grand adventure, you can always come back here. We will have so much fun."

Now, the vampires had stopped talking and smelled the air. Monty realized that the vampires must have detected them somehow. Caezik pulled back the string on his bow and a large black arrow materialized in it. Silently releasing the arrow, it shattered the brightest light in the room causing it to be doused in shadows.

Caezik grabbed Monty and jumped into a shadow. After a momentary blindness, Monty found herself falling into a boat in the river as Caezik disappeared into another large shadow. Within the house, several screams and explosions occurred. Not wanting to waste her opportunity, she quickly untied the boat and pushed herself down the river. With the mansion growing smaller and smaller, she hoped Miranda would be okay, but she knew her mission to save the world would also help Miranda. She promised herself that she would find her again.

Still thinking about her time in the mansion, she almost didn't notice the fog cloud rushing at her. Again, Monty found herself helpless. Getting ready to dive into the water as her only escape, she noticed something move beneath the water. Then, a large wave shot out of the river and swallowed the vampiric cloud. Monty waited to see whether it would reappear. After a few moments, the vampire never reappeared. Instead, a familiar blue face emerged from the water next to her boat.

"Nadalia," Monty said. "Be careful, there is a vampire in the water I think."

"The vampire is dead," Nadalia said. "I dispatched him. They are vulnerable in water, and it was easy for me to kill him as nymphs are masters of the water."

"Thank you for helping me again. How far away is Parn?"

"Another's day ride, but I think I can speed you along."

"Yes, I need to get there sooner than later. I don't want to run into anyone else trying to kill me or capture me.

"I will be glad to help my rescuer. Just hold onto the boat. It's going to move fast." With a sudden jerk, she felt the boat accelerate faster and faster on the river. Somehow, the blue creature was pulling the boat and swimming simultaneously. Monty looked around the edge of the boat, but didn't see any reason that the boat was moving so fast. She tried asking, but Nadalia just said it was one of her many powers. Settling back into the boat, Monty watched the back of the nymph's head, bobbing up and down.

"Will you tell me more about your life before being a nymph?"

"Why would you want to hear sad story," Nadalia said looking back at her passenger.

"I have already seen so much magic and great powers. I would rather hear more about the normal stuff. I think being ugly and fat seems more interesting than being an all powerful sea witch." Nadalia laughed and told her story.

PART THREE

Chapter Nineteen

Tomas Dreams

In a large circular, crystal room that sat at the depths of the Fifth Spire, a beautiful woman slept in midair. She wore a white gown with silver jewelry wrapping around her slender frame. Her soft, fair skin was accented by rose-colored cheeks and full, red lips. Her long auburn hair floated in the air along with folds of her skirt. Tomas watched his wife, Carina, in her eternal sleep.

He often came down to the room when he needed strength and resolve. The sight of her brought back old memories of when Tomas felt truly happy. He remembered waking up and seeing her beautiful face lit by the early morning sun. He always loved the way she kissed him and held him tightly as if she were keeping him from flying away. Carina would pick flowers in the meadows outside their home and create beautiful arrangements. Sometimes, she would make him a crown of intertwined flowers and place it on his head. Despite all his flaws and mistakes, she was the only one that loved him for whom he was. He was the one that deserved to die and not her. Soon, he would correct that mistake and bring her back to him.

"Visiting your dear wife again," Lady Enix said from behind him. "She looks almost like an angel in that room." Lady Enix walked into the room and approached Tomas' wife. The witch was wearing a blue and red feather cloak around her mostly naked body. "I check on her every day and I promise you she is at peace."

"All I care about is our agreement," Tomas said trying to choke back tears. He remembered how he cried into the night while holding her dead body. "You will bring her back to life before you open your portal."

"That is the agreement," Lady Enix said examining Carina.

"She will be just as she was before without the memories of her death," Tomas said.

"As I said before, she will be just as she was before her death. I have already started the preparations. Soon, both of you will be reunited and released from your obligation. Now, we have more business to discuss."

"Who do you want me to kill this time," Tomas said aggravated.

"You don't have to kill anyone, at least not yet." She smiled wickedly at Tomas before returning to her examination. "I need you to take information to General Ameriz. His cannons are almost in place, and I don't want him shooting the wrong thing." Pulling a piece of parchment from underneath her cloak, she handed it to Tomas. Then, she handed a small device known as a realm-walker. It looked like a jewel encrusted brooch that allowed a person to teleport to a preprogrammed location. When they were finished, they would use the same device to return to their original location. Only Lady Enix had such devices, and they proved extremely useful in allowing Tomas to cross the entire realm in seconds.

"Sounds easy enough," Tomas said relieved while looking at the letter and the device.

"Another thing, Lord Commander. Please ask him how his prisoners escaped. I have already informed the emperor of your general's failings, and he was not very pleased. I have put plans in place to make sure your general incompetence does not jeopardize the ritual."

They had received the news in the middle of the night that Calais, Denarith, and Estasia had been captured. They were supposed to be transported to the spire in the morning. Lady Enix remained irritated that they escaped the Fifth Spire and was gleeful that they were recaptured. When she heard of their escape, she became enraged and is seeking revenge against the incapable soldiers that allowed them to escape again.

"I will let the general know," Tomas acknowledged. He looked at his wife again before he pressed the realm-walker jewel. In a flash, he disappeared.

*　*　*　*

Tomas reappeared on the edge of General Ameriz's camp. Looking behind him, he could see the drift and the distant flares of the maelstrom. Proceeding into the camp, the guards and patrolmen quickly saluted him when they saw his armor and rank. Making his way to the general's command tent, he was surrounded by bustling people making their way to various destinations. Some stopped and saluted him while others ignored him. The grey skies seemed to cover everything in a gloom. After a time, he finally got to the command tent that was denoted by black and red stripes. When he entered it, he found a large table surrounded by several officers and the general.

"Lord Commander Tomas, welcome to my camp," General Ameriz said looking up from his studies. "What does Lady Enix have for us today?"

"I have the coordinates for your attack when the ritual begins," Tomas said approaching the table. He handed the parchment to a red-haired officer who handed it over to the general. The general reviewed the parchment and stood up.

"I will take these coordinates to the cannoneers," the general said. "Please accompany me, Lord Commander." Ameriz walked out of the tent with Tomas following him.

They made their way to a group of horses. Ameriz mounted a black steed covered in red barding. Tomas was given a black-spotted grey to use. The general's bodyguards also mounted their own horses. They quickly rode out of camp while the crowds parted ways.

Once they were away from the camp, the horses galloped through the tall grasses of the plains while heading to the towering ethaerium cannons. After a time, General Ameriz slowed his horse down and moved alongside Tomas. "The plan is proceeding accordingly."

"Be warned, general, you have traitors in your camp, and they are loyal only to Lady Enix," Tomas said.

"Of course, I do," Ameriz said smiling. "I would expect nothing else from that witch. I assume she is still angry about the loss of the prisoners."

"Very much so, general," Tomas said. "She has already informed the emperor and shall make you suffer after the ritual is complete. A fate you won't have to worry about as long as the plan is successful."

"It has to be," Ameriz said. "The fate of our realm hangs in the balance. It is actually amusing. On one hand, we will be overrun by crazed corrupted creatures, on the other, we could be overrun by demonic armies. Which poison will you drink?"

"Hopefully none, general. If the plan works, we will have a way to stop the corrupted and we would have destroyed the witch and her portal to hell."

"You know that there is very little chance that this plan will work. Everything has to work exactly as planned, or disaster will be upon us." Tomas knew the plan could fail, but he didn't really care. He just wanted his wife back. "Do you think Lady Enix suspects something?"

"Very likely," Tomas said truthfully. The general was too smart and already knew the answer. "She has revealed nothing to me, but she is extremely confident in her plans."

"There is one thing I have not figured out yet," the general said scratching his beard. "What part do your friends play in her plan?"

"I am not sure. Thankfully, she does not want all my friends dead. Now, the ones that remain are running to the four corners of the realm to escape her wrath."

"That is a good thing as they would probably cause issues."

"Don't worry general, they will stay far away. They don't deserve death for their service to the empire."

"You and your friends learned a great deal about the corrupted. We would not have a way to defeat them if it weren't for you. When this is over, I will make sure that you and your friends are truly honored for their service."

"Thank you general, I eagerly expect it," Tomas said smiling.

Tomas relished the days as a member of Lady Enix's group. They killed many corrupted and stopped several impending attacks. He was highly regarded in the emperor's court. Afterwards, his influence and importance waned as other initiatives were taken up. The young emperor never seemed to like Tomas as he grew up. He always preferred the more bolstering imperial guards who spoke of grand battles and slaughters. With this new plan to finally stop the corrupted, Tomas was finally important again and was given his much-deserved respect.

"There is much to do after we kill Lady Enix."

Tomas only nodded.

*   *   *   *

Later in the day, Tomas made his way back to the camp. After his discussion with the general, they had arrived at the cannons and watched the cannoneers review the coordinates. They entered the coordinates and making the adjustments by moving large cogs and levers. It would take time before the adjustments were complete. Instead of watching over them, Tomas returned to the camp. He still had unfinished business.

As the day was ending, the camp was lit up by various lamps and torches. The crowds were slowly thinning as people made their way to the various drinking and gaming spots. There wasn't an official inn in an army camp, but soldiers would gather in groups around the camp to socialize. Sometimes, traveling bands of merchants would set up shop near the camp to offer services, foods, drinks and exotic supplies. Usually, it provided a pleasant diversion for the soldiers between fighting or during the long days of marching. Here, a thousand men sat idle on the edge of the Drift while they waited for orders. All the soldiers had were diversions especially with all the superstitions around the desert. Unlike the rest of them, Tomas didn't have time for such diversions and waved off sellers as he made his way back to the command tent.

He got off the horse and handed it to a stable boy. Then, he made his way up the street to the edge of the camp to another group of tents. Besides, operational tents like eating and planning, the next largest tents belonged to the general and the officers. The only exception was the imperial guard. Each general had an imperial guard assigned to them as an attache to the emperor. In these assignments, some of the imperial guard

146

would choose a tent just as big as the general since the assignments were not highly regarded in the emperor's court. Valuing utility over luxury, others would choose smaller tents to match the officers. There weren't many of those types left. Thorwyn was not one of those and chose a very large tent to show his superiority.

When he approached the tent, he heard women giggling within the tent. Not wanting to hear anything else, he quickly made his presence known. "Lord Commander Thorwyn, I need to speak with you," Tomas yelled at the tent's entrance.

"Whoever it is, go away," Thorwyn yelled back.

"Thorwyn, it's Tomas," Tomas said. "I need to speak with you."

After some inaudible cursing, Thorwyn emerged from the tent, thankfully with a plain shirt and pants on him. The last thing Tomas needed to see was the man being naked. Knowing how disgusting the man was, he might have done such an act at other times.

"So Lady Enix's lackey returns," Thorwyn said. "What do you want and make it quick? I'm paid up through the night, and I plan to make every second count."

"Lady Enix wants to know more about the prisoners that escaped," Tomas lied. "What was their condition and did anything happen to them while they were guests here?"

"You came to see me about the escaped prisoners," Thorwyn spat. "I know what you are doing. You are trying to put this on me. Well, it won't work. After this assignment, I have already been promised a place back in the court, and I will not let a lackey like you stop me from getting back there."

"How are you going to get back into the court," Tomas said. "You hit one of the ladies-in-waiting."

"Oh, I did much more than that to her," Thorwyn grinned. "It was only her mother that made such a big stink about it. With a few bribes, I got the charges dropped."

Tomas was disgusted and couldn't believe he was openly admitting to bribery. Such boldness and lack of decorum were becoming the new norm in the court, so Tomas had to tread lightly. "I would be careful, if I were you. Mothers hold grudges for a long time that money doesn't fix."

"Don't worry about the lady. With all the attention she got, she was sold off into marriage within a month." A woman's voice from the tent called out to Thorwyn. "Are we done here?"

"What about the prisoners," Tomas insisted.

"They appeared uninjured and in good health," Thorwyn said annoyed. "That little Calais is a nice piece of work. I would have enjoyed a night with her, but the general insisted on following proper etiquette. Instead, I took her clothes and enjoyed watching her walk through the camp with a just a few pieces of cloth."

"Why did you take her clothes," Tomas said.

"She said she didn't have her book, so I had to make sure she wasn't hiding it. We never found it which is weird that a summoner would go around without her spells."

Tomas remembered that Calais didn't have her book at the spire either. She must have hidden it with someone she trusted. Summoners didn't leave their books lying around. With most of her family on the run, there were few places she could have taken it. Most likely, she was on her way to get it back and was using Denarith and Estasia as protection. If they figure out where the book was, they might catch them finally

"What about the other two," Tomas said.

"The champion was oddly quiet which was disappointing. I would have enjoyed beating him." Tomas knew Denarith was not as dumb as he leads on. He could be very tactical if he chose to be and avoided such treatment. If he did mouth off, he would be dead and this disgusting guard in front of him would be dead as well. "Estasia was funny when I put the gem cuffs on her. She thought she was so high and mighty. Instead, I turned her into a drooling rat crumpled on the ground."

"Any word on their escape."

"No, most of the men saw nothing and whoever it was had a key to get them out. I don't really care that they escaped. It is just one less thing that I have to do in this blasted place." Then, Thorwyn got close to Tomas staring him in the eye. "Trust me, lackey, I don't care what you tell Lady Enix. At the end of the day, it is my word against yours. The emperor likes me a lot more than you."

"We're done here," Tomas said not backing off. Thorwyn turned back around and went into his tent. "Another thing, I will let them know to arrest you if you hurt any of those girls."

"No, they won't," Thorwyn laughed disappearing into the tent. "I paid the insurance and their mine to do what I want."

Tomas knew those women would be injured or even killed by the morning. He would have killed the man to save them, but a scandal would prevent him from getting his wife back. She was all that mattered.

CHAPTER TWENTY

The City of Parn

Monty floated down the river in the same small boat she has absconded from the baron's mansion. Now, that she was free from the baron, she allowed herself to relax and just watch the stars in the clear night sky. Everything seemed so peaceful as she listened to rustling trees and the singing insects around the river. Despite the river's current and Nadalia's intermittent course corrections, she felt like the boat just floated on air.

Once Nadalia had finished her sad story, they had only intermittent conversations about flowers or animals around the river. It brightened Monty's mood to see Nadalia much happier being free from captivity. At times, Nadalia loved discussing her dreams of being normal again, but it made Monty uncomfortable since she didn't know how to cure her. She would look down at the medallion that Montague had given her and pondered the idea that it might do more than just find this elusive Ninth Spire.

"There is someone nearby," Nadalia said urgently as her head broke the surface of the water. Pulling herself up, Monty searched the river banks. Nothing seemed out of the ordinary until she saw a black-robed figure standing nearby on the river bank. Quickly, she ducked into the boat hoping that the figure hadn't seen her. Nadalia hid on the other side of the boat.

"There you are, little one," a familiar voice called out. When she heard Djinn's voice, excitement overtook Monty as she jumped onto her feet.

"Djinn, you're alive," Monty shouted eagerly. "I thought the vampires captured you."

"I was never captured," Djinn said. "What vampire could capture me, a master wizard. Besides, I am much too skinny for a vampire to bother with. Now, tell me, where are you going in that boat?"

"Be careful," Nadalia whispered. "We don't know whether we can trust him."

"It's okay," Monty whispered to Nadalia. "He is a friend." Despite her reassurance, Nadalia continued to keep most of her head hidden below the water.

"I am going to Parn," she said turning her attention back to Djinn.

"Wonderful, hold the boat, little one," Djinn said. "I will be right over there." With his large brim hat flopping up and down, Djinn quickly tip toed across the water to the boat while holding up his robe to keep it from dragging.

"That is marvelous," Monty said. "You are walking on water!"

"I am," Djinn said perplexed. Then, he crashed into the water next to the boat and flailed about. "I can't swim! I can't... swim... help!" Monty reached over and grabbed one of his arms and pulled it onto the boat. Once Djinn got a good grip, he pulled himself up into the boat while almost capsizing it.

"You can walk on water, but you can't swim?"

"I wasn't walking on water," Djinn said in a mass of wet robes and a drooping hat. "I was just running really fast."

"Djinn, you are the strangest, kindest wizard I have ever met,"

"Why thank you, little one? That is the nicest thing a maru has ever said about me."

"How many maru's have you met," Monty said confused. Could there be others out there besides her?

"Just you."

"Oh, I thought there might be others. The horrible baron said they were all dead."

"And there might be others out there, but lets hope they are as pleasant as you. How did you meet Baron Verrandrin?" Monty relayed her tale of being fooled by the baron and then lured into his mansion. She spoke of the being held prisoner and then being freed. When she mentioned the hooded man Caezik, Djinn maintained his placid look.

"Did you know him," she said. She really wanted to know whether he was an ally or enemy.

"Of course, I do," Djinn said. "He is a good man and a fantastic archer. If I wanted anyone to kill me with an arrow, I would want it to be him. I wouldn't feel a thing. It was good that he found you. Vampires are a nasty type of corrupted. They suck the blood from their victims, fly and turn into the wind itself. You, however, don't have much to worry about as you don't have any blood. They probably couldn't even hurt you. For that matter, I don't think any corrupted could hurt you."

"Is that why I could cure them," Monty said reluctantly.

"Is that what the baron said," Djinn said quietly. "It's very possible, little one. Montague had been planning this for a long time. If you had such a gift, it would interest a great many people. You should be careful who you tell that too. Such power could be used for great evil. It is good you escaped."

"Do you want my power?" The thought made her cringe. If it were true, she would know then she was truly alone in the world.

"I don't need anymore power," Djinn said. "I can destroy an entire town by making a rabbit disappear in a hat. Why you want to put a rabbit in a hat was something I never understood. I figured it was better to put them in your pocket instead. An orc would keep it there for a snack, but I am no true orc. I should be wearing fingers and skulls of my enemies and dressing far more practical that means fewer clothes and more weapons and armor and jewelry and nose rings. I hate nose rings. They always make my nose itch."

"I am glad you are my friend," Monty said softly. Thinking about her few friends in the realm, she remembered Nadalia. "I forgot. You need to meet my other friend, Nadalia. Nadalia, where are you?" She scanned the water's surface near the boat, but didn't see the blue face or her body. "I don't see her. Where did she go? You must meet her."

"I hope I didn't sit on her," Djinn said as he briefly stood up to look at the floor of the boat.

"No, she is a nymph, but a good one." After scanning the water again, she reluctantly sat back down. "She must be gone then. She believes I will heal her, but I am not so sure I have the power."

"You don't need powers," Djinn said. "Powers don't make you capable, and it seems as though you are doing just fine without them. Keep your wits about you, and you can do anything."

"What's that," Monty said as she noticed several orange and blue lights reflecting off the river's surface. Slowly rising above them like a dark shadow, Monty stared at the massive city walls with lit towers. Gradually, the wind delivered music and distant voices from the massive city.

"Good, we are here," Djinn said. "This... this is the city of Parn. It is one of the few remaining great cities in Adia. It is a nexus of trade between river boats, airships, and trains. Unfortunately, it is run by the empire that means they won't let us in."

"Why?"

"Well, we're strange things, different things. You know, things that don't look like them so we must be feared. Which means, we have to get out of this boat or the city watch will discover us." Monty looked up and could see two large towers monitoring the river with large spotlights. She looked back over and saw Djinn working with an oar to steer the boat back to the shore.

Once they arrived on the shore, Djinn scouted ahead while Monty waited for his signal from a group of bushes. Then, she heard a noise behind her as Nadalia's head emerged from the water. "There you are, where were you? I wanted you to meet Djinn."

"Maybe another time," Nadalia said. "When you do get the power to help us, please don't forget me."

"I made a promise to help you and everyone else that I can. I won't forget you Nadalia." The woman smiled and disappeared below the water.

"Duck," Djinn yelled in a loud whisper. "Duck! Duck!" Monty ducked down reflexively as she looked for the attacker. When nothing came, she quickly made her way over to another set of bushes that Djinn was hiding in.

"Why are you yelling about a duck," Monty whispered.

"We are near the city wall," Djinn said as he ignored her question. "There are patrols out at night, you know, to keep us strange things out of it. We must be quiet and move quickly. Now, I think there is a wagon nearby." She followed him close to the large stone wall that seemed to touch the sky. Near the wall, there was a small wagon with several barrels in the back and several more barrels placed next to the wall.

From on top the barrels in the wagon, Djinn grabbed a cloak, and ripped part of it in half. He handed it to her to put it on. Following his instructions, she suddenly noticed her blue dress had been covered in dirt and soot. Despite its dirty appearance; she didn't want to put on another ugly cloak to hide her beautiful dress. After stroking part of the lace, she reluctantly enveloped herself inside the black cloak.

"Now, I will cast a spell to let us walk through walls," Djinn announced.

"Is that a good idea," Monty said, but Djinn had already started to cast his spell.

As Djinn waved his hands and said strange words, they became encased in a bright light and the wall began shimmering. Then, the wall exploded. Women screamed and guards sounded the alarms. Monty stood inside the massive cloud of dust and debris gawking at the sight of the massive hole in the wall. Then, Djinn pulled her to a group of nearby bushes. "That wasn't supposed to happen," Djinn said as he scratched his green bald head. Instead of the militia men, two men crashed through the bushes and uncovered a small hole nearby.

"Who blew up the barrels," one man said.

"I don't know, but I am not waiting around to be caught," the other man said.

"Is it done," the man said as he watched his companion step down into the hole.

"We got the tunnel past the inn last week," the other man said from down in the hole. "Don't forget to cover the entrance this time. A couple of the militia goons almost fell right into the hole."

"Yeah, yeah," the man said as he stepped into the hole and began to climb down an unseen ladder. Right before he completely disappeared, he recovered the hole with a nearby group of branches and bushes. Near the exploded wall, Monty could hear the militia officers yelling orders to search the area.

"What do we do now," Monty said nervously as she looked at their sparse cover of branches and twigs.

"We follow those two into the hole," Djinn said confidently. "Their tunnel will take us straight into the city."

"What a terrific idea," Monty exclaimed. "I haven't been in a tunnel before. Wait, will they let us use their tunnel?"

"Of course," Djinn said. "No one owns a tunnel just like no one can own a cave. Follow me, little one. We will be in the city in no time." He quickly uncovered the hole and climbed down it just as the two prior people did. After searching for the rope ladder rungs, Monty followed Djinn but forgot to cover the hole. The ladder led to a dark cavern lighted by a singular torch. Further down in the cave, Monty could see another torch lighting their way. Without hesitation, Djinn marched down the tunnel to the distance light. Monty followed closely looking at the glistening; damp walls dimpled with sparkling stones.

The tunnel twisted and turned with several interconnected rooms. Most of the rooms look as though people lived in them. Some of them had weapons while others had mining equipment. One room had a large map of the city on the wall with several tables and chairs surrounding it. After a time, they heard voices in the distance.

"Go back and get my sword," a voice yelled. "We may run into the militia up here." Then, a man was strolling back down the tunnel towards them. The man froze when he noticed them. In a courteous manner, Djinn removed his hat, and grinned at the man. When he saw the tall orc, he stammered as his face turned white. While trying to run and turnaround, the man halfway stumbled but quickly recovered.

"ORCS!"

Frantic, the man was screaming and running back up the tunnels. "The orcs are coming," he continued to scream. "They have invaded the tunnel, and they will burn down the town. Run for your life!"

Djinn put his hat back on his bald green head and continued to smile. Monty checked behind them to see whether there were more orcs, but she saw nothing.

"I see no other orcs," Monty said confused.

"There are no other orcs," Djinn said. "Most city humans tend to have a healthy respect for us." Monty still didn't quite understand as they continued forward. Djinn grabbed a nearby torch to light the dark tunnel in front of them.

"How many did?" a distant voice said.

"There was just one," another voice said. "You know orcs. There is never just one. Our corpses will be swimming in an orc army. They will kill us all."

"Pipe down, you idiot! Let's get into the inn and then we can get the militia."

"You mean the same guards we are trying to avoid."

"Trust me, they will be more interested in orcs than thieves."

When Monty and Djinn reached the end of the tunnel, most of the men had already climbed the ladder. The only one left was the same man from earlier. When he saw Djinn again, he screamed and dropped his torch while scrambling up the rope ladder. Once he got to the top, he looked down and noticed that the torch had lit something on the ground. A small flame sparked and smoked as it followed something into the adjacent room. "I lit the barrels," the man said as he disappeared. "RUN!"

"I think that is our cue to get out of here," Djinn said as he hurried over to the ladder. "Up you go, little one." Monty made her way up the flimsy rope ladder clumsily. "Climb quickly. We have little time."

"What's happening," Monty said as she reached up the top of the ladder.

"Explosion," Djinn said. "Big boom. Run, little one, run!" Djinn climbed quickly after her. Monty found herself surrounded by wooden walls. Djinn leaped into the room behind her and dragged her through a nearby door.

Her senses sprang to life as she smelled hot bread and heard lively music. The hallway was covered in warm light created by black iron lanterns hanging on the walls. Despite her attempt to linger in the cozy environment, Djinn continued pulling her down a hallway and past the main hall where everyone was eating and dancing.

"Where are we going," Monty said as she strained to see into the festive room.

"Through the kitchen," Djinn said continuing to drag her along. As they burst into the kitchen, several people ran screaming when they saw the orc. One woman even threw doughy biscuits at Djinn while screaming something about getting out of her kitchen. "Not much time, little one." Djinn was trying to dodge the floury missiles but got hit by them often enough to turn part of his robe white. "Jump through the window." Before

Monty could position herself, Djinn just tossed her through the open window and onto a dusty, dark road.

Brushing off the dirt from her blue dress, Monty found herself in a nearly deserted street lined with various buildings. The narrow street was lit by several black tall lamps. Several wagons, barrels, and crates were scattered around the buildings. After Djinn landed next to her, Monty followed him behind an abandoned wagon on the other side of road. While taking cover, the back part of the inn and the building next to it exploded.

People poured out of nearby houses to gather around the damaged buildings covered in fire and smoke. Shrieking alarms reverberated through the city causing more and more windows to light up. Fortunately, Djinn and Monty slipped into a nearby alley before the growing crowds of people noticed them.

"Why did the buildings blow up," Monty said as she scanned fiery wreckage.

"It's simple really," Djinn began. "That building next to the inn was a bank. The men must have been building this tunnel to break into the bank and then use the explosive barrels to destroy the vault. Once in the vault, they would steal the gold and gems and then escape back through the tunnel before anyone could pursue them. Instead, they had not quite finished their tunnel and the human running from us accidentally dropped a torch that prematurely detonated explosives. Fortunately for us, the explosion destroyed only the inn's storeroom and part of the bank, so no one was hurt."

"That's good," Monty said slowly as she came to a sudden realization. "Wait, did you know there was a tunnel full of bank robbers with explosives?"

"I had no idea," Djinn said innocently.

"You know more than you're telling me," Monty said with her arms folded.

"I am innocent, little one. I have told you everything."

"Fine," Monty said in a huff. Monty still had her doubts, but decided not to push the issue. With both of them still on the run, it would be better not to get an argument. "Where is this sage at?"

"Oh, that's easy. He is five blocks that way across the well-lit main street." Monty looked in the direction that his finger was pointing and saw large open roadways that were all heavily lit.

"So, how do we get down there with no one seeing us?"

"We disguise ourselves; of course." He reached in his robe and pulled out a large red scarf. He wrapped the scarf around his mouth and part of head. With his very large brimmed hat on his head, he had hidden most of his green skin. "You just have to keep your head down, and your hood pulled over."

As they walked down the streets, more and more people were flooding the streets to gawk at the burning buildings. Other than the crowd, Monty saw more and more guards patrolling the streets. Some were trying to keep order among the watchers while others were searching the alleyways and empty streets. After a couple of blocks, Monty noticed a group of guards were getting close to them.

Djinn led Monty behind a large white statue setup in the middle of a four-way street. Monty peered over the statue's large circular base and watched the militia men. Glancing at the statue, it appeared to be a man pointing a sword into the sky while holding a dagger in the other hand. Slowly, the militia patrol walked down another street.

Suddenly, Monty reflexively spun around when she heard a loud noise behind her. Luckily, it was only a cat knocking over a crate and the patrol didn't notice. Then, she heard cracking. Somehow, she had bumped into the statue hard enough to cause the legs to crack and crumble. Standing back, Monty watched the statue crash into ground.

"Oh, I am very sorry," Monty said. "I didn't mean to damage it."

"Incredible," Djinn said standing next to her. "You destroyed the statue of Parn, the hero."

"You mean the one who was killed by a maru." Monty was mortified. Then, they heard the patrol running back to them.

"Over here," Djinn said as he pulled her into a nearby alley. The patrol broke into a clattering sprint as they rounded the corner. By then, Djinn and Monty were running down the alley and turning down another well-lit street. With another set of guards in front of them, Djinn picked her up and burst through a door in a nearby building.

Unlike the inn's main room, this one was dimly lit, but the air was filled with cooked meat and mead. A makeshift stage had been built with tables as a man danced and sang with a baritone voice. A crowd of women was clapping and dancing with him while several other people were passed out on the floor or on some of the tables. Djinn continued to carry Monty through the room as he maneuvered around toppled tables and snoring bodies. After hopping over a few more clumps of people, he made his way behind the stage and hid in a darkened niche.

Several militia men crashed into the room with their weapons drawn. Monty twisted out of Djinn's grip to get a better view of the guards and the singing man. After the man ended his last verse in a deep, long, reverberating tone, the patrol walked carefully to the stage. The crowd of women giggled and stumble as they fawned over the singing man.

"What can I do for the city guard of Parn," the man called out as he tried to untangle himself from arms and kisses.

"Two suspicious people came in here just now," a militia officer said. "Did you see where they went?"

"Fortunate for you," the man said while looking at dark sinuous brunette next to him. "You found room full of suspicious people. This one definitely needs to be searched for illicit goods." The women stared back at him with lustful lips.

"This is no joking matter," a militia officer chided. "Our city has just been attacked, and I will arrest you and everyone in this building if I have too." Instead of answering, the man on stage had started to kiss a woman's neck. "You stop that this instance!"

"Please," the man on stage said as he stopped kissing the woman and turned his attention back to the militia officer. "Do you have any idea who I am?" The officer just glared at him. "Excuse me ladies, I must properly introduce myself to these distinguished officials of Parn." He hopped off of the stage and bowed deeply in front of the guard. "I am Nashwell Blackengard. My friends call me Nash."

"Wait," the officer stammered. "I've seen you. You're that famous bard who was in that play I saw with my wife. You are supposed to be the greatest bard to have ever lived." After pausing for a moment, the officer returned to attention and saluted Nash. "My apologies, Lord Maestro. I didn't recognize you."

"It's okay, my good fellow," Nash said as he shook the guard's hand. "Theirs much magic and makeup in those productions so some people don't recognize me at first."

"I didn't mean to interrupt your party, but the city is on high alert. It would be my honor to escort you to a safe location."

"Thank you, sir, but I must decline. I have other affairs I must attend. As one of the greatest bards to have ever lived, which you rightly point out, I can surely take care of myself. However, you can assist my guest. They are such beautiful creatures that must be protected at all cost. Would you be so kind as to escort them to safety?"

"It would be my honor," the guard said as several women objected.

"It is okay, ladies, but I promise I will return very soon so we can continue what we started."

Despite their continuing objections and kisses, Nash lead the group of women out of the building with the rest of the patrol. After exchanging several kisses and goodbyes, Nash finally closed the door. With a sigh of relief, he leaned back against the closed door looking at the room filled with sleeping patrons. As he mumbled some indiscernible words, he proceeded to Djinn and Monty's hiding place.

"I knew the explosions were a sign," Nash said moving furniture to uncover their hiding spot. "Apparently, it was a sign that announced the arrival of Djinn, the great chaos wizard."

"Technically, only one explosion was mine," Djinn said. "The others were bank robbers and possibly orcs."

"Let us be clear," Nash said as he helped Djinn stand up. "Blowing up a bank is not a proper solution against bank robbery, and who do we have here." Nash bent down to see under the thick cloak covering Monty. "Why, hello?"

"Monty is her name," Djinn said. "I found her in Smithhaven, and I am helping her get to the sage. That is why I am here, Nash."

"So, he sent the letter to everyone then," Nash said shaking his head. "I told Montague that he couldn't trust the old group. We have all changed and not for the better, I might add. Most of us have sided with Lady Enix while a few of us still stand against her."

"Speak for yourself," Djinn said. "I have not changed at all. I am the same old wizard."

"Well, your smell hasn't improved," Nash replied. "Let me take you to the sarge upstairs before anymore guards decide to show up."

Monty followed them upstairs while hopping over toppled furniture and people. Even the stairs were littered with dirty glasses, empty bottles, and smelly men. While it took Monty more effort to keep up and not get dirty, Djinn simply walked up the stairs with his robe dragging across everything.

"Sarge," Nash yelled as he entered a hallway on the second floor. "It's time to wake up, you old bear. We've got company." Nash started to beat on the first door in the hallway.

"I didn't think it was a good idea to wake up a sleeping bear," Monty said as she caught up with them.

"Don't worry about old sarge," Nash said as he continued to beat on the door. "He is a kind and gentle old man. Also, he is one of the best master-at-arms in this realm. In fact, he is only here to protect us."

"I hate you," an old, half-dressed man screamed as he threw open the door. "I will kill you right here, right now."

"What's the matter," Nash said with a forced smile. "Did you not enjoy the festivities last night? I saw several women looking at you."

"Your hellish music kept me up all night," the man sneered. "What's worse, if people weren't thumping against the walls, they were retching their guts out. I have been in battles that were quieter. Now, stay right here while I go get my knife so I can kill you. Don't worry, a broken bottle will do the trick if I can't find my knife." The man smiled and started to turn around.

"Before you look for that knife," Nash began. "Let me introduce you to our new guests. You remember our crazy orc friend, Djinn."

"So those were your explosions in the distance," the old man said. "I thought it was one of his bizarre play bits."

"Sarge," Djinn said chuckling. "I hope you have gotten over that incident in Blackbay a few years back."

"Oh, I had forgotten about that. Maybe, I will get two knives."

"Last, but certainly not least, this is Monty," Nash said as he directed the old man's attention to her. "Monty, this is Lord Sargent Marek Roen." Monty proceeded to remove her hood.

"This is why Montague wanted everyone to come down," Marek said. "He wanted to show us his animated white statute."

"You're being rude," Monty said bluntly.

"I don't care," Marek said. "The empire is killing hundreds of non-humans and, for some reason, Lady Enix has been freed from her prison. There are a few more important things going on then Montague's toys."

"Definitely not a toy," Djinn interjected. "This little one is a maru."

"A maru in Parn," Marek laughed. "Now, that's irony. No wonder the city is getting destroyed."

"We are taking her to the sage in town," Nash said. "Would you accompany us on this grand adventure?"

"Adventure," Marek said appalled. "While you are prancing around on stage and you are blowing up cities, I have spent the last ten years fighting the corrupted and this blasted empire. I don't know what's worse. The empire is slaughtering the innocent in mass to prevent more corrupted creatures while the corrupted are killing the innocent in mass because they can. I certainly don't have time for toys or silly adventures." Marek slammed the door.

"He's just a rude, old bear," Monty said as she sat down on a stair step. "I don't know what's worse: being called a maru or a toy."

"Don't worry, my darling," Nash said as he proceeded to another door in the hallway. "He is just rough on the outside, but he has a heart of gold on the inside." Monty glanced behind her to see Nash open a door and pull out a yellow overcoat. After putting on the overcoat, he closed and locked the door. "Shall we began?"

"I am getting tired," Monty said feeling a sudden wave of exhaustion hit her. She leaned her head against the wall falling into the blackness of a deep sleep.

CHAPTER TWENTY-ONE

The Sage

With heavy eyes, Monty found herself laying in a large, soft, red chair surrounded by books. Looking to her left, right and even behind her, there were books everywhere. Some lay opened on numerous tables while most of them lined the walls. Books were even piled up on the surrounding floor. Among the books, she found her companions talking quietly at a nearby table.

Djinn and the bard named Nash were on one side while the old bear, Marek, and another human sat on the other side. The human had a big nose, bulging eyes and dark receding hair. He had a slim frame covered in blue and white robes. Out of the three, he was the first to notice her.

"Oh good," the man said. "That little white, statue... the creature you brought wasn't broken after all. It looks like it's moving around a little slow, kind of like a lion right before it rips out part of your throat, which would leave a man lying on the ground with most of his blood gushing out of his missing neck. Obviously, this helps the lion as the man can't fight back while the lion drags him back into the tall grass and eats him."

"She's nothing like a lion," Nash said. "She is completely harmless. She's as innocent as a kitten."

"Do you know how many diseases a kitten has," the strange man said. "Besides, I've watched kittens eat a dying man's face off. He might have lived if he had a face that is."

"I promise I will not hurt you or anyone else," Monty said in a sleepy haze.

"You won't hurt me," the strange man said confidently. "I am the sage. I am told that you had been looking for me."

Suddenly, Monty was completely awake. "Oh please, I need your help," Monty said excitedly. While knocking over several piles of books, she jumped out of the chair and ran to the sage. "Montague gave me this

160

medallion and I need to learn how to use it. I must save the realm." She took off the medallion and put it several inches from his nose. The sage slowly took it from her hand and examined it.

"Quite honestly, I have no clue what this is," the sage said, "but, I recognize some of the symbols."

"That's wonderful," Marek said sarcastically. "This is just another one of Montage's games. It's another clue that will lead to another clue. We took months to figure out his last clues. Luckily, we found it before Lady Enix tried to destroy the realm the first time. We should just stop sneaking around, assemble a large force and imprison her. This time, we will put a guard up so that no one lets her out."

"It doesn't matter who let her out," Nash said. "Besides, she is extremely resourceful and will just find another way out. The only way you will kill her is by destroying her or banishing her to one of planes of hell. Maybe Montague put the answer in that necklace."

"If he did, it would be in code," the sage said as he studied the medallion. "These appear to be archaic symbols from before the Age of Dragons." He walked across the room and looked through books. "Montague never listened to me. I told him that destroying Lady Enix was not possible, but he still had this idea in his head. It was like bad fungus on bread that grew in his head and continually poisoned his thoughts."

"How could he destroy her with that," Monty said as she watched the sage impatiently? He continued to study each part of the medallion in an infuriating slow manner. After all this time, she was so close to the Ninth Spire and the angel, Enikus.

"Lady Enix is a demon," the sage said. "Do you know what a demon is?" Monty just shook her head. He opened a book and began flipping through several pages. "Demon and dragons were once angels. They were caretakers of the planes and all things that were created in it. Some of the angels rebelled against the Divine. They lost and got kicked out. Some fled to the realms of chaos to become dragons, while others went to the various planes and converted them into what some called the nine hells. Don't be fooled, there are more than nine hells. Normally, the dragons and demons can't travel to a plane without being summoned, but then some fool summons a demon and then it summons more. Eventually, the demon armies get a foothold, and they will transform it into another plane of hell. Funny, the demons call it a rite of cleansing. I am not sure what they are cleaning since they are nothing more than diseased cockroaches chewing on the local populace."

"That's why we were hoping Montague would find a way to stop Lady Enix," Marek said. "Instead, we got a toy and a necklace." Monty hated hearing that word. It made her feel inferior and useless.

"You mean a maru," Djinn interjected. A wave of despair crashed through Monty's heart as she remembered the baron's awful stories about maru killing people.

"Stop it," Monty yelled. "I am not a toy, you old bear. I am not a maru. I am just... me."

"I don't care" Marek said. "Millions of people will die because we can't stop this demon."

"Oh leave the little darling alone," Nash said frustrated. "None of this is her fault or Montague's fault. He was one of the few who was trying to stop Lady Enix." As Monty quietly shook from a storm of emotions inside her, Nash came over and put a strong, calming hand on her shoulder. "No need to be sad, darling. The sage will get it figured out, and I got a present for you." From under his large yellow overcoat, he pulled out a red dress with pink ribbons and lace.

Everything dissipated inside her as she stared at the beautiful dress. Filled with glee, she grabbed the dress, and began looking around for a place to change. "This is wonderful," she said as she wiped her tears away. "Where can I put it on? I must see how it looks."

"Through that door," Nash said as he pointed to a door separating the main room from a smaller, darker room. "Don't worry, it's only a small storage room. Quite clean as I don't think he ever used it since most of his stuff is out here on the floor."

Monty smiled as she knocked over more book piles by making her way to the door. Grabbing a nearby lantern, she disappeared into the storage room. Placing the lantern in the corner, its dim, orange light lit up the storage room filled with dust and spider webs. Not caring about the unclean conditions, she quickly changed into her new dress and discarded the makeshift cloak and old blue dress onto the ground. Once the buttons and bow's were tied, she made her way back into the library.

"I cannot believe my eyes," Nash declared from across the room. With a large smile, he made his way over to her. "Darling, you look like a beautiful red rose blossoming on a snowy mountainside." Blushing, Monty looked down and picked at her dress as she looked for words of appreciation. "Allow me to take your hand and escort you to my table." With a reassuring smile, Nash delicately took her hand and walked with her back to the table where the others were sitting. Despite Nash's announcement, Marek was sleeping upright and Djinn was reading a book upside down.

Nash grabbed a heavy book and through it on the table. Marek slowly opened his eyes while Djinn peered over the book in his hands. "May I announce Lady Monty," Nash said while bending over to kiss her hand.

"You look extraordinary," Djinn said. He closed his book and noticed something on the cover. With a confused look, he turned it right side up and then sideways.

Marek rolled his eyes and closed them again.

"I hate to interrupt tea time with Princess Monty," the sage said. "I am trying to concentrate here, and you still don't know how you will kill your pesky demon." Monty was astonished to see the sage surrounded by open floating books. Turning different pages in different books, he moved the medallion along each line of text as if the words themselves would decipher the medallion.

"Are you another member of the Lord's Council," Monty said.

"No," the sage said without looking away from his page. "Sages are not one of the twelve orders of the Lord's Council. We are historians and purveyors of knowledge. We seek knowledge and help others to understand it. Sages preferred not to get involved with the Lord's Council's mission to banish all the dragons. Now, you have a sage helping you banish a demon and the leaders of the Lord's Council too weak and too scared to get involved."

"Just a bunch of rich old men who want everything to stay the same," Nash said. "That way, they can stay rich and powerful in their reign until they die. Then, the next fellow wants everything to be the same, so he doesn't lose any power. It's a vicious cycle. To this day, I don't see them facing down a dragon."

"Don't be fooled," Marek said with his eyes closed. "Unlike us, there are many brave men and women in the orders. It is they who protect this world. The only reason a council was formed was to keep the peace between orders and to mobilize us against great threats like the dragons."

"Well, it is our good fortune they chose not to act," Nash said. "Last time I had to deal with my head of the order, he took my money, and stole my girl. He called it a tribute to the order. In the end, it worked out for me since it turns out that the girl wasn't as clean as she claimed. He was itching for weeks."

"A bard finally getting what he deserved," Marek laughed. "The head of my order threw me in jail for a month for hitting him. I knocked him clean out too with just one punch. The man was a pompous ass and deserved it. If I see him again, I will knock him out, just for the fun of it."

"What about you, Djinn," Monty said. Instead of listening to the conversation, Djinn was scanning the spines of several books. "Did you ever meet the head of your order?"

"Yes, and he is a good man," Djinn said. "One of the best humans I ever knew. If it weren't for him, I wouldn't be a wizard. He has told me it gives him hope for the world if an orc can be a wizard. Everyone else just sees me as a green savage."

"That's the way it works," the sage said in the distance.

"I hope you mean the medallion," Djinn said dryly.

"Well, sort of, anyway, I found it," the sage said as he pushed the floating books aside. "The medallion is a communication device. It is paired with other medallions like it and they can communicate even across the realms themselves. It has 'V' shaped markings with the half circles. It means that this is just a small part of a larger collection." He was anxiously pointing to various encryptions on the medallion. "These symbols mean 'by air' or 'with air' but the next part of the symbols states that a signal or message is sent. Apparently, they were used as communication devices during the Age of Dragons and before. With ethaerium, we didn't need these anymore. No one had written about them or used them in centuries."

"Great," Nash said sarcastically. "So, how do you turn it on?"

"I don't know," the sage said.

A large gust of wind thew open a nearby window despite the flapping protests of pages and papers. Then, a large eagle soared into the library and continued to fly around the circular library in long lapses. Slowly, it descended back to the ground as everyone watched it except for the sage that was still scanning a page. Unfortunately, it made the sage's shoulder its final perch. Unable to maintain his balance with the large bird on his shoulder, the sage fell to the ground in a mass of waving arms, legs, and robes. Unaffected by the sage's lack of grace, the bird simply hopped off the crumbled mass and perched it self on a nearby table.

"They guards are coming," the bird said.

"Nora," Monty exclaimed as she jumped from her chair and ran to the bird. With another trail of disheveled books behind her, she gently hugged the large bird. "I have missed you so much. Where have you been all this time?"

"Don't worry child," Nora said. "I have not been far. I knew Djinn would take care of you."

"Nora, you finally reconsidered my offer after all these years," Nash said devilishly.

"If I mated with you," Nora said in deep thought. "I would have to eat you afterwards. It would be the only way to make the relationship manageable. Don't worry Nash, I am still considering your offer."

"Leave the old woman alone, Nash," Marek said. "It is time to leave."

"Is that the old bear," Nora said as she morphed back into her usual jaguar form? "I am surprised. You still haven't gotten yourself killed in some useless battle."

"Don't worry your pretty little tail," Marek said. "You said there were guards coming. There still might be a chance. Do you have a backdoor?"

"Through the kitchen," the sage said as he pulled himself off the ground. "Just follow the signs that say trash, fugitives and crazy, stupid druids."

"Ahh," Nora said. "I missed you too, sage."

"I surely won't miss any of you," the sage said. "But, be careful out there. I hope you find a way to solve your demon problem. That way, you can come back and annoy me again. For you Monty, I have a little piece of advice. The world's not that bad. There are still a few good people around. Just focus on that little ray of light when you find yourself trapped in darkness."

After saying their goodbyes, they made their way through a back hallway into a very messy kitchen. Pots and counters hadn't been washed in weeks. Small animals, and bugs made their way through the maze of refuse. Without hesitation, the group pushed through the slimy, moldy mess to a smaller wooden door.

Slowly pushing the door open; the group walked into a dimly lit alleyway that was surrounded by a large group of armored men and onlookers. With the early morning sunlight, Monty could see that most of them wore the black and red Parn uniforms. To Monty's horror, two of them wore the black and gold imperial guard uniforms. She shrank behind Djinn as memories of Montague's killers flooded her mind.

"You are hereby under arrest for plotting against allies of our illustrious Emperor, the holy protector of the Dragon Shield," an imperial guard yelled as he stepped forward with his sword drawn. "You will come with us peacefully and be tried in court for your crimes. Otherwise, we will kill you where you stand."

"Blow through the medallion like a whistle," Djinn whispered to Monty. Still hiding behind Djinn's robes, Monty looked at the medallion and blew across the medallion. As she blew, lines on the medallion glowed with a white, bluish light, and then dimmed again.

"Did it work," Monty said in a soft voice.

"That should do," Djinn said.

"Since when is disagreeing with the emperor a crime," Marek said to the imperial guard. "Last time I checked, people could still voice their opinions or is the Empire going to take that away too."

"Step away, Lord Sargent," the imperial guard growled. "I can kill a master-at-arms, especially one as old as you."

"We will see about that," Marek smiled as he drew a rod from his belt. From the rod, a long, spiked chain whip sprang to life. The imperial guard's eyes widened with surprise and clutched his sword even tighter. The surrounding guards closed with drawn weapons.

"Aren't you going to do something," Monty said to Djinn and Nora.

"Nothing is sexier than watching one man stand against an army," Nora said. "Even if he will get killed in the process."

"Don't worry," Djinn said. "Our backup has arrived."

Suddenly, a thunderous light exploded in the sky. As the light faded, everyone stared at large airship appearing directly above them. It wasn't like other airships that were shaped as flying galleons. This one had a wide shallow hull accented by gold and silver plates. Large massive wings of blue sails extended out from the sides of the hull. Three smaller masts were mounted along the deck of the ship.

"What is that," Monty said shocked by the strange sight?

"That, little one, is the Ninth Spire," Djinn said with a wide grin. "It is commanded by the good elf, Lord Captain Maliki."

"He didn't tell me it was a ship," Monty muttered to herself.

"Why did Maliki just show up," Nash said frantically.

"I called him," Monty said quietly.

"You knew this would happen when you used that thing," Nash said. "You might have just gotten all of us killed."

Several beams of white energy lanced out of its hull with each one destroying nearby towers. Fire and debris rained down onto the streets, and several alarms screamed throughout the city. Two small airships approached the massive ship and began firing cannons that appeared as balls of fire in the dim light. Each shot exploded on a bluish force field surrounding the Ninth Spire. The onlookers scattered into the streets and buildings. With more lancing beams, it reduced the small airships into fiery debris reining down onto other parts of the city. Then, a small explosion of light near Marek pulled everyone's attention away from the ship.

An elf with bronze skin was wrapped in a majestic, navy blue cloak. Only a metal, plated arm was visible. Under his disheveled auburn hair, he wore a solid, gold plate over his eyes and a part of his nose. Several people backed up as he scanned the area. Slowly, he moved the plate up onto his forehead to reveal emerald green eyes.

"Maliki," Marek said as he made his chain weapon disappear. "These people don't have to die. Just let them go."

"Navigator," the imperial guard snarled. "I have heard a lot about you. I will be promoted to the highest ranks when I kill you."

"Stop, Lord Commander," Marek pleaded. "You can't kill him. Just let him go. You can arrest me, and I will answer for his crimes."

The imperial guard didn't listen. He and several others charged the navigator. Without moving, his eyes glowed like the sun and the charging men just fell over. Their skin had turned grey and lifeless. Their faces had twisted into a silent scream.

"What just happened," Monty said approaching the dead men. The other guard and militia men fled. Maliki did not follow or hurt them further. Marek just stared at the dead men in despair.

"A navigator can absorb the knowledge and powers of artifacts, books... and people," Djinn said solemnly. "They call it soul reaping."

"I am Lord Captain Maliki," the navigator said as he approached Monty. "You are Montague's great creation. What name did you give yourself?"

"Monty," she said quietly. While she hurt nobody, Monty felt partially guilty for calling the Ninth Spire that resulted in these people's death.

"Have you finally gone crazy, Maliki," Nash ranted. "You destroyed several buildings and caught half the town on fire."

"They had snipers positioned in those towers," Maliki said. "Your death was certain which is what she wants. It is best we leave. More guards and ships are approaching."

"Will you take me to Enikus," Monty said.

"Yes," Maliki said.

"Djinn and I are coming," Nora said. Monty felt comforted to know her two friends would stay with her.

"Of course, I am coming," Nash said. "It sounds as if we are getting the old group back together again. We will have the crazy navigator and the crazy angel. We might stop her if we can avoid burning down cities."

"I am not going," Marek said.

"I don't recall asking you," Maliki said.

In several flashes of light, they were transported to the Ninth Spire.

CHAPTER TWENTY-TWO

Yellow City

"Do you smell that," Denarith said sniffing the air with his long snout. They had been riding most of the night after escaping the army camp. Denarith led the way using his totem sprint while Calais followed on horse. They continually kept Estasia half-awake as she rode slumped over in the saddle. She remained extremely weak from the gem cuffs. Because Denarith and Calais could both see in the dark, they had made good time to the road that led to the Yellow City. Shortly after reaching the road, they had slowed down to watch for camps and other travelers. Now, Denarith was stopped in the middle of the road under a sky full of stars and three distant moons.

"I smell nothing," Calais said sniffing the air. "What is it?"

"I smell death," Denarith said in a deep tone. He walked off the road and into the tall grasses. Calais directed her horse to follow while watching for any signs of movement. From the corner of her eye, she saw Estasia continuing to follow along. More than likely, Estasia was too tired to argue against their decision to investigate the smell.

After a time, he bent down and picked through something on the ground. Calais dismounted to investigate his find while Estasia remained on her horse. Getting closer, the smell of death almost overwhelmed her. Getting sick to her stomach, Calais pressed forward to find several dead bodies mutilated on the ground. None of their belongings had been taken, but they had been torn apart by something strong with claws and teeth. Unable to see very much detail in the dark, she tried to feel some of the sticky remains for anymore evidence of the attack.

"You know what did this," Denarith said looking at Calais.

"Corrupted," Calais said softly.

Over the last several years, her work with portals had taken her to remote places throughout the realm where Calais never encountered the corrupted. It was rare for her to see their destruction much less their attack.

Within the last year, she had heard of more frequent attacks on cities and caravans. Looking at the remains, she surmised that this could be yet another victim of their blood thirsty destruction.

"Can you tell how long they have been dead," Calais said while still examining pieces of flesh. Totem champions had an extremely keen sense of smell and could observe many details that a human would normally miss. If he could figure out how long they have been decomposing, they would know how close the corrupted where to their position.

"They have been dead for over a day," Denarith said. "I can see that their tracks lead away from the city. More than likely, they are ambushing travelers headed for Yellow City."

"They must be hiding in the grass," Calais said nervous peering through the grass blades.

"They are not here now," Denarith said. "I would smell their scent a mile away."

"We should get to the city before we're attacked," Calais said.

"After everything we have been through, I wouldn't mind bashing some heads in. Let them come."

"Denarith, we have to get Estasia to the city so she can recover. I don't have my books, and Estasia can't cast any spells. We need your protection. After we get to the city, you can go and smash all the heads you want."

"I will take you to the city, and then you are on your own."

Bending back down over the remains, she meticulously picked through the flesh and clothes. The clothes were a nicer thread so Calais thought they would have valuable jewelry or coin that they could use. After a few moments, she found what she was looking for.

"It looks like we can at least buy lunch and passage," Calais said pulling out some blood-soaked satchels. Inside two satchels were a large amount of imperial coins. In the other satchel, she found valuable gems and stones.

"That is a lot of coin," Denarith said. He took one bag and sifted through its contents. "No normal trader or courier would carry so much or put it all in one satchel. Robbers would take all their money. Real merchants would hide their riches all over their wagons to make it hard to find. I know, I have raided plenty of caravans and had to search everywhere to find anything valuable."

"It must be for a bribe or a bounty," Calais wondered.

"Something rotten was going on here to be exchanging money so far out of the city," Denarith said. Calais knew that the barbarian tribes did extensive trading with the empire. Usually, the trading would occur in cities where merchants and traders felt protected from any treachery.

"Should we leave it here," Calais said.

"Nope, we will take it and spend it," Denarith said. "The dead don't need it and the corrupted that killed them don't need it. So, we will take it and put it to good use."

That fact that corrupted did not treasure gold or gems made many people fear them. They couldn't be bribed or influenced by the wealthy or the nobility. The corrupted only coveted more power. With few ways to gain more magical powers, they have resorted to control and fear. She had heard stories of corrupted taking prisoners only to terrify them and cause pain. When they got done toying with them, they would discard their victims and move onto others. Captured nobility were especially prized since most of the corrupted came from the lower classes and hated the noble class such as Calais and Estasia. The thought of being captured sent chills up Calais' spine while she re-scanned the horizon for any threats.

With nothing in sight, she turned to Denarith who handed her a satchel of coins. He took the other satchel and gave Estasia the gems by tying it to her belt. Picking through the remains, Denarith found a few more pieces of jewelry. He tried to hand Calais a few pieces, but she refused the bloody trinkets. Once Denarith finished looting the bodies, Calais pulled herself back up on her horse and checked on Estasia that was partially sleeping in her saddle. With Denarith items stashed in his belt and pants, they headed back to the city through the dark plains.

*   *   *   *

Yellow City was a patchwork of buildings, camps and makeshift markets. Unlike many cities, it didn't have a city wall or cobblestone streets. Instead, it sprawled out into many directions in a patchwork of oranges, browns and grays. The most striking feature of the town was the large skydocks that towered above everything else.

The skydocks were giant metal towers that extended into the sky with smaller metal arms pultruding from them at various intervals like limbs on a tree. Nets and wires were scattered throughout the scaffolding to raise and lower cargo. Airships, still designed after the old sailing sea ships, were flying to and from the towers. Some remained docked along the metal arms as people walked on and off the ships. When someone left the ship, the person would walk along the arms known as skywalks to the elevators that would carry them to the ground. Sometimes, people would ride the wires from one skywalk to another. Bustling with activity, the skydocks made Yellow City one of the largest trading hubs in southern Adia. Since the skydocks provided such easy access to the town, it was home to the empire, criminals, rebels, tribes and other oddities. Luckily, Calais and her friends would not be noticed or arrested.

Still mostly naked, Calais tightly held her cloak around her to hide her body. She walked gingerly on the road with her bare feet. After riding most of the night, Estasia remained weak while she leaned on Denarith while they walked to the archway that denoted the entrance to Yellow City.

Since the city had no walls, the archway was only decorative metal scaffolding. Around it, merchants had set up several carts to sell their wares to incoming and outgoing patrons. Some merchants watched them intently while others scoffed at them. Since it was still early morning, the only noise came from the skydocks. The rest of the city remained asleep. Suddenly, another rock stabbed Calais' foot.

"Ow," Calais said. "I wish we could have ridden in with the horses."

"Stealing imperial horses is a capital offense," Denarith said. "They would have arrested us as soon as they saw them. Besides, they will be watching us closely. Anytime I come to one of these cities; most of the militia thinks I will try to steal something or kill someone."

"Wait, I thought you did that anyway," Calais said perplexed.

"I know, it's great," Denarith laughed.

"Oh great champion," a nearby merchant said approaching them. He was covered in a patchwork of robes and blankets and had a thin, crinkled face. "I have lovely jewelry for your beautiful wives." He held up several necklaces made of silver, turquoise, and leather.

"My wives wear only gold," Denarith said abruptly. "I have no interest in your junk."

"This is the finest silver," the merchant said.

"Be gone little man, my wives had a weary night and don't want to be bothered," Denarith said. The merchant tried again, but Denarith just glared back at him. Once the merchant left, Calais shot Denarith an angry look.

"Don't look at me like that, wife," Denarith said quietly. "I will have to punish you if others saw your defiance. Besides, it's a good cover to get us by." Calais rolled her eyes and looked back at the ground, so she could avoid stepping on sharp rocks. He was right, but she wouldn't tell him that. His ego was already insufferable.

"I will play along this once, but don't you dare touch me," Calais said discreetly.

"You should put your arms around me," Denarith said looking at the other merchants. "It would look better especially since you aren't wearing very much."

"Drop dead," Calais snapped at him.

After fending off several other merchants, they finally arrived at the gate. Before they could continue their way through the archway, three armored men with spears, swords, and shields came out from behind one of the nearby shacks and stopped them. "Stop barbarian," the man said. He had a large nose and pocketed face while wearing the Yellow City uniform. "Who are these women with you?"

"They are my wives," Denarith said bluntly.

"This one is dressed a little nice for a barbarian and what is this one hiding under her cloak," the man said. "How do I know that you didn't steal them?"

"We are here of our own freewill," Calais said trying to sound meek.

"Don't speak unless I command it," Denarith barked while yanking her back by her hair. Disoriented for a moment, Calais could feel part of her head burning. Denarith turned back to the city militia men. "Do not listen to her. She is a new wife, and I am still training her." Then, he grabbed part of her cloak and raised it up for them to see her almost naked body. She still only had the red breechcloth and chest wrap. They leered at her hungrily. Feeling violated, Calais avoided their gaze. "You see, she has nothing on her. I dress only them this way so that I don't offend you cultural sensibilities. Believe me, it is cheaper to have them wear tribal gear." He dropped the cloak, but she still looked away from the all the craving eyes around her.

"It doesn't bother me," the militia man said. "I will pay you for the clothes, and they can parade around naked for all I care."

"That is a tempting offer," Denarith said. Calais wanted to hit the barbarian, but she knew that he would retaliate with even greater force. Not wanting to suffer a bruised face or worse, she continued to play her part so that they could get into the city and go on their separate ways. "I paid a fortune for these clothes that I wish I could get back, but I have business here that requires certain dress. Can you get out of our way now so I can conduct this business and get out of this town?"

The militia man glanced at Denarith's axe and stepped out of the way. The other men followed him. Denarith nodded to the man and walked through the archway with Estasia. Calais held her cloak tightly against her and followed him. The men talked quietly among each other and laughed before moving back to their shack. Calais knew that it was at her expense, whatever it was. Leaving the metal arch way, she noticed that the city streets were only simmering with activity as a few wagons moved up and down the twisting streets. With no one paying attention to them, they made their way in-between two buildings that kept them out of sight.

"I can't believe that you did that," Calais said hitting his arm.

"Listen woman," Denarith said annoyed. "Totem wives only speak when they are spoken too. The totem champion is the voice of his household. If I hadn't punished you, they would have been suspicious. I did you a favor and got you in the city. You have your money, and now you can go on your way."

"I will be glad to get away from you and finally find some real clothes," Calais said irritated.

"What about me," Estasia said weakly. "I can barely walk."

"I will never be free from you two," Denarith growled. "Fine, I will take her to the Red Horse Inn while you find us passage. There is a great brothel nearby."

"You're coming with us," Calais said taken aback.

"I never really liked Yellow City, and you need my protection until you get your book back."

While Calais was still upset with Denarith, part of her knew he was right. Estasia and she were extremely vulnerable until Estasia gained part of her power back. Sometimes, it took days for wizards to recuperate. The thought of working with Denarith for the next several days disgusted her. "Very well," Calais said coldly. "I will meet you at the inn." Without saying goodbye, she held her cloak tightly closed and walked down a street to the airship station.

None of the streets went in a straight line making navigation difficult. All she had to do was head to the center of the town where the base of the skydocks were located. As the morning got later, people emerged from their shacks and small homes. Shops opened their windows and doors. Generally, everyone ignored her as they went on their business which suited Calais just fine. The ground was littered with manure, wood chips and broke glass. After avoiding some of the debris, Calais looked for a tailor or an emporium. Closer to the center of the city, she saw a large shop with clothing setup on wooden mannequins outside it.

Hurrying into the store, she opened the shop's door and a ringing bell announced her presence. Once inside, the shop had several dresses and formal suits setup on more wooden mannequins around the floor. Several shelves had folded clothing of various colors. Other shelves just had cloth material. After a moment, a small man with round glasses and a thick mustache hurried out of a backroom.

"Excuse me, but we don't serve harlots here," the man said with a nasally voice. "Leave, or I will call the authorities."

"I am not one of those people," she gasped. "I need traveling clothes. I have money to pay you for it."

"I am sure you do," the small man said. "I don't want that kind of money in my store or have anything to do with your kind. I run a respectable business. Now, go away."

"Please, help me," Calais said. "I need clothes so people like you don't mistake me for a harlot."

"Clothes will not absolve you of your sins. You will have to live with your choices. Now, go or I will call the militia."

"I want clothes," Calais shouted. "Give me some clothing!"

"Very well," the man said calmly. "I will just call the militia."

"Wait," a deep voice said from the back room. "I know her, and you need not call the militia."

A tall, slender elf walked out of the back room. He had fiery hair with deep, yellow eyes. His skin was weathered and dark from being in the sun. He had a roman nose with a high brow. The elf wore loose orange-and-yellow clothing. When she saw the purple sash with the gold pendant, she realized the elf was an old acquaintance.

"Drachid," Calais said astonished. "Is that you? I thought you had left this realm."

"It is good to see you again," Drachid said with a courteous nod. "A merchant's business takes them to many places, and I made my way back here a year ago. I am glad to see you are all right."

"I believe we have completed are transaction," the small man said. "If you don't mind, you can take your associate with you." Calais was repulsed by the man's callousness. Drachid thanked the man for his business and led Calais out of the shop.

"That man was so rude," Calais said while still trying to keep her cloak closed. "Why did you do business with him?"

"The times have gotten worse with the corrupted," Drachid said. "Humans are becoming more suspicious of the elves and some even blame us for the corrupted. While it is not pleasant, I have to make money for my tribe, so we can continue to survive."

"If humans were so terrible, why do business with them," Calais said while she walked with him down the street. "You can just trade with the other fire elf tribes. There are also the orcs and barbarians."

"Many fire elf caravans have gone missing over the last year," Drachid said grimly. "Rumors suggest that they are being killed or captured if they go too close to the fifth spire. There are not that many fire elf tribes to trade with since they won't go near the spires. Their trips take twice as long now, and a tribe cannot make all its own goods. So, we barter with the humans while we can."

"I am so sorry to hear that," Calais said. She knew what was at the Fifth Spire, and she saw no elves when she was a captive. They must have been turned into the fire knights that meant they were dead. She didn't want to tell Drachid since it would only cause his more grief. She didn't want to talk about the Fifth Spire, so she needed to change the subject. "I need some clothes. A nasty imperial guard took my clothes."

"Why did you let him take your clothes," Drachid said perplexed.

"It is a long story, but I need clothes." She carefully stepped around some debris in the road.

"It is a good thing I found you then," Drachid said. "That shopkeeper has only fancy clothes that would have been torn apart in less than a day. I will take you to my camp where I will give you proper clothes that you need and warrant your station."

"I need nothing too elaborate," Calais said. "There are bad people after me and I don't want to be noticed. I also really don't want to put your family in danger."

"I face giant sand worms and crabs," Drachid said plainly. "We can protect ourselves. Don't worry, we will keep you safe."

*   *   *   *

The fire elf camp sat on the corner of two intersecting streets. It had several covered wagons that formed a half-circle around a large fire pit. Work areas had been set up around the wagons. Several elves made leather goods and sewed clothing together within these work areas.

Fire elves spent most of their time wondering the drift and the plains around it searching for rare goods. They were often expert craftsmen and were known for their exquisite products. Part of the reason stemmed from their natural ability to produce, and control fire. They used this mastery of the flame to heat and cool materials with high precision. They used it in all their crafting, even tailoring. Other than engineers, almost no one could match their quality of material that became known as fire-touched. Calais intently watched the seamstress to see how she would use her fire ability.

The elf focused on her tasks and didn't even notice Calais. She moves the needle in and out of the cloth as she guided the string into the seams. The needle moved easily through the cloth, but Calais saw nothing different. With the seamstress not revealing any secrets, Calais turned her attention back to the wagon where Drachid had disappeared.

"I finally found some clothes that would fit you," Drachid said after reappearing in the doorway to the covered wagon. "I hope you like it." He handed her a complete set of clothes. "You can go in the wagon over there and change. Please hurry, I want you to meet someone."

Calais gave her thanks and walked into another covered wagon full of general supplies such as rope, flour, and other vials. Pulling the door shut behind her, she stroked the soft clothing. She was shocked at how smooth and light the material was, but she knew fire-touched cloth was extremely durable. Removing the little clothes she was wearing, she quickly got dress before someone entered the wagon. Sporting a white shirt and a red long jacket with black trim, she also wore black pants and boots. With a proper side satchel and belt pouches, she could distribute her money so it was not all in one place. Noticing a letter at the bottom of the satchel with gold imperial coins, she placed it in her satchel to read later. Then, she delicately placed her drawings and the remaining parchment into the satchel. Taking her old clothing, she exited the wagon.

"I will take those," Drachid said. "He quickly tossed them into the fire pit. Calais didn't object and was actually relieved to see them burn. "Now, come. You must meet someone."

He led her to a group of female elves who wore only a chest wrap and brightly colored pants. Each of them was armed with two curved swords strapped to their back. The elves also had long ribbons of yellow and red cloth that drooped over their shoulders. If it weren't for you, my tribe would have been killed. I would have helped, but, as a dancer, I was called away on another mission."

"Thank you," Calais said. "I knew your tribe was innocent and had nothing to do with the corrupted. It was the right thing to do to send them to another realm." The Lord's Council and the imperial officers were extremely upset with Calais. It was only her talent and being part of the nobility that protected her. Despite the charges being dropped against her and the fire elf tribe, the rest of the summoners distanced themselves from her, even her old teacher. It was the reason she became a portal technician. She hated the thought of helping them kill innocent people, so she chose a new profession.

"We learned much being away from this realm," Drachid said.

"Calais, in honor of your sacrifice, I would like to give you a chance to watch our war dance," Elarid said.

"War dance," Calais said shocked. "Who are you going to war against?" The war dances were ancient rites that few outsiders witnessed. The elves used it to prepare themselves for the coming battle. It was said Sand Dancers used war dances to hone their prowess and powers before a great battle."

"I will explain afterwards," Drachid said. "Please sit down and watch. Elarid is one of the best Sand Dancers of her generation."

"Thank you, father," Elarid said. "I hope we meet again, Lord Conjurer." After another deep bow, she walked away and rejoined the other dancers.

The thought of the elves preparing for war was extremely disturbing to Calais. With Lady Enix trying to open portals to distant planes and corrupted killing everyone, she knew that the only way for everyone to survive in this realm was to overcome their differences and unite. Instead, each race isolated themselves more and more. The empire was pushing out all non-humans from its cities even after all their great contributions. The elves disappeared into the wilderness or exiled themselves to different realms. The orcs and barbarians were trying to kill each other even faster.

Quieting her thoughts, she made her way to sitting area around their camp fire. Drachid followed her and helped her find a suitable seat.

"Drachid, can I draw the dancers," Calais said politely before Drachid moved to another area of the camp.

"Of course, it is our honor to aid a great summoner as yourself."

Around them, she watched the elves set up a large tent to enclose the ritual and prevent outsiders from seeing it. The elves always kept the ritual a secret, but they would never say why. The Sand Dancers were a group that dated from the Age of Dragons. It was claimed by the fire elves that the Sand Dancers had freed them from the dragons' control. Human stories reported that the Sand Dancers were the elite forces of the dragons that slaughtered anyone who rebelled against them. In either case, Sand Dancers were greatly feared in combat by every group in the realm. With the tent erected and the small audience seated, the dancers entered the area and stood in a circle facing the fire.

Wispy, reed music played by a small group of musicians. The haunting melody was followed by drum beats. Then, the dancers moved in smooth; curving dance moves. They jumped and flowed around the fire until the slow music stopped. Drawing their swords and lifting them high into the sky, they waited motionless. Drums started up again but with a fast beat. The other musicians played low tones that gave the music a foreboding tone. The dancers' sword blades ignited into flames, and they spun around in a torrent of fire. They would jump and spin through the air. Sometimes, they would leap over the fire in synchronous patterns. While many moves seemed similar to combat moves, Calais saw nothing that was unusual or secretive. Then, everyone except Calais hummed. The drum beats got louder and faster. Suddenly, the dancers exploded into flames and became creatures of flames.

Calais couldn't believe it. The elves had turned their bodies into fire. From Calais' knowledge, only some of the corrupted had this power. No other creature in the realm could transmute themselves. The idea that the elves deep magic and the magic of the corrupted could be linked fascinated Calais but also terrified her. If the empire knew this, it would give them enough cause to destroy all the elves in the realm. No one would be safe. That is why they are so feared in battle. They would be impervious to damage, and their fires could rip through their enemies unabated. Focusing back on the fiery creatures, they continued to dance and move just as they had done before.

With her summoner's ability, she could see their essence through the bodies of flames. Taking out her parchment, she focused hard so she could draw the dancers quickly. With the audience still humming with the loud drum cadence, Calais' parchment became filled with the dancers' fluid movements. She noticed that the flaming bodies were not just burning erratically, but the flames continued to follow the contours of the elves bodies and limbs. Each strand of hair was it's own flame that fanned around their heads. Once the drawing was done, Calais grabbed her seat as she breathed heavily. Very light headed, she glanced at the drawing to see it was almost an exact drawing of the dancers in their elven form with their blades on fire.

Looking back up, the dancers were spinning and moving faster and faster and then stopped. Their flames dissipated to reveal the dancers again as fire elves. Their clothes and weapons remained intact just as they were before the ritual. The music stopped, and the audience stopped humming. Sheathing their swords, they turned back to the fire and kneeled down. The rest of the audience hummed in a different tone while the dancers remained still. Appearing as if they were in a trance, the dancers focused on the fire in the middle of the tent. It slowly burned down into nothing leaving the tent dark. Each dancer stood up and raised their hands into the air. Conical flames burned above each of their fists. Then, the rest of the elves in the audience stood up and did the same with fires burning above each of their fists. The darkness sank away as the inside of the tent became filled with the bright flames.

"We must never forget," Drachid said in a loud voice.

"We will never forget," the audience responded.

Calais knew this phrase dated from the Age of Dragons. She had been told that the fire elves suffered greatly as slaves to the dragons and sacrificed almost everything to escape them. They repeated this phrase because they wanted none of their generations to forget their hard-won freedom and sacrifices. Unlike the air elves and the water elves, the fire elves had a deep reverence for the past. The fists of flames reminded them they would all fight to the end to defend their freedoms at all cost. It was another sign they were preparing for battle. Wanting to know more about their plans, Calais waited for the ritual to end and watched the dancers file out of the tent. Then, the audience made their way out somberly. Putting her paper back in her satchel, Calais maneuvered her way through the exiting crowd to Drachid.

"What is your plan," Calais said. "Why are you preparing for war?"

"We are not at war," Drachid said. "We must be always prepared for it, especially now. Your empire has sent several bureaucrats and a contingent of imperial guard to test this city for their great protection plan. Some people on the city council would swear allegiance to the empire for their protection. Others want freedom from the empire and protect the city on their own. I am here to persuade the city to be independent. We would offer them protection as long as their city maintained open trade with all.

With all the corrupted attacks outside the city, many people fear that the city will be destroyed and is seeking the empire's protection."

Calais wondered if the coins they had found on the dead bodies were related to the corrupted's attacks. "Please wait here for a moment," Calais said to Drachid as she searched her satchel for the mysterious letter. "I found something on my way here."

She found the letter and examined it closely. It had a broken imperial seal on it. Opening the letter, it discussed in vague terms about an arrangement that more caravans needed to be attacked. It continued to promise land and money if the city agreed to join the empire. If it were to the corrupted, Calais knew this agreement would have angered them greatly since they believed everything already belonged to them. Looking further down the letter, it was only signed as a concerned friend for Yellow City. Finding nothing else on the letter, she gave it Drachid that studied it himself.

"I cannot go to the city council since I am wanted by the empire," Calais said. "You must take it to them and tell them that your scouts found this outside Yellow City along with these coins. This will prove that the empire or someone else is trying to manipulate Yellow City."

"I know about the corrupted and how they frighten the humans. But, the human who wrote this is looking for something more than protection. The political alliances in Yellow City are tenuous. Someone is playing a dangerous game, and I will stop this scheme before the city is tricked into giving up it's soul."

"Thank you, chief," she said. "Here are the coins. I need enough money to book passage and get supplies."

She transferred the money to another satchel. Drachid took the money and the letter. He carefully hid both items within his robes. Calais bid him and his family farewell. Then, she made her way out of the camp and to the airship station. If imperial guards were in the city, she had to hurry before they found her or her friends.

*   *   *   *

She entered the airship station and quickly scanned the room. The waiting room was a large empty area with three people standing in line at the counter. Behind the counter, a large bearded man with round glasses was selling tickets. Further back, Calais watched several clerks moving around the back room full of book ledgers and tall stacks of parchment. She proceeded to stand in line when she heard a familiar voice.

"There you are," Denarith said. He walked through the door she had just come through. "I am glad I caught you in time."

"Done already," Calais sneered at him. "I knew you were fast, but I didn't think you were that fast."

179

"Are you still mad at me," Denarith said confused. "You got to let that stuff go. I hit things, and it always makes me feel better."

Calais thought of several retorts but kept her mouth shut. She wondered if she should just let the imperial guard have him while Estasia and her escape. While a small part of her seriously considered the action, she knew it was wrong and decided to let it slide for now. "We don't have time for this," she said pointedly. "Imperial guards are in the city, so we have to leave before they catch us." She was still too annoyed to care about who might have heard her.

"Good news," Denarith said. "I already got us passage. Come with me to get Estasia and I will explain further."

Surprised, Calais followed Denarith out of the station and down the street. With it being midday, they had to weave through the bustling crowd. Everyone was so engrossed in their tasks that a bomb wouldn't have stopped them. Fortunately, most people gave the champion a large berth that made it easier to walk down the road.

"I didn't want to say anything in the station if there were spies," Denarith said.

"I thought you just bashed spies' heads in when you found them," Calais said.

"I do, but we don't have time," Denarith said. "The imperial guard were at the inn when I went to get Estasia." The Red Horse Inn was situated near the skydock and was considered one of the premier locations for nobility to stay at. It didn't take long for them to get within eyesight of the inn. "It looks as though they are still there. Quickly hide over there." They ducked behind a large wagon. Since no guards or militia men were marching to them, Calais figured they hadn't been seen.

"What is the plan now," Calais said. They had to get Estasia out of there before the imperial guard discovered her. Their options were limited. When Denarith didn't immediately respond, she glared back at him.

"You can disguise yourself as a harlot and then dress Estasia as a harlot to get you both out," Denarith said thoughtfully.

"That's a terrible plan," Calais said. There were so many holes in his idea that Calais didn't want to even think about it. "Besides, I got new clothes, and I will not lose them again. You should dress like the harlot."

"I think a bull-headed harlot would be a little noticeable," Denarith said.

"Oh trust me," Calais said. "You get them drunk enough, and they won't notice."

"I just had an idea," Denarith said amazed at himself. Calais cocked only an eyebrow waiting. "In this area, some of the women talk about an underground network of tunnels where wine and liquor sellers store their barrels to keep them cool. They use those tunnels to move the wine to different locations. They call the tunnels the Barrel Runs.

Calais was astonished. He actually came up with a good idea that made sense. "So we got to another location then sneak through the tunnels to the inn where we grab Estasia and escape."

"So you can be devious," Denarith smiled.

"What airship do we have tickets for," Calais said.

"We have to get to the Dawn's Tribute," Denarith said. "It is on Skywalk 4, Tower B. The captain is a friend of mine."

"Do you know where another entrance is to the Barrel Runs," Calais said.

"I have something in mind," Denarith said. "Follow me."

Calais was worried about following Denarith, especially after the gate. Taking a deep breath, she tried to relax while following the champion down a few side streets. Luckily, they didn't encounter any imperial guards or bureaucrats. When they got to their final destination, Calais became worried again.

They were standing in front of a brothel with loud music and laughter. It was a two-story inn with windows all around it. Some windows were open while others were closed. Calais didn't look at the windows any closer because she didn't want to see anything. Loud music, laughter, and cheering filled the air around the brothel. People wondered in an out of various social classes. Several women were hanging out around the door calling out to passerby's. As soon as they saw Denarith, they all quickly called for him to come back and play.

"I am not going in there," Calais said.

"We don't have to go in there," Denarith said waving back at the girls. "There is a side door to the basement that we can use."

"How do you know that?" Calais said following him around the house into a deserted back alley.

"They use it for special guests," Denarith said. He knocked on it twice, and a woman opened it. She greeted him and led them down into the dark basement. It was filled with pipes, barrels, and crates. The only way out of the room was a dark tunnel, a stairway leading up, and a metal door. The door was guarded by a large man with thick leather armor. He didn't change his expression, but just watched them.

"I am Denarith," Denarith said ducking around the pipes. "Lady Darria is expecting us,"

"I will let her know you are here," the woman said. She wore a light blue dress similar to the ones that the other women were wearing outside the house. She unlocked the metal door, opened it and then closed it behind her. It was too quick for Calais to get a glimpse inside the dark room.

"Hey Kol," Denarith said to the large man. "Here's a couple of coins to let her know I changed my mind." Denarith handed the large man several coins, and the man nodded. Before Calais could ask, Denarith led her down the dark tunnel. Looking back, the large man said nothing or even move.

The tunnel was dark and long. It was mostly carved rock and clay with the occasional wooden beams for ceiling support. The moist air and rock made the tunnel cold. After a while, they came to a locked door. Denarith quickly smashed the lock and opened it to reveal a large store room with several wine racks, barrels, and crates. It had several other locked doors around the room.

"Which way," Denarith said turning to Calais.

"I have no idea," Calais said. "I have never been down here."

"I am a totem of the great bull," Denarith said proudly. "I am not a ground hog."

"If I would have known I would navigate down here, I would have made some notes about the surface streets and buildings," Calais said. Frustrated, she looked around the room and found some signs. "Look, they are actually smart, unlike us with no maps or compass. They put up signs. We go through that door." When she pointed to the correct door, Denarith smashed it's lock and walked through first.

"I knew you would find us a way there," Denarith said. Calais shook her head annoyed and followed him through another long dark tunnel. It was much the same as last one. When they arrived at the basement, it was similar to the other one except it didn't have a mysterious door. No one was in the basement, so Denarith moved up the stairs first with Calais following.

The door opened to a hallway with a warm yellow glow. Gold fixture lamps decorated the hallway walls, and the floor had a red carpet. With no one in the hallway, they closed the door, and walked down the hall where it opened up to a larger room. Along the way, they carefully checked several closed doors for ambushes. Then, they saw an open door.

Looking into the room, Calais found it was full of people dining at large round tables. Servants scurried around the tables filling cups and taking plates. Most people were well-dressed and talking among each other. A table in the corner of the room was filled with imperial bureaucrats and an imperial guard. Not paying attention to the door, Calais quickly moved past the open doorway. Denarith looked around and just shrugged his shoulders. Unable to hide or sneak, he walked casually by the door. Then, they waited on the other side with Calais checking to see whether any of the imperial personnel were coming to them. When she saw them still sitting at the table, she breathed a sigh of relief and started down the hall. Suddenly, they heard Estasia's laugh.

Looking back into the dining room, Calais saw Estasia sitting at one of the tables near the imperial bureaucrats. Luckily, they didn't notice her since her back was turned to them. Not wanting to draw attention to herself, she grabbed a nearby servant's arm.

"I need your help," Calais said. "My friend, Estasia, is dining presently. We received an important message at the front desk that requires her immediate attention. Would you let her know, right away?" Calais described Estasia's appearance and casually pointed to the table. The servant agreed and proceeded into the dining room. Calais and Denarith made their way out of the hallway and into the inn's foyer.

The foyer had large crystal chandelier hanging from the ceiling. The exterior wall was covered in large windows looking out onto the dusty streets. Rest of the room was covered in light yellow paint with a red carpet. A well-dressed man stood behind the counter speaking with a couple that had just entered the foyer through a pair of double doors. Chairs and small end tables littered most of the room. With nowhere to hide, Calais told Denarith to hide somewhere outside while she waited for Estasia. He grumbled and left the foyer. Calais stepped up to the counter and waited patiently for her turn. The clerk politely let her know that she would be helped soon and Calais just nodded. Brushing her black hair back, she watched for Estasia from the corner of her eye.

Estasia finally appeared in the foyer and made her way to the counter. Subsequently, a man stopped her. Calais tensed when she saw the man's imperial uniform. "Lord Master Estasia, I presume," he said with a deep voice. He had a large belly with a flush face. They could probably out run him if needed.

"You are mistaken, sir," Estasia said innocently. "I am Lady Ashlynn Verrakyd." Calais shuttered when Estasia said one of the most feared baronies names. If the Verrakyd barony learned of her deception, it would cause Estasia a lot more problem.

"I apologize, my lady," the man said. He bowed and went back to the dining room.

Estasia made her way to the counter. "I believe I have a message," she said to the clerk. Before the clerk could respond, Calais turned to Estasia.

"I am the message," Calais said.

"What a beautiful outfit," Estasia crooned. "Where did you get it?"

"That's not important," Calais interrupted. "We have to leave. Denarith found us a ride."

"I hope it's not a wagon full of manure," Estasia said dourly.

They left the inn, but the fat bureaucrat had returned. This time, he wasn't alone with another bureaucrat and an imperial guard standing behind him. "Lady Verrakyd, I need to have a word with you," he said calmly. They continued walking out the door pretending not to hear him. "Maybe, I should call you Lord Master Estasia, after all." Then, they both stopped but still did not turnaround. Calais wiggled her fingers at Estasia indiscreetly. Estasia shook her head. "Lady Verrakyd has been dead for six months." Calais sought she heard cows mooing in the distance. "It is not common knowledge, but she was killed in a tragic accident." Then, Calais thought she felt a slight trimmer on the ground. "Now, turnaround and come with us. There is no reason to make a scene in this lovely establishment." The ground trimmer grew. Calais realized what was happening.

"Run," she yelled.

Estasia and Calais threw the doors open to reveal a large herd of cattle stampeding towards the inn. Calais noticed a large sculpture of a horse painted red. Seeing the imperial guard and bureaucrats rushing to them, Calais pulled Estasia onto the red horse while a sea of cows and bulls moved past them. The cattle crushed the inn as the inhabitants screamed. Many of them jumped out of windows. Everyone else in the area was scattering while several militia men were chasing the cows in the distance. The inn crumbled under the flow of cattle. With wood and glass falling around them, they were surprised by a rope ladder falling on top of them.

Looking up, Calais saw the curved hull of an airship floating above them. At the top of the rope latter, she could see a man waving to them to climb the ladder. Not having much choice, Calais climbed the ladder. Estasia tried to follow but almost fell off the ladder. Estasia screamed and held onto a rung with one hand. Reaching down, Calais helped Estasia get both hands back on the ladder. Rapping their hands and feet around the rungs, they started to pull the ladder up. The ship slowly rose into the sky as they were reeled onto the main deck.

"Welcome to the Dawn's Tribute," a man in a blue uniform said. "I am Captain Wyllik, and you know Denarith." Denarith stepped up and helped Estasia and Calais to their feet.

"That was great," Denarith said. "I wish I could have seen their stuffy nobles faces."

"Thanks for the help," Calais said, "but did you have to destroy the entire inn and part of the town."

"I didn't do that," Denarith said. "I was trying to get to Wyk to bring the ship here. I didn't have time to unleash a stampede on the town, but I wished I did." He started laughing.

Calais looked back at the fading town and wondered who had helped them.

CHAPTER TWENTY-THREE

The Ninth Spire

Monty stood on the Ninth Spire's deck. It was like any other galleon-like deck. It had three tree-like masts with webs of rope between the masts and deck. An engraved, gold-ladened railing created a border between the deck and the dim blue sky with scattered, puffy clouds. Maliki was standing on the poop deck while giving commands to ghosts.

Looking around, Monty saw ghosts everywhere. Some ghosts moved up and down the rigging. Other ghosts carried large barrels or chests along the deck until they disappeared into a stairwell. Despite Monty's arrival, they did not notice her presence or respond to her. They would even walk through her companions despite their objections. Their faces were expressionless, and their eyes looked at nothing but seemed to see everything. They made no sound unless they moved a part of the rigging or dropped a barrel. Monty heard only the wind until Maliki approached.

"My crew will take you to your quarters," Maliki said. "Once I am ready, I shall call a dinner where we can discuss our plans further. Until then, I bid you a good rest." As they acquiesced to his invitation, he turned to Monty. "Please accompany me. We have much to discuss."

The guard and militia men who were killed by Maliki, materialized as ghosts wearing the same clothing and armor. Looking at Monty, they had the same dead expression as the other ghosts. They dispersed and moved to some unseen task. "I think it would be best if I went with Nora and Djinn," Monty said hesitantly. She didn't want to be alone with the strange elf or his ghosts.

"This is not a request," Maliki said patiently. "You are the last remnant of my good friend, Montague. As such, I need your help."

"Go ahead child," Nora said looking at Maliki with uncertainty. "Djinn and I will be nearby if you need help."

"Please follow me," Maliki said. While he seemed cold and distant, Monty sensed a warm tone when he said Montague's name. Looking back at Nora again, she gave Monty a silent nudge and comforting wink. Following him, they walked to the upper deck. Maliki stopped and watched a section of the deck expand upward into a cave-like entrance leading to downward spiraling stairway.

"How did you do that," Monty said astonished.

"The ship is a part of me, and I am a part of the ship," Maliki said while flexing his left arm armored hand. "I can make the ship into anything I want, and I can hide its many secrets. At the bottom of the stairs, is one of those secrets."

Monty walked down the stairs following Maliki. It seemed to go down into a bottomless black pit. The only light was from the entrance and a few unseen red lanterns. When the entrance closed up, it became extremely dark and Monty could barely see the steps. After walking down a few turns of the staircase, they finally came to a door. It appeared to be a red stained wooden door with a gold knob. Maliki opened it gently with soft white light pouring out of its seams. Monty followed Maliki, and the door shut itself behind her.

The room was full of stars. They were not just on the distant ceiling or walls, but they actually floated around her in midair. She could even touch them and they would simply float away before moving back into their proper position. Along the walls, she followed blue glowing lines as they formed strange patterns. In the center of the room, was a massive chair that faced a wall that appeared as a black crystalline mirror.

"Welcome to my observatory," Maliki said. "From here, I can see all the realms and planes I have visited. Sometimes, I can even see what is currently happening in a realm. This is what navigators do. We explore places, people and artifacts. We learn and record it so it might not be forgotten."

"You have been too all these places," Monty said in awe. She tried counting the stars but gave up after losing track of the moving stars. "What are these places like?"

"Unfortunately, the same," Maliki said. "Good and evil continue the same, predictable war in each realm. What is remarkable is how each person fights it personally and on the battlefield? Each of them has a part. A widow's crying despair can lead to a town being destroyed while laughter can empower an outnumbered army to vanquish all its foes."

"What does that mean?"

"It is the reason I came back when you called me through your aerogu." He pointed to her necklace. "Lady Enix is one of the many that is trying to destroy this realm in the name of evil. This time, I have chosen to fight against her."

"This time? What do you mean by that?" Monty worried she might have made another mistake by going with this navigator.

"So they haven't told you," Maliki said, turning to her with a raised eyebrow. "Let me show you." On the wall in front of them, she watched her reflection in the black crystalline mirror be replaced by pictures of villages and the corrupted. "Two hundred years after we defeated the dragons, there were reports of the first corrupted. At first, they were only a few. The Lords' Council dispatched them and believed they were darklings... demon spawn. Then, they got more numerous over the decades. The Lords' Council realized that the people themselves were actually changing. After a group of corrupted killed the last emperor twelve years ago, the Lord's Council and the four governors formed a group that would study and eradicate these creatures.

"This team was lead by Lady Enix, a planar scientist, and Montague, a great engineer." The picture on the wall showed a beautiful, exotic woman in a feathered cloak. Her deep, penetrating stare caused Monty to shiver. "The rest of us were picked by the leaders of our orders. Not for our purity, but for our power, and darkness. We were twisted souls who followed Lady Enix's plan blindly. Simply, we were slaughtering innocent people who might turn into corrupted and collected their souls in soulstones." The images showed her friends killing hundreds of people and destroying entire villages. Nora was striking down people with lightning as Caezik struck others with black arrows. A black haired girl summoned monstrous beasts that tore many people apart. Maliki fired white energy bolts from his metal arm that incinerated anyone they hit. Nash slashed and stabbed people with swords while Marek shredded others with his chain whips. Other people she didn't recognize worked in concert with her friends and left a wake of carnage. The horrible sights caused Monty to turn away. Looking back at Maliki, she saw him watching the images with a sad expression.
" Were all those people going to turn into corrupted?" Monty said.

"None of them would turn into corrupted," Maliki said. "Lady Enix had deceived us. With these soulstones, Lady Enix and Montague were to supposed unravel the secrets of the corrupted. Over time, Montague and Djinn learned of Lady Enix's true plan.

"She wanted the soulstones to use as an energy source to unlock the Dragon Shield and unleash hell onto this realm. In the beginning, only Marek, Nora and I believed Montague and Djinn. The others disagreed. Seeking out an old associate of mine, the angel Enikus, he helped us convince the others. The dragon-cursed siblings and their family friend,

Estasia, joined our opposition against Lady Enix. Then, we convinced a bullish totem champion, Nash, Baron Verrandrin, and Tomas."

"The baron became a good man," Monty said bewildered.

"Not exactly," Maliki said with a smirk. "Like many of us at the time, he served only him and his own interest. He felt that he could gain more wealth and power by stealing Lady Enix's power and artifacts, especially the soulstones. They were the key. Montague and Djinn had created a bold plan to use the soulstones to capture her. When she tried to open a portal to another plane, Lady Enix was vulnerable. We sabotaged the ritual and used the soulstones against her to imprison her inside another plane. In the process, a soulstone merged with each of us, so we could access it's power. Afterwards, the group disbanded and we went our separate ways. The empire called us heroes for stopping the portal and imprisoning the demon. No one was a hero. We can never atone for all the innocent blood on our hands."

"If she was imprisoned, how did she get out."

"Someone released her. I don't know who, but it doesn't matter. Now, she wants her soulstones back to reopen the portal. The only way she can get them is by killing each of us. When we die, the soulstone will release from our body and return to the Fifth Spire. Many of us have already been killed."

"What is my part in this?"

"It is not for me to say or know. That is why we shall meet the angel. We must not fail, or another plane will be taken by evil. It is the reason that this plane is never visited or had communications from other planes. There are few good realms left." Most of the stars around the room turned red with only a handful still blue. "They can't kill the Divine, but they can take away everything he loves."

*   *   *   *

Monty leaned on the rail of the main deck while she watched wisps of clouds float by. Below her, she could see dots of trees and buildings. Sometimes, she would try to identify the dark specks on the ground to take her mind off the horrible images she had just seen. Then, they would come back. Her friends had such great power, but they used it for evil. Her thoughts were interrupted by a familiar voice.

"You missed lunch, child," Nora said. "You should eat to keep your strength up."

"Why did you kill all those people," Monty said angrily.

"So Maliki told you," Nora said with a sigh. "It was a complicated time. As a druid, I am supposed to protect nature and the cycle of life. I watched the humans with their ethaerium inventions destroy animals and forests for research and to mine more nodes. I became angry and hateful to the

189

humans. As a human myself, I knew their ambition all too well. While Lady Enix did trick us, a part of me knew it was wrong, but another part of me wanted to hurt the humans. Watching their villages burn, I wanted to feel satisfaction at our victories. Instead, all I felt was anguish and despair. When Montague told me about Lady Enix, I thought that by helping them to stop her plan and imprison the demon I would be relieved of my guilt. It didn't happen. While grateful that we stopped her, I still feel the pain in my soul for each person I murdered."

Monty's anger melted away, and she pitied the cat. "I am sorry for being angry with you." Walking over to Nora, she hugged Nora.

"You are right to be angry," Nora said. "We made the wrong choice and hurt many people. Lady Enix gave us an excuse." She paused for a moment as Monty released her. "I made a promise to you. If you want me to leave, I will go away and never bother you again."

"No," Monty said. "I want you to stay, but you have to promise me you won't do anything like that again."

"I promise, child," Nora said while bowing her head to Nora. "I shall never harm an innocent person again."

"What about Djinn," Monty said. "I don't remember seeing any pictures of him hurting people."

"Unlike the rest of us, he didn't actually kill anyone in the villages. He claimed he had already seen too much death. Before he was a wizard, he was the son of an orc cheiftain. His tribe was one of the more warlike tribes that constantly fought wars with the empire, barbarians and other orc tribes. He saw much death growing up. Luckily, he developed his power innately and his tribe banished him. Another wizard took him in and taught the orc to be a chaos wizard. The idea of an orc wizard seems silly and dangerous, but Djinn is a rather unique individual. It was because of the carnage he saw growing up that made him value life. I always suspected that Djinn knew Lady Enix's true nature."

"Did someone say may name," Djinn said walking up from a lower deck.

"Oh I said your name," Nora said looking back at Djinn. "I said that you knew who Lady Enix was from the beginning."

"Once you see evil, it is much easier to recognize," Djinn said. "Have you heard from Maliki on his search for Enikus?"

"No," Nora said. Monty folded her arms and was becoming impatient. "It takes time to find celestial beings, child. Even navigators have a difficult time."

Feeling frustrated, Monty walked back to the rail and watched the ground. It had been several hours, and she was anxious to get off the ship. Besides Maliki's cold nature, she didn't like the ghosts and avoided them anytime they came near her. They seem to be everywhere on the ship which made her anxious. She hummed to herself to soothe her nerves.

"What is that song, little one?" Djinn said.

"I don't know," Monty said. "I have never heard it before. It just comes to me."

"To sing a song that has never been sung is marvelous," Djinn said. "In a way, it reminds me of the orc chants of death and dismemberment."

"Don't listen to him," Nora said sleepily. Laying down on the deck, she yawned with a mouth full of sharp teeth. "It has a pleasant, sweet melody."

"There is nothing wrong with the orc chants," Djinn said proudly. "They are proud and noble songs that have led many orcs to their deaths and dismemberments. For an orc, it is one of the many ways to show his glory on the battlefield."

Maliki reappeared on the deck near Djinn. Everyone stared at him apprehensively. Wearing the solid gold plate over his eyes, he stared off into the distance for a moment. Then, he turned his gaze towards Monty. "We must suspend our search for Enikus. Our old friend, Caellan Pallendarr, is in trouble. I fear he may be killed soon."

"We must hurry if Caellan is in trouble," Djinn startled. "He cannot die."

"Who is he," Monty said.

"He is a paladin that helped us ten years ago," Nora said. "What's happened to him, Maliki?"

"He has been taken captive by wraiths," Maliki said. "Please hold onto the railing. It will be over soon." Maliki did nothing while everyone else gripped the railings and ropes. Nora continued to nap on the deck.

The ship jumped and shook with a heavy vibration. The surrounding sky melted away into a bright blue flash. After a moment of heavy shaking, she observed the blue glow around them fade away into a dark stormy sky. Near the ship, she saw a tall stone castle standing at the edge of a lake. Thick rain and lightning covered the surrounding area. Then, the surrounding sky exploded.

The ship veered through the explosions with some of them striking its invisible shield. As the ship convulsed with each hit, Maliki stood on the deck calmly while everyone else was holding on to some part of the ship. Through the thick smoke, Monty could see that the attack was coming from the castle itself. As before, beams of white energy lanced out of the ship's hull and struck the castle multiple times. Parts of the castle exploded into fire and smoke as large stone debris rained down into the lake. After a few exchanges of weapon fire, the castle stopped attacking.

"What just happened," Monty yelled through the rushing rain. Her hair and cloak were drenched in a matter of moments.

"He destroyed the castle's defenses," Djinn yelled back as he held onto his large-brimmed hat.

"Is the battle over," Monty said.

"No," Djinn said trying to point to the castle. "It just got worse." Like insects, the castle was covered in ghostly skeletons. The ship finally stopped above the castle, and the rushing wind died down. "It's not the wraiths that are the problem, but what's at the castle's gate." Then, Monty saw it. Lit by several torches, Monty watched a small army trying to break into the castle. "Each time a wraith touches a human; it drains them of their life force. If we don't hurry, the entire militia will turn into wraiths.

"Can they defeat the wraiths," Monty said somberly.

"Not without ethaerium weapons," Nash said as he joined them at the front of the ship. "Where do you think the wraethenu is hiding?"

"Like all pretentious evil creatures, he sits in the throne room," Maliki said. "Nash, you will help the militia down there while the rest of us will face the wraethenu directly."

"Not having to fight the wraethenu is an excellent plan," Nash said. "I am ready when you are."

"Monty can't fight," Nora objected. "She is not safe."

"As a maru, she is immune to their power and will not be in any danger," Maliki said. Surprised, Monty wondered what other powers she possessed.

"I don't care," Nora said. "Stay near me, child, and don't let them touch you."

Monty looked back at the smoldering castle covered with wraiths and began to hum softly to herself.

CHAPTER TWENTY-FOUR

Battle of Castle Krakenjall

Caellan stood in his dark, damp cell staring out a small window at the top of the cell. As the castle above him filled with battle cries and screams, he leaned against the wall watching for any signs of how the fight's status. He knew the local militia was storming the castle and trying to kill its master, and he hoped that Jarmal had brought the ethaerium cannons. Without them, Jerick would slaughter the militia. Returning to a small bench, he slumped forward as his past failures crept back in his mind. Angrily, he sneered back at them.

"I need a drink," he said with a soft gravely voice.

"A drink is the last thing you need my friend," a familiar voice said out of the darkness beyond his cell.

"No, Maliki, you are the last thing I want to see."

"I am sorry to disappoint," Maliki responded in his same aggravatingly even tone. "In fact, I am here to rescue you. Then, I was hoping you would help me destroy the ruler of this castle before he can spread death throughout the region. I assume you know how dangerous this wraethenu is?"

"Yes, I do. He was my friend and cursed with weakness. Just like me."

"Caellan, we have no time for this."

"I thought you were immortal. What do you care about time?"

"He has released his wraiths onto the militia," Maliki said in more urgent tone. "Their ethaerium cannons are still not in place. It is only a matter of time before the militia has been turned into more wraiths, and then they will overtake the villages in the region."

"In what deep, black hell, do you care about saving anyone? You forget, I know what you were before Enikus. I know all the lives you destroyed as a mercenary and as navigator. I know you can never wipe that away no matter how many people you save. So why try to save a village when you can just destroy rather than condemning their very souls?"

"What happened to you? Why have you allowed despair and anger to consume you?"

Quickly standing up, Caellan began to pace in his cell while still ignoring the failed screams of the militia. He stopped and looked at Maliki. Every year, it always seemed that more and more of Maliki was being covered in that strange bronze armor. It was almost as if he were turning into a part of the ship. For a slight moment, he almost felt sorry for the elf who would eventually be consumed by madness after losing all his humanity. Then, he heard the thundering ethaerium cannons firing at the castle. The ground shook, and dust fell from the ceiling. His wife was still up there.

"I lost Jewell," he breathed. "I couldn't see past my own sins to love my wife. So, she left me and joined Jerick's crusade against the nobility. Now, she has turned into one of them, and I don't know how to save her."

"So Jerick is the wraethenu and he turned her into one as well." Caellan just looked back at him. He didn't want to answer because he hated the truth. "You know she can't be saved. Once she excepted the dark powers, part of her soul was consumed. The rest of her soul will wither away over time and all that will remain is an evil creature. You can only release her so she may find peace."

"I will not kill my wife," Caellan yelled. "I will not kill Jerick. It is my fault they finished like this."

"You are a fool, paladin. He chose this path and so did she. It was their choice. You should know this if you remember your training. Your job is to protect those in need. Right now, those soldiers and the innocent villagers need you. We failed to save the innocents once before. Let us not repeat that mistake."

"I don't have the strength to do what you ask."

Maliki fired a beam of light out of his armored hand. It destroyed part of the cell door. Caellan just stood there watching pieces of the cell door collapse onto the floor. Despite his freedom, he did not move wondering if he even deserved to leave.

"You are free now," Maliki said. "You may not have the strength, but together we were powerful enough to banish a demon. Fight with us or leave. It has always been your choice, paladin. I will be in the throne room."

Caellan watched Maliki teleport away in a bright flash. He knew Maliki would kill Jerick and Jewell. If the wraethenu was killed, all its victims would also be destroyed including his wife. There had to be a way to cure them, but he needed time to find the answer. Meanwhile, he had to secure them to prevent anyone else from being harmed.

Leaving his cell, he grabbed his sword and ran up the stairs. Knowing that most of the fighting was in a different part of the castle, he quickly made his way to the kitchen. The castle was laid out very similar to his father's castle, so it didn't take him long to get there. Mostly, the kitchen was undisturbed and still in good condition. Looking at the food elevator, he knew it was the fastest way to get to the throne room. Using several large cast iron pots for the counterweight system, he was quickly pulled most of the way to the upper parts of the castle. Unfortunately, the rope stopped and he found himself stuck. Cursing at his situation, he climbed the rope. With his two-handed sword strapped to his back, he struggled in the small elevator space, and he cursed the rope, the rock and anything else he saw.

*   *   *   *

When Caellan reached the throne room, the battle was in full rage. Pulling himself from the small space, he rolled onto the floor and quickly stood up. His friend had not just summoned his wraiths to the fight, but he had also called skeletal warriors. They were mainly positioned in the large audience chamber. On an elevated circular platform, Jerick was standing next to the red cushioned and gold-framed throne. Behind it, a red curtain gently moved back and forth from the open windows that ran along the audience chamber. Outside the windows, Caellan shuttered when he saw a storm of wraiths still circling the castle. Drawing his sword, he quickly slashed through a nearby wraith. It shattered into a million pieces of light before fading away. Looking for the next foe to attack, he was taken aback to see his old friends.

He couldn't believe that Maliki would bring this circus into such a fight. The crazy, orc wizard Djinn was casting energy shields, strange fireballs and multicolored flowers. Despite their casualties and covered in pink flowers, the undead continued their relentless charge. The animal druid, Nora, crushed the undead as a black bear and then instantly turned into a cat or a bird to dodge their strikes. With swipes of claws and lightning flashing from her mouth, she destroyed more ranks of wraiths and skeletons. Maliki had his army of ghost sailors fighting the other undead. His old companions even had a strange three-foot tall statue that stayed in the back away from the fighting. Luckily, Maliki had not attacked Jerick. He still had a chance to save his friend.

Ducking and weaving through the diving wraiths, Caellan made his way to Jerick. Watching the battle calmly, Jerick did nothing while pacing in his long black and gold-lined robes. His chest armor was made from pieces of blackened bone. On top of his head, he wore the baron's golden crown. They must have been preparing for their supposed ceremony. As Caellan got close, he saw the creature crack a slight smile.

195

"You have finally made it," Jerick said. "Are you here to give my wife and I your blessing?"

"Do not do this, Jerick," Caellan pleaded. "It is not too late. Give up your power and become a human again. You still have time. My friends will destroy you if you don't."

"Let them try," Jewell said appearing from behind the red curtain. "We have a power greater than any lord. We will protect the barony from the conniving nobles and the aloof lords."

"This power is evil," Caellan said. "Don't give into it. It will only destroy you. You will become the same monsters that you are trying to destroy."

"You have said that before," Jewell said. "Would you sacrifice your power as a paladin and as a noble?"

"Yes," Caellan said softly. Jewell stepped back with a surprised look. "I would give it all up if it meant being there for the ones I love, whether it meant protecting them, holding them, or even laughing with them. I know now that I was wrong."

"You are too late, Caellan," Jewell said with remorse. "We had our chance. Now, I have a new life with Jerick."

"You can still be with Jerick," Caellan said. "Give up your powers, and we will let you go free. You can go anywhere you want in this realm, together. I won't stand in your way." Jewell hesitated and looked at Jerick. He glared at Caellan. "Let it go, Jerick. You are better than this. I have known you for a long time."

"Why should I surrender when I have armies at my disposal," Jerick said? "You haven't tasted the power that I have. If you knew how good it felt, you would not give it up either. I will keep it."

"You have made your decision," Maliki said walking to the throne. He was carrying one of his swords in his right hand and a limp skeleton in his left hand. Dropping the skeleton, he raised his sword at Jerick. Looking back at his best friend and wife, Caellan knew it would soon be too late. He couldn't stop Maliki, and he couldn't defeat Jerick without his armor. He knew the Divine would never get him back his armor for all his failures in life.

"Jerick," Caellan called out to his best friend. "You must escape. Maliki will destroy you."

"I don't fear him," Jerick sneered. "His power pales in comparison to mine. Don't worry, I will be merciful and destroy him quickly so he doesn't suffer. "

"And I must destroy you if I will be free," the woman who used to be Jewell said. Using her sword, she lunged at Caellan. He easily deflected her attacks, but he would not attack back. He could never kill her.

"Stop this, Jewell!"

"Never, I will make you pay. I hate you!"

Still blocking each of her attacks, he moved to the side so he could see where Jerick and Maliki were. Jerick had created a sword of shadow and stood ready to fight Maliki. Undaunted, Maliki continued to move forward without even raising his sword. Jewell yelled at him, but he ignored her. He had to get over there somehow.

"Jewell," Caellan pleaded. "I have to stop Maliki. He can destroy Jerick. Please, help me."

"No, I will never listen to you again."

She moved much quicker this time. Caellan could barely parry her rapid attacks. With one successful strike from her blade, she would cut through his body unimpeded. He was running out of options. Finally, he chose. He parried and then thrusted his sword into her stomach. She collapsed around the blade and looked at him with almost human eyes again. Fond, agonizing memories of their marriage and courtship flooded back into his mind. Tears ran down her cheeks as she smiled at him. It was the first time in a long time. With Jewell wounded, he might have a chance to save Jerick.

Caellan looked back at Maliki. Maliki quickly parried all the sword attacks from Jerick. Maliki was the best swordsman in Tallendrall and no one came close to his skill. Surprised and shocked by Maliki's skill, Jerick let his guard down briefly. It gave Maliki enough time to grab Jerick by the throat with his left armored hand. Maliki effortlessly raised Jerick off the ground and impaled him with his sword in the right hand. With Jerick stunned, it gave Maliki a chance to use his soul reaping.

"Don't do it," Caellan screamed.

Maliki was one of the most powerful navigators and could soul reap a small crowd or even absorb a demon. However, they had to control these souls and their memories or a powerful soul could overtake him. That is why navigators never absorbed a dragon or demon. Eventually, the demon would take them over, and they would become the demon. Wraethenu's powers came from demons, but Maliki was too powerful to be bothered by just a piece of a demon.

Caellan watched his best friend, Jerick, slowly dissolve into nothing as Maliki finished ripping away all his soul and memories. For a moment, he thought he saw Jerick with a peaceful expression. Then, Jerick was gone forever. Caellan turned back to his wife who was also dissolving. With the wraethenu dead, he would lose her forever. Choking back tears, Caellan watched his one true love fade away. The rest of the wraiths vanished while the skeletons crumbled onto the floor. Then, his anger overtook his grief.

"I curse you all you wretched people," Caellan screamed. "I hope rats eat out your entrails."

"Who is that," the white small statue asked.

"A pious holy knight," Djinn said. "His name is Lord Knight Caellan Pallendarr. He is a paladin, a soldier of the Divine."

"Maliki," Caellan said as anguish swelled in his chest. "I could have saved her!" Dropping his sword onto the ground, he fell to his knees. It was all too much for him. After everything he had done, it was never enough. No matter how much he tried, it was never enough. From losing his father to losing his wife, he cried out to the heavens as he wished for death to crush him and take him away to his damnation.

Despite the cold stone skin of the small statue, Caellan found himself in the warm embrace of the strange small statue. Her short arms were barely long enough to spread around his broad shoulders. She didn't say anything and just held him.

He barely noticed her touch until he felt something inside him. It was like her warmth of love and peace was flowing directly into his cold soul. Almost painful at first, it reminded him of wearing his armor like the Divine was touching his soul. Startled, Caellan leapt to his feet while pulling himself out of the strong embrace. "What is this? What are you doing to me?"

"Montague made her," Nora said. "Her name is a Monty."

"Montague? Is this what he spoke of in his letters?"

"Montague is dead and has taken his secrets with him," Nora said.

"How? Who killed him?"

"We don't have much time," Maliki said. "Lady Enix has escaped her imprisonment and is trying to reopen the portal."

"So her wickedness has returned to this realm. It is only a matter of time before this realm is flooded by demons."

"Unless we can stop it," Djinn said. "There may be another way to stop the demon, but we must work together."

"Then, you will do it without me," Caellan said. "I am threw saving this realm. Almost everything I loved is gone. I have nothing left to fight for."

"You are still being a fool, paladin," Maliki said. "This fight is not about you or me. It is about the innocent. Don't turn your back on them."

"No, I am a failure," Caellan said. "I will not fail anyone else again. Now, let me be." Caellan sheathed his sword and made his way to the stairwell that led to the entrance of the castle.

"He should have come with us," Monty said.

"Leave him alone, child," Nora said. "He still has many more battles to fight. When he is ready, he will come back to us."

*   *   *   *

Caellan walked out of the castle and stood in the courtyard. It had stopped raining with only the occasional flashes of lightning. Beyond the gate, he could see the militia carrying their dead to burning pyres. Caellan became even more disheartened when he saw all the pyres along the lake shore. Many people died trying to fight the undead. He still remembered the screams from his cell before Maliki came. He didn't realize that the battle had gone so badly. Stepping closer to the gate, he looked among the few standing soldiers for his friend, Jarmal. After a moment, he finally found his friend talking to some soldiers. Walking quickly, he made his way around the courtyard, but was stopped by a voice he had hoped he would never hear again.

"Congratulations on your victory," Lady Enix said. She was sitting on top of the wall next to the gate. She only wore a black chest wrap and a breechcloth. On her back, she had large feathery wings made up of blue, red, and yellow feathers. Her bronzed skin seemed to shimmer even in the gloomy light of the storm. "The great paladin defeated the might wraethenu."

"Did you give Jerick his powers," Caellan said bitterly. The thought that she had manipulated the whole situation with Jerick and Jewell infuriated him.

"No, that was not I," Lady Enix said. "I wish it had been me. I would not have made it so easy. There are other demons in this realm luring you mortals to their doom."

"It is too convenient for you not to have a part in this," Caellan said. "I know you did something."

"Very well, I will tell you since you can't do anything about it now," Lady Enix said with a sly grin. "It is true that I did not have any direct hand with your friend Jerick and Jewell. However, I might have helped the baron and baroness with their village problem."

"That is why they could summon fire creatures," Caellan said thoughtfully. "You gave them enough power to be dangerous but not enough to defeat Jerick. You knew this would happen."

"I knew nothing," Lady Enix said while hopping off the wall and lightly landing in the courtyard. "You mortals are so unpredictable. I certainly suspected that if I nudged Jerick here or the baron there that this might have happened. Jerick could have always renounced his power and became normal again. You just never know."

"I could have saved them," Caellan said looking at the sky.

"Not likely," Lady Enix said approaching Caellan. "You mortals love their power and will do anything to keep it as if you have any real say in the matter. Let me help you forget this matter. I can be very persuasive." She ran a finger slowly down his cheek.

"Away from me," Caellan said pushing her away. "I know your games, witch."

"That is so sad," Lady Enix said while she circled him. "I was hoping you would take the fun way instead of the hard way. I know how much fun paladins can be. I have seduced many over the centuries."

"Do what you must," Caellan said. "I will not comply."

"Oh very well," Lady Enix sighed. "You will be my prisoner and I will take you back to the Fifth Spire." She paused for a moment and then smiled. "Of course, I have to make one more stop, so I can kill your sister, Calais."

Before Caellan could attack Lady Enix, everything went black.

CHAPTER TWENTY-FIVE

A Day of Tribute

As the crew of the Dawn's Tribute got their ship set on the correct course, Calais wondered around the ship getting herself familiar with it. Below the main deck, she found mostly cargo with a couple of crew rooms, the kitchen galley and cannons. The ship was not heavily armor and only had a few cannons below the main deck with a turret and a few cannons above deck. The most investing detail about the ship was all the secret compartments. In each of the rooms, there was at least one if not more hidden panels. Most would have missed the small details but summoners had to have an eye for the minutiae. Some of the panels were empty while others had valuable cargo such as statuettes, jewelry and imperial coins. Calais took none of it and just closed the panels back up. Normally, ships have a few secret compartments, but they were so numerous that Calais could only think of one thing: smugglers. Since nosy passengers made most smugglers paranoid, Calais made her way back up to the main deck.

She always like watching the clouds wisp by as the wind brushed against her face and hair. With the new jacket from Drachid, she stayed comfortable in the cool air. Looking over the side, she watched towns, fields and forests pass below them. The crew was finishing with the rigging and Estasia was laughing with Captain Wyllik and Denarith. Instead of joining them, Calais leaned on the rail at the edge of the ship enjoying the scenery. It didn't take long for Estasia to wonder over to her.

"What do you think of the captain," Estasia said. "He is a very handsome man."

"He is all right, but not really my type," Calais confessed.

"Not your type," Estasia said. "Do you even know what your type is?"

"Do you not have a type?" Calais countered with a smile.

"Why should I be so picky with my wedding fast approaching?" Estasia said. "I have to enjoy life before I am chained to a rich house and husband."

"If you want to be free, then call off the wedding. As a lord, you can renounce your nobility and have all the freedom you want."

"That's what you don't understand. I don't like being a lord or gallivanting around the realms. I enjoy beautiful houses and furniture. I want jewelry and the most fashionable dresses. I desire balls and suitors fawning over me. I need a husband who will protect me and fulfill my deepest desires."

"Nothing sounds more boring than dresses, balls and suitors."

"No interest in suitors? I saw the way you were looking at Rev. Being an air elf, he would definitely keep things interesting under the sheets."

"Estasia! I can't believe you said that." Calais tried not to blush while trying to forget such thoughts.

"Like I said, you should have a little fun while you still have a chance. You won't always be pretty or single."

"I have fun," Calais argued. "I enjoy traveling the world and seeing all its strange wonders, people and lands."

"You mean trouncing through mud to find rocks while being bitten by insects and being sucked on by parasites."

"Funny, that sounds just like one of your balls except for the mud part."

"Oh ha ha, you think you are just so funny. After I get married, I will take you to some of the grandest balls and show you how much fun they can be."

"I noticed something. You never talk about your future husband. All I know is that it's Kris Ryvell, one of the cousin of Baron Ryvell. Have you actually met him and talked very much?"

"Of course, I met him. We have talked extensively. I went with him to a few balls a year ago. He is a gentleman, successful merchant and a celebrated artist."

"I've heard he is one of the more honest and good nobles available for marriage."

"He is a good, decent man. From what I have heard, and he has told me, he doesn't involve himself with nefarious activities like the other nobles have engaged in."

"That's great. It sounds like you found a great husband who will take care of you. So, is he a good kisser?"

"Oh yes, he is a fantastic kisser," Estasia said distantly.

"What's the problem?" Calais said as she noticed something bother Estasia.

"It's just that he is a little boring. He is all business and no play. At times, it feels like he is more interested in his business deals or making a sculpture than spending time with me."

"That's why you want to have fun. You think you will be sucked into a boring life and never have fun again. Trust me, your life will never be boring. Your best friend is a summoner who can't stay out of trouble and you are friends with barbarians, orcs and wizards that will always muck up your life. Then, you add in grand balls and their awful politics. At the end, you will wish you had a boring life."

"For some reason, it feels like I am going to a prison, even though this has been what I wanted all my life."

"Look, if you want to have fun, then I will not stop you. As a friend, I just want you to be careful. Your decisions could backfire. I think you should honor Kris and not do anything stupid like going too far with the captain."

"You are right, Calais. I will start doing that tomorrow. Today, I am supposed to have lunch and tea with the captain in his quarters."

"Ladies, will you join us for some dancing," one of the sailors called out. A couple of them started to play a jig on various musical instruments while the other sailors clapped, sang and danced around.

Smiling, Estasia grabbed the sailors hand and began dancing around the deck with him. After a few turns, another sailor took her hand and danced with her while the previous sailor continued to clap and sing. They tried to get Calais to join, but she promptly refused. More sailors danced with Estasia as they laughed and smiled. Denarith and Captain Wyllik were also clapping and singing. A tall, gangly sailor tried to dance with Estasia, but he lost his footing and fell into the band. The music stopped as the sailor and the band members crashed onto the deck.

"Illium, you are just as clumsy sober as you are drunk," one sailer said helping the tall sailor up. The gangly sailor had a thick bushel of brown hair, a freckled face and a thick chin.

"What would you know about being sober," Illium said smiling.

"I am sober now… sort of," the other sailor said appearing a little tipsy. "Captain, can we break out the spirits?"

"We should arrive at the Amaya docks tonight," the captain said. "With no bad weather on the horizon, I think we are good to have some fun."

Calais was astonished by the captain's decision. She walked over to Denarith and said, "did you tell him about us being chased by fire knights and imperial guards?"

"You need to relax," Denarith said. "I trust Wyk. I have known him for many years. He knows what he is doing, and he's really good at avoiding the authorities."

"I noticed," Calais said unsatisfied. Stepping back to the rail, she watched the fools break out bottles of liquor. Despite her desire to be ready for trouble, she slowly realized that these poor sailors could not help much during an attack. The fire knights or the imperial guard would slice through this ship like nothing. Burying the thought of a potential massacre, she let them enjoy their time while she kept a watchful eye on the horizon.

"We drink to Denarith and our new friends," the captain said with a raised glass. With a loud cheering agreement, the all drank. Then, they poured another round of drinks. When the band started to play again, a sailor waived them to stop.

"I think the lovely ladies would love to hear about our adventures," the sailor said. He had a long gray beard with an old, weary look. "Being sailors, we have been on quite a few adventures. I bet more than any of you noble ladies have had. Crazy Vic, why don't you tell them about the hydra."

"It would be my pleasure," Crazy Vic said while standing up. He had a bald head with a short goatee. He was shorter than the other sailors but definitely much more muscular. "So there I was," he began. "The hydra was looking right at me with its sixteen heads."

"The hydra only had six heads," Wyllik said.

"I disagree, Captain," Crazy Vic said. "I definitely remember sixteen heads or more. There were a lot of heads. They were growling and spitting. One would try to bite me and I would dodge to the left. Another came at me and I would dodge to the right. As they came at us, we would smash their heads and then cut their heads off. Blood was spraying everywhere. Finally, we drove forward with a spiked lance and impaled the beast, bathing us in more blood. Then, we gutted it and sold it for its meat and skin. I was cleaning the blood out my ears for weeks. We not only killed that beast, but we killed dragonlings, corrupted, sandworms, skeletons and even ghosts." The rest of the sailors cheered. Calais stood there baffled by the story. There were so many facts wrong, but Denarith motioned not to say anything. She assumed he didn't want her to offend his friends. "We can kill anything in this realm and without anyone's help, not the empire, not the lords, not the stuffy nobility, not even the Divine!" The sailors cheered even louder this time. Calais shook her head at their audacity and looked over the rail to see if anything was about to destroy them. "We are the crew of the Dawn's Tribute," he yelled to sky. "We answer to no one!" All the sailors leaped to their feet cheering loudly.

The captain quieted everyone down and had the band play again. Still shaking her head, Calais noticed the captain speaking into Estasia's ear while she grinned mischievously. After a few nods and giggles, he took her hand and led her to his cabin. Disappointed in her friend, Calais turned around and leaned against the rail.

"Are you okay," Denarith said walking over to her. "You seem a little tense."

"They are still after us," Calais said. "It's only a matter of time."

"Then, you should get some rest," Denarith said. "We have been running all night. All warriors know it is better to be rested before battle."

"You have been making sense all day," Calais said. "Are you feeling okay?"

"I always make sense, you don't listen." Leaning against the rail, he got a very serious look. "But, you are right. I can sense our enemies gathering around us. Lady Enix is about to strike."

CHAPTER TWENTY-SIX

Enikus

Monty sat eagerly on the railing with the wind blowing through her hair. The Ninth Spire had just transported itself above the city of Bonewalk which was in the Xandia province. It was a city different from Parn. Instead of stone and brick structures, this city comprised mostly of wood with only a few stone structures. Even the city wall's were composed of large tree trunks. Within the forest of buildings, a dense fog was rolling into the city. Monty thought she felt something darker moving with it.

"I have located your angel," Maliki said from behind her. His dark, stoic voice didn't make her feel much better with the dark horizon consuming the sun. "He is in a den of thieves and may not be there much longer. It is time to go."

With a bright flash, Monty, Nora, Nash, Djinn and Maliki were transported from the silent, cool ship deck to a large, warm, dim room filled with loud voices. Like the inn in Parn, she was surrounded by crowds of people laughing, yelling and singing. Men and women congregated around tables covered in food and drink. Some played card and dice games while others were tossing knives at the wall or at each other. Despite their fun, they leered and cursed at the newcomers before moving to another area. Most of the crowd did not see them since they had been teleported to a small, hidden alcove.

"Nash and Nora, you should go keep a lookout outside," Maliki said. "Djinn and I will take Monty to the angel."

"It would be my pleasure," Nash said. "They tried to eat me the last time I performed at a place like this."

"They should be grateful," Nora said. "You would have given them a bad case of indigestion otherwise." She quickly changed from her normal jaguar form to a small bird that quickly flew up a set of stairs.

"Don't worry," Nash said to Monty. "I think she is starting to like me. You be careful and keep your head down." He sauntered upstairs while trying to avoid eye contact.

Maliki, Djinn and Monty made their way through the crowd. Monty noticed that most of them glared at her, but were intimidated by Maliki and the robed orc. After a short time, they finally emerged from the sickening haze of sweat and fluids. In the back of the room, a man sat at a table alone. When they approached him, he grinned with a broad, white smile.

"My friends," the man cheered. With short, dark hair and skin, he looked like any other human wearing a brown overcoat with a black shirt and trousers. "It's been such a long time. Please, have a seat and tell me what you have been doing for the last few years." After shaking Djinn and Maliki's hand, they pulled up three chairs to the table. The man eyed her for a moment with the same happy, wide grin. "What is your name?"

"She's why we are here," Djinn said. "Her name is Monty. Montague made her." The man just stared back unfazed by the revelation.

"Are you the angel," Monty said slowly.

"I am indeed," the man said.

"This is Enikus, known as the wingless angel," Maliki said.

"I am so happy to meet you," Monty said gleefully. "Montague said you would fix everything and make it all better."

"Slow down," Enikus said. "Everything will be ok. You are a maru and the Divine has great plans for you. Speaking of which, I need your help, Maliki. Calais is in trouble and she needs your help. You need to be at the Amaya docks this evening."

"What about Monty," Maliki said.

"Ah, my friend, don't worry, she will be okay as long as you come back."

"Very well," Maliki said as he stood up. "May the Divine bless your travels." With a nod to them, he teleported back to his ship.

"Who is Calais and how did you know she was in trouble," Monty said.

"She's a friend," Djinn said. "She helped us ten years ago to imprison the dreaded Lady Enix, and she is a powerful summoner. By drawing a picture, she can make it spring off the page and come to life." Monty grimaced as she remembered the images of the summoner calling monstrous creatures.

"She's been on the run for months from Enixia," Enikus said. "I have been keeping an eye on her. Now that Enixia has finally caught up with her, Maliki is going to rescue her so they can prepare for the final fight. It will be a glorious battle!"

"Who is Enixia," Monty said.

"You call her Lady Enix," Enikus said. "I remember her when she was called Enixia before she was exiled."

"Montague said you would show me what I must do to stop Lady Enix," Monty said. "What can I do?"

"You're the key to destroying Enixia," Enikus said. "There is a special power you must learn, and I will get you started on that path. Be warned, it will be hard and dangerous. If you fail, she will unleash armies of demons onto this plane. Sounds like fun right?"

Monty nervously looked at Djinn as she was uncertain of what to say. She knew this is what she wanted, but she doubted her resolve. She didn't have any powers and this new power might not be enough.

"Do not fret, little one," Djinn said. "You have the strength to do this."

"I will do it," Monty breathed.

"All right," Enikus cheered. "We will wait here for our cue."

"A cue," Monty asked. "Why are you in this place?"

"That's simple," Enikus said. "I had to stop this pesky demon from possessing a human's soul. Humans make enough mistakes without the help of demons."

"Why don't you just stop Lady Enix," Monty said.

"I am," Enikus said. "I am helping you." Monty just returned an unconvincing look.

"Why do they call you a wingless angel," Monty said as they waited for this cue.

"I was sent here hundreds of years ago to stop a dragon," Enikus said. "To kill him, I had to sacrifice my wings. Since then, I have been trapped on this plane happily helping all those in need."

A loud noise erupted from the stairway at the front of the room. Militia men in brown armor were flowing into the room. With clubs and swords, some of the customers were fighting while others were escaping through unseen hatches in the walls.

"That's our cue," Enikus said. "Follow me through here."

Moving along the wall, Monty followed the orc and angel closely to avoid the rampaging crowds. Like rats, people were streaming though holes in the wall. Some were getting trampled. Some were fighting each other and the militia. Surrounded by the frightening chaos, Monty failed to notice the attacking men.

"ORC," one of the men screamed. As Djinn turned, one man stabbed him in the abdomen with a long dagger. The other man smashed a chair against him. Monty released a horrifying scream.

"You retching filth," Enikus said angrily. Instead of pulling a weapon or casting a spell, he simply flicked his finger at them. The men violently flew through the ceiling and into the nearby swamp. With the men gone, he quickly examined Djinn's wounds.

"Don't worry about me," Djinn said. "We orcs are tough and can stand a few cuts." Despite his reassurance, he briefly stumbled while trying to regain his balance. Monty glanced at his bloody wound apprehensively. "We have no time, and we must move on."

Without argument, Enikus steadied Djinn as they continued forward. To clear their way, Enikus shoved people aside with a simple gesture. Monty ducked as chairs and cups smashed against the wall above her. Holding her hood over her head, she kept looking for more attacks. Fortunately, none came as they approached a section in the wall.

Somehow, Enikus caused the wall to shutter and create a new opening. The three of them carefully climbed through into a dark corridor. Before anyone could follow, Enikus closed the entrance behind them. Djinn snapped his fingers and caused a bright red orb to appear in front of them. Lighting their way and dripping a strange red ooze, the orb remained in front of them as they trudged through the rocky cave.

Their progress was slow as Djinn wasn't moving that fast. Silently distressed, Monty continually looked at her wounded friend who pushed forward without complaint. Maneuvering through the fractured ground, Enikus attempted to keep the wizard steady. As they approached the end of the tunnel, it appeared to be blocked by stone or a giant rock. Leaving Djinn for a moment, Enikus pushed the massive rock aside. Monty looked at him in awe. Enikus just winked and went back to helping Djinn.

*   *   *   *

Dim, foggy light spilled into the cave and they made their way onto a dirt road in the middle of the city. The buildings were built from a combination of wood and stone while covered with bone and skull decorations. Behind them, Enikus slid the rock back against a two-story stone building to close off the cave.

"We are almost there," Enikus said.

Turning onto a larger street, they worked their way through the crowds and vendors. Carts filled with wares lined both sides of the street. Vendors were yelling above each other to announce their various products. Some people were haggling while others were slowly browsing the carts. In the middle, people were moving quickly in both directions with no apparent order. Above the street, people hollered out of second and third story windows. Although no one seemed to notice or care about them, Monty wrapped her cloak around herself like a protective armor. After fighting their way through the middle crowd, they came upon an intersection.

Against large stone buildings, fruit vendors lined the corners of the intersection. The thick crowds and vendors continued down the street while the intersecting street was narrower and much sparser. Enikus directed them to turn onto the narrower street and then he stopped. There was only silence.

All the windows shut and vendors hid behind their carts. Everyone else silently moved into buildings or behind carts. Coming from the other direction, she saw a member of the Imperial Guard leading a large group of militia men. Monty stiffened with fear and horror when she recognized the man as the one who killed Montague.

"Surrender," Tomas ordered. He drew his sword as they continued to approach. Enikus ignored him and continued to help his companions up the street. "I will kill all of you if I have too."

"What's happened to you," Enikus lamented. "You use to be a good person, and now you're just being a jerk." Tomas paused which Monty thought was strange. Then, Djinn fell to the ground clutching his wounded side.

"Don't bother with me," Djinn said trying to ward off Enikus' assistance. "I will hold them off so that you can escape."

"No," Monty said. "You must come with us. I need you to help me through this. You have always been there for me. I can't lose you." Tears were rolling down her cheek now as she looked to Enikus for reassurance. Instead, Enikus returned only a grieving expression. Glancing back at the approaching men, Djinn put his warm, soothing green hand on her shoulder.

"You are the strongest person of us all," Djinn said. "I knew Montague for many years, and he would have been proud of you. Now go quickly." Monty cried out as Enikus pulled her from Djinn.

"You have to deal with me first," Djinn said to Tomas. He pulled himself up from the ground and made his way to a nearby fruit cart.

"What are you doing, Djinn," Tomas said wearily. "I am a member of the Imperial Guard, and I am immune to magic." He turned to the militia behind him who where laughing at the wizard. "You can't hurt me." There was more laughter. "Just give up and come quietly." Then, Tomas was struck by a large tomato and the laughter stopped.

"You're not immune to tomatoes," Djinn said while leaning on a wooden cart. With a darkened expression, Tomas began to make his way to Djinn. While almost carrying Monty, Enikus moved farther and further from the impending battle.

In the distance, Monty saw Djinn throw his hands up into the air which was covered in a purple aura. The sides of the buildings and carts exploded. Directing the stone and wood debris, Djinn sent the militia flying through the air while others took cover. Tomas was continually struck by stone and wood as he tried to get close to the wizard. Turning another corner, Monty could no longer see the battle. More and more explosions and screams could be heard from the battle. Then, there was only silence, and Monty wept.

"We must keep going," Enikus said. "We are almost there." Through teary eyes, Monty nodded. Letting go of her hand, Monty followed the angel quickly up the street. Turning onto another street, they came face to face with another group of the militia with Nash at the front.

Nash was holding a strange metal cannon that seemed familiar to Monty. Then, she realized it was the same device that Tomas took from Montague's house. He smiled and pulled the trigger. It unleashed a massive beam of energy that struck Enikus. Leaving only a burning trail of fire through several buildings behind Monty, Enikus was no longer there.

"So it does kill angels and demons," Nash said surprised.

"Why did you do that," Monty said in horror.

"Don't worry, darling," Nash said as he approached her. "You will know the answer soon enough."

Then, a deep sleep overcame Monty, and she collapsed onto the dirt street.

CHAPTER TWENTY-SEVEN

Dark Wings

The sky turned blood red against the dark outlines of the Amaya Dock. Leaning against the rail at the bow of the ship, Calais watched the docks grow larger and larger. It wasn't as busy as the Yellow City's docks, but looked very similar with three large towers made of metal scaffolding extending from the ground to the clouds. Amaya was a smaller outpost and didn't have as many resources as Yellow City. Since its primary purpose was to resupply ships on long journeys from the river lands of Adia, it didn't have very many visitors at once. Calais could only see a few ships docked, and the skywalks were calm. Everything almost seemed too calm.

"Have you had dinner yet," Estasia said coming up beside Calais. "The captain served me a broiled fish."

"Is that all he served you," Calais said repugnantly.

"Are you still mad?" Estasia said leaning her back and elbows against the railing. "I told you that I would start being a good girl tomorrow."

"Is that because no men would be around," Calais said? "What you did was wrong and you know it. You dishonored your fiancee."

"I am not married yet," Estasia said. "I am just trying to have some fun."

"When you get bored with your husband, will you go look for some fun? You are not ready to be a wife. You want only him for his title and money and that will only satisfy you for so long. Then, you will be caught gallivanting around and humiliated. You will be kicked out of the nobility, and your life will be ruined."

"Oh please, Calais. I already have a mother. I don't need another one."

"You need to call off the wedding and finish having fun before settling down. As a wizard, you have plenty of support to do this."

"Enough," Estasia yelled. "I can't call off the wedding. I have to marry him, and I don't have a choice. It was part of my father's deal to have his lands protected by the empire. I was traded off like some piece of meat for his ambitions. Now, I have to marry some boring, ugly man and bear his ugly children. Before I am enslaved in a business deal, I will have fun with all the men I want."

"I didn't know this was an arranged marriage," Calais said dourly. "You made it sound as if you picked him out in our earlier conversation."

"I picked him, but I picked him from only a few ugly nobles that had money. He was the least ugly and most decent man of the bunch. The funny part about the whole arrangement is that he doesn't want to be married either. So now, we both are doing our duty for the empire to carry on our family lines. Oh how I can't wait to get stuck with a man who doesn't even want me."

"I am so sorry to hear that. I thought arranged marriages were in the past and most nobles were choosing their spouses."

"No noble has chosen their spouse in the last ten years. With empire choosing it's cities to protect, the nobility has been fighting with each other to own an imperial city. No one can be trusted. You were right to leave the nobility. I just wished I had listened to you. Instead, I have to marry. At least, I get to attend lots of parties as long as some backstabbing baron doesn't take our land away."

"Oh Estasia," Calais said hugging her friend. "I have little influence, but I will do everything I can to protect you from backstabbing nobles."

"Thank you," Estasia said holding her friend. "I will always consider you my sister." She paused for a moment staring at the sky. "That is a really strange bird. I don't think I have ever seen that kind before."

Calais turned around and stared at the flying creature as it flew swiftly to their airship. Looking closer, Calais saw that the bird had a head of a lizard, the wings of a bird and a body of a snake. "It's a darkling." Darklings were abominations of nature. Demons made them by merging animals with their dark powers trying to create a superior creature. Coming out of the surrounding clouds, there were more than just one. There was a large flock of these creatures approaching fast. Looking at each other, Calais and Estasia both knew Lady Enix had sent them.

"To the defenses," Denarith roared. Then, Captain Wyllik called out several orders along with the first mate.

Several sailors ran back and forth. Some set the rigging while others manned the cannons. The ones that didn't have specific stations grabbed large crossbows and braced them against the railing. Alarm bells could be heard from the Amaya docks as they manned their own defenses. The ship made a large turn towards the docks to gain additional cover.

Grabbing a crossbow herself, Calais braced it against the railing like the others and aimed it at the approaching cloud. Waiting for a target, she realized that there were hundreds of these creatures coming at them. Denarith stood ready with his axe while Estasia tried to cast some defensive shields. She was still too weak and could barely muster a large enough shield, but it proved to be too weak. The creatures smashed through it and began spitting fireballs at them.

Calais loosed bolt after bolt trying to hit the darklings. They twirled and dived to avoid the crossbow fire. Larger cannons had better luck as they hit several of them at a time. The docks began firing even larger cannons that struck large groups of the spitting creatures. Denarith would swing his axe releasing a blue wave of energy that destroyed several creatures at once. Despite their successful attacks, there were just too many.

The creature's fireballs burned the rigging and sails while damaging the hull. Several sailors were on fire after being hit several dozen times. Estasia did her best at casting defensive spells but could only create cover for Calais, Denarith, her and a few of the sailors. Some of the sailors were being picked up by multiple darklings by wrapping their tails around their arms and necks. Then, the flying creatures tossed their prey over the side. The rest of the darklings unleashed a barrage of fireballs onto the docks.

The ship suddenly lunged to the side and began to drift to one of the skywalks. The helmsman had disappeared, and the captain was fending off the ravenous swarm. The wheel and levers were turning by themselves. Seeing smoke rising from the smoldering hull, Calais knew the engine had been damaged. It was only a matter of time before the ship collided with the skydocks. If the ship collided with skydocks, it would turn the ship into a cloud of splinters.

"We have to get off the ship," she said running to Denarith. "Help me get a lifesail ready."

Denarith followed her to the lifesail which looked like a large boat the was positioned upside down. Normally, a sailor would use a crank to moved the boat into a launch position. The lifesail with their small engine and sails were extremely heavy. Instead, Denarith grabbed the edge of the boat and flipped it over. Then, he pushed it into launch position. Estasia continued to cast shields to protect them, but she was becoming extremely weak.

Before they could board the lifesail, they were all thrown to the deck while the ship skidded against the metal scaffolding and released a high-pitch wail. Several creatures fell to the deck around Calais in pain. Examining the creatures' pointed ears, Calais realized that they must be sensitive to high-pitched noises. With more smoke rising from the hull, she remembered that mis-configured engines would cause high-pitch noises. A lesson she learned almost crashing an airship a few years ago. Grabbing Denarith and Estasia, Calais pulled them below deck.

Smoke filled the dark corridor. She made her way down the corridor with Denarith following her. "Where are we going," he said trying not to breathe?

"I know how to stop the creatures, but we have to damage the engine," Calais said.

"If you damage the engine more, we will fall out of the sky," Denarith said. Calais ignored him and worked her way to the back of the ship.

The engine compartment was positioned in the ship's lower aft. Opening a hatch, Calais quickly climbed down. Denarith tried to go through the hatch, but he was too large. Exhausted, Estasia just leaned against the wall watching Calais go down. When Calais got to the bottom of the ladder, she was surrounded by smoke and grinding gears.

The engine room was filled with pipes, metal boxes, and long rotating rods. Large and small gears turned with each other while some of the gears' axels sparked and whined. With light erupting from cracks in the engine compartments, Calais knew the ethaerium energy containment had already started failing. Once it failed, the ship would plummet to the ground. Moving quickly, she made her way to the other side of the room.

There was a panel with levers and knobs used to calibrate the energy flow and gear movements. Calais made the adjustments that would create the high frequency sound by turning a few knobs and pulling two levers. She waited, but nothing happened. Reviewing the readouts and examining the settings, everything appeared in order. With a loud clang, she turned and saw one of the vertical rods come loose. Calais realized that the rod needed to be reseated in the spinning gear below it for her plan to work. The standard procedure would be to shut the engine down before resetting the rod. With their limited time, this was not an option.

Making her way to the loose rod, she jumped on to one of the heavier metal casings and walked along a narrow beam between more spinning gears. Getting close to the rod, she stepped onto a higher ledge that was level with the large spinning gear. It was several times larger than her and was spinning extremely fast. The large elliptical holes on the inside of the gear made it almost impossible to stand on. She would have to jump onto the rod, and her weight would pull it down and center it enough to be reconnected with the spinning gear below. Balancing herself carefully, she began to pump her legs for the jump.

She leaped forward and barely caught the loose rod. Pulling herself up, she wrapped her legs and arms around it and felt it moving downward. It was moving more slowly than she anticipated, and her hands were getting sweaty. Trying to finding new grips on the rod, it became much harder to hold onto. The spinning gear beneath her looked more like spinning blades that would cut her into pieces. Finally, the rod connected to the gear, and it began to spin at the same speed. She tried to hold on with her arms and legs, but the rod was just moving too fast. Unable to hold onto it any longer, Calais was thrown off the rod and into a metal casing before she dropped to the ground.

Feeling woozy, she pushed herself back onto her side while watching the turning gears. Then, Calais could hear the engine emitting the expected high pitched sound. Smiling at her success, she tried to stand up but lost her balance. Falling back onto the floor, she tried steading herself while finding the room's exits. Locating an exit ahead of her and to the left, she started to crawl along the narrow wood floor. The smoke had become excessive, and Calais couldn't breathe well. Part of her wanted to go to sleep, but she knew that wasn't an option. The smoke and her head injury were confusing her brain. Calais fought each step and watched the exit get closer and closer.

Then, the gears erupted around her. The engine released a loud humming noise. Then, it slowly faded away. Calais knew that the engine had failed, but it imbued the hull with enough energy to keep it in the air. It was a built-in safety feature that all airships had. While they would not crash, Calais had to survive the flying gears and rods that separated from the engine. Unable to move quickly, she became afraid and wrapped herself in a ball to limit the damage from the flying pieces of metal. Then, a large hand reached down and pulled her completely out of the engine room.

Denarith was standing above the engine room entrance and had placed Calais next to him in the smoky corridor. Still dizzy, she fell back to the floor next to the engine door. At closer inspection, she noticed that Denarith had chopped a huge hole into the floor to grab Calais. Estasia put a reassuring hand on her shoulder while she barely could stand herself.

"That was a close one," Denarith said. "You are lucky that I just saw you, or we would be scraping you off the engine."

"We have to get to the main deck to see whether it worked or not," Calais said. She tried to stand up, but she fell down again. "Help me, Denarith. I can't quite stand up."

"You got a nasty bump on your head," Denarith said while picking her up. "So what did we do exactly?"

"I was trying to kill all those creatures using the engine." Calais wanted to give him more details, but her head was throbbing as though a hammer was hitting it. Denarith just looked at her quizzically. Barely able to see through the haze, she felt only the rocking motion of Denarith's steps while he carried her to clear air.

Calais covered her eyes from the bright, red glare of the dusky sky. After Denarith set her on the deck, Calais tried to look around the sky for the flying darklings. "Do you see any," she said to Denarith.

"No, they are gone," Denarith said.

Several sailors were cheering to be alive, but a flash of fire erupted from the deck at the back of the ship. When the fire subsided, Lady Enix stood on the deck with her feathery wings stretched out. Several sailors backed away while the captain approached her.

"Get away from her captain," Calais yelled breathlessly. "She will kill you."

"I am sorry, Calais," the captain said turning around. "It was too good of a deal to pass up." He turned back to the demon. "Here is your prize; Lady Enix, as was promised. Do you have our payment?"

"Yes, my handsome captain," Lady Enix said. She handed him a large bag of coins.

Captain Wyllik looked through it and pulled out a few large gold coins and held them up in the air. "I will tear you apart, Wyk," Denarith roared.

"You were a good friend, but the money was better," Wyk said. "This has to be the best pay day ever." He turned and gave Estasia a wicked smile.

"I can't believe he seduced me," Estasia growled. "I knew it was too easy." Calais would have frowned, but she was too focused on the demon.

"Hand them over, captain," Lady Enix said. "I am very busy, and I don't have much time."

"Maybe she has more money in that little piece of cloth on her," one sailor said undaunted. The rest of the surviving sailors gathered closer to the demon. Still holding their swords and crossbows, they glared at her hungrily. The captain looked at Lady Enix nervously.

"The men feel they deserve a little more money," Wyk said trying to sound bolder than he was. "Especially with the damage to our ship from your little friends, I think extra compensation is in order."

"I was hoping you would ask for more," Lady Enix said with a large grin.

Immediately, the captain heaved in pain while dropping to his knees. Fire erupted from his body. His clothes and skin burned away with his last dying scream. Ashes and bones were the only remains of Captain Wyllik as he crumbled to the ground. For a moment, the sailors backed away in horror.

A few sailors shot her with crossbows, but the bolts ricocheted from her skin as though she was made of stone. Two attacked her with swords, but they were quickly engulfed in flames like the captain. The rest of the crew tried to run, but some fell down while other dropped to their knees.

"Divine help us," one sailor screamed at the sky. Flames engulfed him, and he became a pile of ash and bones. Others cried for help, but their screams were drowned out by the flames.

"We have got to get out of here," Calais said struggling to stand up. Her head was still spinning. Because of the soulstones, they were immune to the demon's attack that was killing all the sailors. However, Calais also knew that Lady Enix had many other ways to kill them. For a moment, Calais saw fear in Denarith's eyes.

Denarith picked her up in one arm and Estasia in another. He ran to the edge of the deck and looked at the nearby scaffolding. The ship was moving extremely slow after striking the docks, but it had drifted too far from the docks for Denarith to jump.

"Jump," Estasia yelled.

"I can't jump that," Denarith said.

"Just jump and I will help you," Estasia said. Looking back, Calais saw Lady Enix getting closer walking slowly along the deck. When she saw the demon's smile, Calais knew the demon was enjoying herself. "Hurry, you stupid barbarian."

He ran back to the middle of the deck and then dashed to the end of the deck before hurtling themselves to the scaffolding. Calais watched Estasia cast her flight spell, but she was still extremely fatigued. It was just enough to give them the additional lift to reach the docks. Then, Lady Enix fired a fireball at them. With hesitation, Estasia tried to cast another spell while Calais pleaded for her to stop. She had little energy, and she was barely conscious. The temporary shield was enough to block the flames, but the blast destroyed the flight spell and threw them to a different section of the scaffolding. Because of the explosion, Denarith lost hold of them. Spinning through the air, they tried to grab each other. Denarith found Calais' arm, and Calais grabbed Estasia. Before falling to the ground, Denarith grabbed a piece of metal jutting out of the scaffolding. They held each other like a long chain.

Calais' head was really hurting, and she couldn't focus on Estasia while she held her forearm. Calais lost her grip on Estasia who hung limp. "Estasia, hold on," Calais cried out. Estasia weakly looked at her but didn't smile. "Don't let go." Then, she felt a sudden jerk as Denarith was losing his grip of the metal beam.

"Look out," Denarith grunted while looking back to the ship. The demon shot another fireball at them. Calais clenched her teeth and eyes as the fireball approached. Then, a black arrow struck the fireball causing it to explode. For a moment, they were engulfed in the fiery heat before they felt the cool air again. Then, something grabbed Denarith's arm holding the metal scaffolding. Straining to look upward, Calais saw her brother Caezik helping Denarith. His black cloak was flapping around him in the high wind.

"Come on, you blasted barbarian," Caezik grunted with a strained face. "I can't hold all of you."

"I am trying," Denarith said. "Just need to get a better hold."

With Denarith moving to get a better grip, Calais felt her hold on Estasia slipping. She was barely holding on to her hand. "Estasia, grab my hand," Calais said. "I can't hold on much longer." Estasia did nothing. "Caezik, help Estasia. You can come back and help the rest of us."

"I can't," Caezik argued. "You are all going to fall if I let go."

"Caezik, don't let her fall," Calais pleaded. "She is too weak to cast any spells. She will die."

"You are all going to die if we don't get out of here soon," Caezik said.

"Hold on, Estasia," Calais said. "Please, hold on."

Estasia threw her head back and smiled weakly at her friend. Then, Calais lost her grip. She watched her best friend plummet to the distant ground. Calais screamed. All she felt was pain and despair. Despite their differences, Estasia had been her best friend. She was the only one Calais felt comfortable talking too. A part of her hoped that the demon would kill her quickly so the pain would go away. Feeling her hand slipping from Denarith's grasp, she involuntarily grabbed Denarith's arm with her other hand with tears running down her cheeks.

Without Estasia's weight, Denarith pulled Calais up while she seized the metal outcropping. With Caezik's help, she climbed onto the metal arm and wrapped her body around it since she was still too dizzy to stand up. Once Calais was safe, Denarith made his way onto the metal arm and deeper into the metal scaffolding to get better footing. They could hear Lady Enix laughing. Without warning, the airship exploded.

Several lancing white beams hastily shattered the ship's hull. The smoking debris fell to the ground and there was no sign of Lady Enix. On the red horizon, Calais saw the Ninth Spire glide to the docks. With a bright flash of light, Calais, Caezik, and Denarith were teleported off the metal scaffolding and onto Maliki's ship before it vanished again.

PART FOUR

Chapter Twenty-Eight

Monty Caged

Monty awoke in a cage. Her dark red cloak and red dress had been stripped off her. Instead, she was wearing a simple, sleeveless, black dress that extended only a little past her knees. She sighed as it made her white marble skin appear even more like a statue than before. Pulling her knees against her chest, she took inventory of her surroundings.

Her cage was a simple wagon being drawn by two horses. Both side walls were just black iron bars similar to wagons in a circus attraction. The wooden floor was covered in dirt and straw as if an animal had once lived there. Surrounding her wagon, several other wagons, horses, and armed men created a large caravan. Some of the guards wore black leather armor while others were far more frightening as they were only composed of red metal and fire. Fortunately, no one was looking at her or paying her any attention which was good.

All she wanted to do was cry. She really missed Djinn and hoped his death was not too painful. Then, she had lost Enikus before he could even show her the secrets of a true power that could have saved them all. While she hoped Nora, and the others were safe, she didn't want them to come and find her. She didn't want to see them die like Djinn or Montague. She didn't want to lose anymore friends. Then, there was Nash.

"Awake are you," Nash said. "I didn't think my spell would affect you that long."

"Why did you hurt Enikus?" Monty said. "He would show me a way to stop Lady Enix and save us."

"After I got Montague's letter, I started to think. Do I die in some vain attempt at destroying or banishing a demon again? On the other hand, should I enjoy all the great things in life and wait for the demon armies to show up and kill me? Either way, I would be dead. So, I chose life and all its great pleasures. Unfortunately, you have to die for that to happen. With that, I give you my sincerest apology. I hope your short life was filled with excitement and pleasure."

"You betrayed all your friends and what's good in the world," Monty said darkly, "so you may have more fun."

"Exactly," Nash said. "Trust me. A good woman and a couple of pints of ale will wash all your past regressions away."

"I hope all your parts fall off," Monty said.

"I see you have been spending too much time with Nora."

"Stop bothering the creature, Nash," a female voice said as she rode up next to the cage. Its soft, alluring tone almost sent shivers up Monty's spine. Wrapped in a black, feathered cloak, the woman wore the same face as the demon that she saw on the Ninth Spire. "I am Lady Enix."

Monty just stared at the thing riding the black fiery stallion. At first, she didn't know what to say to the architect of her misery. She knew she wasn't supposed to hate or wish death on anyone. As she looked upon the thing, the deepest part of her wanted it to die. "Why did you capture me and not just kill me," she said finally.

"You are the key to making the portal work," Lady Enix said. "You're clever creator actually put all his best work and inventions inside you. You're foolish friends could have banished me with you. Instead, I shall use you to open a stable portal to another plane. It was inevitable. I would always win."

"Don't listen to her," a man yelled from another prison wagon. "Don't let that demon poison your mind." Then, Monty recognized the voice and the dirty figure as Caellan. At least, someone is still alive.

"Stop your whining, paladin," Lady Enix said. "If I wanted to poison her mind, I wouldn't need to waste this air. Besides, I want her to know she is extremely important. She will be a great and powerful ally for us. To show you my appreciation, Monty, I got you this." She rode next to another nearby wagon and pulled the cover off. Underneath, a wrapped body laid on the top of the straw. "I have kept your orc friend's body. If you cooperate, I will return him back to life."

"That's not possible," Monty said under her breath as she stared at her friend's body.

"Of course, it is," Lady Enix said as she put the blanket back on the wagon. "As a demon, I can do many things. This is one of my many gifts and my own promise to you." Monty just stared back dubiously. "Think about it. To help you make the right decision, you should have his hat to keep safe. Djinn always loved his hat." She pulled his signature large, brimmed hat from the wagon and tossed it into Djinn's cage. Without moving, Monty just stared at the familiar hat. Lady Enix laughed while riding to the front of the caravan.

*   *   *   *

They traveled in the caravan for most of the hot day through grasslands. While holding Djinn's hat, Monty watched the grasses' hypnotic movement as it moved back and forth with the blowing winds. With the wagons plowing through the sea of grass, they left only two thin trails. Besides, the deep rustling sound of the grass against her wagon and wind, it was strangely silent.

Occasionally, Nash would break out into a song. Then, Caellan would curse at him, but he would say nothing else. The human mercenaries' stoic silence was betrayed by glints of fear in their eyes. The fiery guards' armors made no sound and would only leave a burned trail of grass and not cause any grass fires. In the front of the caravan, Tomas rode silently and never looked at Monty. When Lady Enix was around, she would give orders and the others would follow them silently. Most of the time, she vanished in a bright flaming flash and remained absent for a long time. After a while, Monty saw a large caravan appear on the horizon and the caravan stopped. Everyone stood there and waited in silence.

Monty watched the new caravan approach nervously. This caravan was different. Instead of guards, children surrounded it, filling the air with distant laughter. Instead of wearing armor, they wore plain clothes of brown and white. Their wagons were built to carry supplies instead of hold prisoners. More than anything, Monty saw happiness when she looked at their distant faces. Then, Lady Enix approached them as they got closer.

"Madam," a man called out as he rode a large grey steed. "We are honored to meet you. Your guard has the imperial insignia. Is that truly an imperial guard that leads you?"

"The honor is mine," Lady Enix bowed. "It is true that we are aligned with the emperor's court. Who do I have the honor of addressing?"

"My name is Serut," the man said as he gave a small bow from his horse. "Which way do you travel?"

"We are heading north to transport prisoners to Dragonlock."

"It is good to hear you are heading north. We are also heading that direction. Our town was destroyed by those dishonorable and vile corrupted. We are hoping to find refuge in one of the northern cities so we may be protected by the empire."

"You have a long journey ahead of you."

"It is true, but we are only workers and farmers. We have little protection. In the traditions of Xandia, I ask that you show us mercy and invoke the right of hospitality. Let us eat of each other's food and shelter each other in these storms so that you can protect us and we can take care of your guards."

"No," Caellan screamed. "Run! Run away! She will kill you all. Please run! It is your only chance." He continued to scream, but the man just eyed Caellan with suspicion.

"Oh Serut, I accept your offer," Lady Enix said. "In exchange, I will protect you from everything including yourself. You never have to be afraid again." Serut returned her a confused look.

"Don't hurt them, demon," Caellan continued to scream. "They are innocent. Let them go!"

It happened quickly. The men and women screamed as each one of their bodies were engulfed in flames. Then, they were silent as the flame finished transforming them into fiery armored guards. Even the horses were transformed into fiery beasts. Thankfully, the children were not affected and were running into the distance screaming. The new guards did not follow the children and slowly merged the two caravans.

"You see knight," Lady Enix said. "I am merciful. I spared the children, and they are in the precious hands of your Divine now."

"How dare you speak of mercy when you have just killed hundreds of people," Caellan said angrily.

"I did not kill them," Lady Enix said rebukingly. "I released them from the Divine and his torturous game. You see Monty, it is the Divine's greatest lie. He pretends to give you free will, but instead puts you in the most heinous maze called life. In the maze, he causes that person nothing but agony and despair. He makes them think they are choosing these painful paths for themselves. In reality, he is the one who creates these obstacles to lead you down these painful paths.

"The idea that it is out of love is ludicrous. It is like telling a person who is being beaten that it is for his own good. All it does is make a person numb to the pain so you have to beat him harder. When he can't endure anymore pain, the Divine kills him. Trust me, the Divine loves no one and he enjoys causing nothing but despair and agony. Instead, demons give people strength and show them their path. They never feel pain, anger or regret. They only know love for the one who takes care of them."

"Taking away their freewill is not love," Caellan said.

"Of all the people, I think you would understand the most, Caellan," Lady Enix said. "He causes you nothing but misery as he forces you to make unfair decisions. Instead of you hiding in a bottle, demons can offer you true peace and give you real purpose."

"Don't waste your breath on me," Caellan said. "I won't be poisoned by your words. I am doing a good enough job poisoning myself."

"Trust me, knight, " she said mockingly. "I can smell the poison."

"You should just kill me now," Caellan said irritated. "Dragonlock is months away at this speed. You will tire of me and kill me ,eventually."

"Months," Lady Enix laughed. "We will be there by nightfall. Besides, you are far too much fun to kill off."

In front of the caravan, Monty watched a black cloud grow into a massive black portal with lightning flashing from all sides. Without hesitation, the caravan slowly walked into the inky blackness. Monty held onto Djinn's hat and hummed softly as the darkness over took her.

CHAPTER TWENTY-NINE

The Aftermath

Calais awoke in a soft white bed in a small warm-lit room. Not feeling dizzy or woozy, she carefully sat up while pulling the thick blanket off her. She still had her clothing on from earlier and her red jacket hung on the room's wooden wall. The rest of the room had only a chest and a white glowing wall lantern. When she wondered where Estasia and Denarith were, she suddenly remembered her best friend's death.

Calais' eyes watered with memories of Estasia. While her brothers protected her, she always felt alone until she met a gangly young girl who loved dresses, jewelry and dolls. They had almost nothing in common, but they both loved exploring the strange gardens and forests. They found wondrous animals and strange ruins. No matter what fields they ran in or caves they crawled through, Estasia always found a way to keep her pretty dresses clean. Calais would look like a mud puppy and get in trouble for messing up her fine clothing. Sometimes, Estasia would let Calais borrow a dress so she wouldn't get in yelled at again by her father. No matter what happened, they always looked out for each other?

With each memory of Estasia, more tears ran down Calais' cheeks. When they weren't exploring, Estasia was showing her other parts of life. It was Estasia that taught her how to flirt with boys and what to do during balls. Calais was a terrible dancer, but Estasia's body flowed with rhythm. All the boys loved getting her attention, and she helped Calais get her first suitor. A nice boy who gave Calais her first kiss. Estasia was the only person happy for her since Caellan and Caezik tried to beat the boy up for touching her. Luckily, her other brother, Arturo, helped the boy escape before they found him. Calais' love life was never boring, especially with Estasia's help. When they weren't chasing boys, Calais was always helping Estasia with her studies.

Bringing up her knees against her chest, Calais buried her head, and wept. Calais was the one that pushed Estasia to follow the path of the wizard. When Estasia passed the lord's tests for wizards, Calais aided Estasia in the more difficult aspects of wizardry. Calais loved watching Estasia cast her light and wind spells. It was one of the most beautiful effects she had ever seen. When Calais lacked confidence in her skills as a summoner, it was Estasia that supported her. Calais became one of the greatest summoners ever, all because of Estasia. Calais didn't know how she would get along without her. She felt like a part of her soul had died with Estasia. With more memories of Estasia churning through her head, Calais continued to cry.

After a time, there was a knock at the door. With puffy red eyes, Calais looked up but didn't answer. Her hopes of being alone were dashed when the door opened. Caezik walked into the room and closed the door behind him.

"I am glad to see you're awake," he said hesitantly.

She looked at him and remembered what had happened at the skydock. Instead of helping Estasia, he stayed in the scaffolding helping Denarith. Recalling Estasia slipping from her grasp and falling, she became flush with anger.

"How dare you come in here after what you did?" Calais said indignantly. "You were supposed to help Estasia. Denarith was fine for a few more moments. You could have shadow jumped and grabbed her. She died, because you didn't save her. It is your fault she is dead."

"Are you finished," he said. He paused for a moment looking at her intensely with his gold eyes. She just looked back at him seething. "What you didn't know was that Denarith was injured and would drop all of you. If I hadn't helped him, you would all be dead. I knew how much Estasia meant to you. I was there all those years. I lost a friend too."

"I couldn't hold on," Calais said sobbing. All she could see was her friend falling. "I couldn't hold on. I needed your help to save her. You're my brother. You are supposed to be there to help me. If I were stronger, I could have saved her."

"I was there for you," Caezik said frustrated. "You're alive because of me." He paused for moment pacing in the room with his long cloak flowing around him like a dark shadow. "Denarith told me what happened. She was too weak from the gem cuffs to hold on to you."

"That's not true. If she hadn't used her powers to protect us from Lady Enix's fireball, she would have had enough strength to hold on."

"Estasia knew what she was doing. She sacrificed herself, so that Denarith and you could live."

"If I had my summoner's book, she wouldn't have had to make that sacrifice. I could have protected all of us." Calais had stopped crying. Her eyes and throat were raw. She stared at the wall feeling empty and hollow. "I was just too scared, and I lost my friend because of that."

"What were you scared of," Caezik said confused? "You disappeared as a conjurer after we imprisoned Lady Enix ten years ago. I had heard you were getting jobs on airships and working as a portal technician. You barely spoke with Caellan, Arturo, and I. What happened that made you quit being a conjurer?" He stared at her while she dug up the answer and all those unpleasant memories with Lady Enix.

"I created an abomination," Calais said choking on the words. "Lady Enix helped grow my power, and I could create creatures that didn't exist. It scared me. I no longer just saw the realms as they were, but I saw ways to build new realms. I could have become a plague on this world and hurt even more people." If the other conjurers had learned the truth, they would have exiled her to some other plane. Over time, summoners became strong enough to see the weave of life. Most of them would change the life they summoned into unnatural forms called abominations. The power is so great that most summoners give into the divine-like abilities and slowly go mad. Once the madness takes to hold, many will find their way to another plane where they can rewrite entire realms. Others will try to change the realm to their own image. Calais heard the stories of summoners creating islands and cities of monsters that would kill thousands of people. The idea of her killing more people made her shudder. "It scared me so much that I buried my books. I didn't want to hurt anyone else. Instead, my friends are dying and I can do nothing. It's not fair."

"Of course, it's not fair," Caezik said. "Life is never fair. Do you remember that summer when father wouldn't let you go back to Parn with Estasia? What did Estasia tell you?"

"She told me to go buy a new dress to make me feel better." The thought caused Calais to smile. It actually felt good to smile after crying so much.

"Not that," Caezik said shaking his head. "What did she tell you before that?"

"She said to wear strength and honor like armor and everything will work out," Calais said.

Caezik kneeled down next to the bed to look her in the eye. "You are a strong person, Cal, and you are a good person. We all lose our way, but family leads us back. After our father was killed, I was so angry that I did many terrible things. If it weren't for you and Caellan, I would be dead. It's my turn now. I am here for you, and I will do everything in my power to keep the madness from taking you."

"Thank you," Calais said. She looked at him with her tear-filled eyes. Then, she hugged him. He put a stiff hand on her shoulder. Calais knew he was never very comfortable with affection especially with his family. However, she needed a hug after everything that had happened. Feeling better, she released him, and he stood back up with an awkward silence. She knew he didn't know what to say. Pulling off the covers, she pushed herself out of bed. Both of her brothers were taller than she, and his bulky cloak made him even more imposing.

"So where are we," she said looking up at him.

"We are still on the Ninth Spire," he said. He almost seemed relieved to be talking about something else. "Maliki healed your head wound, and we let you sleep through the night and part of the morning. The rest of us searched for Monty and the others. We learned that Lady Enix captured Monty and killed Djinn. Nora has also disappeared." Calais felt weak again.

"Oh no that poor sweet wizard," she said. "He was the nicest orc I have ever met. Why were Nora and him in Bonewalk?"

"They were taking Monty to see Enikus."

"Wait, the wingless angel is here. He can help us stop Lady Enix."

"He was here," Caezik said correcting her. "People say he was destroyed by some weapon that also took out several buildings. I doubt he was killed, but Maliki can't find him."

"How many of us are still left," Calais said quietly.

"Not counting the ones working with that witch, there are only a handful of us left."

"What do we do now?" Calais said sitting back down on the bed. "There aren't enough of us to fight her."

"Maliki is focused on finding Monty. He believes that she is the key."

"Who is this Monty?"

"That's kind of complicated. I met her once when I rescued her from Baron Verrandrin's mansion. I really don't know why she is so important, but she was made by Montague."

"What do you mean she made him?" Calais said quizzically while looking back up at her brother.

"She is a maru or at least that's what Maliki said."

"If she has a soulforge, then she might be able to control the harmonic frequencies of the portal," Calais said jumping up excitedly. "That is why Montague made Monty. She is the key! We have to see Maliki immediately."

* * * *

The Ninth Spire was a maze. It had been ten years since she was on the ship. Fortunately, Caezik knew where he was going. After walking up and down corridors in the lower decks, they ran into Denarith.

"You're finally awake," Denarith said relieved. "I didn't know whether you would be awake anytime soon. Maliki said you wound was pretty severe and that you might sleep for a couple of days."

Calais thanked him and noticed bandages around his hand and arm. "What happened to you're arm?"

"These scrapes are nothing," Denarith said nonchalantly. "That last fireball slightly burned part of my arm and hand. Caezik showed up just in the nick of time."

"How did you know how to find us?" Calais said.

"Lady Enix bribed a magistrate to sentence Estasia and her parents to death. I used the scrolls magic to find her, so I could warn you."

"How is that possible?" Calais said astonished. "You need a magistrate, a jury, and a regional governor to send a black letter."

"Lady Enix had grown in power and influence over the last year. I tried to find an answer. All I know is that she has the emperor's court support."

"Were you going to kill her?" Calais said hesitantly. With so much betrayal already, she really didn't want to know the truth.

"I was bound to kill her, eventually. A black hand chooses the place and time. I was hoping to wait till after we solved the witch problem. Then, I would try to get the black letters revoked."

Calais had heard the stories about the black hands. Some of them would torture their prey for years before killing them. Others would kill their prey off quickly. That is why so many criminals feared them. They didn't know when death would come for them no matter how much they prepared. "Thank you for your help, Cae," she said. "Estasia would have been grateful for all you've done."

"I know how much she meant to you," Caezik said with a smile.

"Yep, you're a good man despite sneaking into criminals' homes and killing them," Denarith said grinning. "Where were you going, anyway?"

"I have a theory about this Monty," Calais said.

"Monty who," Denarith said confused?

"She is a maru," Calais said. "I think I know how we can use her to stop Lady Enix."

"Maru," Denarith said scratching his head. "Aren't those the constructs that destroy cities and assassinate heroes?"

"Those are just stories meant to scare kids," Calais said. "Montague made her to imprison Lady Enix once and for all."

"Wait, you said 'her'," Denarith said. "How is a construct a 'her'?"

"I don't know," Calais said annoyed. "I am just telling you what Cae told me."

"It looks like a small woman," Cae said. "Don't ask me how it works."

"Enough questions, Denarith," Calais said. "We need to get to Maliki."

Denarith just shook his head in confusion and followed them around more hallways. The inside of Maliki's ship was almost like a small realm itself. It could be set up in any dimension or configuration he needed. Unfortunately, it was configured to be a long walk. Finally, they came to the large double doors that represented the Captain's Quarters.

Denarith started to open the door, but Calais stopped him. She scowled at him while knocking on the door. Denarith shrugged his shoulders and waited.

The doors opened by themselves. It was a large room with several couches, a couple of large tables and a bed. Several pictures hung on the wall of people and events that Calais didn't recognize. Several large windows looked out onto the bright blue sky. The wood furnishings made it a magnificent room. Maliki stood near one of the tables without a shirt. Next to him, Lady Enix had her arms wrapped around him.

"What is she doing here," Calais said hysterically. "Besides Montague, you are the last person I thought would help that witch." Denarith tensely stepped back. She knew he was smart enough not to attack Maliki aboard his own ship. Caezik had already pulled his bow, but he had not aimed it at the demon or Maliki… yet.

"You were wrong my dear Maliki," Lady Enix said. She still wore little clothing and had shaped her wings back into a thin blue cloak behind her. "They believe we are allied."

"They still haven't attacked," Maliki said.

"Is that because they are afraid of me or of you, navigator," Lady Enix said into his ear.

"What is going on, Maliki," Caezik said angrily. "Why is she here?"

"Not by my choice," Maliki said. "Celestial beings can come and go as they please. I am not powerful enough to stop them."

"But you can be," Lady Enix said seductively. "You can reap my soul, and you can gain all my power to go to the farthest reaches of the universe."

"The answer is no," Maliki said sternly. "You would take my soul and bring death and destruction to the few remaining beautiful places in this universe."

"The same old answer," Lady Enix said. "You told me that a year ago after I escaped my prison."

"You knew she had escaped," Calais said surprised. "Why didn't you warn us?"

"I warned Djinn and Montague," Maliki said. "Some of you I could not locate in time, and others did not trust me."

"I am not sure we still do," Caezik said. "You still haven't answered our question."

"I am here to offer you a truth," Lady Enix said letting go of Maliki. She sat down on a table with her legs crossed. "I have the maru so my victory is certain. So, I offer you a chance to live. I will no longer hurt any of you nor try to take your soulstones as long as you leave this realm. As you know, the planar alignment is in progress. Once it ends, I will open my portal and take this realm. If any of you are still here on this realm, I will destroy you. If you try to interfere with my plans again, I will destroy you.

"You have an opportunity for life and glorious lives at that. Calais, you could become the greatest summoner and create realms of beautiful creatures and lands. Caezik, you would be the hand of justice in all the planes. You could destroy people before they hurt the innocent. Denarith, you can take your barbarian tribe to another realm of fertile lands so you can grow your tribe and destroy your enemies. All of you have a chance for glory and power. It is an opportunity that few on this realm will get. I have forgiven you for what you did ten years ago. Now, it is your turn to let go of what happened ten years ago, so you can become the greatest of all lords."

"What about Maliki," Calais said. He had moved away from Lady Enix and been looking out the window. His left arm and body looked like a normal arm except the skin appeared as metallic bronze. "What did you offer him?"

"I didn't offer him anything," Lady Enix said. "He was already planning on leaving this realm. His wanderlust had almost overtaken him." Calais knew little about navigators. Over time, most would leave this realm and travel to other planes and never return. They called it their wanderlust with their thirst for knowledge becoming unquenchable. If they would fight Lady Enix, they would need him.

"Is this true?" Calais said.

"It is true," Maliki said distantly. He turned to look at Lady Enix. "I am leaving, but I will choose when I leave."

"I have made my offer," Lady Enix said ignoring Maliki. "Your other friends have died opposing me. With my fellow demons, we will kill you and all that oppose me. As an old friend, I ask for you to choose life and not death." The thought of her as a friend caused Calais to shiver. "Hopefully, we won't be seeing each other again." With that said, she stood up and bowed before them. After that, she smiled and disappeared in a burst of flames.

"I am not leaving," Calais announced. "Too many of my friends have died for me to run away."

The rest of them did not respond immediately. Maliki returned his gaze to the window. Caezik walked further into the room and sat on the edge of the table. Denarith just stood near the door with his arms crossed.

Watching her silent friends, Calais worried that they might be considering the demon's offer.

"You are not alone," Maliki said finally. "I will fight with you."

"Don't worry Cal," Caezik said. "I am sticking with you to the end. What about you, champion? You have been unusually quiet."

"I don't speak to that witch," Denarith said pointedly. "She will get in my head and make me do things. When I raise my axe against her, I will die which means I will be dead soon."

"Denarith, you are the wisest man of us all," Caezik said chuckling. "What is the plan, Maliki?"

Chapter Thirty

The Fifth Spire

As the caravan exited the black portal, Monty's wagon was surrounded by desert with a red sun slowly moving below the horizon. Crunching against the sand, the wagon made its way up one of the many, curving dunes. With a strong breeze, the straw and dirt flew out of her wagon as the few human guards covered their faces. Against the ground, Monty saw a purple and pink flicker.

Looking farther ahead, she saw a massive wall of purple, pink, blue and white. Contained behind the wall, clouds and lightning twisted violently. Amazingly, it almost took up the entire horizon. "What is that," Monty said to Caellan as his wagon was much closer now.

"It is called the Dragon Shield," Caellan said. "At the end of the Age of Peace, a catastrophic event occurred and created a huge portal that let the dragons enter our world. They enslaved all living beings on this realm and toyed with us for almost a thousand years. The lords fought back and eventually learned how to use the spires to create a wall around the portal to prevent the dragons from entering our realm. In a great battle, we pushed the dragons back through the portal and created the Dragon Shield. To control the Dragon Shield and the spires, the lords built a massive structure on a floating island above the energy field. They call it Dragonlock Castle. It is where the emperor lives, because his family line has a unique power to control the Dragon Shield's machinery."

"Who is the emperor," Monty said watching the lightning.

"He is an impetuous child in his early teenage years. After his parents were killed, he was too young to rule, so a steward managed the emperor's duty. Recently, the steward has disappeared, and the emperor has taken his place on the throne of the empire. Now, the brat makes irrational decisions with his slithery advisors. It is because of him that the realm is falling apart."

"What has he done?"

"When his military is not abandoning the populace to go run and hide in the protected cities, he spends his time at parties and stripping away land and titles from the nobility. I watched old friends lose everything, because the emperor thought their noses were too big."

"That sounds awful." Monty saw a brief flicker in the wall that released a puff of purple smoke.

"Some say the shield is failing," Caellan said. "The emperor and the nobility claim that the shield had always done that. They say there is nothing to worry about."

"What do you think," Monty said.

"Nothing lasts forever, and I am sure the dragons want their revenge. Eventually, the wall will fail, and dragons will destroy this realm instead of enslaving it again."

"Between demons and dragons trying to destroy everything, what keeps this realm safe?"

"The Divine," Caellan said distantly. "They say good will defeat evil. I am not so sure."

She was shocked by his lack of faith. A paladin should have more faith than anyone else. Her deep memories showed her images of paladins vanquishing evil and helping people. Before she could ask the dispirited man anymore questions, she saw a tall, dark silhouette against the purple-flashing wall. It was a large tower surrounded by an outer wall. Occasionally, lighting would launch from the top of the tower and strike the wall behind it. "Is that a spire," Monty said.

"That is the Fifth Spire," Caellan said. "It is one of twenty-four spires used to create the Dragon Shield. That is where Lady Enix will take us to open a portal to hell and then kill us."

*   *   *   *

Monty thought the spire appeared majestic against the purple wall of energy. However, the spire's interior was much different. After passing through its thick gates, she discovered the spire was composed of twisting, confusing tunnels like the intestines of a great stone beast. The dry, stale air was quickly filled with dust from the entourage's stamping boots. Once inside, Nash and Tomas followed Lady Enix into another dark tunnel while Monty and Caellan were led to a narrow circular stairway.

Walking behind her, Caellan had suggested not to struggle and to go along with their demands. Despite every inch of her wanting to fight these people who killed Djinn, she gritted her teeth and complied. She didn't want to jeopardize the opportunity of getting him back, but she wondered if Lady Enix would keep her side of the agreement. In the end, the demon would kill them all unless she stopped it. She just wished she knew how.

Eventually, they reached a small corridor that led to a larger room lined with prison cells. It was another dusty, dark room. Even the iron prison doors showed their age as their hinges wailed when opened. The guards pushed Monty inside the cell. Looking around, Monty found no comforts like a bed or even a chair. It was just stone with some loose chains hanging on the walls. While she watched the guards from her cell, Caellan just slumped into a corner of his own cell. Two fiery guards and a human mercenary waited at the entrance.

Flames suddenly erupted from the floor of the larger room. After wincing from the bright light; she saw the thing they called Lady Enix emerged from the fireball while it quickly dissipated. This time, Lady Enix was wearing very little clothing and had two large colorful, feathered wings. The human mercenary just watched her while the fiery guards did nothing at all. Then, Monty noticed a wrapped body on the floor behind the demon.

"I hope you don't mind your quarters," Lady Enix said. "You need to stay here for a little while we make the necessary preparations. I don't want you running off, at least not yet. Per our bargain, you and Djinn may leave freely once you have helped me."

"I don't trust you," Monty said. "How do I even know you can bring back someone from the dead?"

Without saying a word, she walked over to the guard. In a fluid motion, she drew the weapon from the guard's scabbard and stabbed him in the stomach with it. Clutching the handle of the sword that went completely through him, he dropped to the ground, gasping for air. Surrounded by his pooling blood, he quickly died. Sickness overwhelmed Monty as she stared at the dead body.

"You horrible creature," Monty said. "You didn't have to kill him."

"Of course I did," Lady Enix said. "Before I can resurrect somebody, they have to be dead." She picked up the limp body with one hand and breathed a blue flame into him. The body spasmed and convulsed. After a moment, it stopped, and Lady Enix gently helped him back on his feet. Monty was astonished to see the dead man alive once more. Raising his head, he saluted Lady Enix and showed no sign of a lethal wound. She returned a salute, and the man thanked her and walked out of the room. "You see now I have the power to bring back Djinn as long as you help me. That is the only way you will get back your friend."

Monty hesitated. She didn't want to help that thing, but this was her chance to get back Djinn. Everything would be much better once Djinn was back. Then, he might kill this thing and stop the demons. As she pondered her options, Lady Enix noticed her hesitation.

"I will let you think about it," Lady Enix said. "You can tell me when I come back. If you need anything, please just yell." Then, she vanished from the room in a ball of flame. The guards left, and the room was quiet and dark.

CHAPTER THIRTY-ONE

Before the Last Kiss

In the lower levels of the Fifth Spire, Tomas walked down a long corridor to the room where is wife slept. He refused to think of her as gone since he would soon be reunited with his beloved. With the curved hallway being so dark and bleak, he became distracted and allowed his mind to dream of their future life together. He needed her to be alive, so he could be whole again. Then, he heard a clattering from a nearby room that dragged his mind away from his longing thoughts.

Looking around, he saw no one else in the hall. There was only an open door that led to another dark corridor nearby. Carefully, he approached the dark opening. Out of the darkness, Nash strolled into the main corridor where Tomas stood.

"Good evening, Tomas," Nash said courteously. He continued to pass Tomas as if nothing were wrong. Tomas looked back down the corridor and realized that it came from one of the spire machinery rooms.

"What are you doing Nash," Tomas said. "Why were you down there?" Nash stopped and turned around. He was wearing a large yellow overcoat covering his brown and black leather outfit underneath. His right arm held a large satchel against his back. Tomas eyed his satchel suspiciously.

"I was just checking on spire's generator to make sure it would be ready for the ceremony," Nash said.

"I didn't think performers knew much about ancient machinery," Tomas said suspiciously.

"You would be surprised at the skills I have picked up over the years."

"What are you really up to?"

"Nothing, I am on my way out."

"So you are leaving us? What about your commitment to Lady Enix? She may still require your services."

"I frankly don't care what she requires. I already betrayed my friends for her. If it weren't for me, she wouldn't have caught Monty in Bonewalk. Now, she can open her portal, and I will enjoy my few remaining days with beautiful women."

"You're the spy that has been sending her messages from Parn and Maliki's ship."

"That's all true," Nash said looking away from Tomas. "I did what I could to stay alive. If not, the demon would have killed me months ago. Now, I have to worry about an apocalyptic army and an angry angel. My odds are not looking so good."

"I thought you killed the angel. You used Montague's weapon. It should have killed him."

"Nothing can kill an angel or demon. The only reason Enikus killed that dragon is that he sacrificed a part of himself. He gave up his power to travel among the planes and back to the Divine. In turn, he was granted the power to kill the dragon. Montague's weapon may be powerful like the ethaerium cannons that were used to injure dragons, but I didn't sacrifice anything. Trust me, Enikus will be back, and I will pay dearly for what I did. It's time to have some fun while I still can. Why don't you come with me?"

"I can't," Tomas said dourly. "I have a promise to keep."

"A promise to Lady Enix," Nash said with disbelief. "You can't trust her. She will turn on you. Even if she gave you your reward, there will be a catch. There's always a catch with demons."

"I am sorry, my friend," Tomas said with a sigh. "I cannot go. I still have to take care of something."

"If you change your mind, take one of these," Nash said throwing a realm-walker at him. Tomas caught it and looked at it carefully. Tomas knew there was more to Nash's story than just self-preservation.

"You still haven't told me what you were doing in the machine room," Tomas said putting the jewel in his pocket.

"Since the demon can't read your mind because of your soulstone, I will tell you what I can. I just made some minor modifications to the generator that runs the defenses."

"You're helping Maliki," Tomas said with apprehension. "He hasn't once reached out to me. Why does he still trust you after your betrayal?"

"He doesn't," Nash said. "Maliki and I have never gotten along. Let's say he never has been a fan of my self-indulgences. Here, we mutually benefit from my assistance. If he kills the demon, then I am free to continue to enjoy life and not get killed by a horde of demons. If he dies, I have one less enemy to worry about. Either way, I win." He finished with a big smile.

"I can't believe you," Tomas sputtered. "I spent the last year trying to protect our friends, and you are trying to get them killed."

"Killing Montague was not protection."

"I had no choice. I had to kill some of them, but I argued to save as many as I could. When this is over, I wanted our friends to remember that I helped them and protected them. They will understand that I couldn't protect all of them."

"That's the difference between you and me. You care about what they think of you. I don't care about what they think of me. They are a bunch of self-righteous, tormented souls. All they focus on is their sins from ten years ago. Some of them ran from their sins trying to escape them. You embraced your sins and their glory it brought you. But, a few of us diluted our sins with drink and women. In the end, our sins make us weak and vulnerable to creatures like Lady Enix. The only way to defeat her is by accepting our past and forgiving ourselves. I, for one, can't do that so I accept that I am one of the villains on this stage we call life."

"We were heroes," Tomas said angrily. "We saved this realm, and we will do it again."

"Keep telling yourself that, my friend, but there is no salvation for all those horrible things we did ten years ago." With that said, Nash turned, and walked down the corridor. "She will betray you," he said as he got further down the hall.

Tomas watched him with disgust but wondered if he were right. Had he made a bad deal with the demon? Was she going to go back on her word? The thought made him cringe with fear. Hastily, he made his way down the hall. He had to know

*   *   *   *

Tomas walked into the crystal room where his wife's body levitated above the floor. He paused for a moment admiring her peaceful appearance. As before, her body appeared to be an eternal slumber. While her eyes remained closed, Tomas felt as though she was reaching out to him like a silent plea for help sprung from her lips. Unable to provide her any comfort, he watched Lady Enix cast spells around her. The witch was the only chance his wife had to live again.

"I bring news of the preparations," Tomas said once the demon finished a spell. "We have completed the soulstone configurations, and the portal is fully charged. We are ready to begin the ceremony."

"In time, there are a few more preparations I have to make," Lady Enix said with here eyes closed as if she were concentrating on some point on the ceiling. "Have all the remaining mercenaries meet me in the control room. I plan to give them their final payment before releasing them."

"What about me?" Tomas said indignantly. "You said you would resurrect my wife as long as I helped you prepare the portal. I have finished my part, and I expect you to bring her back to life. You have been taking weeks casting all your spells. You did it with the other mercenary in a matter of seconds. Why is she not alive yet?"

"The other mercenary was just a parlor trick," Lady Enix said with an evil grin. "He is nothing more than a walking zombie under my command. I had to show the foolish maru I could save her friend."

"Are you going to bring back Djinn?" Tomas said. With so many friends dead, he had a glimmer of joy with one of them being brought back from the dead.

"No, I have no intention of bring back that wizard after all the pain he caused me. I despise him so much I wouldn't even bring him back as a puppet. He and Montague had been a thorn in my side for so long I am glad they are both dead now."

"You will bring back my wife," Tomas said with pleading eyes.

"Your wife resurrection is soon at hand," Lady Enix said. "Soon, she will be awake and you can continue your miserable relationship."

"We were not miserable until that night. We were happy. We loved to be around each other."

"Remarkable, you lie so often that you lie to your own self. She despised you. I have been reconstructing her soul and memories. I have seen how much she hated you and your lies. Did you know she never lied once to you?"

"That night, she had lied about whom she was with. I saw her sneak back in and then have the gall to lie to my face that she was not with another man. If she had only told me the truth, I could have found the other man and stopped him from seducing my wife."

"That is so funny." Her strange laughter echoed through the chamber. "She told you the truth. She was never with another man."

"Then, where was she?"

"She was with her brother. The same brother she hid from you. She was trying to save him so you didn't kill him."

"Why would I kill her own brother? I loved her and her family. I would never actively hurt anyone close to her."

"He had turned into a corrupted, and she was trying to help him find his way back. She thought there was a way to turn him back while you would have destroyed him."

"She could have told me. I would have listened to her and tried to help her." Tomas was lying to himself. He hated the corrupted and would have destroyed it, no matter whom they were related too.

"She knew better. She thought she knew you better is before you killed her."

"You promised that you would never speak of that."

"You mean when you became so angry that you took out your sword and ran it through her gut like she was some dog."

Tomas stepped back. The memories of his bloody blade piercing her beautiful stomach churned his stomach. He remembered her eyes as she stared at him in horror. She looked at him like a monster. Even then, she used her last dying breath to say "I love you" to him. In return, he kissed her lips gently. His heart shattered that day and his life ended while holding his wife's bloody body.

"Stop what you are saying," he cried. "I need her to come back to life." He knew the only way to remove the painful memories was to bring her back to life. "I did all this for her. So, I can save her. That is why I released you from that prison. That is why I made the deal with you. You save her, and I help you open the portal. The portal is ready to be opened, and I expect to walk out of here with my wife." He was shaking with anger.

"Your wife will walk out of here today," Lady Enix said sinisterly. "She will wake up and come for you. She will remember all those terrible things you said to her and all the lies you told her. She will know all the people that you have murdered for her salvation. When she finds you, do you think she will be happy or upset?"

"You were supposed to wipe away the memories of me killing her. That was the deal."

"I wiped away those memories of you impaling her, but she will remember those murderous eyes when you pulled your sword. When you speak, Carina will only be reminded of your jealous rage. Do you think she will ever forgive you and run back into your arms?"

Tomas just stared at the demon. In that moment, he realized that the demon was right. He had made a terrible mistake. If Tomas brought her back, she would only know more pain when she looked at him or when she saw her brother as a corrupted. He wanted to save her and bring himself salvation. Instead, he has cursed her by bringing her back to this realm of anguish and death.

"I changed my mind," Tomas said shivering with fear. "I want her to stay dead. You can keep your portal."

"It is too late," Lady Enix said placing her hand on the woman's abdomen. "She will be awake soon, and she has so much to tell you."

"No, I will not see her again."

Tomas ran out of the room while Lady Enix laughed. He had to escape the spire quickly. In the dark corridor, he pulled out the realm-walker jewell. Looking back at the distant room, he hoped the spire would be destroyed before his wife awoke. Maybe, she still escaped the agony of life. He knew what he had to do, Focusing on the jewel, he used it to leave the spire forever.

CHAPTER THIRTY-TWO

Darkness

Monty just sat in the darkness. Normally, she would have sung her normal song, but it never came to her. While she believed it was the right decision to save Djinn, it didn't feel right. Instead, she felt sick with anguish, wrapping her arms around herself tightly. Nothing would make her feel any better. She was alone and helpless.

"So, what is your plan," Caellan said in the distance.

"I haven't gotten all the details worked out yet," Monty said. "Basically, I will only make her think that I am helping her until Djinn is resurrected. Then, he will help me find my special power that can destroy the demon." After she said it out loud, it didn't seem that great of a plan but that was all she had for the moment.

"So you plan to outwit the demon," Caellan said wryly. "Don't you know you can't outwit evil? It will make you think you're winning, but then it will stab you in the back when you're not looking."

"What do you know of outwitting anything," Monty said sourly. "The only thing you seem to be good at is giving up and wallowing in despair."

"What do you think we did ten years ago," Caellan said. "With over six month's of secret planning and scavenging, we had a plan to outwit this demon creature. Instead, she waited until we were complicit and slowly assassinated each one of us. With most of the old group dead, she has possession of most of the soulstones again and will reopen the portal to some hellish realm. The only thing we did was delay the inevitable and strengthened her."

"There is still a way to beat her," Monty said. Then, she saw a faint light coming up the stairwell. "Someone is coming." Caellan didn't respond, but Monty didn't really care. She was tired of his dour mood.

As the light got brighter, it revealed a cloaked figure carrying a lantern. The figure's gate was slow but soundless. Walking to Monty's cell, she watched the lantern's bright light release a thousand shadows within her cell. Monty just stared at the approaching light.

At the cell door, it slid a metal tray into Monty's cell. With a grating whine, it stopped itself only a foot from the door. Dark food filled the tray's crevices. Looking up from the food, Monty saw a woman's slender face hidden in the hood.

"Eat up child, it will give you strength," the woman said. Between the familiar voice and the weathered eyes, Monty recognized her friend.

"Nora, you're alive," Monty whispered eagerly. "I am so glad you escaped. Are you okay? Where have you been?"

"Careful Monty," Caellan said. Covered in shadows, he leaned against the bars of his cell. "How do you know this isn't some trick like Nash? How do we know she isn't working with Lady Enix?"

"You don't," Nora said annoyed. "I guess you have to trust me." She gave Monty a wink and smiled before walking over to Caellan's cell.

"Why is that," Caellan said bitterly. "Druids care only about nature such as the strong devouring the weak."

"You are so boring," Nora said. "We value balance. Sometimes, the weak must survive so they can become strong. Regardless, rampaging demons are not good for any kind of balance. Now, are we done with philosophy?"

Caellan didn't respond. Monty watched him smolder while looking for words. After a moment, he dropped his head down in defeat with a disgruntled expression.

"Besides, I took only this horrible form so I could give you this." Nora pulled a large two-handed sword from under her cloak. It was the same beautiful sword that Caellan had wielded at the castle. Caellan grabbed it and pulled it into his cell. He held the blade upright and studied it for a few moments. "So, tell me, knight, do you trust this druid now?"

"Why did you bring this?" Caellan said. "I have no use for it here. It will only prolong the inevitable."

"Perhaps," Nora said thoughtfully. "I brought it, so you can protect her."

"I can't protect anyone," Caellan said as he put down the sword. "I, especially, can't protect those close to me and will only fail again."

"The only thing I care about is protecting her," Nora said pointing to Monty. "I don't care about you or your self-pity. Montague and Djinn both died to save her, and I will gladly die for her. If you want to die so badly, you should do it for someone like her."

"Djinn won't be dead for long," Monty blurted. "I can save him."

"Tell me something, child," Nora said. "If you work with that demon to save Djinn, how many people would die in the process? Would Djinn want that?"

"There is a power he is supposed to help me find," Monty said.

"How many people are you willing to kill for this power," Nora said darkly.

Monty was taken aback. She never realized her quest could actually hurt people. "If I don't get this power, how am I supposed to help? I don't have a magical sword or ship. I can't cast any spells or change into animals. What am I supposed to do?" Trying to hide her tears, she buried her head in her arms. "I want it so bad, but I promised I wouldn't hurt anyone."

"That is why you must protect her," Nora said to Caellan. "She is a far better person than we were. We chose power over good and paid dearly for it." Silently, Caellan turned away from Nora.

"I will protect her," he said after a few moments. "You are right. She is better and far more powerful than we."

"What powers," Monty said with tears running down her cheeks. "I have no powers. I can't do anything except sit here."

"Power does not come from magic or items," Nora said returning to Monty's cell. "Power comes from within you. Listen child. As long as you believe in yourself with confidence, kindness, and faith, you can achieve anything. That is the true power. It is a power that can bring down tyrants and destroy all evil either directly or indirectly. Your part in this is just as important if not more important than ours."

Monty slowly stopped crying while she thought about all the people that have helped her. She remembered the maid, the corrupted and the assassin who saved her from the baron. While looking at her dear friend's body, she thought about the funny wizard, the kind druid, and the strange navigator who guided her to the angel. Even the sour sage and cranky sergeant brought her a small smile. They had all given up so much to help her, and now she would throw it all away.

"I hate not knowing what my part is in this adventure," Monty said quietly. "I don't know whether I will live or die, but I want you to know I appreciate everything you have done for me. I won't let your sacrifice be in vain."

"You are a good creature and let no one tell you differently," Nora said smiling. "I must go now, but I won't be far."

"Nora," Monty said as the druid made her way out of the room. "You look nice as a human. You should take that form more often."

"Maybe, but I am not about to give up my tail, and cat naps," Nora said before disappearing.

*   *   *   *

Monty sat in the darkness for hours until somebody came. Thinking about her mistakes, she felt like days had passed. Occasionally, she would focus on a faint glimmer of floating light in the distance. Still in a gloomy state, Monty didn't care if it were a reflection, magic, dust, or some kind of spirit. It reminded her she had not been completely forgotten. With the approaching footsteps, she forced herself out of her stupor and prepared herself for whatever came next.

"Are you ready to do your part," Lady Enix said as she approached Monty's cell. There were two fiery guards escorting her. The demon ignored Caellan's deadly stare. Looking back at Monty, Caellan nodded and gave her a reassuring smile.

"I… I can't… I cannot go along with your plan," Monty said. At first, she was nervous, but she gained confidence with each word. "I won't betray Djinn's memory by hurting other people."

"So, you are much weaker and foolish than I thought," Lady Enix said. "Don't worry, it means death will come much quicker." She took chains from one of the fiery guards and released them. Instead of dropping to the floor, they briefly hovered in midair before flying through the bars of Monty's cell. Wrapping around her, Monty cried out in pain as the chains glowed red hot.

"Stop that," Caellan shouted. "If you want to torture someone, you should torture me. You listen to me you cursed creature." Monty cries became louder as the pain increased. "Stop hurting her."

"What will you do?" Lady Enix said to Caellan. "You have abandoned the Divine and so you have no real power to hurt me. You are useless, and I promise you that your death will be full of pain. Now, you will have to excuse me. I have a realm to end."

After Lady Enix opened the cell door, the chains levitated Monty into the air. Bobbing gently in the air and still in pain, Monty floated after Lady Enix as she and her entourage left the room. Caellan continued to yell curses and obscenities at Lady Enix until he was left in the dark.

CHAPTER THIRTY-THREE

The Tower Wizard

In a flash of light, Calais appeared in a dark forest. She was surrounded by several old trees with gnarled faces staring at her with grim expressions. Many of them had lost their leaves and stabbed the grey night sky with their twisted branches. The ground was mostly dirt and dead leaves that crunched under her feet. Occasionally, she would hear a call from an owl or the squeaking chirp of a bat. No other movement could be seen among the tree trunks. Feeling suddenly alone and vulnerable, she wrapped her arms around herself and walked to the dark tower in the distance.

While the rest of her friends made plans to attack the spire, Calais had to get her summoner's books. If she were going to be of any help at all, she needed her magic. Unfortunately, she knew she had little time, and Maliki refused to travel near the tower.

Navigators and Tower wizards had a deep dislike for each other. Their views on the universe were very different, and they often fought with each other because of it. While the navigators explored the planes and collected artifacts, tower wizards saw themselves as defenders of the realm that included any artifacts. They regarded the navigators as thieves and meddlers. To make matters worse, she remembered stories of tower wizards harnessing energies from within the realm and could damage or kill the navigators, if they got too close. While many other orders within the Lord's Council didn't care about their feuds, Calais felt the realm was worse off for each tower wizard or a navigator killed because of their disagreements. Calais knew Maliki harbored no ill-will to her brother, Arturo, the tower wizard, but he preferred not to take any chances. Maliki got as close as he could and teleported her with a few miles of the tower. Although it was not very far, the dark, decaying forest made if feel much further.

Calais walked for a long time, but the tower seemed no closer than before. Feeling tired, she wanted to stop and rest. The weariness of the last several tragic days still hung over her. She leaned against a twisting tree trying to get some of her strength back. Then, a flicker of light caught her attention. Straining her eyes, Calais saw a distant fire.

She made her way to the fire trying to move with stealth. Not knowing whether it was a friend or foe, Calais didn't want to take a chance since she was all alone. Getting closer, she saw a dark figure leaning against a tree. He stayed motionless and didn't appear to notice her. Using her ability to see in the dark, she saw more of the figure's details with each step. It was an older man with light armor. He had no visible weapons. Without warning, he pointed a finger directly at her.

"You can stop right there," the old man said. "It's no use sneaking up. I heard you a mile away." A broad smile appeared on Calais' face when she realized who he was.

"Marek, you're alive still," Calais said running over to her old friend. "Where have you been? I thought Lady Enix had killed you."

"No, the demon hasn't killed me yet," Marek said. "Believe me, I will not sit around and wait for her. I have been trying to assemble in army, but everyone wants to run away from her or help her. The imperial army wouldn't give me any soldiers and the Lords' Council have refused my request. I hoped your brother, Arturo, would help me fight her. Instead, he hides in his tower and won't even open the door."

"You will be happy to know we are not running anymore," Calais said kneeling down next to him. "Maliki, Denarith, Caezik, and I are getting ready to attack Lady Enix at the Fifth Spire. I am only here to get my books from Arturo, so I can be more effective."

"You finally came to your senses," Marek said. "I would be happy to lend my skills to destroy that witch."

"You realize that this is a suicide mission, right," Calais said. They needed his help, but she also needed him to understand the danger.

"I love suicide missions," Marek said with wide grin. "You can count on me." Then, Calais remembered that the hardened veteran wasn't afraid of anything and loved it when the odds were against him.

"Thank you, sarge," Calais said putting her hand on his shoulder. "I am glad there are few of us still out here."

"So where are these books," Marek said standing up.

"In the tower with Arturo," she said. "He is one of the few people in this realm I truly trust."

"I don't know that I trust him, but I didn't have many people I could turn too. He was always a strange fellow."

After Marek gathered his supplies and put out the fire, he walked with her to the tower. Marek lit a lantern so he could see his way through the dead brambles. No animals or insects made any sounds, and Calais heard only the wind blowing through leafless branches. Occasionally, she would put her hand on the grey, almost-lifeless tree trunks. Something bothered Calais about the dead forest. She couldn't put her finger on it.

"There is something strange about this forest," Calais said while they continued walking.

"Have you met your brother," Marek said. "Like I said, he is a very strange fellow indeed. Most likely, he is doing some weird experiment."

Like Calais, Arturo enjoyed his studies. He always found the sciences most fascinating. Instead of sword practice or hunting, he wanted to learn more about the surrounding plants and animals. Because of their lack of interest in such areas, Caellan and Caezik often derided or distanced themselves from Arturo. This caused Calais and Arturo to be closer as they grew up. Mostly, she loved debating various ideas and theories with him, but he tended to have a more cynical view of the world. Calais always blamed his cynicism on him being adopted by her father.

She remembered the day he came to her home. Being only a year apart, they were both very young. Her mother had passed away when she was two years old, and her father refused to remarry. Instead, he adopted a boy several years later. He claimed the boy was as special as the rest of them. Arturo had black straight hair and pale skin. Unlike her gold eyes, he had black irises that made is eyes appear like black starless nights. His quiet demeanor differed greatly from her boisterous brothers. He would not speak with anyone for days. He just nodded or shook his head. One day, he saw her with a flower in her hair while she danced around the room to a performing minstrel. He said she was the prettiest dancing flower he had ever seen.

For a while, she was the only person he would talk too when he was not buried in books. Over the years, they remained close, but something always bothered her about him. Not knowing what it was, Calais never spoke of it to anyone. While her father treated him like his own son, Arturo had enough problems with her brothers. After their father's death, they all went on their separate ways. Arturo kept in touch with Calais but he never reached out to his brothers. Sometimes, he claimed he had no brothers. Despite her attempts to keep the family together, Calais knew her brothers never reached out to Arturo either. Their father's execution was the last time they were all together.

After walking for some time, they finally came to the door to the dark tower. A cold wind blew around the tower sending shivers up Calais' back. Marek gave Calais an uncertain look and pounded against the door. Usually,

Arturo would have met Calais on the road before they even got to the tower. Instead, they were knocking on the doors like strangers. After knocking a few more times, the doors finally opened.

The tower's interior appeared completely dark. Knowing her brother would never hurt her, Calais stepped into the entryway. Marek followed behind her slowly. Once they were fully inside, the doors shut behind them. Something in the darkness ahead of them moved. They stood their ground as the shadows and light slowly coalesced around an approaching figure.

"Welcome to my home," Arturo said with a deep bow. He had long straight black hair that framed his pale, elongated face. He had a hawkish nose and black searching eyes. Long black robes covered his thin, angular frame. "I am so happy to see you again, Calais." He gave her a long, embracing hug. The stench of his unbathed body was almost unbearable. Afterwards, he smiled at her and shook hands with Marek. "It has been a long time, lord sergeant."

"Indeed, it has, Lord Master Arturo," Marek said grimacing. "I see you still don't bathe or clean your tower." The bit of light in the hallway revealed clutter and trash pushed against the stone walls.

"Well, I am very busy with important work and don't have time for those little things," Arturo said with a weak smile.

"Arturo, I am here for my book," Calais said. They had to move quickly. Arturo had a nasty temper that could be bad for them. Like navigators, tower wizards had full control of their tower's interior and could create almost anything they wanted. No one ever survived an angry wizard's tower.

"Of course," Arturo said grinning. "You must first dine with me. I want to hear what has been going on in the outside world."

*   *   *   *

They had a small dinner of sausage, cheese, and beans in a small room. The only light came from lit candles that hung on the stone walls. The table was a plain piece of rectangular wood with a wooden leg at each corner. Arturo sat at one end of the table picking at his food while Marek sat next to him eating ravenously. Calais sat across from Marek and only ate a few bites. Since the skydocks, she had regained little of her appetite.

After savoring each bite, she would continue her tale of their escape from Lady Enix and all the places they had gone. Arturo listened intently and only asked a few questions here and there. He appeared extremely sad when he heard about Estasia's death. Calais knew he had always been infatuated with her, but she never returned the affection. Estasia preferred men of action to men of science. Once she completed her tale, she quickly explained that she needed to get her books to fight Lady Enix.

251

"Will you join us," Marek said after cleaning off his plate. "A tower wizard would be a valuable asset."

"I must decline," Arturo said. "I have extremely important work that I must complete."

"Your work will mean nothing when the realm is overrun by demons," Marek said.

"There is more going on with Lady Enix than you realize," Arturo said. "What the general said about destroying the spire is correct to an extent. I don't know the full details, but my spies report that they are attempting to capture the demonic souls."

"That can't be true," Marek said aghast. "They would be fools to play with demons especially their souls. What would they do with them?"

"I don't know," Arturo said swirling around the last of his wine. "Some of them fear the corrupted so much that they are willing to do anything. That is why you must go to the tower and try to stop Lady Enix. I must stay here and work on my contingency plan if you fail."

"What contingency plan," Calais said. "People have been trying to stop the corrupted for decades now. I imagine demonic armies are much worse than the corrupted."

"In the last couple of years, I have found the answer. I have figured out a way to transform the souls within the corrupted. Come, let me show you."

They all got up from the table and followed Arturo. Marek gave Calais a questioning look, but Calais just shrugged. With everything going on, Calais really didn't care about solving the corrupted problem especially with the potential of an invading demon army. However, she still cared about her brother, so she let him show her his new experiments. They walked down a long corridor before entering a large chamber.

The floor was covered by bones and several corrupted were chained to the wall. They were the animal-like corrupted appearing as wolf-man hybrids. When she got closer, Calais noticed the skin was slowly falling from them and their hollow eyes looked only at her. She didn't see any ferocity or anger. Her summoner abilities allowed her to see that there was almost no life inside them. All she saw was a strange spark inside them she had seen elsewhere.

"These corrupted are undead," Calais said stepping back. "You ripped their souls out of them and turned them into soulless monsters."

"These soulless monsters are controllable," Arturo said proudly while looking at the strange creatures. "We have nothing to fear from the corrupted any longer. I have found a way to change their souls and make them compliant. They will become an unstoppable army."

"Who's unstoppable army?" Marek said disgusted. "Taking away a man or a monster's soul is terrible, because you take away their freewill. They are nothing but machines. Besides, if you can take away a corrupted soul, does that mean you can take away a human soul?"

"The application would be similar," Arturo pondered. "The empire and I have been talking about the ability to manipulate souls for many years now. You could create an army of drones that work and fight without complaint or needs. The human bodies are remarkable devices we have yet to reproduce in machines. Why recreate the wheel when we can just repurpose the body?"

"We are talking about a person's soul," Marek said angrily. "Their soul make them who they are. Changing their soul or damaging it is completely immoral. It goes against everything the Divine teaches."

"I have no use for the Divine," Arturo said nonchalantly. "I can see and manipulate the realm around me. Why do I need the Divine? What can he give me I can't learn on my own?"

"You are a fool," Marek growled. "You are playing with forces you can't possibly fathom and will destroy you and everyone around you."

"Enough," Calais yelled. "Both of you need to stop. Arturo, please take me to my room so I can get my books. Marek, I will meet you at the tower's main door and we will leave."

They promptly left the chamber, and Arturo led her up a long stairwell. Grateful, Marek disappeared into a hallway that led out of the tower. Arturo tried to apologize, but she rebuffed him. Soul manipulation was a terrible act, and she couldn't believe he would do such a thing. After a short time, they came to the door to her room. She entered the room with Arturo standing outside the door.

It was a small room with a bed, a chest, and a large bookshelf. Looking at the shelf for a moment, Calais saw many books she had owned growing up. Many of them were out-of-date science books, and some of them were nonsensical children stories. Calais didn't understand why he would keep them. Turning her attention to a blank stone wall, she carefully pressed a few stones to make them open into a secret chamber. Summoners could store their books in special inter-planar spaces to prevent thieves from getting them. The downside is that there could be only one access point. She knew Arturo's tower would always be a safe place, so she hid them here for safekeeping. Reaching into the small space, she pulled the large dusty tome, a jeweled dagger, and a carrying satchel out of the niche. With the items removed, the stone wall closed up and reverted to a flat stone wall.

Sitting on the bed, she carefully thumbed through it. Many creatures of different realms populated the pages. She stopped briefly at a picture of a squad of air elves flying spiderlights. She had drawn it during one of her visits to see Rev. Part of her missed him and hoped he was safe. Before closing the book, she remembered the pages she had drawn at the military camp.

Calais delicately pulled out the pages from her belt satchel and infused the pages into her book. After a few moments of the book glowing, she saw that the pages disappeared and then reappeared as new pages at the end of the book. It still had many more blank pages. With the book back in the carrying satchel, she hung the satchel over her shoulder so it lay across her body. Then, she positioned her red jacket over the satchel and hung the sheathed dagger on her belt.

Stepping out of the room, Calais found Arturo hovering near the door. He had a leering gaze. "What are you doing," she said anxiously.

"I want to show you something," he said excitedly. "I didn't want to tell you about it in front of Marek. He wouldn't understand. Come with me. I have made a breakthrough."

"Then, lead the way," she said.

They walked down the stairwell and went into a small corridor that led to a large red door. Arturo walked hastily to the door and unlocked it. Calais followed him, but she kept her distance. While he was always a little odd, his strange behavior seemed even more unusual. When he opened the door, he walked in and motioned her to follow.

She walked through the door and found her self at the edge of a large circular chamber. A large cylindrical capsule hovered in midair at the center of the chamber. It had several hoses connected to it that extended from the walls. There were giant holes in the roof and the floor of the chamber, and the mysterious whirring machine shot bright beams continuously through each opening. Looking at the dragon carvings on it, Calais quickly recognized the device.

"This was father's machine," Calais said astonished. "He never got it working. How did you figure it out?"

"I don't want to go into the details now," Arturo said enthusiastically. "I actually figured it out. Father was using it to harness the energies from the land to counteract the dragon's curse. I can drain the land and use that energy to rebuild our homeland."

"You mean the curse he caused on the land," Calais said suspiciously. Growing up, she didn't notice it immediately, but the blight on their land spread over the years. Some say her father created a terrible spell that had backfired cursing their land. Obviously, he denied it and eventually found a way to save the land using Starlight Trees. Then, Calais remembered the forest outside.

"You are killing the forest like the blight did in our homeland," Calais said accusingly. "This is why they executed father, because he was using dragon magic. The council will kill you."

"It is necessary," Arturo said dispassionately. "I need the energy from this land if I shall cure the blight in our own land."

"This is like stealing," Calais said frustrated. "You are taking land from one baron and giving it to our own. What you are doing is wrong."

"I don't understand," Arturo said furiously. "Of all our father's children, I thought you would understand what he was trying to do. He was trying to cure the land of the dragon's blight. He knew he had to hurt people and the land if he would save everyone else. You are as closed-minded as Caellan and Caezik. I thought I knew you were better, but I was wrong."

The tower was shaking with his anger. Shadowy tentacles arced through the air. She had to distract him somehow if she would escape. Looking back at the machine and the hoses, she had an idea and hoped it wouldn't kill them all.

Calais pulled the dagger from her belt and sliced through several hoses. As a gift from her father, the dagger was made of a special metal that allowed its sharp edge to never dull. It took only one swipe to cut through each of the thick hoses. Hot steam and yellow gases bellowed from the broken hoses. Arturo cried out in fear and had his shadowy tentacles grab the loose hoses. With his focus taken away from Calais, the tower stopped shaking and all the candles seem to reignite. Seeing the staircase through the small corridor, she dashed out of the room.

With the way down blocked by fallen debris, Calais raced up the stairs. If she could get to the roof, she might summon something to get her to safety. Running upward, she heard several explosions from the chamber she had just left. Calais didn't want to see Arturo hurt, but she had to keep him distracted long enough for her to escape. After a long climb, she finally came to the top level. Throwing the door open, Calais rushed into another long corridor that went around the tower. She only had to find the stairs to the roof.

Running through the hall, she threw each door open. Most rooms were cluttered storage rooms or guest rooms. When she threw open another door, it appeared empty. Then, she heard a familiar voice that warmed her heart.

"Wait, help me," Rev shouted. Calais looked back into the empty room where she saw Rev shackled to the wall.

"How did you get here?" Calais said grabbing a key off the nearby wall. She carefully removed the shackles from Rev. "You should have left this realm already."

"I tried to leave, but I was attacked by your weird brother," Rev said rubbing his wrists. "Some strange black cloud enveloped me and brought me here. He said I couldn't leave because he didn't want you to find me. He has some really weird obsession with you."

"I have no idea what is wrong with him," Calais said. "He has been using father's dragon machines, and I think it might have caused him to go crazy which is why we have to get out of here."

"My spiderlight is on the roof," Rev said looking at a jeweled display on his wrist.

"Great, now we have to find the ladder to the roof," Calais said running back into the hall.

"I smell no fresh air," Rev said joining her. "Trust me, I know air."

Without warning, the walls and floor shook. The lanterns went out around them. Her brother had regained some control, and now he was after them. Calais pushed Rev back into the room where he was held prisoner.

"What are we going to do now," Rev said.

"We don't have much time," Calais said. "I can feel the tower's interior starting to change. Soon, we could be in the basement and never escape."

"Then, summon something," Rev said tapping her book satchel.

"I don't know whether I can," Calais said pulling out the book. "I am scared. If I lose control, I could kill people. I could hurt you." She stared at the book in terror. Rev gently pulled her chin to his calm face.

"Do you want to kill people," Rev said.

"No, I don't want to hurt anyone," Calais said anxiously.

"Then, trust yourself," Rev said. "I know your heart, and you won't hurt anyone."

They looked at each other for a long moment, but the tower shuddered again. Almost losing her balance, Calais returned her attention to the book. She opened it and thought about what was needed for this situation. In the distance, they heard Arturo's voice.

"You have no escape," Arturo said. "I know you don't understand, but in time, you see I am right. I will show you how I will cure the blight and the rest of the world of these celestial curses. People have to die to save this realm. With your help, we can change all the living things on this realm as they should have been created. Don't be afraid, I can show you. You have no where to run. These stone walls are impenetrable."

"Your brother is one crazy fool," Rev said shaking his head. "No one should have to die, and mutants are never the answer. I met a few in a bar once, or they could've been really ugly humans. I can't say, but mutants are definitely not friendly. They through me against this stonewall and…"

"That's it," Calais said as the book pages flipped to a page that displayed a large stone giant. "We are surrounded by stone walls. I can use this stone shaper I saw on Occraendrall. They are very rare to see since they live within the rock cliffs. I was traveling…"

"I bet it was wonderful," Rev said over the rumbling tower. "You need to cast that spell quickly."

With a deep focus, she concentrated on the image. Since she was out-of-practice, it took longer for her mind to grasp the image. After a few more moments, it became easier to feel the image and the rest of the images in the book. Her mind stroked the life forces that the book contained, and the memories of conjuring came flooding back to her all at once. With a renewed vigor, she mentally grasped the image and pulled on it. The book glowed, and the stone giant dragged itself from the page.

The stone shaper was made of boulders and smaller rocks but still was shaped like a large human. It ducked down in the small room waiting for her command. Then, Calais told it to force its way to the roof. The stone giant raised its arms and pushed against the ceiling. Feeling it struggle against the tower wizard's magic, Calais focused her energy on the giant increasing its strength and power. The ceiling collapsed around them with a thunderous roar. The stone shaper made sure nothing fell on her or Rev. Above them, Calais could see grey cloudy skies. With another mental command from Calais, she made the stone shaper pick them up and placed them gently on the roof of the tower. Seeing the spiderlight, Rev jumped on it and started the activation sequence. After putting her book in the satchel, Calais sat behind him and put her arms around his torso. She silently thanked the giant and caused him to dissolve into glittering sparkles while he returned to her book.

"You cannot leave," Arturo shrieked. "I need you! You must stay here. Please don't go, my dancing flower."

Before she could answer, Rev activated the spiderlight, and they flew off the roof into the grey sky. Looking back, Calais saw the tower was enveloped in black tentacles. In the corner of her eye, she saw movement on the ground. A figure was running away from the tower. With closer inspection, she realized it was Marek.

"We have to save Marek," she said in Rev's ear. "He is below us in the forest."

"You brought that crotchety old man with you," Rev said annoyed. "Do we have to save him?"

"Yes, we do," Calais said rolling her eyes. "You must hurry before Arturo gets him."

"Fine," Rev said.

He threw the spiderlight into a stomach-churning loop, and they dove back to the ground. With the wind rushing against her face, she held onto Rev tightly. Black tentacles shot out of the tower trying to grab the spiderlight. With quick maneuvers, Rev avoided them before leveling out above the ground. The vehicle twisted and turned around the dead trees while streaking towards Marek that was still running. Once they got to Marek, Rev slowed the spiderlight down and flew next to the fleeing sergeant.

"Get on, sarge," Calais called out. "It is the only way we will escape Arturo."

"I hate flying," Marek puffed. "I would rather die of a heart attack."

"Just get on," Calais said. "We have to get to the Fifth Spire if we will help Maliki."

Grumbling, he jumped on the spiderlight behind Calais. The vehicle whined under the heavier strain of three people. Rev flipped some switches, and the vehicle raced into the sky as it headed for the Fifth Spire.

"Are you okay?" Calais said looking back at Marek.

"I will be fine as soon as I throw up on you."

CHAPTER THIRTY-FOUR

The Widow's Touch

Caellan surged with anger as he watched Monty get taken away. He didn't know what the demon had planned, but he knew Monty would die in great pain. Of all people in the realm, he knew she did not deserve that fate. Fiercely pulling on the bars, he was ready to rip apart the cell and the spire itself. He yelled and screamed until their lantern light finally vanished.

Finding himself in the quiet darkness, he jerked himself away from the bars and kicked them several times. He knew it wouldn't do any good, but it felt mildly cathartic. After walking around his cell and striking the walls in fury, he calmed down and finally think straight. With a flick of his wrist, he made his sword reappear in his hands. A paladin could never be separated from his holy weapon.

Focusing on the sword, Caellan made it glow with a soft white light. Able to see the surrounding area, he looked around for some clue on what to do next. He knew little about spires or their portal technology, and it would be extremely difficult to fight Lady Enix and her guards alone. He knew Nora was nearby, but she would still not be enough. Then, the light showed him what he must do.

With two swipes, he sliced away the cell bars and walked over to Djinn's body. Looking at his friend, he cracked a small smile remembering the crazy, good-hearted wizard. Caellan knew he needed crazy. He hoped he still had enough of the Divine's grace to do this next part.

The widow's touch was a power that few understood. Even the paladins didn't really understand it. It was a ritual that few performed in their lives and even less talked about it. The few stories that Caellan had heard spoken of the Divine himself moving through the paladin. Some described it more than a curse. Once a paladin knew the ultimate love and power of the Divine, they saw only the evil taint that covered the realm. Some went crazy while others put down their swords to help the sick and helpless. He hoped he was strong enough to save Monty before going to crazy himself.

Caellan knelt down next to the body and placed his hands upon the empty shell. Breathing deeply, Caellan focused his energies through his hands. Nothing happened and Caellan wondered if he were already crazy. Then, he felt a warm energy moving through him.

It enveloped Caellan's eyes in a warm, white light. The room and body tore away from him, and he found himself flying through his homeland. He recognized the groves and pastures he played in as a child. Then, he saw his home, Castle Pellandarr, standing tall in a shining light. Getting closer, he saw four towers burst from the ground around his home. The shining light faded, and darkness over took the land. At the bottom of each tower, he saw Caezik, Calais, and himself lying dead. His father's body laid in the fourth tower. Then, the towers shuddered, and each one became a tail for four stone scorpions. They stabbed the castle with their massive stone tails, and it slowly bled and crumbled. A massive earthquake shook the land as a head with a crown of horns, and an elongated snout emerged from the remains of his home. He had never seen a dragon before, but the awful sight made Caellan shudder. Opening his snout to reveal many rows of jagged, sharp teeth, the dragon breathed flame on the land. Everything was destroyed including the scorpions.

Suddenly, the flames and dragon vanished, and Caellan found himself standing on charred land. Caellan's sword rested against a burned tree. Next to the sword, Caellan saw Djinn laying their peacefully while holding a beautiful, white flower. As the sword glowed, other flowers grew around Djinn. The tree grew while releasing a thousand leaves along it's growing branches. After only a few moments, the charred land was replaced with beautiful fields of white trees and flowers. Then, Djinn's eyes opened.

Caellan found himself back in the dark room next to Djinn that was sitting up. Like waking up from a deep sleep, Djinn just yawned and stretched his arms out. Slowly, he stood up, and felt his green bald head.

"Ah, Caellan," Djinn said surprised. "When did you get to Bonewalk and have you seen my hat? I seem to have misplaced it." He searched the room, low and high, as if nothing had happened. Caellan just sat there in shock.

"Did you see the vision too?" Caellan said.

"What vision?" Djinn said. "I only recall falling asleep after I was stabbed by Tomas. I dreamed about some strange white light."

"Djinn, you have been dead for over a day now," Caellan said in shock. "The Divine let me save you." His head was still swimming with images from his vision.

"Dead, that's not possible," Djinn said confused. "I should have seen fields flowing with blood of endless battles with lots of… chanting… and singing."

Then, Caellan remembered why he brought the orc back to life. "We must hurry," Caellan said standing up. "Monty is in trouble, and I need your help to rescue her." Caellan picked up his glowing sword and noticed the wizard was still looking for his hat. "The hat is in the cell over there. Monty protected it while you were 'sleeping'."

"Oh, how thoughtful of her," Djinn said as he found his large brimmed hat. He brushed it off and slowly put it back on his head. "Now, I am ready to save the day."

Without checking for guards, Djinn nonchalantly exited the room and made his way down the stairs. Surprised, Caellan quickly looked around for any alerted guards and caught back up with Djinn. "We need a plan," Caellan said in a loud whisper.

"We have a plan," Djinn said. "We kill the guards, stop Lady Enix and save Monty."

"We need a strategy," Caellan insisted. "We are severely outnumbered." As they exited the stairway, they entered a large hallway. Several fire knights rushed at them. Without missing a step, Djinn effortlessly waved his hand while releasing several large bolts of energy. The fire knights were disintegrated in a large explosion of energy. "Well, maybe we're not quite as outnumbered as I thought. What about the chaos effects? I noticed no green flowers, blue haze or anything else strange."

"I never created green flowers," Djinn said indignantly. "I know exactly what I cast and what needs to be cast. Like any good chaos wizard, I just channel those energies into the effects I want. Right now, Lady Enix and her minions don't deserve flowers."

"You mean, you did those bizarre effects on purpose?" The wizard remained silent, but Caellan knew the truth. The orc wizard was truly insane. In their current circumstances, Caellan knew a crazy wizard would be more helpful than a sane one. Shrugging his shoulders, Caellan followed the wizard without further questions.

As they continued down the long hallway, a large eagle flew towards them and changed into a black jaguar. "I have scouted the area, and the defenses have been brought down per the plan," Nora said while walking next to them. "There were eighteen guards stationed outside and a few dozen patrolling the halls. There are about thirty guards in the main chamber."

"So, she will be used as a capacitor to open a stable portal to another plane," Djinn said. "It's exactly as Montague planned."

"What do you mean?" Caellan said shocked. "Are you saying she is supposed to die?"

"Oh no," Djinn said dismissively. "We were going to use her to permanently banish Lady Enix before she could escape or be released. While we were too late in preventing her escape, we have a chance now to stop her."

"How does Monty stop a demon?" Nora said.

"That's easy," Djinn said. "She just has to redirect the portal to ensnare the demon and banish it from the realm."

"How does she do that?" Caellan said. He was never very good with portal mechanics or magical theory.

"Don't worry," Djinn said. "I have a plan."

"Once we attack, do you have a plan for all guards in the spire who will come to the demon's aid," Caellan said.

"Don't worry knight," Nora said. "Reinforcements are on their way and will dispatch any remaining guards." She could only mean the other lords that helped them before. He was not sure how many were still alive, but they needed all the help they could get. With Djinn and Nora not sharing the details, Caellan knew he could trust them so he reluctantly stopped asking questions.

Despite Nora's warning, they found no other guards as they carefully maneuvered their way through the maze of corridors. Caellan knew little about the spires and no one was sure why there were so many hallways with few rooms of machinery. Fortunately, Djinn knew how to navigate his way through the large tunnels and led them to the spire's control room. Strangely, no guards were stationed at the entrance.

"Are you ready?" Nora said to Caellan. He took a deep breath. It had been ten years since he was last in this room. There was nothing more horrible than facing the wrath of a celestial being. It was not her power, but her eyes and the way they seemed to tear his insides apart. "You have the faith and the strength to do this knight. She needs you."

"I am ready," Caellan said as he drew his weapon. He wasn't lying, but a part of him didn't know if he was strong enough for this. He just hoped that he could hold out long enough for someone to save Monty after he died. The thought of death gave him a sense of peace.

*   *   *   *

Casually, Djinn walked into the control room while Caellan and Nora inched their way in cautiously. The room was just as he remembered. At the center of the room, Monty floated above a large circular diadem surrounded by twenty-four pedestals. Many pedestals held a soulstone that was pumping blue light into a river of energy that was continuing upward from the diadem. Bounded by chains, Monty was in the middle translucent blue energy flow. In her dusky woman form, Lady Enix sat in a raised control chair next to the diadem. Being on the ground floor of the control room, Caellan also remembered that there were two other levels above them that were probably filled with fire knights. This level had many fire knights who all turned at once towards the three visitors.

"Welcome heroes of the Fifth Spire," Lady Enix announced. "You have the great honor to witness the end of your realm. Don't worry. It won't be much longer before an army of demons burns your precious realm and free you from your mortal imprisonment. If you wish to spare yourself such a fate, return your soulstone to one of the pedestal. I won't make such an offer again."

"You must excuse me demon," Djinn said. "I do not care about your prattling. Monty, can you hear me, little one?" Monty returned only a weak smile. "To save us, you must sing your lovely song."

"It doesn't matter what you have planned," Lady Enix said. "You will all die even if it means killing you several times, wizard."

"It is up to you now, little one," Djinn said. "Your song is one of your powers. You must sing. We need your help."

Caellan stood in his battle stance, watching the fire knights. He stayed close to Djinn and Nora as they slowly approached the diadem. After further urging from Djinn, he could hear singing in the distance. The fire knights readied their weapons with the singing getting louder. Then, the energy around the diadem changed. The blue translucent energy fluctuated and pulse with white rings.

After studying the control chair's console, Lady Enix glared at Monty angrily with her eyes erupting in flames. "I will kill you for your insolence," she said. Her sensual voice was replaced by a deep growling. "I will kill you all." Veins of fire were now running across her body. Her skin became hard like stone with her hair being replaced by a crown of horns. "I will succeed in opening this portal and your tiny deaths will be in vain." With a mouth full of sharp teeth and eight burning eyes, she surrounded herself with giant, fiery wings. Caellan watched in horror as she transformed into her full demonic form. "Kill them, my children of fire."

Without warning, the fire knights swung their swords at the three of them. Caellan quickly parried each jarring blow then skillfully struck back. Even with their fiery, hard plated armor, Caellan's holy sword sliced through the demonic creatures easily. Djinn dodged and struck several of them with energy bolts. Some of them disintegrated while others were thrown back. In her nimble jaguar form, Nora lithely dodged each attack as she ran up and under the tall fiery creatures. Still in a full run, she breathed a storm of lightning upon her attackers. If the fire knights weren't torn apart by the cat's claws, they were disintegrated by the lighting. Despite their gains, more fire knights were flooding into the lower level from the upper areas.

With crackling screams, the fire knights were running along the ceiling and walls. Their attacks became more and more numerous as Caellan was having trouble parrying the multitude of sword attacks and their long-range fire bolt attacks. With some spewing lava-like fire from there the helmets, he had to dodge to the side and move further from the others. Finding himself surrounded, Caellan killed the ones he could, but was forced to parry a growing number of attacks. He knew it would be only a matter of time before they would break through his defense. Then, Lady Enix struck.

With an outstretched hand, Lady Enix fired a massive bolt of fire at the singing maru. Hanging helplessly above the diadem, Caellan watched in horror as the fire exploded around Monty causing her to scream in pain. Burning away part of her black dress, her white skin was singed with black burn marks, but she kept singing.

Caellan knew he had to protect her. No creature could withstand the full power of a demon, not even a maru. Gritting his teeth, he stopped defending and drove his attack forward. With each swing, he killed a fire knight, but two more would take their place. While his sword was unaffected by the fiery disposition of his attackers, his clothes, and light armor were quickly being burned away. Using his sword's point and shoulder, he smashed his way through the group of fire knights as they all tumbled to the ground in a fiery explosion. With searing pain from his burned upper right arm and shoulder, he looked up to see the demon strike Monty again.

Lady Enix slowly walked down the stairs and fired one bolt after another. Each time, Monty cried out in a pain, and her singing became weaker and weaker. Pulling himself off the ground, he rushed to Monty. Her eyes had gotten weak, and most of her skin was blackened. She had little time. Fortunately, the demon didn't notice or care about the approaching paladin.

"You will die now, maru," Lady Enix said. "When you return to the Divine, tell him how you failed to save this realm." Pointing her hand at Monty, Lady Enix unleashed a jet of fiery energy. Without thinking, Caellan threw himself in front of the attack and blocked it using his two-handed sword.

Caellan tried to hold his ground, but the stream of energy pushed him back to the blue flowing energy of the portal. The heat slowly burned away the rest of his tunic while clawing at his skin. Pushing against the rush of energy and the searing pain, he screamed in defiance. Then, he felt a surge of power giving him even more strength and power.

It had been a long time since he wore his armor. The paladin armor was a special gift from the Divine that made them impervious to most attacks. First, the armor wrapped itself around Caellan in flowing white energy. Then, it hardened into a silvery full plated armor adorned with a white cloak. No armor in the world could match the perfection and beauty of the paladin's armor. Despite its beauty, most people feared the appearance of it on the battlefield. It was said a paladin could survive a dragon's attack. From under his visor, Caellan noticed Lady Enix hesitate before pressing her attack.

With the armor, he held his ground, and heard Monty sing louder than ever. Her melodious voice echoed through the chamber giving him strength. When he tried to push the attack back, the demon replied with an even stronger attack. Unable to push forward, he did the only thing he could and stood his ground. With a group of fire knights rushing to him and barely able to resist the demon's attack, Caellan knew he wouldn't be able to protect Monty much longer.

Suddenly, the chamber's wall exploded as a vehicle crashed into Lady Enix and spun into another wall. Free from the demon's attacks, Caellan quickly dispatched the five fire knights that were charging at him. Returning his attention to the crash, Caellan could see three vehicle passengers lying near the smoking wreckage. Lady Enix was already on her feet and was preparing to execute them. Caellan had little time to stop her.

Chapter Thirty-Five

The Battle

Calais saw Lady Enix approaching the three survivors. Still, light-headed from the crash, she fought with her satchel to pull out her summoning book. Lady Enix had taken her full demon form, and it wouldn't take long for her to kill them all. Worse, groups of fire knights were preparing to attack. Just as she got her book out, the demon was already upon them. Calais knew she couldn't summon anything before the demon attacked in full force. She tried to scoot back to the wall while pulling the book opened. She needed a little more time.

Then, the paladin struck the demon from behind. She instantly recognized her brother's armor. She had only seen it once but never forgot its beauty. The demon turned to the paladin and knocked him back with a blast of flaming energy. This was just the time she needed to prepare her summoning spells. Calais knew the armor would protect him so she focused on protecting Rev and Marek.

Opening the book, she quickly turned to the defensive spells that were all photographic drawings and diagrams. Focusing on a picture, it flew off the page and caused a wall of stone to erupt from the floor. With Rev, Marek and Calais protected from the demon, Calais turned to other pages and summoned her other creatures. More drawings floated up from the pages and made several full plated men with spears and shields materialize in front of her. They immediately attacked the fire knights trying to flank the wall. As her creations provided cover, she turned to her other companions.

Marek had jumped to his feet but appeared dazed from the crash. Seeing the fire knights, he grabbed his chain whip handles from his vest and took a standard battle stance. His chain whips ejected from each handle like long tendrils. "This will be fun," he yelled. He flicked the whips at the knights causing them to shatter in a burst of flame. As more rushed him, he tripped several fire knights while dodging other fire knights' sword attacks. For a moment, Calais marveled at how deftly he handled himself in battle especially with multiple foes. Unfortunately, Rev did not fare so well.

Calais ran over to him and looked for serious injuries. He was unconscious and didn't appear to have any serious injuries. "Wake up Rev," Calais said quickly. "We are in trouble. Please wake up!" She shook his body and slapped his face.

"Stop hitting me," he said groggily. His eyes opened, and he sat up. "Were did you learn first aid?"

"Sorry," Calais said. "I am more familiar with portal mechanics then physiology. Let's get you on your feet. We are surrounded by fire knights and Lady Enix is really upset." When she tried to move him, he cried out in pain.

"Would you stop trying to help?" Rev said. "My leg is broken, and my side is on fire. Help me over to the wall. Maybe the dumb things will mistake me for an ornament. Gently!" Calais did her best to move him quickly but carefully. Admittedly, she wasn't great at the latter. Once they got him to the wall, he drew out his crossbow and sword. "Okay, you have done enough." Then, he surprised her with a kiss. For a moment, she stared back at him, breathless. With shock, awe, fear, joy and love exploding inside her, she kissed him back even harder and longer. Finally, she pulled her lips from his and stared into his deep blue eyes. "Go help your friends." With an embarrassed smile and renewed vigor, she pulled herself from him and charged into battle.

With fire knights swarming the control room and her friends being surrounded, Calais decided it was time to even the odds. Still protected by her walls, she threw the book onto the floor and closed her eyes. The book flew open with pages flipping back and forth while she focused all her magical energies at it. Stopping on a page, the drawings flew out of the book and quickly formed into the summoned creature.

An army began to immediately form around her. Behind her, ethaerium cannons began blasting groups of fire knights. In front of her, a group of armored soldier quickly engaged the fire knights and forced them back. Beside her, sand dancers began to whirl around in a dervish attack against the flanking fire knights. Above her, air elves with spiderlights strafed their enemies on the upper platforms. The control room was filled with the roar of battle while Calais focused on each creature.

With the fire knights confused, her friends quickly took the advantage and began decimating Lady Enix's forces. With each earth shattering explosion from her cannons, Nora tore apart each fire knight that wasn't killed in the blast. Marek coordinated his attacks with the summoned soldiers and decimated the enemy's ranks. A familiar wizard jumped onto a spiderlight and released havoc with lightning, fire and ice. Caellan fought Lady Enix while protecting someone in the forming portal. Despite their successes against the enemy, she could feel her mind wane.

The only limitation of a summoner was the number of creatures they could manage. As each creature struck the fiery metal armor, she could feel its strength. Every time a creature parried a knight's powerful blow, she could feel its fear. When a knight disintegrated into a hot, fiery death, she could feel its joy. Each time a summoned creature was slain; she could feel its pain. While the strain continued to mount against her, she had to keep pushing. Calais refused to let her friends down even if it meant her death.

Lady Enix finally noticed her minions losing the fight while Caellan struck her continuously with his holy sword. Grabbing the paladin by the neck, she threw him against the wall and pinned him there with metal debris. Releasing exploding balls of flames from her hand, they decimated most of the summoned soldiers with Marek diving for cover. Calais directed all her cannon's attacks against Lady Enix to stop her, but the demon was unfazed. The cannons exploded with a wave of the demon's hand. The blast threw Calais forward with the rest of the debris.

"Calais, are you okay," a familiar voice said. As the smoke cleared, she saw a green face looking down at her.

"Djinn," she said trying to catch her breath. The blast had partially covered her with stone and metal debris. With the smoke clearing, she suddenly felt the sharp crushing pain of the debris. "I am so glad you are alive." The pain was exquisite. "I would hug you, but I can't get up right now."

"I can fix that," Djinn said. With a wave of his hand, he made the stones fly off her. The pain seemed to lessen with each removed stone, but her body still hurt from the blast. Several fire knights attacked him, and he dodged each one while striking them down with large bolts of purple energy. Pulling her up, she tried to hug Djinn but fell on him instead. Luckily, he was taller and caught her.

"I don't know whether I can do more," Calais said. She could barely stand with pain shooting through her body.

"Fortunately, I need a portal mechanic and not a summoner," Djinn said in a comforting tone. "The portal will open and Monty hasn't had time to realign it. We need to slow it down."

"Get me to a control panel," she said gritting her teeth.

Turning to a charging fire knight, Djinn quickly dispatched the armored foe with another blast of purple energy. Through the smoke of the fallen creature, Lady Enix approached them with her hand emblazoned with fire. Calais thought she saw a smile as fire lanced toward them. Djinn tried to jump out of the way with Calais, but they both toppled onto the debris with the fire screaming over them. Unable to get out of the way, more flames lanced at them. This time, a figure blocked the attack.

Maliki stood over them using his left metallic arm to project a shield around them. Infuriated, the demon shot a massive amount of energy at Maliki, but he resisted and stood his ground. Calais thought she was in an oven as the shield was being surrounded by the hot fire. Out of nowhere, a hand grabbed Calais and pulled her away from the attack. Thankfully, it was her brother, Caezik.

"What took you so long?" she said wincing in pain.

"Lady Enix had a few more defenses in place other than the spire," Caezik said. "Luckily, Maliki dispatched them quickly, and we got here just in time." Pulling out his black bow, Caezik fired several arrows at Caellan to release him from the pinning metal shrapnel.

"It has been a long time, Cae," Caellan said after standing back up from the long fall. Then, he stopped before coming much closer and just looked at Caezik. "I am glad you are here."

"It's good to see your armor again, Cael," Caezik said.

"This is not the time for a family reunion," Calais said. "And, I really hurt." They both just looked at each other. "Where did Djinn go?"

"The champion's got him," Caezik said. "I can get you over there."

"Wait," Calais yelled as they were enveloped in black shadows before appearing next to Djinn and Denarith. "I hate shadow jumping. It makes me sick, and I already want to throw up."

"Take her," Caezik said as he passed her over to Denarith. "I will provide you some cover." He smiled before disappearing into more shadows.

"You don't look so good," Denarith said as he propped her up.

"I am fine," Calais said sourly. "I just need help standing up." Wrapping his left arm around her, he helped steady her. "Is Maliki okay?"

"He's actually holding the demon back," Denarith said surprised. Peering through the smoke, Calais saw Maliki dodging and blocking the demon's blasts with his armored arm. After blocking each attack, he blasted the demon with white lancing energy from the same armored hand. As each blast hit the demon, it would be knocked to the ground before jumping back up to it's feet to fire even more flame bolts at Maliki. Despite his cloak being burned into tatters, it appeared to Calais that he was actually winning.

"We must get to that control panel to help Monty," Djinn insisted. "She won't last much longer."

"Lead the way," Denarith said. He was almost carrying her with just one arm instead of helping her walk. Calais didn't mind since the pain continued to grow in her body. "The crazy orc said something about some portal-beeping-wiring-thing that would fix that blue stuff over there."

"I am not crazy," Djinn said. "I am just eccentric."

"You're an orc that can repair a magical portal," Denarith said. "That makes you a crazy orc. That is a good thing, because I don't like normal orcs."

Two fire knights charged Denarith. Moving Calais out of the way, he parried both of their attacks and smashed each knight with his large battle axe. "We got to hurry," Denarith said. "I want to kill more of those fire creatures before you make them go away with your portal thing."

"It's right over here," Djinn said pointing to a metal box bolted on the lower part of the wall.

As they neared the box, the entire control room shook with loud explosions outside the spire. The box blew up with hundreds of sparks. "The army has already started their attacks," Calais said. "We have little time." Emerging from the ceiling above Monty, she saw a webbed framework of steel rods and spheres moving downward into the blue energy. "You see, the tower's defenses are coming online and the surge of power will only make the portal open faster."

"Too late," Djinn said. "The portal is already open."

Underneath Monty, Calais watched the floor dissolve into a view of black, rocky land. Unfortunately, Calais knew that Monty would not continue to float in the portal. Eventually, she would drop into the plane below her or be destroyed by the portal's energy. With a portal already active, she wouldn't be able to deactivate it in time to save Monty or stop the demon invasion. The only way to stop it now was to destroy the portal, the spire and everyone in it.

"I know what I must do," Calais said somberly.

"We are with you, love," Djinn said with an encouraging smile.

Before Denarith could respond, the demon appeared in front of them with a bright flash. The demon pulled the dragon spear from Denarith's belt and caused it to expand into a long, wicked spear. Denarith swung his axe, but Lady Enix caught the axe's handle with her other hand. Too focused on freeing his axe, he didn't notice the incoming spear and was impaled against the wall. The force of the attack threw Calais from Denarith's grip. Dazed from hitting the ground and feeling the pain from her previous injuries, Calais watched Djinn blast the demon with a flaring, energy attack.

"Don't do it, Djinn," Calais whispered. She knew that wizards could only channel so much energy. With the amount of energy he was directing against the demon, he would die soon. Out of nowhere, Nora appeared next to her. "We have to help him."

"It is too late for him," Nora said sadly. "Can you stop the portal?"

"Get me to that control chair," Calais said. "I will stop all this."

Growing into a much larger jaguar, Calais pulled herself onto Nora's back and held on as tightly as she could to the short slick cat hair. Positioning himself between Monty and the demon, Maliki added his own energy attack against the demon while Nora bounded past him to the control chair. Looking behind her, Calais saw Marek and Caellan fighting the main group of fire knights with a separate group pursuing her and Nora. Several other knights tried to attack Nora, but she quickly dodged their oversized swords. For the ones she couldn't dodge, they were destroyed by flying black arrows. Unable to see Caezik, Calais thanked him silently as they got to the stairs leading up to the control platform.

It took only a few leaps up the stairs before they were at the elevated control chair. Calais jumped to the control chair, and Nora blasted a group of fire knights following them. Black arrows destroyed the few knights that escaped Nora's lightning breath. Free from pursuit, Calais used the portal controls on the control chair to recalibrate the portal.

"Where is the invasion?" Nora pondered.

Calais looked up at the portal. Instead of an army of demons, bright white orbs of energy floated upward into the machine of metal webbing above Monty. "I have seen nothing like it," Calais said bewildered. Watching the machine disintegrate the white orbs, Calais scanned the monitors but found no explanation of what was happening. "I am not getting any strange readings from the portal or that strange device. I see some kind of faint life emanating from the orbs, but I can't tell what they are." Calais wondered if this is what Arturo was talking about with the demon souls.

Flames and energy exploded from the demon as it unleashed an enraged bellow. Maliki was thrown into the portal and disappeared. Djinn crumpled onto the ground next to the wall in a smoldering heap. Pulling the spear from the charred body of the barbarian, she threw it directly at Monty. An idea sprang into Calais' mind, and her summoning book appeared in front of her. It flipped to a certain page, and s stone wall sprang up instantly between Monty and the spear. As the spear embedded itself into the wall, the demon turned to Nora and Calais. Seeing the demon's rage, Calais began to furiously press buttons and turn dials.

Rearing back, the demon fired a massive ball of flame at Calais. For half a moment, Calais thought about jumping off the chair. With the thoughts of everything that her fallen friends had sacrificed, Calais stayed in the chair to finish her adjustments. Seeing that Calais wouldn't move, Nora transformed into her cloaked human form and wrapped her large black cloak around both of them. Calais tried to adjust a few more settings when the flaming ball exploded and everything went dark.

*   *   *   *

Monty continued to sing with tears running down her cheeks. Her friends' pain and suffering filled her with so much anger and sadness. She wanted to reach out and strangle the nearby demon. Instead, she was supposed to sing and stop the portal. Part of her didn't see the song's effectualness anymore while staring at the black rocky land below her. Each note became harder and harder to push out as the terrible demon hurt her friends. Watching a massive explosion consume the control chair, she intoned the song's last note and was too disheartened to repeat it for the eighth time. Then, everything changed around her.

The portal changed the black rocky land into white, shining clouds. The energy around Monty turned completely white and finally released her. She fell downward into the shining clouds. The control room dissolved around her into a blue shimmering light.

After the bright flash, Monty was falling through brightly colored nebulous clouds. Free from her chains, she looked up at a large white sun shining above her and then saw darkness below her. Everyone else was falling around her. Her deep memories told her that this was the ethaerium and that she would be destroyed in a matter of seconds. This was proven true as all the fire knights dissolved into fading orbs of light. Looking for her companions, she was suddenly struck by a fiery blast.

The demon streaked toward Monty with fiery wings. Despite her clothes being in tatters, Monty tried to dodge the attack by twisting in the air. Instead, she was struck again by the demon's painful blast. Helpless, Monty could not escape the screaming demon as it grabbed her by the throat. The demon's touch made of fire, and energy burned relentlessly. Monty punched back in vain. The unbearable pain filled her entire body. With no one else to help and nothing left to do, she reflexively reached out to light above for help. Finally, it reached back.

The light flashed, and something inside her changed. A warm energy sprang from her heart, and the pain faded. The demon shrieked and couldn't release its grip from Monty. The demon's hand holding Monty's throat turned black and hard. Then, the demon's arm turned to the same hard stone. Slowly, the rest of the demon twisted into a misshapen, shrieking, dark statue. The white and black statues fell interlocked through the prismatic clouds.

Seeing the distant suns, something in her deep memories changed. Monty could see faint lines connecting all the suns with the light above her. On some, she could see red lines connecting to a distant group of swirling clouds. Monty realized that the strange clouds were called the planes of

272

chaos, the home of the dragons. She could also see how the dragons were slowly draining the suns and their realms of all life. Despite the Dragon Shield, she knew the dragons were still draining her realm unless the portal could be closed forever. With this knowledge, she realized her other abilities and powers. With one of them being strength, the maru smashed the demonic statue into dust. Free from the demon, she enjoyed the solitude, and peace as she watched the speckled clouds.

Then, the black silhouette of the Ninth Spire burst from the clouds. Watching the clouds roiling off the ship's sails and hull, Monty cried out with happiness. If Maliki survived, she knew others might have lived. Waiting with eager anticipation, she was finally teleported onto the main deck.

Nora who was still in her human form removed her black cloak and placed it around Monty. Before Monty could say anything, the druid hugged her with joyful tears running down her cheeks. Once she released Monty, Nora checked her face, her arms and hands like a doting mother. "I am so glad that you survived," Nora said as she tried to hold back more tears.

"Me," Monty said in disbelief. "I thought you had died in that explosion on the chair."

"Don't worry about me," Nora said. "This cloak was given to me by my father, and he said this magical cloak would always protect me. His love has protected me for centuries, and now I want you to have it.

"Oh Nora," Monty said as she looked at the beautiful fabric. "I can't take this. I can't take your father's cloak."

"My dear child, he was the nicest man I had ever known, and he would want the person who saved his daughter to have his cloak. I know you may not realize now, but you saved us. You saved us all."

"A great hero indeed, little one," Djinn said sitting down next to her.

"Djinn, I am missed you so much," Monty said with an ecstatic hug. His skin and clothes were burnt, torn, and bloodied, but his hat was in perfect condition. "How did you come back from the dead?"

"That fellow in the shiny armor," Djinn said. No longer wearing his paladin armor, Caellan leaned on the railing and obliged Monty with a deep smile. Behind him, Caezik who was still wrapped in his dark cloak, nodded approvingly at Monty. On the other side of the deck, Marek saluted her with a somber look. Near him, several other people were sitting down as they tended to their wounds. For a moment, she wondered if she were dreaming. None of them should have survived the fall through the portal.

"The ethaerium kills all living things," Monty said to Djinn. "It should have torn you apart."

"I rescued them," Maliki said walking to Monty. His cloak and clothes were still burnt and shredded. "Being thrown through the portal first allowed me time to call my ship and grab anyone else who might fall through the portal. Fortunately, you and Calais shut down the portal and pulled the demon out of our plane."

"Is the demon dead," a woman asked. She was the same woman who Nora had protected on the chair.

"Yes," Maliki said. "The Divine channeled his power through Monty and turned the demon into ashes. One way or another, Montague's and Djinn's plan actually worked."

"So this was your plan the whole time," Monty said. "You wanted to throw me in a portal with a terrible demon and get yourself killed." Before Djinn retorted her claim, he noticed her half-grin and just shook his head with a wide grin.

"Monty, may I introduce you to our dear friend, Calais," Nora said. "She is one of the best summoners in the realm and a good portal mechanic." They exchanged greetings and then Calais introduced Monty to her other companions. Denarith sat against the railing with several bloody bandages wrapped around his arm and abdomen. Near the half-conscious barbarian, Rev had fallen asleep with splints placed on his leg and arm. Marek just grumbled at Calais and Monty.

"Now, what's wrong, sarge?" Calais said disapprovingly.

"He is just a grumpy, old bear," Monty said.

"Of course, I am grumpy," Marek said. "I survived the battle that means I have to live several more years on that miserable rock. Speaking of which, how much longer are we going to be floating around out here?"

"Very well, sarge," Maliki said. "I will set a course for your miserable rock."

In a flash, they were again back above the purple maelstrom. Scorched earth and rubble had replaced the fifth spire. The rest of the towers erupted with lightning as the maelstrom roared against the Dragon Shield. Watching the purple and blue flashes, Monty remembered her true purpose.

"The Fifth Spire is no more," Calais said. "That only leaves fourteen spires to maintain the shield. Who knows what other damage the military caused when they fired their cannons at the spire. If a few more spires are destroyed, the shield will collapse."

"I will fix it," Monty said quietly.

"How are you going to fix the shield, child," Nora said.

"That is my true purpose," Monty said. "I shall close the maelstrom. I am just not sure how yet."

"We will come up with a plan that will hopefully not include demons this time," Djinn said.

"No you won't, wizard," Caellan said. "You are coming with me. I have to go home to Castle Pellandarr."

"Why are you going back," Calais said. "You told me you would never return there."

"I have too," Caellan said glumly. "I had a vision that showed me that our home is in danger. The wizard and I are the only ones who can save it."

"Then, I am going with you," Calais said.

"No, you're not," Caellan said. "You need to help Monty with the maelstrom. No one knows more about portals and realms than you. The world will be a much better place without the maelstrom."

"I hate it when you make sense," Calais said disgruntled.

"You can't tell me no," Caezik said gruffly. "I am coming with you."

"I welcome your company," Caellan said with uncertainty. "It will be a difficult task for us."

Djinn walked back over to Monty that was gazing at the distant horizon where the bright stars met the dark land. "I guess I am stuck traveling with the paladin and terrorizing ignorant humans." Djinn said shaking his head. "Where will you be going, little one?"

"I must go back to Parn," Monty said. "I have a promise to keep." She had to find her friend because she had the power to cure the corrupted.

Chapter Thirty-Six

Carina

Tomas stood on the cliff above the Drift and watched the Fifth Spire explode in the far distance. He quietly hoped that his friends survived, and his wife was finally given peace. All of it happened because he had failed as a husband and as a soldier. It was his fault he let the demon out to terrorize the realm. If it had not been for the empire's plan to steal the demons' souls, they would have executed him. Instead, he must stand by and watch the empire try to control the demons. After seeing what Lady Enix was capable of, Tomas knew the empire would fail, and an army of demons would still crush the realm. He wondered if the general would listen.

"Lord Commander Tomas," General Amirez said behind him. "We have just received reports that Castle Dragonlock captured many souls during the transference."

"That is horrible news, general," Tomas said looking down. For once, he could not lie. "You won't be able to control them."

"I wouldn't worry about that," the general said reassuringly. "Because of your friends' research ten years ago, we know how to contain them. Soon, we will harness their power and create powerful soldiers that will make the empire invincible." He walked up to Tomas and put his hand on Tomas' shoulder. "It is a great day for the empire."

"I watched many of my friends die over the last year," Tomas said while fixated on the roaring maelstrom. "One demon almost destroyed the entire realm. How does the empire plan on controlling an army of demons?"

"I am not privy to the details. Actually, I never really understand what the engineers were saying half the time. All I know is that Zilvary has some mechanized contraption that will use the demons' energies. We will have the power to finally destroy the corrupted once and for all. Thanks to you. I have been ordered to bring you back to Castle Dragonlock where we will receive commendations from the emperor himself. Come now, lord commander, an airship is waiting for us."

General Amirez turned around and walked through the forest of the giant ethaerium cannons. The towering barrels were still smoking from their barrages against the Fifth Spire. Soldiers and craftsmen worked on dismantling them for transport to their next assignment. A group of horses were waiting for the general and Tomas. Reluctantly, Tomas followed the general, and mounted a horse after the general hopped onto his own horse. They both rode back to camp with a contingent of bodyguards following them.

"You know the empire will fail," Tomas insisted. "They won't be able to control the demons, and the realm will be destroyed."

"My dear lord commander who said anything about saving the realm."

*   *   *   *

Down in the dunes of the Drift, a group of men sat around a campfire with several wagons and horses anchored nearby. They were talking nervously among each other after seeing one of the spires explode. Figuring that the area would be swarming with imperial soldiers, the group decided it was best to head south at first light. After all, they didn't want the empire finding all the stolen goods they were carrying. Still talking, one of the men stood up and drew a sword at an approaching figure in the dark.

The men stopped talked and stared at woman. She wore a beautiful white dress with long auburn hair. The man lowered his weapon at the strange sight. They didn't know what to make of a woman not dressed appropriately for traveling through the shifting sands of the Drift.

"Careful, boys, it could be a corrupted," one man said.

"I think it's a ghost or a spirit of some kind," another man said.

When the woman got close enough, she held out her hand. "Please help me," the woman said. "I am lost, and I need to get back home. I need to find my husband."

"We would be happy to help you," one of the man said standing up. "What is your name?"

"My name is Carina," she said.

"Welcome to our camp," the man said. "Please sit down and warm yourself. The Drift can get mighty cold at night." The woman took her seat and looked around at the leering men nervously.

"Do you have anyone else with you," the man continued. "How did you get out here dressed like that?"

"I don't remember how I got here," the woman said. "The last thing I remember was arguing with my husband. He was very angry."

"Hmmm, it sounds like he dumped you in the Drift for you to die," another man said repositioning himself next to her.

"My husband would never do that," she said appalled.

"You have no gear, no weapons and a slip of a dress, that could easily be cut off," the man said sneering at her while putting his hand on her leg. "How else would you explain you being out here?"

The woman appeared frightened while staring at the man's hand on her leg. The other men chuckled. A few got up and approached her while others continued to drink and watch.

"Don't worry, we will be gentle," the dirty man next to the woman said while stroking her hair. "At least, we will be for part of it."

Suddenly, a fire knight landed in the camp fire and drew his oversized sword. Several men cried out in terror while a few began running. The woman in the white dress just sat on the log like a statue. With a few swipes, the fire knight cut down the men around the fire. Then, he fired several flame bolts at the running men. Each bolt hit and incinerated its target. Finally, alone with the woman, the fire knight sheathed his sword and bowed before the woman.

"Thank you," the woman said. "You arrived just in time to save them from a more painful death. They tried to hurt me, but I would have torn them apart, piece by piece. I think I would have enjoyed listening to their screams." She pondered for a moment while staring at the sliced up bodies bleeding into the sand. "Do you have a name?"

The tall fire knight simply bowed.

"It is very good to meet you, Faellan," she said with a single nod. Somehow, the woman could hear his thoughts, and knew she had complete control over him. "We have much work to do before I see my husband. I want everything to be perfect."

Faellan cocked his head and looked at the woman quizzically.

"We are going home in Adia," she said staring at horizon. "I must gather supplies and prepare my home for my husband's return. During that time, I will need you to protect me. As a noble woman, I have many enemies and I must not be distracted. I must show Tomas how much I truly love him."

Carina just smiled while feeling the hole in her stomach.